SAFE DISTANCES

Sage's Story

Susan Michalski

GEODESY

BOOK 1

Copyright © 2013 CreateSpace
Susan Michalski
All rights reserved.

ISBN:1492135151 ISBN-13: 978-1492135159

3/10/2014

Gordon,

You can lead a horse to the library, but you can't make him read your book. Thanks so much for reading mine! Without readers there is no point in writing! Susan Michalski

DEDICATION

For Skye, the girl who changed my map and navigates like no other.

Contents

Chapter 1 (Gifted)

Our secrets, hidden safely behind the stones and mortar of our private little prisons, keep us in and others out. Breaking down those walls is hard and often futile work. You have to be willing to get dirt and blood on your hands.

The sun is coming up over the houses on the next street. Any moment the door of the main house will creak, and Ethan will creep out into the half-light of dawn. We have been here in the old lady's garage apartment over-looking her pool for a week. We're here because of Ethan and his twin sister, Elena, but I have yet to meet them. I'm not allowed to "know" them. This is my mother's rule.

My mom, Rachel, is a shrink of last resort. People hire her to solve the problems of the kids that they never wanted who are now fucking up their lives. My mother's job is to save these desperate parents from their kids or maybe she's supposed to save the kids from their parents. I'm not sure she even knows which it is.

Finally, the door groans, and I lean closer to the glass. As Ethan moves away from the house, he glances over his shoulder like he has done something terribly wrong. He walks haltingly like a little boy held too tightly in check. His hair falls around his face in soft light brown curls with gold highlights that catch the rising sun. Even from this distance I can see that his features are delicate, sweet cherry-red lips against white skin, a small turned-up nose, a gently sloping jaw, and soft, sad eyes like a Botticelli angel. He strips the towel from his waist and abandons it on the deck. I watch the muscles in his slight shoulders and the curve of his back in the instant he takes to lower himself silently into the water. He moves quickly like a tiny animal, fragile and skittish. I find it hard to believe that he is my age, 17. A slow ripple runs the width of pool as he disappears under the water. He is there and gone so fast that I can almost believe that he is a figment of my overactive imagination. In my journal I've named him "Mouse."

This is the opening I have waited for. I grab my running shoes from beside my bed and slip through the half-opened door. I'm confident I can get out without waking Rachel because last night she stayed up watching the movie that was supposedly written by her celebrity crush for the thousandth time. She complains about how facile it is, how people don't just suddenly recover from life-long trauma like that, but she loves it anyway. I think she secretly wishes that one of her patients would open all up to her and reveal their deepest secret pain, and then suddenly the kid would be able to have the life that he was meant to have. All her hard work would come to good, and someone would be forever grateful to her. The sordid reality that she can't accept is that her job amounts to the extraction of secrets. In the process maybe she helps one or two patients a little, but she isn't ever going to forge some bond and intuit the very thing the kid needs to hear to make his walls crumble and his fear dissolve. I know she thinks she can, but she can't. Stone and mortar cannot be melted by fire or tears.

I slip past her door and down the stairs to the kitchen. I'll put my shoes on once I'm outside. I turn the dead-bolt slowly, keeping it from clicking. Breathe. Turn the handle and open the door part way, so it doesn't groan. All that's left is the screen door.

"Sage?"

I freeze. The small question floats down from upstairs. I contemplate ignoring it.

"Sage! What are you doing?"

"Going for a run, Madre. Back in a flash!"

I hear her hesitation. She wants to stop me, but she knows that it will only delay the inevitable. "You know the rules," she finally sighs.

"You bet!" I say cheerily. I don't wait for her to change her mind. On the porch just a few feet from the edge of the pool, I bend to slip on my shoes without untying them. As I stand up, Ethan glides in to the wall and surfaces. Our eyes meet for a moment before he looks away. The water dripping on his face gives the impression that he is crying. I lift my hand and give him my sweetest grin, but instead of smiling back, he frowns and swims away. He reaches the opposite end of the pool, and in one easy movement he is out of the water. In the instant it takes me to inhale and speak, he has scooped up the towel, and the screen door has banged shut.

"Another time then, Mouse," I say to the air.

I walk slowly to the end of driveway, hoping he'll change his mind and come back out, but he doesn't, so I keep my word and head up the street at an easy lope.

My mother tries to keep her client files put always unless they are actually in her hand. She's thinks she got a lock on security, but half the time she's so preoccupied she couldn't find her head without a map. Makes spying easy, too easy almost. Once she was out walking, and she left her keys on the table. I was able to read Finn's file, part of it anyway.

Name: Euan Finnian Mulcahy
Age: 17
Referral Source: Criminal Court
Charge: Arson

I only had time to glance at the top page before she realized that she hadn't taken the keys and came back. No matter. I wasn't caught and besides, Finn would tell me the rest, and when he did, the triumph would be that much sweeter. My mother would never get him to tell her his secrets, but he would tell me, eventually.

I met Finn six months ago at our previous apartment after his third appointment with Rachel. I made sure that I was taking out trash at

2:50 when he was leaving. I wore a little strappy handkerchief top, ripped jeans shorts, and no shoes. I smiled shyly, he nodded, and watched me walk down the driveway and back up to the house. Since then, when Finn's appointments are over, he circles around the block. On the next street over I jump on the back of his motorcycle, and we ride out to the lake.

Sometimes we jump from the cliffs naked into the freezing water and giggle as the fish nibble at our white flesh. Sometimes we make out, and I can look into the deep water of his eyes and pretend that he can see into the blackness of mine. I like to sweep his shock of straight dark hair across his ruddy cheek and kiss him where his skin dimples when he smiles. It would be easy to pretend we could someday be in love, except for the absent way he looks away as he pulls me in.

My mom is clueless. Finn is wily; he knows how to string her along. He'll feed her just enough to keep her thinking she is getting somewhere, so she keeps him out of jail. But with me . . . I let him think he's working me, but I'm in control.

I wonder if he'll be meeting her here, at the old lady's house now. I hope Rachel hasn't referred him out to take on the twins full time. I'll have to look in her planner. She never locks that up.

The sun is fully up, and heat is already beginning to weigh heavy on the day when I make my way back into the yard. The old lady, the twin's grandmother is bent over plucking dead flowers from their stems and tossing them into a heap. She moves quickly with purpose, a strong woman who flatly refuses to age. I have to admire her in a way, even though she hired my mother to solve her problems. How bad could they be? Mouse certainly couldn't cause her too much worry. It must be the girl that makes all the trouble, I decide. Maybe she does drugs or gets violent and that's why my Mouse is so scared. Iron Lady looks up from her task and waves a flowered glove at me, attempting a hard smile. I wave back noncommittally and push open the door to the apartment.

My mother is dressed and ready, puttering in the kitchen. She hands me a glass of juice that I down in two swallows.

"How far?" She asks.

"I don't know, three miles maybe. It's too hot, and it's not even July. You out of here already?"

"I have a few minutes." She pauses. I wait for the inevitable question. She takes a sip of coffee and sets her mug down on the table. Tap tap tap on the side of the mug with her thumb ring and inhale, then, "Did you meet Ethan or Elena yet?"

"I know the rules, Mother."

"You can meet them, Sage, you just - "

"Can't know them!" I finish for her. "What would be the point then? You meet people so you can know them. That's how it's supposed to work."

A moment of silence passes, so she rises from the table to pour me a mug of coffee. She's gathering her thoughts, always so careful about constructing her arguments, preparing her oratory to have the correct spin. She wouldn't want to do me any damage. I might never recover, after all.

"The people I work with are not like you." She begins with an old standby. Build me up to emphasize the divide, discourage rather than disapprove. "I need to keep my life separate so the work is about them, not about me." That's a good one. Make me a partner, complicit in the crime of prying open their walls. "You need to respect my work by keeping a careful distance." As if distances between people can be wrought with such purpose. As if she keeps any "professional" distance.

Keeping my voice measured and eyes completely engaged with hers, I say, "Sure. Do your job. I won't interfere. Promise, Mama." Our old lovey name gets her every time. She smiles back at me, appeased. We drink our coffee in companionable silence while I steal glances at her planner, and she enters and crosses off appointments. Finn isn't on her schedule this week, but his dad's number is scrawled in the margin, so I memorize it. This is a bit of unforeseen luck. Now I can call Finn; I don't have to wait for him to show up here.

A sharp rap on the door makes me jump. It's the old lady. "Hey, Rachel," she calls through the screen before my mom can open it.

"Lily, come on in."

"I can't stay but a minute. Just wanted to invite you and your girl over for supper tonight. Give you a proper welcome."

Quaint! I am property without a name. My mom reads my grimace.

"Sage and I would really like that. What can we bring?"

I must be dreaming. She accepted a dinner invitation that includes me and clients. I can hardly breathe waiting for the other shoe to drop.

"Just bring yourselves and maybe some wine if you like."

"Absolutely," Rachel says.

"Well, I got some errands to run. We'll see you 'round six then," she says to me.

"Sweet," I say as coolly as possible to suppress my elation.

Iron lady harrumphs, but I know adults love when you talk to them like they're kids too.

"I'll walk back over with you, Lily," mom says putting her mug in the sink and scooping up her stuff. "Stay out of trouble, Kiddo. Oh, and maybe you could think about helping with the unpacking if you have nothing better to do." She kisses the top of my head, and the door bangs shut before I can formulate an appropriately sarcastic retort.

I can't believe my luck! Tonight begins my foray into the minds of the mysterious twins. Suddenly, I remember I have a call to make.

Finn's father answers the phone, and I hang up without saying anything. Who knows what my mother tells these people about us, and it would be disaster if he recognized my name. "Sage? As in Dr. Evan's daughter, Sage? Why in the hell would you . . . ?" It could get ugly. At least there was no chance of him recognizing this phone number on his caller ID. The line was here when we moved in, so the display name would be Paige, the old lady's last name. And what are the chances that he'd know her?

With no Finn adventure in the offing for the day, I get on the phone and talk to Jo for a couple of hours. Jo Zinn has been my BFF since kindergarten. She knows my warts, and she still talks to me. I consider that about as close to a miracle as can occur in this less than magical world. Jo has street smarts, and she is gorgeous in a tough girl kind of way. The weird thing about Jo is that what you see is what you get. I have yet to run into a single wall with her. But she isn't just like that with me. That's what the whole world sees. Maybe that is the biggest mystery of all to me. Maybe that's why I talk to her everyday even when she is half way around the world visiting her dad for the summer. I need to know that there is world out there without secret prisons, and I need her to save me from breaking bones when I smash into all the walls in this world, maybe especially my own.

"Let it go," she advises. "No good will come of this."

"Let it go? This is the most fun I've ever had at this game."

"Really, I don't trust this guy and I don't even know him."

"You aren't listening, Jo Jo. I'm in control here."

"You aren't listening, o-wise-one. Can you say playing with fire? No pun intended."

"Ha. Ha. Ha! Stop worrying. I don't want him; I just want to break him like a horse."

"Before your mom does?"

"Interesting idea. A horse race. I like it!"

"You aren't gonna win."

"You wanna bet?"

"And encourage you? Not me! Really, Sage."

"Really, Jo Jo. Last word!"

"Ugh!"

"Sorry. It had to be done."

We invented "last word" in the 4th grade. It has kept us from getting really mad at each other for eight years now. It could be the secret of our friendship. I tell her about the twins and dinner that night with the Iron Lady. She is as stunned as I that my mother accepted the invite. "Careful with that, too," she warns. "Your mom is up to something. I'd bet on it." Then she has to go for piano lessons.

My mom comes in around 5:00 looking a little like Saint George after his first round with the dragon. She trudges up the stairs and turns on the shower without even stopping to give me the usual ten minute check-in quiz, thereby piquing my curiosity even more. What could be happening over in that house that would make Saint Rachel, champion of the mentally scarred, come back with her tail between her legs and well, mentally scarred? She comes down twenty minutes later almost completely herself again.

"Help me find the wine," she says.

"Sure. So . . . how'd it go today?" I ask a bit too brightly perhaps.

Mom stops rummaging in the narrow pantry and steps out from

behind the door.

"Sage," I recognize her we-need-to-get-a-few-things-straight tone and sit down at the table. She joins me and continues. "This is not a game." Ooh she's already hit a cliché, not on her game tonight at all. "Lily's family has been through a lot. Please . . ." Her voice trails off.

"Please what, Madre?" I'm curious, but also a little uncomfortable. It's not like Rachel to be at a loss for words.

"Just practice some sensitivity. Okay?" Her phrase ends in a sort of sigh, and I don't know if she is done or not, so I wait a beat.

"Okay."

I'm about to get up and retrieve the wine from the cupboard where I unpacked it when she adds, "especially with Ethan."

"Okay." I repeat a little more forcefully because suddenly I feel like I'm being accused of something. "Anything else?" I ask.

She sighs again, and I know there is more, but she opts out of a confrontation. "Let's find the wine. I don't want to have to run to the store."

Very strange indeed. I put the bottle on the table and then head upstairs to brush my hair and change into a skirt. It's important to make a positive first impression. I decide against make-up. Wouldn't want the poor boy to think I'm coming on to him. I put on the tiger-eye bracelet that my mostly-absent father gave me for my seventh birthday. My mother refers to it as my talisman, but not without a trace of bitterness. When I get back down, my mother is already on the tiny porch, clutching her bottle of Merlot. She smiles nervously and moves so I can get out the door. "Sometimes I wish I still smoked," she says, but maybe not to me. I put my arm through hers, and we walk past the pool to the door that Mouse disappeared so quickly behind this morning.

Before Rachel can knock, the old lady is there. She gives us both the once over before letting us in, and I almost expect her to retract her dinner invitation if we don't pass inspection.

"Well, come on in," she finally urges as if we were the ones delaying our entrance. My mother puts her hand on my back, ushering me in first. I haven't been in the main house yet. The kitchen is comfortable and old fashioned with slate floors, yellow walls, a large farmhouse table and warm wood counters and cabinets.

"Nice place," I say.

The old lady is pleased. "Did it all myself," she brags. "Laid those stones and built every scrap of cabinetry. Even made that table and those chairs."

"Incredible," my mother chimes in. I wonder how she doesn't already know this.

"Have a seat, you two. Dinner 'll be ready in just a few minutes."

Instead of sitting down I wander over to the archway between the kitchen and the living room, hoping to catch a glimpse of the infamous twins. No one is there, but the room is impressive with its high-beamed ceiling and sparkling clean wide-planked floors. A wide staircase curves down into the room. I can hear voices above that tempt me to go look, but before I can take a step forward, Iron Lady is beside me.

"Please, sit down. I'll show you the rest of the house after we eat."

My mom meanwhile has opened the wine and is pouring two glasses. She hands one to the old lady and throws me her "best behavior" look. I sit.

"Would you like a glass of lemonade, young lady?"

"Thanks," I say. The suspense is killing me, so I turn my eyes from the door to ask, "So it'll be just the three of us eating then?"

"Don't be ridiculous!" A musical voice comes from behind me.

I jump because it seems impossible that anyone could have appeared there in the space of time that I had looked away.

"So we finally meet, Sage." The girl continues, extending her hand to shake mine. "Rachel has told us all about you!"

"Uh. . . Oh, hi," I manage to stammer. "Interesting. Rachel hasn't told me a thing about you. It's Elena, right?"

My mom is frowning at me. She hates when I call her by her first name in public.

"She apparently told you my name." Her eyes are cerulean blue and her hair the warm golden brown of a lion's coat. It's cut short so that it curls a little around her ears and just down her neck, stopping at the nape. She's at least a head shorter than I am and dressed in a gauzy white blouse with long sleeves that billow out at the wrists and jeans that cling to her tiny waist and hips.

"Hi, Rachel," she says warmly to my mother, who then gets up, walks over to her, and embraces the little thing like an old friend.

"Where's your brother?" Iron Lady's cold voice breaks the cheery little spell Elena cast upon her entrance.

I watch the girl shrink and wonder if she might disappear if her grandmother speaks again. "He says he's not hungry."

A storm brews in Iron Lady's eyes. "We have guests, and he will join us. Either you bring him down or I will!"

I look at my mother, half expecting her to intercede, but she's studying her glass of wine like the secrets of the universe lie at the bottom.

"I'll get him," Elena breathes, and she's gone just as suddenly as she arrived.

The old lady sets a stack of plates piled high with silverware and cloth napkins in front of me.

"Stop gawking and make yourself useful, girl," she snaps.

My mother gets up from the table and follows her back to the stove.

"What can I do to help, Lily?" she asks, and I wonder if she's talking about the cooking. I take advantage of the moment to gulp some of Rachel's wine. It burns a little in my throat.

"Nothing much to do, but thanks, Rachel." Her voice has lost some of its ice.

My mom comes over and rearranges the silver. I can never remember which side the forks go on. Probably because I eat most of my meals over the sink. By the time we've poured lemonades all around, the old lady has placed the steaming lasagna on the table along with homemade bread and salad.

"Looks great!" I say, suddenly starving. My mother and I sit down, but Iron Lady walks past the table and through the living room to the bottom of the stairs.

"Our guests are waiting!" She yells with a warning note. Then she marches back to sit at the head of the table. "Let's just give them a minute," she says to us.

My mother faces the open doorway, but I can't see through it from my angle. Iron Lady is directly in line with the door, so I watch her breathe heavily as though she's counting. I crane my neck, but my mother pokes me in the ribs, forcing me back into my seat. Then just as I expect Iron Lady to blow a gasket, I hear footsteps on the stairs.

Elena comes through the door first and behind her holding tightly to her hand is my "Mouse." No one moves or speaks as Elena takes the seat across from me, and Mouse sits across from my mother and beside his grandmother. Elena's eyes travel to each of our faces expectantly, but Mouse keeps his shining eyes on her. He is almost visibly shaking.

"Shall I serve, Grandmother?" Elena says smiling nervously.

"Ethan," Iron Lady addresses the boy. Slowly he shifts his gaze to the old woman. "Say hello to our guests."

Mouse swallows and looks tentatively at my mother. "Hello, Rachel." His voice is sweet and melodic like his sister's but lower. It makes my heart pound in my neck.

"Hi, Ethan. Thanks for joining us." My mom's voice is the one she used to talk to me when I was little. I don't remember when she stopped using it, but I'm startled to hear it now. My head is spinning a little trying to figure out what's going on here. "This is my daughter, Sage."

He glances my way but only for a fraction of a second before he looks down at his hands. "Hi, Sage," he mumbles into his lap.

I have no idea how I'm supposed to respond, and I'm contemplating one of the several off-beat sarcastic greetings I have perfected for awkward occasions, but I hesitate too long. Everyone is suddenly staring at me.

"Okay, okay . . . Now that we have all been introduced to death, can we eat?" I mean to lighten the mood, but I come off sounding like a brat. This whole scene is so weird.

Thankfully, Elena stands up to serve, and I notice that Mouse is still clutching her hand. Very gently she uses her free hand to extract the other. Mouse looks like without his hold on her, he might fall.

The food gets served somehow without further comment. It gives us all something to focus on during the long silence that follows. The clinking of silver on china is almost deafening. I rack my brains for a conversation starter while wondering where the famous Rachel repertoire has gone.

Iron Lady's voice makes everyone jump. "So you are a senior this year, Sage?"

I swallow my mouthful of food without chewing it fully. "Umm, yes. Finally, a senior."

"You don't go to Elena's school though, do you?" I look at Elena and Mouse. Why would it be her school and not his, I wonder.

"Where do you guys go?" I ask Elena.

She smiles her magical smile. "I'm at Lawrence. Where are you?"

"Bell. You're seniors, too?"

She pauses to glance at Mouse. He hasn't eaten a bite, but he keeps rearranging the food on his plate with his fork. He looks up when he realizes we're watching him.

"What?" He asks Elena like she's asked him a question. They sit silently looking into each other's eyes. I can almost hear the conversation they must be having, but an eerie silence hangs over the table.

My mother is observing with her therapist eyes, and Iron Lady is watching me, critically.

"Not a trick question." I use one of my mother's favorite lines.

"Elena's a senior," Iron Lady says.

Another lengthy silence ensues, but this time I use the lull to study the twins. Ethan's translucent gray eyes are trained on his plate. Elena's eyes keep darting between her grandmother and Ethan. I can't decide which of them is more nervous. Iron Lady looks from my mother to me and back again, avoiding any chance of eye contact with the twins. Perhaps one or more of us say, "Please pass this or that," but by and large the meal is finished in silence.

"Is everyone ready for dessert? Everyone except my picky grandson." Iron Lady's voice is thick with annoyance.

Elena throws me an apologetic look. Mouse looks like he wants to crawl under the table. Inexplicably, I want to do something to draw him in, make him feel better.

"So, Ethan, do you swim on a team?" It is my only point of reference with him. All of a sudden I am in the spotlight again. Iron Lady's motion is suspended, and my mother raises her eyebrow. I feel like I need to explain myself somehow. "I see you . . . him . . . In the mornings . . . sometimes . . ." I hear my own voice trail off.

Mouse sits up a little taller and even glances at me a couple of times. "I . . . I like swimming," he manages.

"Me too."

Ethan smiles a little, and I feel like I have accomplished something huge.

Then it all falls apart. Elena gets up to clear the plates, and my mother nudges me to help, so I get up and move around to the other side of the table until I am standing behind Mouse. As I reach over to take his plate, I register the heat radiating off of his shoulder. He has on a long-sleeved white shirt like his sister, and I think, he must be awfully hot in that. In that instant, he absently reaches down and rolls up his sleeves, first the right arm then the left, as though he has suddenly realized that he is indeed a bit warm. Then time simultaneously speeds up and slows down. His left forearm is covered with an angry red burn scar that runs from the elbow all the way down to his fingertips. I gasp involuntarily. Ethan pulls his sleeve back down to hide the scar and looks up at me. His eyes are so childlike, begging for comfort or acceptance.

For some unfathomable reason I reach down and put my hand on his shoulder. I barely have time to consider how delicate his bones feel under my fingers before the ground begins to tip and the room spins, my perspective shifts oddly, and it feels like I am sitting at the table across from Rachel with panic rising in my throat. The skin on my left arm burns, and I desperately need to get out of that room, the spinning sensation intensifies along with a sharp pain in my temples, and I'm standing over Ethan again.

He jumps up like I've set fire to him. His sudden movement knocks his glass to the floor where it shatters and splashes lemonade and ice all over me. Shocked by the flying glass and the cold hitting my legs, I drop the stack of plates. They clatter and crash on the stone floor in cacophony of chaos.

Elena crosses from the sink to Ethan's side as he melts into big frightened tears. Iron Lady's brows are knit in disapproving frustration, but she doesn't move from where she stands serving the apple pie. My mother by contrast flies into a flurry of righting the wrong even before the pieces have stopped flying. By the time I can move again, Ethan and Elena are gone. I can hear Mouse's sobs from another part of the house, and I wonder what alternate universe has just collided with this one.

While my mother and the old lady are bent over cleaning up the mess, I circle around to the other side of the table to finish my mother's wine in a single gulp. And then like the other "children," I make my exit. Slipping out the door, I cross to the far end of the pool that is shadowed and private. I slip off my sandals and sit with my legs dangling in the cool water. Just breathe, I tell myself, but my heart is beating like I've been chased, and I can't think. The wine burns in my gut now, my temples are imploding, and the world is still spinning a little too fast. I wish I had thought to grab the bottle. Across the pool through the screen door I watch my mother and Iron Lady bustling about. In the window above them, Elena and Ethan sit facing each other. I tear my eyes from their scene and focus on the ripples I make cross the pool with my feet.

My pulse is returning to normal when Elena suddenly appears and sits beside me.

"Sorry about all that," she offers in her musical way.

"What exactly are you sorry for?" I ask.

"My brother, my grandmother, the whole thing. I don't know." She takes off her shoes and sits down next to me.

"Shouldn't I be the one apologizing?" It comes out like an accusation.

"What for?" She levels me with her blue stare.

"I made your brother cry, broke all the dishes, caused this mess!" Her obtuseness frustrates me, and my temples are pounding harder again.

"Ethan will be fine. He just doesn't like to be touched."

"You think?" She doesn't offer any more information, so I blurt out, "And what's up with the school thing?"

"Ethan's home-schooled." Her voice stays even and calm; it's maddening.

"Any particular reason?" I ask after a beat.

"Ethan will tell you if he wants you to know."

I'm seething, but I don't know why, so I stop talking and try to concentrate on the water.

Then the freakiest thing of the whole strange night happens. Elena puts her hand on mine. In an instant all the anger, guilt, headache, and nausea evaporate. Like magic it's gone. I look up into her cerulean eyes and jump away.

"What the hell did you just do?"

Elena smiles with tired eyes, looks down, and says, "I have this gift."

Chapter 2 (Playing with Fire)

Once the mortar begins to crumble, there is no turning back; there can be no flight from the darkness that someone else reveals.

The next morning I wake when it is still dark. I try to think of something normal to keep from thinking about them, but against my own will I find myself at the window waiting. I have no idea how long I stand there, but when the door finally creaks and Mouse slips into the light, I am able to breathe again. Back and forth he glides beneath the water and up to the surface for a moment. I don't hear my mother come in and stand beside me, but I am not surprised to find her there watching with me.

"Okay, Mom, give me something here. Is it autism? Some kind of brain injury from a fall? What's his deal?"

"No, Sage, not autism. He's never suffered a brain injury. Now you give me something. Why do you need to know? What are you doing here?"

I think about it for a long time. What bone can I throw her without totally tipping my hand? More importantly, what is it she wants to hear. "I don't know. Maybe I can help him." When I hear the words out loud, I wonder if they're true.

"Hmm, maybe," my mother kind of echoes back. We watch Ethan in silence as he slips from the water to the deck so gracefully. He wraps the towel around his waist and turns to look up at my window. I take a step back, but I know he's seen me. For a split second I feel embarrassed and guilty, and then it dawns on me: he knew I was watching him. Maybe he's known since the first morning. I get the same light-headed feeling I had when I saw the burn scar on his arm. My mother has stepped back from the window too, but not for the same reason. She's watching me with a worry furrow creasing her brow.

"It has something to do with that burn on his arm, doesn't it?" I say.

"You know I can't tell you anything specific, Sage."

"Then tell me something general, anything."

She formulates her next phrase, practicing in her mind, and finally she speaks. "Think of Ethan as stuck in time. The past 13 years haven't really happened for him. He's really only about four-years-old."

I think about it for a few seconds. "Well, a little who, what, when, where might be nice."

"That's more than I should say already. Come on, Herbie, don't be mad."

"Not with the dorky nickname, Madre!" She is trying to distract me.

"Not with the pseudo-Spanish again," she mimics, laughing.

I pick up the nearest item, a dirty sock, and hurl it at her head.

She catches it rather nicely and takes aim at my belly. I flinch, and she pegs me in the face.

"Very nice!" I feign anger.

"Last one down makes the coffee." She bolts out the door before me. We jostle each other down the narrow stairs and end up falling into the kitchen at the same time, giggling. A knock at the door stops us short.

"For you?" she asks me.

"Please. My only friend in the world is a gazillion miles away." I say. By the time I flip the dead-bolt and get the door open, no one's there. "Guess they were in a hurry," I say. I am about to shut the door when I notice something on the porch. I go out, pick up the delicate origami flower, and bring it inside.

"This yours?" I ask my mom, handing it to her.

"Not mine." She examines it carefully and hands it back to me smiling. "I think it's for you. Your name is on it, here under the leaf, with a picture of something."

She hands it back to me, and there on the underside of the leaf is my name in lovely miniature letters and beneath that is a tiny but unmistakable drawing of a mouse.

My mother must think I am crazy because I drop the thing on the table like it's on fire and walk out the door in my boxers and t-shirt. Before I make it to the Paige's house, Elena comes out.

"Hey there, nice outfit!"

"I'm not in the mood for chit chat. How the hell did your brother get my book. Is breaking and entering a hobby of his?"

"Slow down, Sage. If you're missing something, Ethan is the last one in the world who would have --"

"I'm not missing anything! God, don't play dumb!"

"What do you think he did?" Elena's voice comes back as hard as Iron Lady's, and I realize how ridiculous this will sound if I am wrong somehow.

"Your brother left me little gift just now!"

"What are you talking about?" Elena's hands are on her hips, and her eyes are shooting ice daggers.

"I'll show you." I reach out to grab her arm, but half way there my hand veers away as I remember the last time I touched her. It's an obvious move that she doesn't miss, and her eyebrow raises. "Come with me," I say.

Elena follows me into the apartment. My mother has gone back upstairs, and the flower lies on the kitchen table where I dropped it.

"One of E's flowers!" The shock in Elena's voice is palpable. "Where did you get this?"

"Where did I get it? Try to keep up, please! I just told you. He gave it to me."

"That's impossible!"

I think about slapping her to wake her up, but I don't have to. She picks up the flower, turns over the leaf and sees my name there in her brother's handwriting. She shakes her head in disbelief.

"Clearly possible!" I say.

"I don't get it. Why would E give this to you?"

"That's not the question you should be asking! And he didn't give it exactly; he left it."

"Why are you so pissed off, Sage? Don't you get it? This is a completely amazing thing!"

"Got it! That's the question! The first one."

"So . . . ?"

"Oh, you want me to answer the question?"

Elena shakes her head like she doesn't want to know or maybe she doesn't appreciate my sarcasm. Then she heads for the door still holding my flower. I circle around and block her exit.

"Look at the picture under my name." I demand.

Elena looks at it closely. "So what. It's a mouse. Is it supposed to mean something?"

I'm beginning to believe she doesn't know anything about my book. "What it means is that your brother read my journal!"

I am expecting the fight to get good at this point. After all, I am accusing her brother of a crime, sort of. But instead of defending him, she smiles. I have no idea what to do, so I grab the flower out of her hand just to make her stop smiling.

"You wrote about my brother in your journal?" It's like an accusation or victory for her.

There is no good way to respond, which makes me more defensive. "I write about everyone! That's not the point."

"I think that is the point, Sage."

"Then you're wrong! The point is that the only way he could know that I call him Mouse is if he read my book!"

Elena is nearly laughing. "Are you sure it's the only way he could know?"

"How else would he know? I haven't told anyone about him . . . you all. . . ."

Elena sidesteps around me, smiling even wider. "Don't be so sure about that. Ethan has a gift too." Then she's gone. I watch her get in her grandmother's truck and pull down the driveway past my door. I cannot imagine what gift she might be talking about, and I don't really care. I just want to have some normal conversation with some normal people.

My mom comes down carrying her coffee, notebook, and planner.

"Everything okay?"

I roll my eyes in response and throw the flower down in the middle of the table again.

"I won't be back till dinner tonight. Do you think you can get the rest of this kitchen stuff put away today?" She is half way out the door by the time I answer.

"Sure," I say, but I have no intention of doing anything at home.

She comes back in. "Please, Sage. We need to work together as a team."

That cheesy line worked when I was six, and it still works. "Okay, Mom. Promise."

She closes the door, and I reach for the phone. Jo will be away for another six weeks, and I really need to see someone normal, well comparatively anyway. I'll work on unpacking later. I punch in the first six digits of Finn's dad's place and tap the phone against my forehead while Jo's warnings play on a loop in my head. Then I dial the seventh digit and put the receiver to my ear.

Finn answers on the fifth ring, "Yeah?"

"Nice phone manners," I say.

"What? Sage, is that you?"

"Yeah." I mimic his tone.

"How'd you get this number?"

"I'll tell you if you come get me and take me out to the lake."

"Hmm. 'kay, but I have to be back by 2. I have an appointment with my shrink."

"Oh, I see. You aren't in crisis I hope."

"Very funny. You better watch out or I'll have to tell her about the chick who's stalking me."

"Now who's the comedian? I'll be in front of the Exodus Cafe in 30 minutes. Don't make me wait." I hang up on his "ooh" noises, feeling very much in control.

Finn shows up 20 minutes late, just about the time I am going to give up and head home. His timing is perfect. I have worked my way past annoyed and into worried, so I end up glad to see him instead of pissed off. He takes his helmet off and puts it on me. That move gets me every time. The first time I rode on his bike he explained it to me like this. "It might look bad for me in court if I killed my shrink's kid."

It would kill him for me to think he cared.

The ride out to the lake is probably my favorite part of our outings. I don't have to come up with witty repartee or triple think every move and every word. I just wrap my arms around Finn's waist, press my thighs into his and let the hills roll by while a random sound-track plays in my head. I don't think there's anything I like better than being on the back of Finn's bike. I have a good feeling today. I am definitely going to have something to write about tonight.

When we get to our spot, it's deserted as usual. Finn sits on his bike and stares at me after I've dismounted and removed his helmet.

"You gonna stay awhile?" I ask a little nervously.

"Maybe." He flashes me his dimples, but he doesn't move from the bike.

"What? Is my hair on fire?" It's out of my mouth before I can stop it.

Finn's dimples go as flat as his eyes. I am not supposed to know about the arson part since he hasn't told me about it, but I do know, and he's probably smart enough to see my panic. To play it off, I pull my t-shirt over my head and undo my bikini top in a single move. I step forward and kiss him before running off the cliff that leads to a 15 foot drop into the cold lake below.

After I hit the water, I stay under for a minute, savoring the icy silence. My heart is pounding from the fall, the cold, and my mistake. I need to play my cards closer to my chest. I feel Finn hit the water inches from my head and dart out of the way. We surface at the same time.

"Refreshing!" Finn's dimples are back, and the sun is shining in his eyes.

After we swim around for a while, somersaulting, floating, and diving to the bottom to bring up handfuls of slime to fling at each other, Finn suddenly disappears. I am spinning around looking for him when I'm suddenly pulled under. He grabs me tight around the waist and holds me against him as he pulls me toward the shallow water. When we surface and stand up, I am totally breathless. His heat and strength scare me a little, but when he kisses me and our tongues touch, I want to get even closer. He has one arm around my waist and the other travels from my face to my neck and down. I shiver. Then he starts kissing my neck, hard. I plant both palms on his shoulders and push hard.

"No marks! Damn it, Finn! Stop!"

He lets go and laughs at me. "Scared your mommy will find out about us, little girl."

"You have more to be scared of than I do."

"Oooo," he laughs some more and steps toward me.

I splash him. "Cool off, Lover-boy!" Then I dive away and swim back over to the cliff. He follows at a safe distance.

We get out and climb the rocks like lizards. At the top of the cliff we sprawl on our backs side-by-side and soak up the hot sun in silence. I think of a thousand things to say, but I keep my mouth shut. Finn needs to be the one to talk I decide. Finally, he props himself up on one elbow to look at me. "What has Rachel told you?"

"Nothing. She can't. You know that." I get up and walk over to where I dropped my clothes.

"You didn't answer the question," he yells from the rock.

I slip on the t-shirt and go back to him. "Finn, Rachel hasn't told me anything about you." I can look right in his eyes because I'm not lying. "I can't exactly ask her. Like, hey, Mom, tell me about that hot guy with the motorcycle. What's his damage? Can I?"

"I guess not." Finn lies back down and closes his eyes.

I sense my chance. "I can't ask her," I say evenly, "but I can ask you. Can't I?"

I wait for Finn to move, but the seconds tick by. I wonder if he heard me. I can barely hear his reply when it finally comes. "Go ahead, ask. I dare you."

Not what I expected. My voice breaks when I say, "So, Finn, what is your damage?"

Before I can react, he has me pinned on my back with my arms under his knees and his face an inch from mine. I crane my neck up to kiss him, but he bites my lip.

"OW! Play nice!" I say.

He sneers. "Play nice? What are we playing at here, Sage."

He's starting to scare me a little. "I don't know." I try to push him off me, but he is too strong. "I thought we were having fun," I say.

"You having fun now, Sagey?" He kisses my nose.

"A blast! Get off me."

"Please? Where's my please, little girl?"

"Fine, have it your way. Get off me, please."

"See how easy that was." He rolls away from me. I jump to my feet and start walking away. "Come back, Sage. Don't be mad. I was just playing." I keep walking past his bike toward the road. "Come on, you can't walk back," he yells.

"I'll hitch," I yell, but we both know I won't.

"Come back. I'll tell you what you want to know." I pause for a step, and he knows he's got me. "I know you want it," he says into the breeze.

I turn around and go back as far as the bike. "Go ahead then. Tell," I say keeping the bike between us.

"What? Tell what?" he asks getting up and coming over.

"Anything. Why you have to see a shrink."

He looks down and frowns. He's embarrassed I think, but before I can blink, Finn's wall is back up.

"Court order. I was arrested. My dad has money. I got a hot lawyer. I'm white and only 17. I got a shrink instead of serving time. Sweet deal if you ask me. And you are my silver lining."

"How do you figure?" He's distracting me from what I want to know.

"I get sent to a shrink and maybe I don't get cured, but I get you." He's moving forward, so I step back.

"Uh uh, not so fast, Mr. Smooth-talker, cured of what?"

"If you want to know that, you have to come here." I hesitate, so he adds, "Don't be scared. I won't hurt you."

I take a step toward him, and he grabs my wrist and pulls me in. I let him kiss me.

"Cured of what?" I demand, trying hard to get free of his grasp.

"We aren't so different. Are we?" he asks, twisting my arm till it starts hurting.

I keep my eyes locked on his and lean away from him. "What are you talking about?"

"You like playing with fire too." I am pulling as hard as I can when he lets go, and I stumble back and fall flat on my ass. He throws the helmet to me where I sit and gets on the bike.

"Get on. I'll take you home." He guns the motor.

I put the helmet on, pick up my bikini top, shove it in my pocket, and get on behind him. All I can think on the way home is how little information I got and how much it might have cost me. Short fuse, short memory, my mom used to say about one of her boyfriends. I hope she is right in this case, or I will never get to the inner sanctum of Euan Finnian Mulcahy. When we get to Exodus, I hand him the helmet and flash him. I am rewarded with a smile, dimples and sparkles and all.

"I showed you mine!" he says. "Your turn."

I am confused by the non sequitur. I flash him again.

"Not those, though I don't mind the second helping. Tell me how you got my dad's number?"

I hesitate a second. "I saw it in Rachel's planner and memorized it."

"Hmm. Later, Stalker-girl."

"Later, Fire-boy."

He doesn't smile, but he gives me a wink before he puts his helmet on. I breathe a sigh of relief as I walk home. Finn seems okay, and I have plenty of time to unpack.

I eat lunch, put on some music, and get to work, leaving Ethan's flower where it lay. I can't bring myself to throw it out, but I don't want it in my room either.

Before I start unpacking more boxes, I rearrange what Rachel has already put up. She has no gift for organization, and if I left it to her, the plates and pots would be in the same cupboard. We move a lot, so we travel pretty light, and it doesn't take me long to get all the boxes unloaded and broken down. I take them out to the trash cans beside the main house and stop to wade on the pool steps for a few minutes.

When the truck comes up the drive, my first instinct is to run back to the apartment and lock the door. Instead I stay in the water. Elena gets out of the truck and waves to me, nice as can be. I wave back, no need to be nasty after all. She goes around to the other side and heads into the house with an arm load of groceries. I am coming over to offer her a hand, but instead of Elena, Ethan comes through the door. Maybe four or five feet separate us by the time he realizes I'm there, and we both stop.

His hair is all mussed like he just woke up. Curls fall over his forehead and neck. I am a little startled to realize that we are the same height. He glances at me shyly. My anger from the morning has long since dissipated. He looks so sweet and vulnerable that I cannot imagine harshing on him.

"Hi, Ethan," I say, softly.

"Hi, Sage." He looks down at the ground and rocks back on his heels.

"Do you want some help with the bags?" I motion toward the truck.

"Sure," he nods and smiles a little.

I keep my distance while he reaches in for some bags, and he waits a couple of steps away while I load up. We walk back to the house together. My mom is on her way out when we get to the door, and I know that she must have been watching from the kitchen. I open my mouth to tell her that I am helping, not socializing, but she puts up her hand to silence me.

"See you tomorrow, Ethan," she says as she lets us in.

"Bye, Rachel," he says, eyes shyly on the ground.

Elena is in the kitchen putting things away. "Is that it, E?"

Ethan looks at me. "Yeah, I think we got it all," I say.

Elena turns around, surprised by my voice. "Sage?" She looks at me and then Ethan and gives me a knowing little wink.

I give her my best 'shut-up' look. "Yup, that's me," I say coolly, putting the bags on the table and turning to go.

"Can you give me a hand?" Elena is trying to put a cereal box on the top shelf of the cupboard that she can't reach. Ethan and I both step forward and almost collide. I quickly recover and step back to let him through, but we make eye contact and my stomach flip flops. Something like a conversation without words runs through my head leaving me dizzy. Ethan helps Elena while I stand awkwardly, trying to regain my balance.

"You okay, Sage?" Elena asks after she's turned around. I watch Ethan take her hand. They do the weird twin thing they do when they look at each other, and I expect at the moment she knows more about what just happened than I do.

"I better get back," I say finding my footing again.

"Thanks, Sage." Ethan's voice is so sweet and unexpected. I

suddenly wish he would ask me to stay.

"Yeah, thanks," Elena echoes.

I am about to push the screen door open when I remember the flower. "Oh, uh, Ethan, thanks for the flower. It's . . . uh . . . really beautiful," I stammer.

Ethan's cheeks turn scarlet as he moves behind Elena like a shy little kid, but he smiles too, and I'm happy to leave him like that.

I'm about to turn and reach for the door handle when the sound of a motorcycle engine startles me out of the moment. I look toward the street just in time to catch a glimpse of my mother on the back of Finn's bike wearing his helmet. Inside the apartment I glance at the clock, 2 pm on the dot. I dial Jo's number in a daze.

"No way! It can't be what you're thinking." Jo reasons. "Saint Rachel, champion of the defenseless and downtrodden, would never fool around with a client! Pull yourself together, girl."

"It's just one more weirdness in a series of severe oddities," I protest.

"Relax. She's just getting him to trust her by showing him that she trusts him. It's a classic shrink-like ploy. Don't you think?"

"Right, Jo Jo. Lots of shrinks ride around on motorcycles with their patients. Admit it. I am not entirely off-base here."

"Okay, but your mom is not exactly a normal therapist. You need to spend less time worrying about what your mom is doing with Finn and more time worrying about what you are doing with Finn."

"Can you say 'progress?' I made actual progress today."

"What progress? He told you something you already knew. Plus he didn't even really tell you. Can you say 'dangerous?'"

"Oh, Jo Jo, don't make me resort to 'last word' again."

"Okay. I gotta go practice anyway. Later."

My room pulses with silence after I hang up the phone. I take my journal down to the kitchen and nuke a cup of old coffee. I am at the table trying to formulate a coherent thought, absently fingering Ethan's flower. A tap on the screen door wakes me up. It's Elena. I close my book.

"Busy?"

"Not really."

"Come swimming with us."

I hesitate because of the rule, but I am really in a mood to defy Rachel, so I say, "I'll be out in a minute."

I go up and change quickly. Outside Ethan and Elena have set up a volleyball net across the pool. I stand on the porch for a minute watching them splash around. Elena is wearing a long sleeved t-shirt and boy shorts that fall past her knees. She's so tiny and cute that it almost pains me that she's not showing more skin. Elena squeals as she misses the ball and goes for it under the net, but from the bottom of the pool Ethan grabs her leg and pulls her down. He makes it to the surface before her and gets the ball. She comes up coughing. "Lanie, you okay?" Ethan hurries to her, and she grabs the ball from him laughing.

"No fair!" he protests, but his whole face is smiling. Elena turns and sees me standing there.

"Hey, you! Come on in. E needs some help. I'm kicking his butt."

"I think we can turn that around." I slip into the water beside Ethan and give him a wink.

"Serve, Lanie!" he yells.

The game is on with rules that are constantly changing and lots of yelling and splashing. I am careful not to touch Ethan, but I can't keep from staring at his scar when he isn't aware that I'm looking. Every time we make a point Ethan laughs. The sound of it makes my chest tight and my head spin, kind of like when our eyes meet but less intense. I don't want the game to end, but we score the required 15 points, and Elena spikes the ball out of the pool in mock defeat.

We have all collapsed on the pool stairs when the motorcycle roars up the drive. I jump up, but realize there is no way for me to make it into the apartment without being seen, so I sit back down. Rachel gets off the bike, hands Finn his helmet, and stops to take in the montage. I expect her to summon me home or at least give me the classic now-you're-in-trouble frown. Instead she waves to us casually and heads into the apartment. Her lack of reaction has me stunned. Then Finn turns off the motor and dismounts. My head begins to buzz. Did he actually tell my mother about us? Elena rises to meet him, and suddenly I realize he is not coming over to talk to me.

"Finnian Mulcahy!" Elena says icily, moving quickly across the deck to meet him.

"Nice to see you too, Lanie." Ethan flinches at the sound of his nickname for his sister.

Elena stops Finn's progress around the pool with a hand on his chest. "Leave Ethan alone. Or better yet, just leave," she says, as Finn jumps back out of her reach.

"Nice try, Elly-Mae. Don't pretend you aren't happy to see me. I've kind of missed you." Finn's voice is sincere. "I see you're making friends with Sage. What's up, Sage?" he yells. I raise a hand, but I stay where I am next to Ethan. "Hey, Ethan, you got yourself a girlfriend?"

"No!" Ethan mumbles.

"Better watch out for her, Ethan. She likes to play with fire. Don't you, Sage?" Ethan looks at me, confused.

"It's okay, Ethan," I say quietly.

"What about you, Elena, you up for some fun sometime?"

"Go home, Finn," she says.

"Come on, don't be like that. We're tight. Aren't we, Ethan. We all need to stick to together 'cause we're all the same."

"Stop it, Finn," Elena pushes him back a step.

"Okay, okay. No need to get physical." He gets back on his bike, and starts it, but he doesn't put his helmet on or pull away.

"Sorry, Sage," he yells over the roar of the motor, "You can't be in our club . . . unless you can get your bastard of a father to murder your mother."

For a moment the only thing in motion is Finn's bike. My mind clicks around his words until I hit upon the revelation that holds the three of us momentarily suspended. The next sound is a sharp intake of breath beside me. The tears have already begun to fall down Ethan's cheeks. I ache to take his hand, but Elena is already there with her arm wrapped around him. I don't watch them go. The door slamming reminds me that I am alone, stuck in this horrible moment with dust filling my lungs, and rocks settling around my feet.

Chapter 3 (Truth or Dare)

Guilt and anger are bound together in the darkness behind the wall. When the stones crumble and light pours in, it's hard to tell them apart.

The evening passes somehow. Darkness brings relief from the heat and the surreal swirl of the day. I sleep easily, but my mostly absent father makes his way into my dream, where he becomes a glittering dragon, lays on top of my mother, pressing her into the bed and burning her alive with his fiery breath. I wake up unable to scream or breathe. Dawn is still hours away, but I'm afraid to go back to sleep, so I go down to the kitchen with my journal.

Ethan's flower rests where it fell on the table. At least a hundred tiny folds must have been made to create it. I close my eyes and imagine Ethan's long slim fingers creasing and turning the pink paper over and over. Suddenly, the paper turns orange and morphs into flame, reaching up and licking his arms. My eyes pop open. I'm sitting in the kitchen with my book open in front of me and a trickle of sweat creeping down my back. I get up to make coffee.

I take my mug, book, and pen out to the pool and sit with my feet in the water. The dim morning light is enough to write by and the cool water keeps me alert. Ethan will be out soon to swim, I hope. I want to write about him and Elena, but I can't.

I write about Finn instead. His mother is dead. Everything else I know about Finn pales in light of this fact. I had assumed that Finn was like me, semi-abandoned. My father left me a long time ago; I wasn't even three, so I don't remember a world where he was anything more than an inconsistent visitor. When I was little, I made him holiday cards with hearts and stars, hand and foot prints, drawings of him and me separated by the width of the paper. I'd keep them in a special place, so I could give them to him when he'd unexpectedly appear. Frequency and duration of his visits varied from year to year, generally amounting to a couple of visits a month for a few hours. He always brought along the girlfriend du jour, who either resented my presence or doted on me. There were also stretches of Thursday night dinners at the same restaurant. Then just when I thought I could rely on him at least for this, my mom would pick me up from school instead of him. I'd pretend to be happy to see her. I'd say I didn't want to have dinner with him anyway. Mom would take me for ice cream or a movie, and we'd skip dinner altogether. She made sure I knew it wasn’t my fault, or hers. Maybe she wanted me to blame him, get angry, but I couldn’t.

I thought Finn’s mom was like that, around but not around. Now I see him as a small boy, crying for his mother, all alone. I understand why he pushes me away, and why he pulls me in. I think of the silent comfort I might offer with my legs wrapped around him and our hands pressed together. I want him to be here now, riding up on his bike, looking for me, reaching out his hand, honest and vulnerable, instead of hard and sarcastic, choosing me to comfort him. It's a pointless fantasy.

Instead I picture his father, a taller heavier version of Finn with the same dark hair. I saw Sean Mulcahy once when he came to meet my mom. I imagine his eyes flash in a moment of anger as he wraps his hands around the throat of a small red-haired beauty with blue pleading eyes and rosy cheeks. The image almost makes me laugh. By Finn's account his father is as bland as two-day-old oatmeal, and about that warm, not the type to commit a crime of passion, not the type to execute a successful cover-up. My mind reels with the possibilities and the questions. I resolve to get online this morning, and if I can't find the information on the net, I'll go to the library as soon as it opens. Something like that must have made the local newspapers, assuming it was a local crime.

I'm still writing about Finn when the door finally creaks. Ethan comes out wrapped in a towel. He wears it like a blanket around his shoulders. His soft curls create a halo with the dawn light behind him. He smiles when he sees me and half waves. When he gets closer, I can see that his eyes are dark-rimmed and swollen. Instead of getting in the water, Ethan sits next to me, and pulls his knees into his chest.

"Hey there," I say. "You okay?"

Ethan nods, and hunches up his shoulders like he's cold.

"Going for a swim?" I ask.

"Maybe. I don't know." He looks at my book, still open in my lap. "Are you writing about what Finn said?" He pauses for a second and adds, "I don't like him." I close the book.

"Why?"

"He's mean. He scares me."

"How do you know Finn?"

"He went to my school when I was little, and he used to live near us. Elena was friends with him, sort of, I think." Ethan talks to the water as though he can't say words and look at me at the same time. When he finishes, he looks up, our eyes connect, and he reaches over and touches my hand.

Suddenly, I see what Ethan is feeling. It's like a dream where you somehow become someone else. The air is crisp and cold. Elena and I are sitting on swings, but not really swinging, in the nearly empty school yard. My (Ethan's) chest is tight and my throat is raw like I've been crying. A sing song voice reaches out to us from across the field "Elly-Mae! Elly-Mae! Come out, come out; it's time to playay!" I look up and see a younger Finn sauntering toward us, leading a group of other boys. Every muscle in my body tightens with fear and loathing. "Hey, Peethan! Wanna play with the big boys?" I feel the heat of humiliation washing over me. Elena rises from the swing to meet Finn halfway. My jaw locks in anger when he kisses her, but I am helpless in the face of the gang of boys. Elena steers them away as she glances back at me over her shoulder, but it doesn't quite quell the panic rising in my throat.

Ethan breaks the connection and looks away. When I return to my own head, it feels like it might split open. I can't find my voice. My first rational thought is that my overactive imagination just ran amok, but Ethan is rubbing his temples too, glancing carefully at me, gaging my reaction.

"Finn scares me," Ethan says quietly, stretching his legs into the water.

I nod. We sit silently while I gather my thoughts. I watch Ethan kick his legs at intervals and count the rings eddying across the pool.

"Ethan?" He looks up. "What just happened?"

He licks his lips and fidgets a little, pulling the towel more tightly around himself. "I don't know. I mean, I know what you mean, but I don't know what it is." Then his eyes start to fill with tears. "I'm sorry. I shouldn't have . . ."

"No, Ethan, it's okay." Instinctively, I move closer to him, reach out my hand to comfort him, but I pull back before touching him. "It's okay. Really."

He wipes his eyes with his palms. "Okay." He looks like he's going to say something else, but he stops and looks over at the apartment. My eyes follow his to the upstairs window, the window in my room. Rachel stands there looking down at us. Then Ethan turns back toward the house for a moment as if someone has called his name.

"I gotta go," he mumbles, standing up. "Bye, Sage."

"Bye, Ethan."

I watch him go into the house and miss him immediately. There is nothing left to do but face the music with my mother. At the door I pause to work out a strategy. I decide to start on the offensive. When I open the door, Rachel is coming down the stairs carrying her coffee mug.

"Spy much?" I ask, turning my back to her at the sink.

"Relax, Sage, you aren't in trouble."

I turn around to see if she's kidding. "For real? All these years of 'no fraternizing with my clients,' and here I am caught in the act, and I'm not in trouble?"

Rachel raises an eyebrow - so annoying. "Rules change."

I take a minute to absorb this shift, "And?"

"And what?"

"The rules of this new game are?"

"It's not a game, and I'm not sure what the rules are. We'll decide as we go. Okay?"

"Let's see if I understand correctly. Not a game; no rules; Rachel is unsure. Now I know the apocalypse is coming."

"Can you please drop the snide?"

"I'm not sure."

"Fine, then. I'll see you this afternoon." Rachel brushes by me, sets her coffee mug in the sink, and scoops up her planner and laptop on her way to the door. She stops with her hand on the handle. I think she might turn and finish the fight, but she talks to the door. "The laundry is taking over your room. Please take care of it today."

"Come on, Madre. You can't just leave."

The screen door slams. I sit down on the floor with my back against the cabinets, close my eyes, and breathe. The phone rings, sending my stomach into my throat. I let it ring until the machine picks up.

"Oh, hi. I thought you were home, Sage. It's me, Elena. Call me." I scramble to the counter and pick up the receiver just before she hangs up.

"Hey. Hey? I'm here."

"Hi. Wanna do something?"

"You mean like hang out or something?" It's a stupid question, and I sound bitchy. "I mean, sure."

"Coffee at Exodus?"

"Works for me. Is Ethan coming?" I realize too late how it sounds.

She doesn't bother to suppress the giggle. "He's with Rachel. See you outside in a minute."

I run upstairs to change out of my pajamas, brush my teeth, and run a comb through my hair. On my way down I shovel all the laundry from my bedroom floor into a basket and push it down the stairs like a sled. I haul the load outside. Elena is already waiting at the foot of the stairs.

"Give me a sec," I call over my shoulder on my way to the washing machine in the garage on the other side of our apartment. I am just about to start stuffing the washer when Ethan and my mom come out of the house. Ethan is carrying a laundry basket and my mother is behind him. When he sees me at the washer, he turns around to go back in the house, but my mom urges him on.

"Yours can wait, Sage," my mom says, moving my basket out of the way with her foot.

I take a step back, and Ethan starts loading sheets into the washer without even saying hello. He looks upset so I say, "Cheer up, Ethan it's only laun . . . dry." My voice trails off because my mom is giving me a shut-up-and-go-away look, and Elena is motioning for me from the driveway.

"Come on, Sage, let's go." She's calling to me, but looking at Ethan.

"Okay." I consider chalking it up as another bizarre moment in my more and more bizarre life, but by the time we are two houses down the street I have to ask. "So what was up with all that?"

Elena stops walking. "Let it go, Sage."

We start walking again, and I am waiting for Elena to say something, but she doesn't. "Come on, Elena."

"Sorry."

Then it dawns on me. “My mom’s been at this for a while,” I say. “He’s not the first bed-wetter she’s treated.”

"If you know so much, why even ask?" Elena says, walking faster. I know I crossed some line, so I stop talking. We make it all the way to the cafe in total silence.

When we get there, the place is humming. Exodus is a haven for freaks of all ages. A gray-haired lesbian couple owns the place. The decor smacks of garage sale kitsch with turtles that light up, faux cubist art done in oil crayons by some kid or housewife, and lamp shades with glass beads that sit atop ceramic flamingo heads. Seven tables fill the center of the room and old sofas from the Goodwill line the outer walls. The first time I walked in I knew I'd found my people.

The girl behind the counter has worked here since she was fifteen, before the lesbians bought the place. She's a total bitch who'd be fired from any self-respecting cafe, but her acerbic attitude appeals to this crowd. A couple who look stoned from the night before make out on one of the couches in a dark corner. A wannabe poet in his 30s sits on another couch with his laptop; he's actually wearing a black beret – albeit twisted backwards. The girl at the counter makes eyes at him, but he either doesn't get it or isn't interested. A fat guy with glasses is arguing with one of the owners about the size of the stage. Some geeky college guys are playing chess by the door, and a couple of middle-age hippy-chick moms are bouncing babies and laughing at the unexpectedly ordinary lives they've found themselves living.

Elena and I wait forever for the barista to get around to making our lattes. In a loud voice I threaten to go behind the counter and make the drinks myself, which Elena thinks is hilarious, but the counter girl doesn't appreciate at all. Elena is still laughing when we sit down.

"Girl, you need to get out more," I say half-joking.

Elena's laugh evaporates. "I have to take care of Ethan."

It is the defining fact of Elena's life. I hear it in her voice through the vague din of the meaningless chatter surrounding us. I don't hear a hint of resentment, though.

Elena continues. "People don't get it, you know. They look at him, but they don't see. They expect something he'll never be."

"Never? Really?"

Elena smiles sadly and shakes her head. "Really. When our mom died, that was it for Ethan. He just gave up or something. I don't fully get it either."

"What about you? It happened to you too, right?"

"It's different for me. I had to grow up fast to take care of my brother, and it wasn't an end for me, it was like a beginning in a way."

"Your gift."

She nods.

"But what about Ethan's gift?"

Elena looks up, feigning surprise. "Sooo, what has Ethan been sharing with you?"

"You'll have to ask him," I say, taking a page from her book.

Elena laughs again. It's a sweet genuine, unexpected sound. She bends her head to sip her latte. The way her head is tipped reminds me of Ethan. She smiles again, and I realize that her question was a test. Her brother doesn't keep secrets from her.

Because it seems to me that I passed, I ask, "What happened to your mom?" I know the minute the words are out of my mouth, I shouldn't have asked, and I half hope she didn't hear me.

Elena raises her eyebrows and pushes her chair back. After a long hesitation, she says, "Truth is, Sage, I don't remember anything about what happened to my mother. All I know is that a massive fire burned our house to the ground. My brother and I were rescued, but my mother died. My father took off that night never to be seen or heard from again. Grandmother reluctantly adopted us, probably mistakenly thinking that our father would be back for us any time. The details are a complete blank for me."

"Is it like that for Ethan, too?"

She looks down and frowns exactly like him. "I don't know. I guess I don't want to know. But even if I did, there's no way he would talk about it."

Wrong again, Ethan does keep secrets from Elena. Elena sighs and closes her eyes in resignation or frustration maybe. I want tell her that Rachel will save then both, but it would be bullshit. I have no faith. Something suddenly occurs to me, though.

"Okay, this is a stupid question, but what about your gift? Why don't you just, you know, heal your brother?"

"Now why didn't I think of that?" Her sarcasm startles me. We sit in silence, while I feel stupid, and Elena feels . . . . I can't imagine what she feels, actually.

"Sorry I snapped. I think the healing thing short-circuits or something because we're twins and he's a part of me. I can't 'heal' myself either," Elena says.

"It's like Cassandra," I say. "You know, a downside to every gift."

"Who?"

I shake my head, embarrassed. "You know, the Greek witch chick, she could see the future, but no one believed her."

"That would suck!" We both laugh. Then she waves her hand to fan away any lingering emotion between us like smoke. She takes another sip and a pause before turning back to me with a mischievous glint in her eyes. "Enough about me. I have a few questions for you."

"Should I be scared?"

"Maybe," she laughs.

"Go ahead. I can take it. Let it fly."

"What's up with you and my brother?" She tries to keep her voice light, but I know now why the friendly invite was extended.

She has a right to be suspicious and protective, so I suppress my usual urge to be flippant. "I like Ethan."

She smiles coyly, "Obviously. But that doesn't really answer the question, does it?"

"I guess not." I have no idea what the answer is. Though, for some reason I desperately want to give her one.

Elena leans in toward me and touches my hand. "Don't expect too much. Okay?"

A shadow passes over us, making us look up simultaneously.

"Girl talk. Ooooh. I hope I'm not interrupting anything about me."

Finn's sudden presence makes me jump.

"Did I scare you, Sage?"

"You wish." In my head he's holding me down again, and my heart is pounding louder than the music, but I flash him a smile.

He's already turned from me to Elena. Her eyes have gone from soft to ice cold, and her arms are crossed over her chest.

"So they let you out this morning," Finn says to her.

"What do you want, Finn?" Elena asks.

"I think you know, Elly Mae."

"Go away."

"Come on, it doesn't have to be like that. It's a beautiful day. Can't we hang out, party a little?" Finn's eyes are sparkling, and his dimples make me want to kiss him. Maybe Elena will opt out.

"What do you have in mind? Pulling legs off spiders? Scaring kids on a playground? Or are we setting fires today? Oh yeah, you probably did that yesterday. My bad." Elena says.

"Ouch. Come on, Elena. It'll be fun."

"Fun for who?" Elena asks. I am prickling with the anticipation of getting more of Finn's story.

"Whom." Finn says. "Fun for whom? I'm surprised at you, Elena, slacking off in your responsibilities as miss perfect. Shame. Shame."

"When did you become the grammar police? Last time I checked you were failing English for the twelfth year in a row."

"Oh oh oh. Stabbed again. Through the heart."

Now Elena is smiling grudgingly, and I'm not even there anymore.

My stomach turns, and I have to look away. The acerbic barista is standing over the beret guy. He smiles absently, but his eyes keep wandering back to the words on his screen, and every few seconds he types something even though the girl is leaning over showing her cleavage. The stoned couple unravels themselves from each other, and the girl wobbles off toward the restroom. The chess boys are hunched over the board like they're planning to move the pieces telekinetically. I contemplate leaving, but despite that third-wheel feeling gnawing under my skin, I want to know what will happen next.

"Sage wants to. Don't you, Stalker-girl?" I turn like a puppy at the sound of my name.

"What?"

"Go to the creek. Come on, keep up here."

"I should go home," Elena says half-heartedly.

"Time to change baby brother's diaper?"

Elena gets up and heads for the door. Finn looks at me, amused.

"Yeah, that'll make her want to go," I say.

Finn chases after her, and grabs her arm. She doesn't try very hard to pull away. I watch from the table as I finish my latte. I can't hear what Finn says to her, but the tension drains from Elena's body, and I know he's convinced her somehow. I half expect that they are going to go off and leave me behind, but Elena comes back in and motions for me to join them.

We decide to get Iron Lady's truck since we can't all ride on Finn's bike, and I can't exactly ask for my mom's car. Finn and I wait outside while Elena goes in to finagle permission and the keys from her grandmother. I'm standing by the pool feeling wildly anxious and uncertain about being here with Finn when he comes up behind me. He presses his body against mine, pretending that he's going to push me into the pool. "Why so quiet, Stalker-girl?" he whispers in my ear. The memory of fear washes over me, but I press back against him to feel the rush his body gives me.

"What's with you and Elena." I ask.

He turns me around and looks into my eyes. "Jealous much?"

"Arrogant much?" I try to push him away, but he pulls me closer.

His mouth is right by my ear. I can feel the moist heat and smell the bitter sweetness of his breath. "It's you, Sage. All you." I stop fighting. I weave my hand into his thick black hair and bring his mouth to mine. The door slams. I jump away from him, suddenly afraid of who our audience is. Elena jingles the keys in our direction to get our attention. When I turn back around, Finn is looking up at one of the upstairs windows, smiling. A sour taste rises in my mouth as my eyes travel upward. We *were* playing to an audience. Ethan.

My stomach hurts remembering how Ethan felt when Elena was the one kissing Finn. But I am not Elena I remind myself. It's not much comfort.

We pile into the front seat of the truck with me in the middle. As we pull out of the driveway and down the street, I strain to catch a glimpse of Ethan in the window. Elena drives silently, and on the other side of me Finn wears a self-satisfied smirk. In the small amount of space I have, I pull my arm forward and elbow him hard in the ribs. He grunts with the pain, I hope.

"What was that for?" he asks.

"Play dumb, you prick!" I am shaking with anger now.

"Hey, you were the one macking on me. Besides what's the big deal? Afraid your little boyfriend will be mad at you?"

"Shut up!" Elena and I both yell at the same time.

The growling and clunking of the old truck motor fill the silence that follows. I wonder why Elena doesn't turn around and take Finn back to the cafe, or better yet, dump him on the curb right where we are. I'd suggest it, but . . .

Sugar Creek Park is a sprawling nature preserve with trails and a wide clear-water creek branching through it. Only a few people come to the preserve to jog, swim, hike, and forget that they are in the middle of a city. The air is fragrant with pine when we get out of the truck. The nearby water and hills make the air feel ten degrees cooler. I decide to hike them out to a place in the creek where it widens and opens into a small waterfall that empties to a deep pool. The spot is off the trail, usually deserted, and one of the places my father used to take me when I was little. I lead the way as Elena and Finn follow.

"Where we headed?" Finn asks.

"You'll see," I say.

"You aren't going to push me off a cliff or anything are you?" he asks.

"You'll see," I say.

Elena laughs.

"You planning on helping her?" Finn asks Elena earnestly.

"You'll see," Elena says, and I laugh too.

"That's better," Finn says. "Now we're having fun."

When we get to my spot, it's deserted. Elena inhales deeply, taking in the scene. Then she kicks off her shoes, rolls up her pants an inch or two, and splashes into the stream. Finn strips off his shirt, shoes and shorts, and chases after her in his boxers. Elena turns around and splashes him. Undeterred, he overtakes her, throws her over his shoulder, and jumps over the falls. Elena's scream echoes off the stone walls and hills around us.

"You prick!" Elena yells, sputtering as she surfaces. Finn is laughing.

I take off my shirt and lay back on the hot rocks to bake in the sun.

Their voices recede into the landscape with the birds, bugs, and flowing water. I am standing at the window with Ethan, looking down at me and Finn kissing. "I'm so sorry," I say, taking his hand. His face is wet with tears, but he isn't crying. I turn and pull him into my arms. I bury my face in his soft curls, smell his sadness. I suddenly realize that the tears on his face are mine as I melt into his warm embrace.

A splash of cold water jolts me upright. Elena is standing over me, dripping. "Wake up, sleepyhead."

"Wouldn't want you to miss out on the festivities," Finn comes over with his clothes in hand. He fishes around in his shorts pocket and pulls out a baggy, pipe, and lighter. He makes a big show of emptying the pipe and packing it with fresh herb. "You ladies do want to partake, I assume." Elena looks at me and shrugs. I wonder if she's ever gotten high. I nod coolly like I do it all the time, but the truth is I've only been high a couple of times, and I wasn't wild about the experience.

Finn hands me the pipe and lighter. "First hit's yours, Stalker-girl." I awkwardly flick the lighter several times unsuccessfully. Finn laughs. "Need a hand?"

I glare at him and finally get the thing lit. I put the pipe to my mouth, the flame to the pipe, and inhale deeply. The strange bitter taste makes me want to gag, but I suppress the urge and pass it to Elena. She takes a small puff, barely inhaling, and passes it back to

Finn. Finn holds the pipe in one hand and brings the flame to life in a single deft stroke. As he stares into the light, his eyes go blank, and he just stays there with the pipe poised on the way to his mouth. The clock ticks oddly in my head while Finn stares at the tongue of fire. Elena reaches over and touches his hand. He flinches like she's startled him, and his eyes flash red for an instant. Then he regains control and laughs low, shaking his head.

"Nice try, Elly-Mae, but you know I don't play that game. Save your hocus-pocus for someone who needs it."

Elena looks away. Finn brings the pipe to his lips and lights it. On the next pass, Elena takes a deeper hit. As we pass the pipe, the mood relaxes.

Elena breaks the silence. "I can't believe this place is right in the middle of the city!"

"Amazing that rich people aren't living here in their McMansions," Finn says.

"How'd you find it?" Elena asks.

"My so-called father used to bring me here a long time ago," I say.

"Got some daddy issues, Sage?" Finn shows off his dimples and narrows his eyes.

"Does that turn you on?" I ask, sliding closer.

"Oh yeah, baby." He runs his hand up my arm suggestively.

Elena giggles. "Me too! I have daddy issues too."

Finn jumps up like a panther and pounces on her. She easily rolls him off her and onto me. We collapse into a hysterical dog pile. When the hilarity ebbs, Finn gets up and packs the pipe for another round.

"Okay, girlie girls, are you down with a little game."

"Who you calling a girlie girl?" I jump up and posture like a boxer.

Elena falls over giggling again as Finn takes the challenge and postures back.

"I can take you," he says.

"You can take me where?" I ask with a wink.

Elena cannot stop laughing.

Finn sits back down and motions for me to do the same. When we are all facing each other in a triangle, he lowers his eyes mysteriously and then looks up slowly.

Elena collects herself and leans in. Our foreheads are almost touching when he says, "Truth or Dare."

"Oh, yeah!" I can hardly contain my enthusiasm.

"What?" says Elena.

Finn and I turn to her in mutual surprise. "You never played Truth or Dare?" I ask.

"I guess not."

Elena's reality becomes clear to me. She's never had a slumber party, or snuck out at night, or gone to summer camp, or gotten high.

Finn is already going over the rules for her when I tune back in. "Last one to go gets to ask whoever they want a question. If you don't want to answer the question, you can take the dare. Once you say, 'dare' there's no going back. You have to do the dare. "

"I don't know," she says. "Can I watch?"

"Truth or Dare is not a spectator sport," I chime in.

Finn smiles and nods. "I should have guessed this would be right up your alley, Stalker-girl."

"Shut up," I say taking the pipe and lighter from Elena. "Elena should go first."

"What do I ask?"

"Anything you want to know," I say.

"Make it something juicy," adds Finn. "You want the person to take the dare."

"That reminds me," I say. "Truth or Dare is like Vegas. Whatever we say or do here, stays here. Agreed?"

"Agreed." Finn and Elena say in solemn unity.

"Go ahead then, Elly-Mae, draw first blood." Finn takes another hit.

Elena looks uneasy, as she turns to me. "Okay, Sage, have you ever had sex?"

My eyes get big as Finn dissolves into a puddle of mirth. "Oh yeah! That's how to play the game, Elena. You nailed it on the first try."

There is no good answer. If I say yes, then I'm lying, and Finn will probably know. If I tell the truth, then . . . "Dare," I say loud enough for the word to echo off the canyon walls around us.

"Make it good." Finn says, not at all disappointed by my evasion.

"Hmm. I dare you to jump over the waterfall."

"Too easy!" Finn protests.

"Naked." Elena adds.

"Better."

"Whatever," I say but my hand shakes a little as I fumble with the clasp on my bra and slide off my shorts. Finn makes approving little noises that are not silenced by my stabbing glances in his direction.

I climb up the rocks to where the creek flows open and wide. The instant my feet enter the cold water, Finn and Elena fade away again like I have fallen asleep on the rock again. I look out over the creek in front of me and imagine that I am the only person who has ever been here. I watch the water eddy in a hurry to get somewhere downstream. I turn around and move slowly toward the edge of the falls. The water flows faster and faster. I almost lose my footing on the rocks, dizzy from the pot, but I flail my arms and somehow manage to stay poised on the edge.

In the distance over the din of swirling crashing water I hear Finn chanting. "Jump. Jump. Jump. Jump. Jump." My heart beats in time. No different than at the lake I tell myself stepping over the falls. A moment later, the water rushes over my head and an invisible hand pushes me down into the swirling cold. I want to stay there in that semi-darkness, but I am already floating toward the surface and back to reality.

Elena and Finn are still laughing at me when I get back to the rock.

"You are so a virgin," Finn accuses.

"Nice try, genius, but I already did the dare, and I don't give freebees." I put my bra and shorts back on. "My turn." I look at Elena. There are a thousand questions I want to ask her, but they are all about Ethan or things she claims not to remember. I turn to Finn instead.

"Finn. What happened to your mother?"

Finn's dimples fade. His eyes narrow and then close. A moment later he opens them and trains them on mine like lasers.

"You bitch, you stupid fucking bitch!" He stands up threateningly; and Elena jumps up and takes his arm. He easily shakes her off. For a few seconds he looms over me, and I remember the flash of violence from the lake.

"I'm sorry," I mumble coiling back, bracing myself for a physical attack.

Instead of hitting me, Finn walks away. A couple dozen yards from us he takes the lighter out of his pocket. He flicks it open, igniting a tall flame. He brings it so close to his face I'm afraid he'll burn off his eyebrows. Then he flicks it closed. He repeats the pattern again and again in faster and faster succession. I rise slowly so I am standing beside Elena. The movement makes Finn stop. He throws down the lighter and starts pacing in a circle. He is saying something to himself, but I can't make it out. His breath starts coming in gulps like sobs. Finally, Elena runs forward and steps into his circle. She puts both of her hands in the center of his chest. He doesn't resist this time and in a few seconds he's breathing normally again. Elena drops her arms and walks past me into the creek. Finn sits down with his back against a tree.

I walk over and retrieve the lighter. Finn looks up at me. His eyes are cloudy, confused. I move closer and extend my hand to help him up. He takes it but doesn't rise, so I climb onto his lap facing him. The dampness from his boxers soaks through my shorts. I wonder if this makes him as breathless as it makes me.

"I'm sorry," I whisper. I rest my other hand on his cheek, so I can lean in to kiss him. He lets me, but he doesn't really kiss me back. He holds me there close to him, though. With our eyes locked in a voice I can barely hear, Finn says, "He shot her. My father shot her because of me."

We sit like that in silence for a second, maybe two, maybe two hundred. Then Finn gently pushes me up, takes the lighter from me, and walks back to the rock for another hit. I follow and sit next to him sharing the bowl.

"Come on, Elly-Mae, it's your turn in the hot seat," Finn calls out; his voice is still a little shaky.

Elena has waded nearly across the stream. She turns and makes her way back.

"Maybe we should head home," she suggests.

"Not until you go," Finn says. "Truth or dare, Elly."

"Be nice," Elena pleads.

"Well, I'm not going to ask if you're a virgin cuz we both know about that." Finn raises his eyebrow and engages his dimples. Elena blushes crimson and lowers her head just like Ethan.

"Too much information," I say. And it is. I don't want to know that Finn and Elena . . .

"Just ask the question," Elena says.

"Why is your brother such a freak?"

I think Elena is going to blow a gasket, but she stays cool and without missing a beat says, "Dare."

Finn smiles wickedly. He wanted her to take the dare. "Take off your shirt and pants, and then kiss Sage . . . on the lips."

How typical, I think, and boring, but Elena seems thrown. She's shaking her head.

"I'll kiss Sage, but I am not getting naked for you," Elena says.

"Come on, nothing I never saw before. Besides, this isn't a negotiation; it's Truth or Dare, and you took the dare, so take off your clothes already."

Elena hangs her head and undoes the buttons of her blouse. She stands for a second with it hanging open, pleading silently with Finn. But instead of mercy he reaches over and yanks it down off her shoulders. I am stunned to see scars and cuts up and down both of her arms. They aren't deep, but they are thick and jagged like they were made by something dull.

"Happy now?" she asks without looking up.

"Pants too," Finn says coldly.

Elena stands and drops her jeans around her ankles and steps out of them like a ballerina. The same kinds of cuts run up and down both legs.

Elena looks down at me. "Let's get this over with so Finn can get his rocks off." I stand up facing her.

"Make it good, girls," Finn says.

I don't know why, but I reach down and take Elena's hand in mine. She smiles sadly and leans in. I am surprised by how soft and sweet her kiss is on my mouth. We stay with our lips gently touching too briefly. After we separate, I lean in and kiss her again quickly. She throws her arms around my neck and pulls me into a warm comforting hug. Encircled by her healing arms, a sense of complete belonging and love fills me. A tear is running down my cheek when she lets go.

"Ooo, you girls are so hot!" Finn howls. Hikers two miles away probably hear him.

When she's caught her breath, Elena says, "We should go home." We all retrieve our clothes and put them on. Elena leads the way out of the woods and back to the truck. Finn and I follow, keeping our distance from her. Inside the truck my thigh rests against Finn's. I want to hold his hand, but I resist the impulse. He looks out the window at the passing cars and scenery. Maybe he senses that I'm staring because he finally turns to face me.

"Always the Stalker-girl." He says it sweetly. "Man, that was some bad weed, wasn't it?" Elena and I agree. Elena turns on the radio, and we all half sing along. It feels almost normal. We drop Finn off by his bike without any prolonged good-byes and head home.

Elena pulls into the garage, and I follow her toward the main house. At the door, she stops. "I don't really want to talk right now, Sage."

"I need to square something with Ethan."

"Really?"

"Earlier he saw me and Finn from the window." I point. Elena eyes travel up.

"Oh."

"I should explain."

"Sage, that isn't a good idea. Just go home."

"I need to talk to him. Okay?"

She hesitates then says, "Okay, but . . . no expectations."

In the kitchen Iron Lady smiles when she see Elena, but goes steely again when her eyes take me in. "Where's Ethan?" Elena asks, handing her the keys.

"Upstairs watching TV, I think. Elena, he's had a bad day. Sage can visit tomorrow."

Elena considers it for a minute and then says, "No. It'll be fine." I follow Elena up the stairs. Ethan is laying on the floor curled up on his side under a blanket with his back to the stairway. The TV is playing some ancient cartoon show. He looks so small, and for the first time it really hits me that he is more like a four-year-old than a teenager.

"E, there's someone here to see you." At the sound of Elena's voice,

Ethan sits up and turns around. He's sucking his thumb. When he sees me, he pulls it out and hides his hand behind his back. I feel like have intruded into some private world where I have no business, like it really *isn't* a good idea for me to be here. My stomach turns. Elena puts her hand on his shoulder for a second or two, and he looks up into her eyes. Then she nods to me and leaves us alone. Ethan sits up cross-legged, pulling his blanket around his waist. I sit on the floor across from him. He won't look up. I have no idea what to say to the little boy in front of me, but I know I have to say something to make it okay for him.

"Hi, Mouse." The nickname slips out unintentionally. It makes him smile.

"Hi, Sage."

"I'm really, really sorry," I start.

Ethan frowns and finally looks up fleetingly. "Why did you kiss Finn?" The question is far more direct than I was prepared for.

"He tricked me. He wanted you to see."

"I know, but why did you kiss him." Ethan's voice has an edge of accusation, frustration.

"Well . . . that's not easy to explain."

"Please, tell me."

"I guess I like some things about Finn. Those things made me kiss him."

"What things?" Ethan is not letting me off easy. I look around trying to figure out what to say. "Sage?"

"I'm thinking."

"What about me? Do you like those things about me?"

The question floors me. I feel like a rib spreader has been applied inside my chest. My throat tightens. "Oh, Ethan, I like you in a much better way than I like Finn."

He sits quietly thinking about my answer, his face still troubled. I want to brush the curls from his forehead and kiss it.

"Okay," he finally says. He turns back toward the TV and lies back down. I sit for a couple minutes watching the show beside him. The next time I look over, he's sucking his thumb again. When I finally get up to leave, he doesn't notice.

I walk down the stairs, past Iron Lady in the kitchen, and out the door. My shoulders ache from the effort of excavation, and all I want to do is sleep.

Chapter 4 (In Your Hands)

When the walls begin to fall and the air becomes thick with the dust of revelation, there is a moment of regret when you want to run from the ruins, when you suddenly no longer want to see what was buried inside.

When I drag into the apartment, Rachel calls from the living room. "Jo called. The message's on the machine."

"Thanks," I say, but head up the stairs without stopping to listen to it.

I'm about half-way up when Rachel calls, "Sage?"

I pause where I am. The last thing I want to do right now is dance with my mom. First, she'll know I've been toking. Second, I have no idea what Ethan said to her about Finn's orchestrated scene. "What, Mom?"

"You okay?"

"Fine."

"Come down here, so I can see your pretty face."

I curse my luck, run a hand through my hair, and edge back down. I poke my head into the living room from the bottom step. My mom is sitting on the sofa with her feet tucked under her. She is writing up her session notes. Luckily, the room is poorly lit by one small window on the back wall, and a single table lamp next to Rachel. On any other day, I would curl up close to Rachel and try to catch a glimpse of her notes. Today I have more information than I can process already. Rachel looks tired too.

"Here I am," I say quietly.

"Did you have a good time with Elena?" I weigh her tone, wondering if she is fishing, wondering if she knows about Finn.

"Sure," I say.

"Where'd you go," My head hurts so badly I want to cry, but I answer calmly.

"Down to Sugar Creek by the falls." Always keep the story as close to the truth as possible. I learned that from my father.

"Are you okay?"

"You already asked me that. Don't I look okay?"

"Relax. I heard you up last night. That's all."

"I'm fine, Mom, just tired. Okay?"

She pauses to take me in fully, and I am waiting for the inquisition to ensue. Instead, she sighs and says, "Why don't you take a nap. We can do Chinese for dinner."

"Thanks, Madre." I give her a genuine smile. "You look like you could use a little rest too."

"Gotta finish my notes--"

"--while they're fresh," I finish for her.

"Sleep tight, Herbie."

I'm already asleep by the time my head hits the pillow. Hours later I wake to the sound of the shower pounding and the phone ringing. I don't get up to answer it. I roll over onto my back and watch the ceiling fan turn like helicopter blades. I wish I could just fly away from here, away from Finn's guilt, and Elena's scars, even away from Ethan. Maybe not forever, though.

A male voice comes over the answering machine. "Sage, it's Daddy. I'm in town, and I thought you could come stay with me for the weekend. Call me, Princess." Click.

I think about running down and erasing the message, pretending I never got it, but he would blame Mom and give her shit about it. It pisses me off that he makes it sound like he lives so far away and that seeing him is some kind of rare treat. I hate him, but not really. I know when I call to tell him I don't want to spend a lousy weekend watching sophomoric comedies in his ugly apartment, it will come out, "Sure I want to see you. I can't wait." And I'll go. I always do.

The shower stops. A few seconds later Rachel comes in wearing her silk bathrobe, drying her hair.

"Oh, you're awake. Was that your father on the phone?"

Suddenly the phone rings again, and we both jump. "You can get it," I say.

"Don't think so. It's for you." She walks away shaking her head.

I take a deep breath and pick up the receiver by my bed. "Hey, Dad," I say without much enthusiasm.

"Can't say anyone's ever called me that before. I think I'm insulted."

"Jo Jo? I thought you were my dad calling back."

"Clearly. What's he want from you now?"

"Only my whole weekend. It totally sucks."

"Just say NO, ya know."

"He's my father."

"He's a jerk, a freak, a prick, a . . . " Jo's voice rises.

I move the phone away from my ear. The blood pumps in my temples again, and I yell louder than I intend to. "Shut up, he's my dad."

The line goes silent, and for a second I think Jo's hung up on me. Then she says, "Sorry. I actually called to tell you I got asked out."

"On a date? No way. That's great. Right?"

"Do me a favor; don't sound so shocked. Okay?"

"Sorry, it's not you. It's just who under the age of thirty gets asked out on dates anymore?"

"Me, obviously."

"That's totally inspirational. Who asked you?"

"One of the guys who takes piano with my teacher here."

"You going?"

"Hell yes! We're going to the symphony. Total nerd outing."

"Perfect, Jo Jo," I laugh.

"It kind of is, isn't it? A good geek is hard to find."

"You know it! Hey, I gotta go," I say because my mom is standing in the doorway, shaking the car keys.

"Seriously, Sage, tell your dad to go to hell. He doesn't deserve your loyalty."

"Yeah, yeah, yeah," I push her dark tone to the side in my mind. "Have fun on your dork date."

"Hey, no need to be pejorative!" We both crack up.

"Later, girlfriend."

"Later."

"Ready to go?" Rachel asks.

I am suddenly painfully aware that I haven't eaten all day, unless you count a latte as actual food. "I'm starved."

"China Cafe?"

"That'll do. Give me two minutes."

I meet Rachel in the kitchen. She hands me the keys to her ancient Volvo, but I pass them back. "I'm too hungry to drive," I explain. Rachel accepts my excuse.

At the restaurant we order and engage in a mock debate about the advantages and disadvantages of diet and regular coke. After the food comes, we settle into comfortable silence while I stuff my face as fast as I can. About the time the food hits my stomach, I begin feeling sane and comfortable for the first time in days. I don't even want to start in on her about riding on Finn's bike. It would be too easy to ruin this perfect moment.

"What are you grinning about over there?" Mom asks.

"Nothing. It's just nice to hang with you."

Mom smiles too. "It reminds me of when you were little."

"Before you were a shrink." I don't mean to sound accusing.

Mom pulls her mouth to one side and wrinkles her eyebrows. Then she changes the subject. "You spending the weekend with your dad?"

"I don't know, probably."

"Good. I think it would be good for you to get away for a couple of days," she says.

"Why?"

"The Paiges are a little intense. I just think it would be good for you to have some distance. Keep perspective."

"Sounds like you're the one who needs a few days away."

"Impossible. You'll have to take them for me."

We both smile. "Why the change in rules this time?" I keep the tone light.

She makes the face again and keeps eating. Her silence annoys me, but I know that repeating myself is not going to make her answer. So I throw out, "Ethan still sucks his thumb."

She puts down her chopsticks and raises an eyebrow. "I know."

"Did you know Elena cuts?"

"Yep."

We sit in silence again. Then Mom says, "You have to understand that they have been through something really horrible."

"How do you know that?" I ask.

"Lily."

"What did she tell you?"

"Sorry, I can't go there, Sweetie. You know the rules."

"I thought the rules were different now."

"Not all of them. You ready to get out of here?"

"Sure."

We gather up the leftovers and head home to spend the evening laughing at an old Woody Allen flick, another one of my mom's favorites. After the movie, Mom heads up to bed, and I lie on the living room floor and open my journal. I write about what Finn said and how he said it so heavy with guilt. I write about Elena's scars and our kiss. I close my eyes to relive it, but in my mind I am kissing Ethan, so slow and gentle, like a whisper. I can almost feel his curls brush against my cheek. I close my book and head up to my room. There in the corner is my basket of laundry, washed and neatly folded. I make a mental note to thank my mom in the morning.

I wake up early enough to hear Ethan come out for his swim, but I decide to stay in bed. When I don't hear splashing, I get up and go to the window. Ethan is standing there, looking up forlornly. He smiles and waves when he sees me. It makes me laugh. I wave back and then head down the stairs and out the door.

"Hey there, early bird," I say.

"Hi, Sage. Where were you?" Ethan looks at the ground and shuffles his feet.

"In bed, sleeping."

"No, you weren't." He glances up.

"How do you know?"

He shrugs and mumbles, "Just know."

"Hmm," I smile. After a couple of seconds he smiles back. "Go ahead and swim. I'll just sit here and hang out," I say.

"Okay." Ethan tosses his towel down and slips into the water.

I sit by the deep end with my feet immersed. He swims under water the length of the pool so fast I almost lose track of him. He surfaces just inches from me. He grins and pushes off from the wall, glides and pulls himself over the water with a graceful strength. His shoulders, arms, and legs are tight, maybe even more than Finn's. When he comes back again, he pauses to look at me. With his golden curls slicked back off his face I can appreciate the slate gray color of his eyes and the long blond lashes around them. My eyes move down his face to the strawberry red lips, and I remember how it felt to kiss Elena. As he pushes off the wall, it occurs to me that Ethan has never been kissed like that and that I could kiss him right now this morning. A shiver runs down my spine.

Ethan emerges again next to my feet. He stands for a moment glancing shyly up at me like he wants to ask a question. Before I can say, "What's up," he splashes me full on, soaking me from head to toe. I scream in surprise, realizing too late how loud I am for how early it is. We both scan the houses guiltily and then look back at each other, a little embarrassed. I reach toward the water to splash him back, but he's already ducked under. I get up on my knees and lean forward, waiting for him to surface. When he does, I reach down, lose my balance, and tumble into the pool head first. For a moment up becomes down, so I stop moving. Before I can kick to the surface, a hand closes around my arm and pulls me up. Ethan doesn't stop swimming until we are at the stairs. At the same moment we both look down in astonishment at his fingers wrapped tightly around my wrist. He immediately lets go and draws his hand into his body like it has been injured. Then he starts shaking his head and mumbling, "Oh no oh no oh no."

"I'm okay, Ethan. It's okay. It's okay." I motion for him to sit down on the steps, which he does. Focusing on that action seems to calm him a little. I sit down a safe distance away and take a few deep breaths; Ethan follows my lead. He is still cradling his arm.

"Are you alright?" I ask.

He nods, but he doesn't look up. I take a few more deep breaths this time for my own benefit. Ethan finally lets his arms go so he can use them to brace his body as he rocks back and forth. His curls fall over his eyes, and his lips are moving, like he's having a conversation with someone I can't see. Suddenly, he looks up right into my eyes and says, "Then don't go!" It sounds like we are in the middle of an argument, and somehow I missed the first lines.

"I . . . I'm not going anywhere," I stammer, looking around to see if maybe he's talking to someone else.

"You decide, you know. You decide." Ethan is shaking. His voice is almost adult, lower and more controlled than I've heard him speak.

"I decide what, Ethan?" I say it as calmly and as softly as I can manage, but I'm shaking too.

He looks confused, frustrated liked I should be following. "You don't have to go with your father. Be mad! Don't go!"

"What are you talking about?" I whisper.

Ethan closes his eyes, inhales deeply, and lets out a shaky sigh, the kind that comes after a long hard cry. When he speaks, he's a little kid again. "You're so mad, but you go see him whenever he wants. You never tell him. You never tell anyone."

I'm speechless. He's right, of course. I look away to try to figure out how he knows this, and my mind flashes on the origami flower in my room and my book of secrets.

"Are you cold?" Ethan asks. I realize that I'm still shaking.

"A little, I guess." We get out of the water, and I sit on the deck while Ethan gets his towel. He places it carefully over my shoulders, and though it may be my imagination, I think his hands touch me briefly. The towel smells like Ethan, honey, lemon, and moist rich earth. I breathe it in deeply.

After he sits down, I ask, "How do you know about me visiting my dad?"

"I don't know," he shrugs. "I don't want to talk about it."

I pause before going on. "You didn't read my book of secrets, did you?"

He shakes his head and pulls his shoulders in like he's trying to hide.

"It's when we touch, isn't it? Something happens when we touch."

He nods. I can see the tears welling up in his eyes, but I can't stop now. "Does it work with everyone? Everyone but Elena. That's why she can touch you." I figure it out as I'm talking. "But you and Elena can talk without talking. That's different somehow. Isn't it?"

The tears spill over and run down his cheeks. I take the towel from my shoulders, inhaling his scent one more time. Then I move closer, and put it over him carefully, without touching. I sit down again, a little closer than before. "Why are you crying, Ethan?"

His words come out in little gulps, "You won't be my friend. If you know things, . . . you won't like me."

I want so much to touch him, kiss him on the cheek, kiss him on the lips, show him he's wrong in a way that words can't. But I know that's not possible, not yet.

"I will always be your friend, Ethan, always."

He shakes his head in disbelief and cries silently into his arms. I try again. "Hey, you just saved my life. In some cultures that means I'm responsible for you now. I have to be your friend. Okay?"

I know he is not convinced, but after a minute or so he looks up, wipes his eyes, and draws in a couple of shaky breaths. "Please, don't go," he mumbles.

On cue my mom appears on the porch in her robe with a cup of coffee in one hand and the phone in the other. "Sage, it's your father. He wants to come get you now," she yells.

I look over at Ethan, and he shakes his head. "Please, don't go." He is louder this time, more desperate.

"I'll be back tomorrow, promise." I stand up to leave, but Ethan reaches out and grabs my hand. For an instant everything goes black, and I feel a flash of fear, like waiting for the impact after the screech of tires. My arm suddenly feels white hot, like a smoldering coal has fallen onto it. I open my mouth in a silent scream. I can't pull away, but not because of his grip. I am looking at Ethan, but we aren't at the pool by his house anymore. My peripheral vision puts me in a bedroom with a mattress on the floor and a corner desk with a computer screen flashing WARNING! I blink hard, and the vision fades. Ethan is staring into my eyes and his are sparkling with bright tears.

"Please."

"Sage," my mother's voice sounds really far away. I look down at my arm and then over at my mother who's taken a step toward us, her mouth open in alarm. I shake my head to stop her advance, and she freezes a few steps from the porch.

I turn back to Ethan. Though I can barely inhale, I manage to say, "I have to go. He's my father." Ethan lowers his eyes and lets go. I rub my arm as I watch him stand and walk slowly toward the house with his head down. Elena opens the door to let him in.

"That wet t-shirt thing isn't working for you," she says, wryly. My eyes are still on Ethan. "He'll be fine, Sage. See you tomorrow." I nod.

"Sage, phone!" my mom yells.

I run over. She shoves the phone into one hand and the coffee into the other. I sit down on the steps, inhale, and say, "Hi, Dad."

"Princess! You ready for a big weekend with your old man?"

"Sure," I sigh.

"Love the enthusiasm."

"Best I could do on such short notice this early in the morning."

"Oh." He pauses for a moment then goes merrily on. "Come on. We're going to have a great time. We can go swimming and catch a movie, something your mom won't let you see. We'll have a blast."

"Can't wait."

"You don't have to. I'll be there in about ten minutes." He misses it again. You always know when someone isn't paying attention because they miss the sarcasm.

"Perfect." I hang up without saying goodbye, and I drag my dripping self up the stairs and into the shower. I don't care if he has to cool his heels waiting for me. I've done it plenty of times for him. While I am rinsing my conditioner, Mom comes in without knocking.

"So he'll be here in like five minutes. You gonna be ready?"

"That's the plan."

"You'll have fun," she says like she is reading out of the *How to Divorce Well* handbook.

I step out of the shower, and she hands me a towel. "No, I won't. He'll fill me up with popcorn and candy, take me to an R-rated movie to piss you off, and then he'll get bored and go in the other room to 'take care of some business.'"

"Been there, done that," Mom says half under her breath.

It makes me laugh. "No worries, Madre. I got it covered."

"You always do," she says, and then pulls me into a hug. I let myself melt into her for a couple of seconds before I pull away.

I throw on the outfit at the top of the laundry basket and start digging around for a couple of others. My mom comes in with my toothbrush, hairbrush, and bath stuff.

"Oh yeah, thanks for folding my laundry yesterday."

My mom drops the stuff on my bed. "I didn't fold your laundry, Sage."

I am just about to ask her who did when my hand brushes against the folded paper. I carefully move the clothes aside and find another of Ethan's origami creations, a butterfly made of silver and copper paper.

Mom steps up beside me to get a look. "Ethan." we say it in unison, but with inflections that couldn't be more different. We stand looking at each other, waiting for the other to offer some explanation that neither has.

The horn honking in the driveway dissolves the moment. I carefully slip the butterfly into my pocket and stuff everything I can grab from the bed into my backpack and start down the stairs. Halfway down I turn and run back up, remembering my journal lying in the middle of the floor where it had fallen in the night.

Chapter 5 (A Thousand Words)

From far away it is not so hard to watch a disaster in progress; it's someone else's pain after all. You take comfort in your arms, legs, smooth safe skin. You hold the oxygen in your lungs and let the tears course your cheeks.

"Who's your little boyfriend?"

Ethan presses his hand against the upstairs window. My stomach turns over, remembering the searing heat of that hand on my arm. His fear flashes through me again, and I wonder what he feels when he touches me.

"Hello, earth to Sage. Come in, Sage."

"What?"

"Please tell me he's not one of your mother's nut-jobs."

"Could you be a little harsher?"

"Oh, god no. Sagey, please tell me you aren't --"

"Whatever, Dad!" I yell, cutting him off.

"Touchy, touchy. Let's start again. Hey, princess. It's great to see you. What's new?"

I roll my eyes and turn my head to the window. He turns on the radio to a lousy old rock station with too much base and lyrics that repeat over and over until you want to kill the singer. He sings along, oblivious.

After an eternity, we pull into the parking lot of his favorite greasy diner, the one he's taken me to on every visit since I was six.

"I thought we'd try someplace new." He laughs at his own joke.

In front of the restaurant a gaggle women decked out in clothes that are too young and tricolored hair makes eyes at my dad as we walk in. He smiles and waves. They wave back.

"Ick!"

"It's called being friendly. You might try it sometime," he says.

"Again, whatever, Dad!"

He laughs a little too hard. "We are going to have so much fun this weekend. Aren't we?"

The hostess tells us that the wait is twenty minutes, but Dad flirts with her, such as she is, and we are seated in ten. The price we pay for her favor is returning her smile every time she passes to seat another customer. I'm not sure what annoys me the most, the funky sweaty smell of my dad's deodorant, the bitter coffee, the burnt toast, the crappy elevator music, or the shock art displayed for sale around the dirty walls. I survive, but I wait outside while he pays the bill. I am actually relieved when we are back in the car. Without asking, I know where we are headed.

"I am so glad you are finally old enough to see real movies," my dad says, pulling into the multiplex.

"You've been taking me to R movies since I was ten. What are you talking about?"

"You know what I mean. Now you can really enjoy them." He throws an arm around my shoulder and ushers me through the parking lot like we're on a date or something. I want to shake him off, but I don't. It's easier to let him have his ego moment or whatever this gives him. At the window he buys the tickets without asking me what I want to see. I don't really care because all I can think about is Ethan. We have half an hour to kill before the movie starts, so I go back to the car to get my book and a pen. I tuck the butterfly carefully between the pages.

The movie turns out to be okay, a typical violent thriller, but the characters are somewhat unique and mildly interesting. After the movie, we go to the park where he always took me as a kid. I'm not sure if he expects me to climb the monkey bars and ride the swings, but I sit next to him on the bench and open my book. He doesn't try to make conversation, so I'm free to lose myself in the morning's memories. I relive the shock of cold and the sudden fire of Ethan's hand closing on my arm, pulling me up from under the water. I focus on the stormy gray of his eyes, holding his glaze longer than I could in reality. In slow motion his hand reaches up and touches my cheek. He leans in and kisses me deeply. In that instant his mind opens to me, and he tells me everything that happened to him without words. I can hardly breathe.

"You okay, kiddo," my dad asks.

I jump at the sound of his voice.

"You were breathing kind of funny. You okay?"

"Fine," I smile, embarrassed. "Just homework," I lie. "We have to keep a journal for English class."

"Wow, they make you do that every year? Pretty boring stuff, huh?"

"Oh, yeah."

"So how is school this summer?" He's laughing at me.

"You think you're so smart. But, it's a summer assignment, so we don't get rusty, you know." He is so annoying.

"Whatever," he says mimicking me.

"It's true."

"I think you're writing about your boyfriend."

"Which one?"

"Now you're just trying to scare me."

"No, seriously, which one? The pyromaniac or the serial killer?"

"Very funny." An awkward moment passes while I try to come up with another come back. Then he says, "You ready to make like a tree?"

"That wasn't funny when I was six, and it still isn't funny."

"Then why are you smiling?"

I get up and walk away ahead of him. In the car I examine Ethan's butterfly. Under one wing is the mouse picture. I study its miniature perfection.

"Whatcha got there, kiddo. You've been mooning over it all afternoon."

"'Mooning?' Nice word, like, Daddy-o."

He reaches over and snatches the butterfly from me as he steers onto the highway. I try to get it back, but before I can grab it, he's switched it to the hand farthest from me. "Pretty butterfly; it needs to be free," he laughs.

Then he holds it out the window. I'm yelling, "No," when he lets it go. I sit back in my seat stunned.

"Sorry, Princess. That was an accident. I was just goofing, really."

We drive to his new apartment in silence while I fight back my bitter tears, and he acts like nothing's happened.

His newest place is on the other side of town from chez Paige in a fairly decent complex for him. I make a mental calculation of the number of places Dad has taken me since I was six. Friends' houses where he couch surfed, rooms he rented in questionable houses with even more questionable roommates, some high end pads like the Victorian in town a couple of years ago, but those places were short lived. I remember a dozen places at least. I take in the affluent ambiance as we pull in the circular drive. Palm trees sway in the breeze, totally out of place for this area of the world. The flowers lining the road are planted in artistically random patterns. A swimming pool with a waterfall and hot tub is visible behind the castle-shaped rental office. Dad stops at a kiosk and punches some numbers into the keypad.

"I haven't picked up my electronic eyeball thingy from the office yet," he explains.

"Sure." I wonder if he's squatting in someone else's place. If I ask, he'll have a hundred plausible lies prepared. Once when I was eight, I told my mom, "Dad lies a lot. You just have to understand that about him; then it's okay." Words to live by.

When we get out of the car, he tries to take my bag, but I snatch it away from him. He leads me up to a third floor apartment in the back of the building. I am not sure if I ever know what to expect, but it is what I expected somehow. Dark and almost unfurnished. One framed sports poster of a bike race leans against the mantle as the sum total of art. A leather sofa that's too large for the space takes over the living room. A big screen television sits on the floor opposite the sofa like it has just been delivered yesterday. A plethora of other audio and electronic equipment sits carefully shelved beside the TV. A couple of bars stools by the counter offer seating for dining since he has no table. In the bedroom a crowded corner desk, a bedside table, a mattress on the floor and a dorm style floor lamp round out the furnishings. I go to the fridge, hoping for a coke, but all he has is eggs, orange juice, and beer.

"I need a coke," I state from in front of the opened fridge.

"Back toward the office, next to the pool, there's a machine. 80 cents. You got it, baby?"

I shake my head, but he isn't even looking at me. He's settling himself in front of the computer in the bedroom.

This is the worst moment of every visit. Faced with no distractions, we struggle for a way to be together. I am determined not to let my guard down, even though I know that no matter how hard I try I will eventually give in. My mom says every little girl craves her father's love and has a right to believe in it, and I do. I don't trust him, and I know he will let me down, but he will also call me his princess and curl my ear. I will weigh those moments more heavily than all the others and keep my faith. I hate myself for being such a sucker, for not just kissing him off and getting on with my life.

After I settle onto the sofa with my book and pen, he goes to the fridge and cracks a beer. The best way to escape from myself is to fill my mind with someone else. I close my eyes and lean my head back. Ethan's butterfly flutters before my eyelids like a flame licking at my mind. I don't want to be here. I realize suddenly that that fact has nothing to do with my dad. If I am here, there's no chance of seeing Ethan, or Elena for that matter. I wonder if Ethan is missing me too. I wonder if he knows what I'm feeling. When we touch, can he see my secrets, too? Does he know what I really want from Finn? Does he know that I kissed Elena? Does he know that I was thinking about him? Could he even understand any of this jumble of emotion. "Stuck in time." Whatever that means. A person can't just age without growing up. Can they? Does he know that he's stuck and could he decide to become unstuck somehow?

I sit up and fill the page with questions . Then I close my eyes and relax against the pungent cheap leather. I conjure Ethan curled on the carpet under the baby blue cotton blanket sucking his thumb. A butterfly distracts me and I rise to follow it down the stairs and outside by the side of the pool. I watch Ethan put the towel over my shoulders, and I hear his voice strong and controlled telling me not to go. I feel his skin hot on mine as he holds my arm. The butterfly flutters through the image dissolving it.

I wake up sweating, a blanket over me and a note with two $20s taped to it sitting on my stomach.

"Out on business. Be back in a bit. Order a pizza, works. Love, Dad."

Nice! Business my ass. I don't even want to know what kind of business he's out on. I'm pretty much stranded, since Rachel has a strict non-interference policy, and Jo might as well be on the moon. Resigned, I call Pizza Paul's, order a plain cheese pie, salad, and a coke and turn on the TV. I flip through all 100 or so channels twice, but nothing holds my attention. I toy with calling Finn, but reject that idea before it can take hold. I wander out onto the balcony to watch the dog walkers two stories below. Not much to look at there. A couple of little yippy dogs with yuppie owners sniff each other's butts and then growl indignantly. The porch has glass sliders into the living room and bedroom. The glow from the computer on the desk in the corner of the bedroom catches my eye just as the knock comes at the door.

I pay for the food, give the hot pizza guy a smile and a huge tip, and retreat to my prison. For the most part I avoid my dad's bedroom, and I respect his one inviolable rule. But the computer is on and open, beckoning with its light. Besides I'm pissed at him, really pissed, so I decide to do a little surfing while I eat. He'll never know, I tell myself. What could I possibly do to his computer? I ask myself. I grab a slice and leave the glass of coke I poured on the kitchen counter.

My dad is not much for rules. In fact he loves breaking my mom's rules. Still he has issued a single edict that up until now I have not broken: never touch his computer. I always thought the rule existed to keep me from breaking it or erasing something important.

I sit down and hit the explorer icon. I Google Finn. A bunch of garbage comes up. MySpace for some wannabe musician with the same name, a couple of hits on just Finnian and just Mulcahy. Then at the bottom of the page is a hit on Sean Mulcahy, a news story. I think that Sean might be Finn's dad's name, so I click on the link. The headline comes up, *"Attorney Cleared of Charges in Wife's Death."*

The year seems about right. Jackpot I think, but the link takes me to a page that says the article is archived. To get to it I need to create an account and pay for a subscription. I have absolutely no luck! Still it is one more clue. I get my book and jot down a few lines. Just because Finn's mother's death was ruled accidental doesn't mean it was.

I turn back to the computer and think about playing a game. Out of habit, I open the documents tree where I keep saved games. No games, duh, so I hit "Music." I scan down the list, but I don't recognize a single band. Then I realize that the names aren't bands; they're girl's names: Trixie, Sandy, Roxy. A little wave of nausea washes over me. I know this is the moment when I should do the right thing, let my dad have his secrets, and walk away. I know this, but I can't. I click on Roxy.

A girl or woman made to look like a girl is sitting on bed with a pile of stuffed animals. She is naked and without hair where a woman should have it. I feel sicker. A music track is playing something I have never heard; it is cheesy and Sinatraish, a paradox to what is happening on the screen. The woman is alone through the entire video, but what she does to herself is both astonishing and horrifying. When the screen finally freezes at the final frame, I struggle to find footing. The ground has melted away under my chair and my heart is pounding wildly, but not in a good way.

"So what," I say out loud. My voice is like cold water in the face, so I continue. "All guys are into porn. No biggie." My heart rate is returning to normal. Then my eyes light on video camera a few feet away on the floor. The blood rushes in my ears again, and I beat it back with a word: "coincidence." The camera being there could mean nothing. I really need to stop being so dramatic. I want to let it go, to click the x at the top of the page, close the video and turn off the computer. I really really want to, but again, I just can't.

I stare at the blurred frozen image of the girl-woman and the bed behind her. My heart drops as I suddenly recognize the monkey, kangaroo family, baby panda, snake. The animals on the bed are mine or they were what suddenly feels like a long time ago. I bite back the tears of anger burning under my lids as I listen to the tick tick tick tick tick of the clock. Finally, I get up. My legs are shaking as I stand, trying to decide what to do. I have to get out of here before he comes home. I don't know if any of this is illegal or dangerous in some way like drugs, but my intuition tells me I need to cover my tracks. I clean up the pizza, drink the coke, and put the leftovers in the fridge. Then I pack up my bag and put on my shoes. Once I know I can jet out the door, I return to the bedroom to deal with the computer.

I click the x on the video. The list of "Music" files is still up. Subconsciously, I scan the names. Just before I click the x to close the list, my eyes glimpse a familiar name: Josephine. It's too late though. The window closes. I hit the sleep button.

Then I literally run from the apartment. No way, I tell myself. There's no way it can be what I'm thinking, but it could be. Terrified that he is going to pull up and see me, I take the path that runs behind the apartment buildings out to the main road. On the street, I make my way past a convenience store. I don't go in because it's the kind of place he might stop to buy lottery tickets. I've never lived in this part of town, but I remember passing a Starbuck's on the way in from the movie.

By some miracle I find it. I'm sweating from running and walking. I order an iced latte, pay for it with some of the change from the pizza, and collapse into a big faux leather chair that sticks to my skin. After a few minutes, the cool air begins to slow my racing thoughts a little, and I realize I need a ride. I think about calling Rachel, but my fingers have another idea. What exactly could I say to her anyway? How could I begin to explain what I should never have seen?

After calling Finn from the Paige's phone, I programmed his number into my cell, so I wouldn't forget it, as if I could. He picks up on the second ring.

"Yeah"

"Hey, Finn."

"My little stalker." He sounds surprised.

"Yeah. Actually, I need a favor."

"Oooh, an opportunity for you to owe me something. Too good to pass up. I am at your service, sweetheart."

"I need a ride. I'll text you the address."

"You okay?" The hint of genuine concern in his voice melts me.

"See you soon?" I manage through the welling tears.

"Sure." I am grateful that he doesn't try to keep me talking.

I compose myself enough to get the address from the barista and text him. Then I sit back down to wait. I have no idea what to do with this information. I am so angry, I can hardly breathe. My chest feels like it is collapsing in on itself, and I want to scream or pound something, or sleep for the next five years. I want to go back in time and never see the stupid computer. No, further back. Never get in the car with my father this morning. I should have listened to Ethan. Did he know something like this would happen? I can't go there right now.

I have to talk to Jo, or not. If he has a video of Jo, it must be without her knowing about it. No way she would do that on purpose. Maybe it isn't even her; maybe it's just a name he borrowed. The names can't be the girls' real names. I get up and head outside to pace in the heat and approaching darkness. Finn takes an eon to get here. As he pulls up on his bike, I wipe my eyes. I do not want him to see me like this. Pull it together, girl, I tell myself. He takes off his helmet and studies my face before handing it over to me.

"What are you doing all the way down here, all alone?" he asks.

"Long story," I say quietly.

"I'm thinkin' we got all night," he says a little coyly.

I put on the helmet and nod. I have nowhere else to go.

Finn takes me to his house. His father is away on some business trip. I know it's a setup. I'm working on half a brain and my emotions are so raw I can't use it. I take the beer he hands me and down it in about a minute. I take another. I wave off the pot he offers, and he puts it away without smoking any himself. He puts a movie in the DVD player about some guy who loses his memory, but the story is told in chunks backward and I can't follow it. It seems an odd choice for a come on, but I am starting to think he isn't going to put me through the moves.

I fall asleep in the corner of the couch. When I wake up to pee, the TV and all the lights are off, except one in the back bedroom. After using the bathroom and stripping down to my t-shirt and underwear,

I make my way down the hall expecting to see Finn still awake. He's asleep, curled in a corner of the bed with no blankets, wearing only a pair of boxers. He looks so sweet and vulnerable. I don't want to be alone, so I carefully lie down next to him. The light is bothering me, so I turn it off. I lay for a long time listening to Finn breathe, inhaling his smell. I love this feeling, like we are a couple, married or something. I relax into it.

Finn's screams break through my dreams, and I am thrust awake violently. I fumble for the light switch, but I can't find it in the dark.

"Finn, wake up!" I yell. "Wake up" Finally, he stops yelling and sits up, breathing heavily, shaking from head to toe.

"Turn on the light. Please, turn the damn light back on!" His voice is far away on another plane, but the desperation is contagious.

This time I find the cord, pull it, and flood the room with yellow. Finn throws his legs over the side of the bed so his back is to me.

"You okay?" I put my hand on his shoulder. I can't tell if he's crying or just breathing hard. He doesn't pull away like I expect him to, so I sit up on my knees and wrap both arms around him. We stay like that until his breathing matches mine. Then he turns around and comes up on his knees to face me.

Even though we have kissed hundreds of times, this kiss is different. It means something. For once I don't control it or calculate the next move; I just kiss him back. He pulls me in tighter. I let him take off my t-shirt. I let him lay me back onto the bed. I pull him down into another kiss. His breath is hot on my face as he fumbles in the drawer beside the bed. For a moment I am perplexed by this interruption. He finds what he is looking for. Then he sits back on his heels and looks at me.

"You ready for this, little girl? Are you really ready." He holds out the condom.

Part of me wants to laugh; part of me wants to run. I think for a minute about the implications. My mother's words come back to me. "Be sure, be really sure because you only get one first time." I hear her add, "Everyone you have sex with becomes a part of you and takes a part of you with them, so choose your partners wisely." I look Finn up and down. Do I want a part of him? Definitely! Do I want to give him part of me? I'm not so sure.

"Tick tock, little girl. The offer IS time limited." He smiles down at me, runs his hand across my face, neck, and down. I shiver.

"Make me sure." I say. He leans down to kiss me. I push him back up. "Trust me. Tell me. . . "

"Sage, please don't ruin this." His voice is desperate like when he wanted the lights on. His cocky smile fades, and he looks down helplessly.

"Okay, Finn. It's okay." I barely recognize my own voice. I take his hand and bring him back to me. Our lips touch so soft, so tender for a moment. Then his tongue is in my mouth, and his hand is on my thigh.

In the next instant, he pulls off his boxers with one hand, rips open the package with his teeth, and rolls on the condom. I barely have time to blink. The roller coaster is poised at the top of the tracks; then it breaches the summit.

I close my eyes and try to capture the moment like a photograph, so I can always remember. I keep Finn's eyes blue, hooded with pleasure. I capture Finn's touch so sure, so heated, grazing my nipples, caressing my thighs, belly, breasts. I store away the hum of his moans, his labored breathing, and his voice whispering my name. I memorize his smell, musky and heavy like olive oil and cinnamon. I savor the taste of his mouth and skin, acrid and yeasty from the beer. I absorb the moment when he is suddenly inside me, and I feel like I am a part of him, completely outside of myself, yet strangely complete.

Then it's over. He bears down, holds his breath, exhales like he is expelling his very soul. For those couple of seconds, we are suspended in time and space. I envy his release.

When it's over, he collapses onto me smiling and sweating, then rolls over.

I feel like I have been suddenly pushed from a sauna into a snow bank. He reaches over me to grab his shorts and then struts to the bathroom swinging them from his finger. I fight back the impulse to hurl sarcasm at him from the bed. Instead, I find my t-shirt and underwear and put them on. I roll over to face the wall. What part of myself did I give Finn? I wonder. My heart aches and my stomach hurts. I have never felt alone before this moment. I have been lonely like everyone else, but this is different. This is alone. It is a feeling that defies tears, that weighs me down to this bed like lead chains. I close my eyes and hope it passes like a hangover.

When Finn, gets back, he curls up, spooning me, and in an instant the stars fall back into alignment.

"Not a virgin anymore, Sagey. How does it feel?" His voice is low and sleepy.

"It feels surreal," I say pulling away a little to turn off the light.

He pulls me back into him.

"The light stays on." It's an order, so I lie back and close my eyes.

In a little while his arm goes slack, and his breathing comes even and rhythmic. Despite the glare, I finally drift off safe under Finn's wing.

I wake up to the smell of coffee. Finn is gone. I find a robe in his closet. I follow the smell into the kitchen. Finn is dressed and sitting at the kitchen table flipping his lighter open and running his finger through the flame before closing it again. He stops when he sees me there.

"You snore," he says smiling. "Coffee's on the counter. I don't have cream, but I think there's some sugar somewhere." He starts to get up, but I motion for him to sit.

"Black is good." He's put a clean cup out for me, sweet. I fill it and sit in the chair closest to him. He leans in and kisses me. He's brushed his teeth already. I pull away thinking how horrible my breath must be. "Give me a sec?" I say getting up.

He puts his hand on arm. "Where do you think you're going?"

"To brush my teeth."

"Sit yourself back down. You can do that later."

I sink back into the chair, take a sip of the coffee and try to think of something to say.

Finn stares at me like he is waiting for a movie to start. He's slouched back with his arms crossed over his chest.

"What?" I finally say.

"What? You're asking me, what? I think it's about time for you to spill it, girl."

"Spill what?" I say, but yesterday is already falling like hail around my shoulders. I want to crawl back into Finn's bed and pretend this is home.

"Don't you have parents who care?"

"Parent." I say.

"I see, Daddy did something. That explains the location. Weekend visitation, hmmm."

"Don't start, Finn."

"Don't start what, Stalker-girl? You been digging at me since the first day you shook your little tail feathers my way."

"Whatever, Finn?" I get up to leave, but Finn grabs my arm and keeps me there.

"Look, I only want to help. Not like you. You only want to know."

I feel the heat of frustration rising up my neck. In three seconds flat I go from zero to seeing red.

"Right, Finn. I just want to know. Do you want to know what I know now? I know that Finnian Mulcahy, motorcycle riding, beer drinking, bad ass is afraid of the dark." I hate that I say it even before it's out of my mouth.

"You don't know shit!" He knocks over the chair getting up, and I half expect him to hit me. "So what's your damage, Sage? Daddy play touchy with you? Mommy ignoring you? You are such a cliché. Can't deal with your own shit, so you have to get in everyone else's. Poor little Stalker-girl."

I get up and grab my bag on my way to the bathroom. I turn on the shower, so he can't hear me cry. I let the hot water pour over me and try to wash all of it away. I want to be home and safe, but I'm not sure I could find "safe" in a dictionary. I cry until it hurts too much to go on.

When I open the bathroom door, Finn is standing there with his head hanging. He reaches down and takes my hand. Then I am crying again, and he is holding me against his chest and kissing my head.

"I'm so sorry, Sage. I didn't mean to . . ." His voice trails off. "I should take you home. Your mom is probably losing her mind."

"I know."

He stops the bike about a block from the Paige's house. I take off his helmet and kiss him deep before I hand it to him. "Thanks, Finn."

"No sweat." He pauses and I wait.

After an awkward silence, I say, "Later."

"Yeah, later, Stalker-girl." I don't watch him put on the helmet or ride away. I just walk.

I try to clear my head, to think of a plausible lie about where I have been and why. I expect drama and recrimination, maybe a couple police cars, but when I get up to house, there's nothing. I take out my phone and check the time, 10:45. I admit to myself that the apparent lack of interest annoys me. Still, I'm relieved that I may not have to explain anything.

The door is open, so Rachel sees me before I walk in.

"Hey, Sage? What are you doing here? I didn't even hear your dad's car." She gets up to kiss me on the cheek at the door.

I am stunned into silence. He didn't even tell her I was MIA, the bastard. I hate him even more. "Oh . . .um . . . he had to work, so he brought me back early and left me at Exodus so I could get some coffee."

"Okay. I have someone coming over in a minute. It's important and work-private. Can you make yourself scarce for a little while?"

"Sure, Mom." I head up the stairs. At the top I notice the door to my room is closed, and I'm pretty sure I left it open. My hand is on the handle when Rachel's voice drifts up.

"Oh, I almost forgot. There's a little surprise in your --"

I can't hear her anymore because I've opened the door to at least a hundred paper butterflies of all different colors suspended from my ceiling. I feel like I am in a spring meadow in someone else's dream. "Ethan," I whisper. I go to the window and look out, hoping he will be there, even though it is much too late for his swim. I am about to turn away when he comes through the screen door carrying a basket of bedding. His expression, somewhere between sad and angry, confirms what I suspect, so I don't open the window and call to him. I turn back to my beautiful gift and feel inexplicably guilty. My phone rings. I know who it is. I turn it off without answering, lie down on the bed, and let my mind float away amid the butterflies from my sweet, sad, broken little Mouse

Chapter 6 (Once in a Lullaby)

At the end of the storm when the wind has died and everything's left shredded and ugly, beyond repair or redemption, a rainbow arches across the sky; the peace of that moment might almost make the loss bearable.

I don't mean to eavesdrop, but the man's voice is booming and my mother responses are high-pitched and excited. Something about the timber makes my heart beat hard and my hearing more acute.

"I'll need some more information to be absolutely sure," the man says.

"I can't believe you found him so fast," my mom says. "Give me a sec, and I'll get Lily."

I hear the door bang, and the voices go silent. I start to drift off; then the door bangs again.

"Evnin', Mr. Raymond. Rachel says you found him." Lily's voice is low, but her words are clear.

"Let's not jump the gun here. I found a lead. I need to verify some information." The man sounds nervous. "You say he left here thirteen years ago."

"That's right," Lily says. "October 17th."

"The time frame is right then. Did you bring a picture, Ms. Paige?"

"It's right here. It was taken at his wedding a long time ago. Will it do?"

"I think so."

"What now, Mr. Raymond?" My mom is nervous too. I can imagine her knee bouncing up and down as she taps her thumb ring.

"I'm gonna go down there and check the guy out. Make contact and nose around a bit. I'll know more then."

"Thank you so much," my mom says.

Iron Lady mumbles her gratitude. The next thing I hear is footsteps and the door banging shut. Who the hell are they looking for? And why are they all so nervous about it? I get my book out and jot down what I remember of the conversation. I'll be able to concentrate better later. I'm finishing up when the house phone rings. My mom doesn't answer, so she must have walked the man out. With each ring my head feels like it might explode, and I almost throw up when the images from my father's computer flash in my head. Bastard. The ringing finally stops. I am up and pacing around my room when I hear the door slam again and my mom's footsteps on the stair then a gentle tap on the door.

"You awake, Sage?"

"Come in."

"So what do you think? Can you believe this?" She gestures in a circle around the room. I let my eyes follow the sweep of her arm. And despite my agitation, I smile.

"Elena helped hang them, but Ethan made all of these. Elena said he's never done anything like this before, not even for her." My mom seems really worked up about this.

"Cool." I have no idea what she wants me to say.

"Sage, you need to listen to me carefully. This is really important."

"Okay." I sit up.

"Ethan's making some huge steps toward joining the world here, and you are his test case. Do not disappoint him. If you fail him, he may never reach out again. Do you understand?"

My stomach goes queasy. "Jeez, Mom, nothing like a little pressure, you know."

"This is not about you, Sage."

"Uh . . . yeah, it is. Me and Ethan." I want to add "and Finn."

Mom nods her head. "Fair enough. Just be sensitive to what this boy has been through."

My eyes well up, and it takes all my self-control not to scream, "What about what I've been through?" Instead I go to the window so she can't read my face. "Sure, Mom."

She waits there for another minute without talking and then finally gets up and goes back downstairs. I let the weight of what I've already done to Ethan and the fact that I cannot hide it from him sink in until I can't breathe. Suddenly, my mind flashes on Elena and the night by the pool. I could use a little peace, and I don't really care where it comes from at this point. I just hope she's at home. I find my phone under the bed where I threw it and dial the Paige's house number. I make a mental note to get her mobile when I see her. I'm relieved when she picks up.

"Sage? I thought you went to your dad's this weekend."

"It was a bust. Can I come over and hang out?" I try to sound casual.

"Sure. Hey, did you see-"

"Yeah. Thanks. See you in a sec." I feel a little bad about cutting her off, but I'm barely holding it together, and chit chat is more than I can handle.

I pace around the room for a few minutes trying to figure out what to do if I see Ethan. I want to thank him for the butterflies, but I can't go near him. If we touch, he'll know about Finn. I'm not sure how much he understands about sex and all that, but he will know enough, too much. I really need Elena, so I take a deep breath and head down the stairs. My mom stops me in the kitchen.

"You okay, kiddo?" she asks.

"Fine. I'm just gonna go over and thank Ethan for the butterflies."

"Great idea."

Elena meets me at the door. She's dressed all in creamy white like an angel or a goddess. Her blue eyes meet mine, and I have to concentrate hard to keep from throwing myself into her arms and weeping. I push past her, scanning for Ethan. When I turn around, her back is to the door, and she's studying me.

"No cops, I swear." Her smile feels like hot water on a recent burn. I turn away.

"Sage?"

"Sorry, Elena. I probably shouldn't be here. I'm just gonna go home."

"Don't think so! Come on." She takes my hand and leads me up the stairs. We cross through the TV room where Ethan and I talked a couple of days ago, down a long hall. The door at the end opens to big bathroom. Elena's room is to the right. There is another door to the left, Ethan's room perhaps. It's closed, so I can only guess.

Elena's room is simple and elegant. The ceiling is sloped with dormers and beamed, like an attic room. At the far end her huge canopy bed takes up one corner. It's draped with white gauze. The comforter is blood red. The rest of the room is spotless, uncluttered like a room in a bed and breakfast. She has a heavy low pine bookcase next to one of the window seats that's so organized it could be painted on the wall. The small roll-top desk beside it is closed, but I know if I opened it, nothing would be out of place. Elena walks over a huge fluffy white rug that covers part of the golden wide planked floor and sits on the red velvet bench at the foot of the bed. The wall opposite the windows is covered with the most amazing art work, all perfectly framed and artfully arranged.

"Damn." I say from the doorway, forgetting my churning emotions for a second.

"What?"

"Your room is . . . well . . . damn!"

"Is that good?" Elena blushes, surprised by my reaction.

"Uh, yeah." Elena gives me a few minutes to take in the paintings. They are stunning, obviously done by the same artist. One is a face with just the eyes peering over the edge of the frame, sad, yearning, searching surreal eyes, nearly lost in a landscape behind them. In some of the paintings a white wolf peers out from behind a tree, a rock, a broken down house. The images are realistic, but fractured, and the colors range from warm to hot, only the wolf or the eyes offer an oasis of cool on the canvas.

"Yours?" I ask.

Elena grants me her silvery bells laugh. "That would be a little egotistical, don't you think. Guess again."

"Ethan," I whisper, incredulous.

"You got it. Pretty incredible, that twin of mine." I know she means it, but her tone hints at sadness too.

"Amazing." Now that I know the paintings are Ethan's I can't look at them without thinking about what I've done. I turn back to Elena.

"You should see my room," I say trying to lighten my mood.

"I did. I helped Ethan hang the butterflies last night, remember?"

"Ugh. That's embarrassing."

"Did you like them?" Elena's tone reminds me of my mother's, excited, hopeful, a little too intense.

"How could I not? It was exactly what I needed." Saying the words brings back the torrent of guilt and fear that keep crashing into me in heavy waves. The tears well up again, and there is no beating them back. Elena jumps up as I sink to the floor under the weight of all the emotions I don't want to be feeling.

"This is so fucked up," I moan rocking forward on my knees. "Please, Elena." She's kneeling beside me, her face contorted in indecision. "Please," I beg, but she doesn't reach out to me. She isn't even looking at me. Her eyes are fixed on the door behind me.

The weight of his presence is crushing. I give in completely to my tears, curl down and bury my face in my knees. I'm helpless to whatever's coming next. I want more than anything to be able to get up and run from this room, but even if Mouse wasn't blocking the doorway, I couldn't summon the strength. I just let go and wait for the silence of falling ashes that must follow an explosion.

I hear Ethan's tentative footsteps, like paws padding over the floor and onto the rug. I feel Elena's breath on my neck as she leans over me. I try to concentrate on its warmth. The floor vibrates a little as Ethan crouches beside me opposite Elena. I wish I could hear the silent twin conversation passing between them. Time is stretching too far. The wait is growing bigger than the ache, and I feel a little lighter. My tears slow and my breathing though shaky is no longer ragged. Finally, I push myself up and wipe my eyes with the back of my hand, embarrassed by the display I put on. Ethan's eyes are wide with confusion or fear. His cheeks are red almost feverish. I wonder if he touched me. I turn to Elena.

"Thanks," I mumble avoiding her eyes. I hurry to my feet, desperate to get out of there.

"I didn't-"

"Why are you crying?" Ethan interrupts, his voice loud, on edge.

I look at Elena for help, but she although she is standing beside me, she offers no easy way out. "I . . . can't-."

"Something really bad happened," Ethan answers for me, "something about your father. I wish you didn't go. I tried to tell you." He's shaking.

"Oh, Ethan. It's not your fault." Before I know what I'm doing I'm crouching beside him with my hand on his arm. The room spins like a carnival ride, and I'm in Ethan's head. His grandmother's voice grates against my nerves, "You stupid boy! When are you going to grow up!" The heat of shame and helplessness is consuming. I am looking at the floor and the puddle under my feet. I can shut out the harsh voice but, there is nothing I can do to shut out the overwhelming powerlessness and humiliation. As I slip further from myself, I fight to keep my own mind blank. Suddenly, I'm in my own room, smiling at the mess of it, picking up the trinkets on the dresser, examining the photos around the mirror. "Come on, E, let's get this done," Elena calls from far away. My heart is huge with longing. Then suddenly the room goes black. My head is heavy and empty. Slowly, my eyes focus on Ethan's. My hand's still on his arm, but I'm back in my own head.

Ethan did not fare as well on his trip through my psyche I fear because tears are coursing his cheeks. I expect him to pull away, run, withdraw forever from the world like Rachel predicted. Instead he stays squatting on his heels, holding my hand tightly, crying quietly. After a couple minutes, Elena separates us. She pulls Ethan gently to his feet and leads him away from me. I stand up to leave, but I'm so dizzy and nauseous that I head for Elena's bed instead of the door. I'm briefly aware of the soft crimson velvet and Elena's delicate summer breeze smell, before I fall asleep.

Just before I wake up, I dream that I'm standing in the warm rain. The wind is whispering through the trees and breathing into my face. I feel at peace in the center of the storm. I don't want to return to the world, but I can't stay in this in-between place. I roll over with a groan and push off the blanket that someone, probably Elena, put over me. Rain drops trickle down the windows in little rivers.

"You're finally awake?" Elena's voice startles me.

"Jeez, girl! I didn't know you were here."

"Sorry," she laughs. "but it is my room, ya know." She gets up and goes to the window. She turns back around to say, "Hey, you want go for a swim?"

"Uh. It's like raining, isn't it?"

"Ethan would tell you that's the best time to swim." I get up and join her at the window. Ethan glides back and forth gracefully as the rain dots the surface of the pool.

"Probably not a good idea," I say.

"He already knows." Elena is standing behind me now.

"I figured. How much does he understand?"

"Enough," she says.

"So that's it then. I totally blew it. Didn't I?"

"What are you talking about?" Elena says without a hint of sarcasm.

"Ethan. Duh! I totally broke his trust. I mean I had sex with Finn."

"No shit!" Elena says it quietly, maybe hoping I won't hear her. Then she laughs ironically. I don't much appreciate her mirth in the midst of my guilt. "You are so self-centered," she says, barely able to control herself. "Ethan isn't really capable of thinking of you like that. I thought you understood."

"But he hates Finn. And besides you and Finn . . ."

She stops laughing and steps back. "What . . . Oh my god. Ethan. You got that from Ethan's memory. That's incredible. Tell me what you see. How does it work?"

"I don't know." Elena is really starting to bug me at this point. "You should know better than me."

"Better than I, not me."

"Whatever. How does it work for you?"

"That's different. We're twins. It's like hearing someone else's heart beat across the room, like a whisper in the back of my mind. I've learned to listen to it. So has he. Is it like that?"

"No, not even close. It's more like trading places with him, borrowing his thoughts and feelings, becoming him for a moment and seeing through his eyes."

"So what did you see? About me and Finn."

"Nothing, actually." Now I get to laugh at her.

"What do you mean nothing? How did you know?"

"Finn gave you up at the river. Don't you remember?"

"Yes. I mean no. I actually don't remember," Elena admits.

"Enough about you; back to me. Is Ethan mad at me?"

"Mad? No, not mad."

"Then what?" I'm about to explode.

Elena's answer comes slowly. "Afraid for you, I think. Afraid of losing you. Maybe a little jealous of Finn. The thing is whatever he's going through, he's never felt that way before and doesn't really understand what's happening. So it's not about you. It's about Ethan. Don't screw it up! Get down there and swim in the rain with him."

"Okay. Okay. Why does everyone think I'm going to screw this up? I'll go home and get my suit."

Elena hands me a bag. "Already got it."

I take it from her roughly, but I smile too. "You coming?"

"I'll be down in a little while."

Ethan's swimming back and forth reminds me of a blind hamster I once had that ran and ran in its wheel all night long, thinking it was escaping into the world. It always seemed surprised to step off the wheel and run into its own house. I watch him for a couple of minutes, not sure of how to interrupt. Then as if he knows what I am thinking, he stops mid flip-turn and stands up.

"Are you gonna swim with me?" he asks quietly.

"I didn't come down to stand in the rain, pleasant as that might be." His smile warms me enough to venture down the pool stairs. Once I'm in the water beside him, I'm even less sure of what to do or say. He rolls over on his back like manatee and floats away for a minute. Then he executes a partial flip and comes back to where I'm standing awkwardly.

"Wanna make a whirlpool?"

I think back to the pool parties I attended years ago when I had friends and how we would all swim as fast as we could in the same direction in a big circle, trying to make a vortex appear. "Sure. Why not?"

I follow Ethan as he jogs around the edge of the shallow end. His narrow muscular shoulders taper to a perfect waist. I have a tough time not thinking of Finn and how he looked walking away from me this morning or was it yesterday. It seems so long ago, not real at all. As Ethan dives forward and begins to swim, I follow just beyond the turbulence of his strong kick. It doesn't take long for me to fall hopelessly behind. When he's almost an entire lap ahead, I cheat and swim through the middle of pool. He turns just in time to catch me.

"You can't do that," he scolds, brows knit in serious concern. "You'll break the whirlpool."

"Sorry, Ethan." I hang my head in mock regret.

"It's okay," he says. "We can stop if it's too hard for you to keep up."

"No, Ethan. I can do it. I was just kidding around." But even though he dives away to start again, I stay rooted to the spot. I have to do something to make it right. Ethan swims back to where I stand, trying to figure out what to say to not screw it up. He looks up at me warily and asks, "Why aren't you swimming, Sage?" The rain is falling harder now, and the wind is picking up.

"I feel terrible about . . ."

"Finn," he finishes for me. "You liked it, what he did to you." Ethan looks up at the darkening sky and moves closer to me. "Then you didn't. You cried. He hurt you. Your father hurt you too." He pauses for a couple seconds, then measures his trembling words. "I won't ever hurt you, Sage."

I look into his innocent gray eyes. "I know that, E. I don't want to hurt you either." He's staring at me intently, biting his bottom lip, like he's deciding something. The wind swirls around us, and we both shiver.

"I think a storm is coming," I say. "We should get out of the pool." But we don't move. When a bolt of lightning slices open the horizon, Ethan takes another step toward me, his eyes wide and anxious. A crash of thunder makes Ethan put his hands over his ears and close his eyes. When it stops, he grabs my hand and pulls me up the pool stairs.

Just as another low rumble of thunder erupts, I lose myself. The rain is falling in torrents, but I am in another place. A woman is calling, "Ethan, Ethan, come in, baby. You need to come in out of the storm." I'm afraid to go to her even though her voice fills me with a warm sense of comfort and love. Behind her a man's low voice curses. "Goddamn it, boy, git in here now!" My stomach feels like it has been punched, and I'm fighting back tears of frustration, fear. "I can't come in, Mama. Come here, please. You can't be there; something bad will happen. Please, Mama, don't make me come." The crash of thunder shakes the ground, and I wake up in my own head, standing by the pool.

Ethan is pulling me toward the house and saying, "We need to get in out of the storm." I'm myself and I'm still holding his hand. It's burning hot. We're both dripping wet and shivering when we stumble through the kitchen door. Elena's coming toward us and Iron Lady's standing by the window where she's been watching. We stop in our tracks, and for a moment everyone is motionless. Ethan is the first to move. He looks down at our hands still laced together. Elena and Iron Lady follow his gaze. I hold on more tightly, and his eyes find mine for more than the usual fleeting instant, and then the most amazing thing happens. Ethan smiles, not a nervous flitting smile, but a full-on, eye-crinkling smile. A crack of thunder chases his smile away as the fear returns, but he doesn't run to Elena, he moves closer to me. Slowly, I bring my free arm around his shoulder and hold him. His wet curls crush against my cheek as he presses lightly into me.

"You're dripping all over my clean floor," Iron Lady says almost gently. "Get yourselves upstairs and dry off." It's an invitation to stay, to hold onto this miracle a little longer. Ethan and I go up the stairs together with Elena trailing behind. Iron Lady follows us to the bottom of the stairs, but doesn't go up. He leads me to the end of the hall and hesitates at the door to his room. Elena steps in, her voice muted and far away. "Sage, your clothes are in my room. I'll get you a dry towel." I wait a second longer, so Ethan can be the one to let go first. Then I close the door behind me in Elena's room and let out my breath. I didn't even realize that I had been holding it. I go to the window and look out into the deluge. The sky flashes bright, and thunder shakes the house as it echoes out across the yard. In the bathroom next door Ethan and Elena's voices, perfectly harmonized by an act of nature calm me. Maybe ten minutes later Elena comes in with the towel she promised.

"Don't go anywhere," she says handing it to me. "But feel free to take a shower." Through the open door Ethan waits for her with a towel around his waist. He waves at me. Then I watch them disappear behind the door to his room. In the shower I turn the water as hot as I can stand it and get in with my bathing suit still on. After a while, I take it off, wring it out, and hang it on the towel bar. I wash my hair with the honey shampoo that smells like Ethan. I get out and wrap myself in the big soft towel. The door to Ethan's room is still closed. Back in Elena's room I find my clothes neatly folded on the bench at the foot of her bed. From the bottom of the stairs Iron Lady calls up that dinner is ready. I meet Ethan and Elena in the hall. He's wearing sweatpants and a long sleeved shirt. I am freezing in my tank and shorts. Ethan's curls are brushed out neatly and tucked behind his ears. My hair must look like Medusa. Elena looks me up and down.

"Tell grandmother we'll be down in a minute or two," she says sending Ethan tentatively down the stairs. She pulls me into the bathroom and starts brushing my hair out. She tugs the brush gently down the length of my straight dark locks like someone who is practiced at caring for a child. The AC blows right on us and my teeth chatter. She tucks my hair behind my ears like Ethan's and signals me to wait by the door. Then she slips into Ethan's room and comes out with a sweatshirt. It's light blue and smells so sweetly of him I think I may drown in it. Elena brings me back to shore.

"How did you do it?" she doesn't wait for me to answer. "You know that no one, and I mean no one has been able to touch him since the . . . since our mom died, except me. Not Grandmother, not a single person at school, not even Rachel. No one."

I wait till she out of breath. "I don't know. I was inside his head and then I wasn't. It must be Ethan controlling it. I don't think it was me."

"You're wrong, Sage. I think it was you, something you did."

"Girls, we're going to starve to death waiting on you down here. Iron Lady's voice is only mildly annoyed, but we hurry down the stairs. In the kitchen Ethan is seated at the same place at the table he sat during our first dinner. Elena goes to the chair beside his but stops; they do their twin thing. Then she smiles and motions me to take that seat. She crosses to the other side. Ethan smiles shyly as I join him on the far side of the table.

"Hey, that's my shirt!" his voice is happy and musical. Iron Lady raises a single eyebrow.

"I hope it's okay. I was cold. Elena got it for me." Iron Lady seems satisfied by my explanation.

"I like it on you," Ethan says, looking down.

"Me too," I say, and without thinking I touch his hand. My stomach flips over, and the dizziness starts, but I focus on the moment: the gray of Ethan's eyes, the smell of his shirt and the tuna casserole, fresh baked bread, the tapping of the rain on the window, and I manage to stay put in my own head. Ethan's concentrating too. He's squeezing my hand hard. Then he relaxes, and I can see he hasn't gone into my head either.

"Let's eat!" Elena says a little too loudly. Without taking her eyes off us, Iron Lady begins serving and passing the dishes around the table till we each have one. Ethan doesn't let go of my hand, but it works out okay because he's left handed and I'm right. Ethan eats at least two helpings while he and Elena chatter about this and that. There's no lull in the conversation, and even Iron Lady smiles and laughs a few times.

When we're all done, I get up and help Elena clear the dishes. This time when my hand is drawn to the heat of Ethan's shoulder, he smiles, and I only feel a little disoriented. I stop at the sink to look out across the back yard. The light is burning in the garage apartment. Rachel's at home.

"I guess I should head out. Thanks for dinner. It was awesome." I don't mean to sound as wistful as I do. The chorus of objections is unexpected.

"Don't go, Sage. Please stay." Ethan's adamant.

"Grandmother, Sage can spend the night here, right." Elena isn't asking.

Iron Lady looks at the three of us. Then she turns to Ethan, "Are you sure, boy?" Her question is full of implied context that I am not supposed to be privy to.

Ethan blushes and shrinks down in his chair. I think Elena says something to him silently, because his chin comes up. Then he nods solemnly to his grandmother.

"Then it's okay with me."

Ethan and Elena both cheer.

"I'll just go tell Rachel what's going on," I say heading for the door. "Back in a minute."

I sprint through the rain and throw open the door. Reality hits me hard in the gut. My dad is sitting at the table with Rachel. The sight of him makes me want to hurl. I avoid making eye-contact.

"Hey, Mom. I'm gonna stay with Elena tonight. Okay?" I don't want to hear my father make any comments about Ethan, so I keep him out of the equation.

I don't wait for her answer. I run up the stairs and close the door to my room. My phone is sitting in the middle of the bed where I left it. It's blinking. I want to ignore it, but I can't. I swipe it on. Eight text messages and five calls. All the text messages are from Finn. He must have gotten my number from Caller ID when I called from the Starbucks. I should have borrowed a phone. Three of the calls too. Only two calls from good old dad.

I sit on the bed to read Finn's texts.

Number 1: 12:03 pm - *Hey, stalker girl, you know the number. Use it.*

Number 2: 1:43 pm - *I meant today - not next week.*

Number 3: 2:32 pm - *Really? WAY?*

Number 4: 3:18 pm - *One simple text-that's all I'm asking.*

Number 5: 4:07 pm - *R u mad?*

Number 6: 5:21 pm - *U R KILLING ME*

Number 7: 6:11 pm - *Still waiting.*

Number 8: 7:03 pm - *AURDOD (assuming u r dead or disconnected)*

Poor Finn. The calls are more of the same. The first is all sweet and I want to talk to you. The second is getting pissed; the subtext being 'call me back, you bitch!' The third is defeated and sad under the bravado and quips. I want to call him, but I don't want to talk. The guy who invented text messaging should be sainted.

"Separated from my phone all day. Sorry to stress you out. Not mad. Not close. Just busy. Call you tomorrow."

The reply is almost immediate. *"WE"*

Typical. He spends the whole day texting me, and when I finally text him back, I get the sum total of "Whatever." Not even the whole word, just a cheesy abbreviation. I smile in spite of it and picture him smiling back, blue eyes sparkling.

For just a second I wish I was spending the night in his bed again. Then I remember the roller coaster ride I took there, and I'm happy that it's Ethan and Elena waiting for me downstairs.

After I get my stuff together, I contemplate leaving the phone behind, but realize that if Rachel gets curious, I'm in serious trouble. I plan the strategy before I head down. I'm just going to make a beeline for the door. No chit chat. I know it's a lame plan, but it's all I've got. Before I even make it down the stairs, Rachel starts in, "Sage, where are your manners? Your dad is sitting here and you can't say hello."

"Hello, Dad," I say maneuvering around the table toward Mom. "Goodbye, Dad. Bye, Mom." I stop to kiss her on the cheek. There is no ensuing third degree, so I am guessing dad divulged nothing about my little disappearing act. He's so good at this shit, it makes me sick. Of course there would be questions to answer if he told her that I took off, questions that I might answer with information that he cannot afford to have out and about.

The rain has slowed a bit, and Ethan is waiting for me by his back door. "Mouse! You're getting all wet," I scold lightly.

"I saw your father through the window," he says.

"I'm okay, Ethan." The lines on his forehead tell me that he's not convinced. "Really," I assure him opening the door to the warm kitchen.

"Games or movies?" asks Elena from the sink where she's finishing the dishes.

"Movies," Ethan and I say in unison.

"Perfect," she says, drying her hands.

In the room at the top of the stairs we get settled in. We queue up Netflix and choose a light comedy that I've never heard of. I curl up in a corner of the overstuffed couch. Ethan sits next to me crisscross. Elena stretches out on the floor in front of the couch. Outside the rain is pouring down again, but the thunder and lightning are only a memory. Big windows at either end of the room reveal the darkening sky. Not long into the movie Ethan lays down and puts his head in my lap. The fight to stay in my own mind is easier, but I wouldn't call it effortless by a long shot. I smooth his soft curls from his face and watch him struggle not to bring his thumb to his mouth. It's a battle he soon loses. I turn my attention back to the movie.

A little while later Iron Lady comes up the stairs with a load of laundry that she takes down the hall to Elena's room. She stops on the way back and pretends to watch the movie with us for a few minutes. Then she signals to Elena. They have a brief conversation in whispers, and Elena comes back and gently reaches over to remove Ethan's thumb. He curls up on his side with his knees closer to his chest, his whole body tensing from the implied reprimand. His shirt comes up a little on his back, and before he can reach around to pull it down, I see the top of the diaper he's wearing under his sweats.

A look of panic flashes in his eyes, and suddenly I am in his room with Elena, towel around my-his waist. Elena is standing by the dresser in the corner of the room, opening the top drawer.

"No! Lanie." My (Ethan's) voice is desperate but hushed. "Please. I'll be good. I promise I'll stay dry. Please don't make me." She hesitates for an instant.

"Ethan, don't do this. You know it will be much worse if you have an accident. Plus, Grandmother will be furious if you wet on the couch. It will be okay, I promise. If you wear sweatpants, she won't even know." A feeling of defeat settles in as I reach over and take the diaper she hands me.

Then I am no longer looking at Elena. I am back on the couch looking at Ethan with queasiness in my stomach and a dull ache beginning in the back of my head. His eyes are filling up, and he makes a move to sit up, but I put my hand on his shoulder and gently lay him back down. I rub his back in circles until he relaxes again and glue my eyes to the television.

Our control over the switching places thing is clearly not perfected yet. But I wonder who slipped up, him or me. In the instant before it happened a kind of question passed through my mind. I wonder now if I am the one controlling it.

The pain in my head is growing exponentially with each passing moment, but I don't want to move from this spot. Ethan reaches out and touches Elena who has been so involved in the lame plot, that she missed all the drama. A couple of seconds later she gets up and goes downstairs. She returns with cokes for me and her and two Advil that she casually deposits in my palm as though I've asked for them. She is instantly back into the movie so I don't bother to say anything. It makes me a bit uneasy, though. I have to wonder what other information Ethan is getting from our physical contact.

By the end of the movie Ethan is so sound asleep that his thumb has fallen out of his mouth and his hand is resting by his cheek. I have been dozing on and off. Only Elena has made it all the way through. She gently shakes Ethan awake and leads him down the hall still mostly asleep. I have just stretched out on the sofa when I notice that the rain has stopped. Suddenly, the most beautiful voice I've ever heard drifts down the hall from Ethan's room. It's a song I recognize from my mom's hippy music collection.

" *Yesterday a child came out to wander/caught a dragon fly inside a jar/fearful when the sky was full of thunder/and tearful at the falling of a star.*" Joni Mitchell's "Circle Game." I sit up so I can hear better. From my vantage point I catch Iron Lady sitting half-way up the stairway. Our eyes meet, and she motions me over. I sit next her, and we listen to Elena together.

"We can't return; we can only look behind/From where we came/And go round and round and round/In the circle game"

She sings it all the way through as the boy is 10 then 16 and 20. When she stops, Iron Lady says with a husky voice. "She sings him to sleep every night just like their mother did." Then she wipes her eyes brusquely and goes back down stairs to the kitchen.

My grandfather told me once that love comes in many flavors, but mostly people think it is only love if it's vanilla or chocolate. The very wise or adventurous might recognize strawberry too. Still, if we can open our minds and hearts, we can taste many more flavors of love. I think that lemon flavored is Iron Lady's love for the twins. My love for Finn is cinnamon, but I love Ethan like peaches and cream. I lay back on the couch and in an instant drift off in a cool sweet dream of whip cream and cherries. I hear the click as Elena closes the door to Ethan's room. Halfway between sleeping and waking I say, "Mango," out loud.

Elena looks at me quizzically. "Mango ice-cream, that's how I love you," I say reaching for her hand. I am sleepy and dreamy, and I have no idea why I say it, but Elena kneels beside me smiling.

"Perfect. I love mangos." Then she leans down and kisses me lightly. Strangely, she tastes exactly like mangos. I let her lead me down the hall the same way she led Ethan. After we crawl beneath the eiderdown of her big soft crimson bed, I long for a lullaby. I settle for curling up against her and listening to her breathing until I drift blissfully away from the earth.

The next morning I'm the last one up. Alone in the big bed, I'm coaxed awake by the chattering and clattering from downstairs. Ethan's begging to come wake me while Elena scolds him to be patient. Iron Lady must be cooking because delicious smells of bacon and coffee are wafting around me. Rachel is there too, asking for more coffee. I can't remember ever sleeping so deeply in my whole life. The sun streams brilliant through the curtains, and the birds perform a symphony in the trees outside the window. The storm has passed, and I think I'm ready to sort through the ruble of the last two days.

Chapter 7 (Out of Mind)

Beneath each pile of debris lies another and another. Each layer excavated is more compressed than the one above until the internal heat of all that is hidden creates a molten river that no one in their right mind would want to traverse.

I have a tough time turning down Ethan's pleas for a swim, but Rachel backs me up by insisting that Ethan has some "work" to do with her. I promise him that I will come back later in the day, and he relents without giving in to the tears that threaten. Elena wants to go shopping, but I beg off that too. I have to find out about Jo and the video, plus I owe Finn something, though I'm not sure what. I seriously do not want to see him, but I can't figure out why.

I'm shocked anew when I open the door to my room and am greeted by the hundred butterflies fluttering in the breeze of the ceiling fan. There's no way I can keep my game face on in here. Luckily, Rachel will be hours with Ethan, so I go down to the kitchen. I dial Jo's number and stand by the sink, looking out over the pool and the Paige's yard. How many days has it been? A week maybe a little more, and Ethan and Elena are a part of me already. Finally, she answers. I sit at the table so I can concentrate.

"Sage! Stranger. Where ya been?"

I don't know where to begin. I have so much to tell her, but I can't be distracted.

"Sage are you there? You called me."

"Sorry. I was kind of lost for a second."

"To what do I owe the honor of a return phone call? I was thinking that you might be breaking up with me. You aren't breaking up, are you?"

We both laugh. "No way. BFF's forever right?" I say.

"Except that's redundant. Forever forever," Jo points out. "So how was your visit with your dad." she asks, biting off the last word like piece of burnt bagel.

"The usual," I say, but my voice breaks just a bit.

"What happened," Jo asks full of concern.

"I broke the rules," I say. She waits. "Went in his room and worse . . . I used his computer." Silence.

"Doesn't sound too serious," Jo offers, but I hear the question in her voice.

"But it was. He has stuff on his computer. Nasty stuff."

Jo cuts me off. "So what? All guys are into porn! You shouldn't look at his stuff if you don't want to see it."

"I didn't say anything about porn. Why did you assume that?" I ask pointedly.

"He's a male over 13 and under 70, nasty equals porn. Not a big leap and not a big deal," but Jo's pitch is rising.

"Jo Jo, it wasn't just porn. It was girls, like young, like me and," I pause for emphasis, "you."

Jo's silence stretches on, and when she finally says something it's not what I expected, not by a long shot. "Sage, do NOT fucking go there. Child pornography is a federal crime with serious consequence. You want your dad in jail till he dies? That's what will happen. But know that he won't go down easy. You have no idea what he's capable of. LAST WORD on that subject forever forever."

Not exactly a confirmation, but I'm sure now. If I open that file, I will see Jo doing something awful, something my dad made her do, something he filmed. I catch a sob coming up from my throat, and I swallow it down again.

"Sage? Are you still there?"

"Hmm." I literally can't speak.

"What's happening with fire-boy?" she is trying to sound cheerful, upbeat, but it's forced.

"We did it!" I say it angrily, when I regain the use of my vocal cords. "I left my dad's without tell him I was going, and I called Finn. I stayed over at his house, and we did the deed."

"OMG. Didn't see that coming at least not this soon. So what was it like?"

I want to scream at her, *"Tell me what it was like for you?"* But I know whatever happened on that video was not Jo's idea, and it was not pleasant.

"It was scary and sweet and awful and scary and amazing. I haven't called him. It was two days ago."

"Sage! You have to call the boy! What's wrong with you?"

"I don't know. I wish I knew, trust me. I wish I knew."

Jo takes a maternal tone with me. "Please tell me you used protection."

"Jo! Actually, we did. Finn was on top of that, no pun . . ."

Jo giggles out of control and it's contagious. It feels so good to laugh with her. So normal, but I am desperately afraid that nothing will ever be normal again between us.

"There's more," I say sobering up.

"You have been way too busy, my friend."

"Speaking of busy," I suddenly remember that Jo has a life too. "What happened on the ultimate geek date?"

"I thought you'd never ask. The music was amazing."

"Don't really care about the music! How was the boy?"

"Cute and totally awkward. He tried to kiss me. It was kind of a fiasco of bumping glasses and clashing braces."

"Okay loving the picture of the fiasco geek almost-kiss. Are you going out again?"

"Are you kidding?" Jo says. "Of course we are."

Another round of giggles takes over.

"Damn I miss you!" My eyes start brimming over at first from the laughter.

"Six more weeks, Sage. Hang in there for six more weeks. So what was the something more? Spill."

I flash back to Ethan curled up with his head on my lap, sucking his thumb, how we trade places and how I am the only one who can touch him. Talking about any of it feels like a huge betrayal. I remember his eyes when he said he would never hurt me, and I promised him the same. I pause.

"No biggie. I watched a movie with the mysterious twins last night. Pretty normal and boring. I'm sure you have practicing to do."

"Okay, yeah. I always have practicing to do. It's not easy being a virtuoso. Something tells me that there was nothing normal or boring about being with them though. I guess Rachel's rule is null and void in this case."

"Looks like it," I say passing it off. "Happy practicing."

"Call Finn. Right now."

"Sure thing. Right now. Promise."

We hang up, and the 10% battery alert goes off. It would not be good for my phone to die in the middle of a conversation with Finn. I go back upstairs to find my charger. I find my book instead. After I spend over an hour writing about Jo, I remember Finn and the dead phone, and I plug it in.

Rachel comes in a bit later and makes her way upstairs after tidying the kitchen and writing her notes. I wonder what she "works" on with Ethan and Elena. The therapy she does with Finn seemed pretty much like straightforward shrink-and-couch stuff, but after the motorcycle ride, I'm not so sure about that either. She knocks lightly before she comes in even though the door is technically opened.

"Hey, Madre."

"Kiddo. Whatcha doing?"

"Waiting for my phone to charge. Thinking about cleaning up my room."

"Wait let me get the smelling salts, I may faint," she half-jokes.

"Have you seen Elena's room? It's like luxurious and perfect."

"Yes, Elena likes to keep everything tidy and perfect, but, Sage, I like you untidy and imperfect. You know what I mean?"

"Sure, Madre," I get up and give her a hug. While I start to put away the clothes that are scattered around the room, Rachel sits on the bed, watching and looking at the butterflies. I think I hear a motorcycle and casually glance out the window in time to see Finn's bike cruise by. This could be a problem.

"Hey, Mom. Are you done with the Paige's for the afternoon?"

"I think so. Why"

"What do you say we get out of here and go for a hike or something." The one thing Rachel loves more than breathing is hiking.

"What a nice idea. I'll go get my hair up and shoes on."

The minute she leaves I text Finn. *Who's the stalker now?*

He texts back immediately. *Come to XODs. I want to see you.*

I reply, *Wish I could. R is here. More later.*

He types, *Later then. Don't make me come over there.*

I send, *Don't joke about that,* just as Rachel comes back in.

I stick the phone in the back pocket of my shorts on vibrate.

"Who you texting?"

I almost say Elena, but Mom will know where she is. "Jo Jo."

"What's up with Jo this summer? I miss seeing her face."

"She had the ultimate geek date, with a real live geek, awkward good-night kiss and all. Can you believe it?"

"A good geek -"

"- is hard to find," we say it in unison and laugh.

"Thanks for sparing me the whole dating drama, Sage. I'm not ready yet. I'm so glad we're on the same page with that." I feel exquisitely guilty. If it were anyone but Finn, I would so tell Rachel all about it. I really do trust her to be awesome about the sex stuff, but it is Finn, and I can't change that.

"Let's go," I say, leading the way down the stairs.

We drive out to one of my mom's favorite trails. It's kind of off the beaten track and a bit more technical than the casual hiker's trail. A good part of it follows an old stream bed that's insanely rocky. Then it hugs the edge of steep hill as it circles down into a ravine. When there's been rain, the stream careens down a cliff some 20 feet above the basin into a shallow pool at the bottom where it disappears underground. Getting to that waterfall is like a reward for making it down the trail. It's hard going, and we concentrate rather than talk. I'm really content to be doing this with my mom right now, but a hundred things are tugging away at that contentment trying to trip me up.

At the bottom the waterfall pours down heavily thanks to last night's rainstorm. Tiny rainbows are glancing off the falls in a couple of places. I immediately remove my shoes and splash into the pool. Rachel does the same. We stand together under the cool water and let it pour over us like a shower. Then we climb up a couple of feet to a ridge behind the water curtain where we can sit and stretch our feet into the falls.

"This is so perfect," Rachel says. "We need to do this more often."

"Like every day," I say.

Rachel looks at me long and hard. "Do you know how much I love you?" she asks.

"Mom, I know you love me. I do." For a second I think she must know about Finn. She's going to confront me.

"I just feel like I'm missing out on things in your life. It's scaring me a little."

What am I supposed to say? She is missing things, and there are things she doesn't know and even things she doesn't want to know about me. I want so bad to tell her everything, about me and Finn, about Jo and Dad, and Ethan and me, and me and Elena, but I shrug instead.

"What do you want to know, Madre?"

"Nothing in particular," she says. She sees the wall, and she knows how to work around it. She is a therapist after all, and my walls are made of paper compared to Finn's and Ethan's. "Remember when you were little? After a play date, you would sit me down to debrief. That's what you called it. 'Debrief.' You were so serious about analyzing every incident and conversation. I loved that. You know it was one of the reasons I went back to school to become a therapist. I wanted to help you understand all the stuff you were feeling and going to feel."

"I never knew that," I'm astonished that I sent her down this crazy path.

"You were such an intense child, so empathic. You struggled so much with all the emotion you were channeling all the time. I thought I could carve you a path since there was no way to lighten your load." She pauses; then her voice goes all soft and sad. "Now I'm not sure that I've been any help at all to you or any of the kids I treat."

"Rachel, get a grip. You're like St. George, out there slaying impossible dragons so people can live in peace. You so help all your kids, me included. Look at how far Ethan's come in like one week."

"Ah, yes, Ethan. Whatever progress Ethan's making it's because of you, not me. Surely, you can see that."

"No way. He let me in because of you," I want to believe what I am saying for her sake.

"It's all you, Herbie. Ethan's an empath like you I think, but his circuits are on overload. Somehow he recognizes that you can help control that overload. At least that's my current hypothesis."

"I think it's much simpler than that. Seventeen-year-old boy meets pretty girl and his hormones do the rest."

Rachel laughs out loud and splashes me playfully. "That in and of itself would be miracle enough for Ethan. Maybe wanting you will be enough to make him want to grow up."

"You think he doesn't want to grow up? You think he likes being . . . how did you put it? . . . stuck in time? I think you're wrong about that."

"Why?"

"When we touch, I know exactly what he feels because it's like I am him sort of. What he feels is mostly shame and helplessness. He knows-" suddenly I stop myself. I'm such an idiot. Rachel led me down this path for this very purpose. She wants to know what makes Ethan tick. Maybe she even suspects that we trade places.

"He knows what, Sage?"

"Nothing, Madre. I shouldn't be talking about this."

"Why not? You have an opportunity to really help him. What do you mean you become him?" Her curiosity is relentless.

"Haven't you ever touched Ethan accidentally?" I wonder now if my experience is somehow unique.

"Yes, the very first time I met him. It was like having another person in my head or being in a dream. It gave me an intense headache, but I didn't really experience what you just described."

"Maybe you should stick with your empath theory. I really can't talk about what I see; it's not my information to give. Understand?"

"Sure." After a long silence she adds, "I'm glad he has you."

I suddenly realize why I don't want to see Finn. I don't want to hurt Ethan. My heart wants to see Finn, but for some reason my mind doesn't. And Ethan doesn't want me to see Finn. Coincidence? I think not. I'm left again puzzling over who is controlling the crossover and what information exactly is crossing.

Rachel has already moved on. "What do you think of Elena?"

I hesitate, thinking about the two times we kissed. I lick my lips. "Mango," I say smiling.

"What are you smoking over there, Sage," Rachel laughs.

"I guess I'd hate her for being so perfect if I didn't like her so much."

Rachel laughs again. "Was the sleep over fun?"

"Not exactly fun in the sense of gossip and pillow fights, but it was good, really good."

"I think that was the first sleep over Elena ever had," Rachel adds wistfully.

"Because of Ethan?"

Rachel nods. "She protects him. Most people wouldn't understand."

I think about the scars on her arms and legs, "But she can't help him," I add.

"What was that?" Rachel asks. I suddenly realize that she knows nothing about Elena's gift. Why would she know? One more secret to hide. It's getting exhausting keeping track of all of them.

"Nothing, just that she enables him, right? She makes it possible for him to be a four-year-old because she takes care of him like one."

"Of course, you're right." Her eyes are shining like this is a revelation to her, and I'm suddenly worried about the damage I have just done to their little microcosm.

"I could be totally wrong!" I say, trying to back pedal.

"No, you're totally right. You ready to head back? I heard you promise Ethan a swim today and by the time we get back, today will be almost gone."

"Sure."

We get our shoes on and hike back up to the car. The return trip is all uphill, so chit chat is out of the question. On the ride back I immediately fall asleep and dream I'm on Finn's bike facing backward with my legs wrapped around him. I feel like at any moment we might crash because the fog obscures the road under the bike making it seem like we're riding on clouds. I'm jolted awake when Rachel pulls into the driveway and stops. I had just begun to enjoy that feeling of impending collision around every turn.

Faced with two obligations, I opt for the one that I think is more pressing. After I change into my swimsuit and grab a towel, I head across the patio. Ethan's at the kitchen table helping Elena make cookies, though it's questionable how much help he's actually being. He's half standing, half sitting in the chair, reaching across the table, stealing a bit of dough and eating it whenever she isn't looking. When he see me at the door, he jumps down and runs to open it. I brace myself for his hug by putting my thoughts squarely in the moment, just in case we lose control, but after a couple dizzy seconds, it's all good.

"We made cookies for you," Ethan says grinning.

"Yes, I can see how much you're helping," I say. Elena laughs, but Ethan looks down embarrassed.

"I helped. It was my idea and I measured and stirred," he mumbles, pulling his hand from mine.

I take his hand back. "I was joking, Mouse. I love cookies." I kiss him on the cheek and his ears turn red. Elena laughs again. "Do you still want to go swimming, Mouse?" I ask.

Ethan looks at Elena for permission. She nods.

"When the buzzer goes off, take out the ones in the oven and put these in for eight minutes," she instructs on her way upstairs with Ethan. Maybe I was right about her enabling him. Surely he can get a swimsuit on without her assistance. I try not think about it. The buzzer rings, and I follow Elena's instructions. Finally, they come back down, and Ethan and I head out to the pool.

We try to make the whirlpool again, but I just can't keep up. When Ethan laps me, he grabs my foot and tickles it till I scream. Then he leap-frogs over me, and the race is on again. Of course getting enough momentum to create a respectable whirlpool with only two people in a pool this large is pretty hopeless, so I turn around when he is halfway to catching me, and pretend to be swimming against the current to break it. We meet in the middle and rough-house to get around each other. We're both laughing out of control as we do mock battle, preventing each other from going forward. I've never seen Ethan so unguarded and happy. In mid-splash he stops and throws his arms around me, hugging me tightly. I am taken utterly by surprise. I wrap my arms around his back and press my cheek to his. We relax into each other belly-to-belly, chest-to-chest. The heat of his body is intense like the time Rachel had pneumonia and had a 103 degree fever. I wonder how anyone can run that hot all the time. I lose myself in his heat and smell, but I stay in my own mind.

Then suddenly he tenses up, and as my hearing comes back into focus, I make out the sound of a motorcycle engine. I pull away from him carefully and turn around slowly. Ethan clings to my arm, but takes a step behind me. I can feel him trembling. Finn idles the bike at the end of the driveway. I can't see his face because of his helmet, but his body language says rage. Elena comes tearing out of the house. I guess Ethan called to her telepathically or something, and she hurries toward Finn. She says something we can't hear from the pool, and Finn replies. One more exchange then he pushes her away as she tries to touch his arm. "15 minutes," he yells toward me and speeds off.

Elena stands looking after him for a few seconds before turning to us. I can see she's seething under her patient smile. "Ethan, you need to get ready for dinner. Go inside." He reluctantly lets go of me and makes his way slowly to the stairs. I follow a little behind. He stops on the deck to retrieve his towel and look back at me and Elena. "Now, Ethan. I'll be up in a minute." Obediently, he disappears behind the door.

Then Elena rages on me. "What the hell are you doing, Sage?" I'm stunned and silent. "You cannot screw with Finn. He's not a nice person, and he's not going to give Ethan a pass. You're putting yourself and my brother in real danger. Jeez, Sage. You need to go do damage control, and you better make it good because if you aren't convincing, you may find yourself waking up to a conflagration one night, or worse he could take it out on Ethan, who, by the way, doesn't understand any of this crap. Fix this now! He's waiting for you at Exodus; you have 15 minutes, so step on it."

I nod helplessly. I have no idea what I'm fixing or how, but the thought of anyone hurting Ethan because of me is more than I can bear. I take the stairs two at a time and throw on my shorts without underwear. I grab a shirt with a built in bra, slip on my old Tevas, and race down the stairs. Rachel is standing in front of the door.

"Where's the fire, Kiddo?" she asks.

"Mom, not now, please. I need to go do something important."

She doesn't move. "What's so urgent and important? Start talking, Sage."

"It would take too long to explain, and I am down to eight minutes. Please let me go. I'll explain when I get back." I'm in tears now.

She hesitates and then steps back to let me through. "One hour, Sage. Then I want it all. No lies. Where are you going?"

"Exodus. I have my phone. One hour. No lies. I promise." I hurry past her without a hug or kiss, thinking - *what the hell am I going to tell her?*

I run all the way to the cafe. When I get there, I'm drenched in sweat. Finn is sitting at an outside table. He fidgets with his motorcycle helmet, pretends he doesn't see me running up. I decide to play it cool.

"Hey there, stranger, can I buy you a cup of coffee?" It doesn't sound very suave since I can't catch my breath.

He grabs my arm and pulls me to him. He kisses me hard, really hard. Then he just stares into my eyes until I pull away. "Now you can buy me a cup of coffee."

I go in and signal to the bitch behind the counter that I need two cups of coffee. She shoves them at me, splashing on the counter. I'm not in the mood. I shove the money at her dragging it through the spill.

"Nice," she says, looking me up and down. "That your boyfriend?" she motions toward Finn.

"No," I say out of reflex. "I mean, I don't know."

"You better figure it out, my friend. He's pretty pissed off at you, so my guess is that he thinks he is."

"Tell me something I don't know." Like I need a total stranger telling me that. Then something occurs to me. "Hey, wait a minute. How old are you?"

"Why do you want to know?"

"Just answer the damn question," I say.

"Twenty-four," she says.

"Can you tell me something?

"Maybe."

"If you, you know, do it with a guy, what does it mean? Am I his girlfriend now?"

"Okay. Well, I guess it depends on the guy. You did it with that guy?"

"Yeah. Thanks for nothing." I walk away.

"Sounds like buyer's remorse," she yells after me.

I struggle to open the door with the coffee and end up spilling some of it down my shirt, but Finn doesn't get up to help. I put the cups at places opposite each other rather than side-by-side, and I sit across from him.

He looks at me like I slapped him. "So that's how it is, Sage?"

"I don't really know how it is, Finn, but you're scaring me."

"Good," he says, but his tone softens. "How am I supposed to feel, Sage?"

"I don't know. I don't even know how I'm supposed to feel."

"You don't seem confused about how you feel about that freak!"

"As if you're so normal! This is not about Ethan, and you know it!" I know it's a lie before it comes out of my mouth, but I don't want his anger directed at Ethan.

"Then tell me what it is about. One day you're giving it to me, and the next day I don't get so much as a fucking text message because you're off playing touchy feely with that Paige kid."

"Kid being the operative word here. You can't seriously be jealous of Ethan!"

"Sage, he was all over you, I'm not stupid."

"Actually, Finn you are kind of being stupid," I smile at him. "When I needed help I didn't call Ethan. I called you. And what you saw this afternoon was two friends hugging, no one was all over anyone. Trust me."

"I want to believe you, Sage, but he really screwed things up for me before, and I don't trust him. I don't want him to screw this up too." His tone is a little calmer.

I'm not really sure what Finn thinks *this* is, but now is not the time to try to define it. "The truth is, Finn, I'm still kind of messed up about what happened at my dad's."

He thinks about that for several seconds. "You wanna talk about it?" It comes out as a challenge.

I had intended to just change the subject, but I realize that I actually do want to talk about it, and Finn is just the person I want to talk to. "I saw something I wasn't supposed to see."

"Snooping around? Imagine that!"

"The sarcasm is not appreciated. Do you want to hear this or not?"

Finn smiles at his little victory. "Go ahead; I'll be chill."

I take a minute to go back to that afternoon in my dad's apartment. "So I was bored, and my dad left me alone at his place. I decided to use his computer to surf, but when I opened the desktop, there were all these files with girl's names."

Finn's eyes get big, "Is this going where I think it is?"

"Uh huh. So I clicked on one."

"And you watched it?"

"Yup."

He sits back and looks at me with something like admiration. "You are full of surprises, girl!"

"Don't get excited; I didn't enjoy it. It was disturbing and sad. But that isn't the point either. In the video there were things in the background, familiar things, my things."

It takes Finn a couple of beats, then he leans forward, "Your dad made the videos. Bummer for you, but not really criminal or anything, unless the girls were underage." The last word comes out in slow motion because my hands are shaking so badly that my coffee is spilling over the sides. He takes the cup from me. "Shit."

I hold back my tears. "There's more."

He gets up and moves to the chair next to mine. He holds both my hands, and waits for me to steady myself.

"One of the names of the files . . . was . . . is . . . someone I know, but I don't know if it's really a video of her or if he just used her name for the file."

"Does it matter?"

"Duh! Yes!"

"Must be a good friend, " he says.

"My bestie."

"Crap." After a few seconds he asks, "Are you sure you want to know?"

"I HAVE TO know!"

"Sorry, forgot who I was talking to." He grins sweetly.

"Nice." I feign annoyance, but suddenly I really want to kiss him.

"You've got three choices," he says. "Ask your friend, ask your dad, or get back on that computer. My guess is that one and two are out of the question."

"Yup. The third may be impossible too, since my dad might suspect that I know something."

"Right, because you took off."

"I actually tried to talk to my friend, but she isn't going to tell me anything. She 'last-worded' me, so I can't talk about it anymore, like ever."

Finn looks at me like I'm speaking a foreign language. "I have no idea what you're talking about, but it seems to me that leaves your dad."

"No way. I can't even look at him. How am I going to talk to him?"

Finn laughs. "Sage, you're the queen of getting people to tell you their secrets."

"Really, then why haven't you spilled your guts yet?"

"You know a hell of a lot more about me than any other girl I've . . . . Never mind. Does your dad know why you left the other night?"

"No. He doesn't know anything," I say.

"How much trouble are you willing to cause yourself to get a look at that file?"

"You think I should tell him I snuck out to see you, and I won't talk to him because I am afraid he'll narc to Rachel. You're kind of brilliant!"

He grins. "I like to think so. Did you leave any evidence that you were on his computer?"

"I covered my tracks pretty well, so this might actually work. I'll definitely get in trouble, but it'll be worth it."

"Problem solved. Now let's get out of here," Finn says pulling me a little closer.

"No can do. Rachel gave me one hour, and it's nearly up."

"That's bullshit!" He slams his hand down on the table, making me and the cups jump.

"Don't you dare get mad at me. I'm the one who has to go home and face the inquisition. She wants the truth this time. So instead of being so selfish, help me figure out what to say."

"I think you can cover it, Sage. You are about the best liar I've ever met," He gets up and picks up his helmet.

"Can I get a ride home?"

"No can do," he mimics me. "Then you might have to tell her the real truth."

"Thanks for nothing," I say, but I smile.

I'm rewarded with a very sweet kiss and a very sad sigh. "Later, Stalker-girl."

"Later, Finn."

I watch him get on his bike and peel out of the parking lot. I have a ten minute walk home to figure out what to tell Rachel. Coming up the driveway, I still have no clue what I am going to say.

I expect to see Rachel waiting by the door or at the very least sitting in the kitchen, but she isn't even home. The car's gone, and the apartment's oddly silent. I go upstairs to take a hot shower. There's a note taped to the bathroom mirror saying she went to dinner and the movies with Benjamin. I say a silent thank you to Ben for granting me this reprieve. Ben is her best friend and more like a dad to me than my "real" dad. He used to live with us when I was small, but he moved out when he married Joshua and they bought a place together. They're the happiest couple I know. We rarely see them now even though they live only a few miles away.

I stay in the shower until I can no longer stand up. Then I get out, go to my room, and lie on the bed with my journal. I write about Elena and the mango kiss until I fall asleep, leaving a long line across the page. I hear Rachel come in at some point. She stands in my doorway for a long time, but I pretend to be asleep. We can talk in the morning, maybe by then I will have come up with a plausible story.

I hear Rachel's alarm at 5 am. Too early even for Ethan. She gets up and hustles around getting ready. I'm awake, but I'll wait till she's gone to get up and go for a run. Around 5:30 she comes in and kisses me on the forehead. I open my eyes a crack. "Where you going so early?" I mumble.

"Doctor appointment for Ethan." She sounds nervous.

"Good luck with that."

"I hope I don't need it. I arranged it early so the place would be empty."

"That was nice," I say rolling over.

"Go back to sleep. I'll wake you when we get back."

I pretend to acquiesce, but the second the door closes, I'm up, throwing on my sneakers, and putting my hair into a high ponytail.

It's already like ninety percent humidity and the air's as still as death. I struggle to breathe for the first two miles, then decide that it's not really worth it to torture myself. I walk the third mile home. At the end of the driveway I notice that Rachel's car and Lily's truck are still there, and I wonder if they're back already. Ethan's hysterical cries reach me halfway up the driveway. I stop to listen with my stomach in knots.

"No! No! No! I'm not going. I can't! Please just go away." He's sobbing, so every word is followed by a sharp intake of air as he half-screams half-cries them out.

Iron Lady's voice cuts through Ethan's cries like a knife. "Ethan Michael Paige! You stop this nonsense NOW. You're being ridiculous, boy!"

Elena is crooning desperately in the background. "It's okay Ethan. Come here. You don't have to go. It's okay. Please stop crying."

Rachel's let's be reasonable tone is nearly completely drowned out, "Ethan, no one's going to hurt you. They just need to get some pictures of your insides and then we can leave. They . . . " The crash of glass shattering on the floor cuts her off, and jump-starts me. I sprint to the Paige's back door.

I hesitate before going in. I'm in no way prepared for the chaos of the scene.

Ethan is backed into a corner at the far end of the kitchen with Elena trying to reach out to him from one side, and Rachel trying to talk him down from the other. Even if he could get past Elena, Iron Lady is blocking his access to rest of the house, her arms crossed over her chest angrily. Every chair has been over-turned and there are broken plates, food, and glass all over the floor. With one hand Ethan's pulling the front of his t-shirt down trying to cover the dark wet stain on the front of his khaki shorts and with the other he's grabbing anything he can reach and throwing it at Rachel and Elena to keep them at bay. There's a puddle at his feet. His face is red and tear-streaked, his expression terrified and determined in equal measure. I'm not sure what I can do to help and I almost turn around, but there's one thing I share with Ethan that no else does, and maybe I can . . . .

I let the door bang loudly behind me. It's enough to suspend the drama. Everyone freezes, staring at me. I take a deep breath and close my eyes. I imagine myself under the waterfall at the ravine yesterday, and I let a sense of peace wash over me. When I open my eyes again, the only noise in the room is Ethan's plaintive crying. Rachel steps out of the way to let me pass. Ethan shrinks back a little, but he lets me come close. I whisper in his ear, "Just let go." He closes his eyes and nods. I brace myself as he lets me wrap my arms around him.

There's no spinning this time. It's more like being slammed in the chest. I can't breathe at all because of the crushing terror that instantly fills my mind and body. I am in a hospital and the pain in my left arm is excruciating. The cacophony of sounds and voices is deafening, but I make out one voice. "His mother is dead; the girl is unconscious, but the boy saw the whole thing." I'm soaking wet and shivering violently. Everyone, everything around me looks so big. A pretty nurse smiles and puts a blanket around my shoulders, but when she touch me, she pulls back with a start and her hands fly to her temples, her face is twisted in agony. She looks at me like I hurt her. It's scaring me even more. "Mama! Mama! Help me Lanie! Lanie!" Now I'm screaming, but I'm all alone with all these strangers standing around me.

The pain, fear, sorrow, it's too much, just too much. My mind starts shutting down one sense at a time. Silence, sweet silence. Mouths moving, feet running, but no noise. Everyone who touches me draws back hands to heads. Slowly, they all back away until no one is touching me. Better, much better. Gradually, I lose the feeling of cold, of wet, and the pain in my arm grows numb, every inch of me numb. Now the bright light in the room grows dimmer and dimmer until it's midnight blue, cool dark blue of the night sky. The hospital smells waft away. The smell of burnt flesh is replaced by honey. Why honey? I think. I smell coffee and urine. The sharp smell shocks me back to the present. Ethan has relaxed in my arms, he tenses a little when he returns, but he's calmer. My knees are shaking, but I force myself to move. I maneuver Ethan past Elena and Lily up the stairs. At the top he pulls away from me a little.

"Are you mad at me?" he asks quietly.

"Mad?" I have a hard time finding my voice, and my vision is still blurred.

"Everyone will be mad at me. I didn't go to the doctor. I broke all the dishes. I wet my pants." His chin is trembling. I try to focus on it.

"No, Ethan, I'm not mad." My knees start to buckle. "I don't feel so well."

"Lanie!" Ethan calls, but I don't know if he says it out loud or in his mind. Elena is there a second later. Next thing I know I'm sitting on the couch and Elena's face looms in front of me.

"Go home, Sage. I can take care of it from here." There's an angry edge to her voice that sounds like it's coming from another room, but her eyes are full of concern. Ethan's begging, "Please don't go," but not out loud.

"It's okay. I'll stay here. I just need to rest for a minute." I lie down and watch Elena and Ethan go down the hall hand in hand. Then it all goes blank.

When I wake up, I have no idea how much time has passed or where I am. I hear voices far away, but I can't make out what they're saying. I move my head with some difficulty. My neck is unbelievably stiff. It finally comes to me that I'm in the Paige's TV room upstairs. For a second I think it's two nights ago, and the movie has just ended. I expect to hear Elena singing, but something's wrong. Daylight pours in through the windows. Bit by bit it all comes back in reverse order: Elena worried and angry telling me to go home, Ethan asking if I'm mad at him, my mind shutting down one sense at a time, the hospital and the horror of hurting all those people, the scene in the kitchen, my miserable morning run, Finn at the cafe, hugging Ethan in the pool, hiking with Rachel. It's all back.

I must have been sleeping for a while because I really need to pee. I struggle to sit up and wait for the dizziness to subside. I'll search cabinets for Advil if I can make it to the bathroom. I stumble down the hall and open the door. Elena looks up from where she sits wedged between the sink and the tub. Long lines of blood trickle down her leg and drip onto the floor. She palms whatever she's using to cut.

"Get out of here, Sage," she mumbles, but the command lacks conviction.

"I need to pee." I use the toilet, flush, close the lid, and sit down.

"You can go now," Elena says.

"I don't think so," I say, rubbing the back of my neck.

"I'm not going to stop just because you're here."

"Yes, you are." I hope I'm right.

I'm wrong. Elena bends over her leg and goes back to work carving into the flesh on her shin. Long thin lines of blood, orderly, controlled, and brilliant crimson crisscross her alabaster flesh. I watch her face, expecting to see pain, tears, grief. Instead I see release, relief, like Finn's face when he climaxed. I reach over and snatch the thing she's cutting with out of her hand.

"Give it back," she hisses. Now I have her attention. "Damn it, Sage, give it back!" Her face contorts with the pain I was looking for a moment ago. "You have no right!"

"Why are you doing this to yourself?" I ask quietly, massaging my temples.

"Because it feels good!"

"Are you crazy!"

"I think that's the general consensus." She smiles sweetly and puts out her hand palm up.

When I open my fingers to examine her cutting tool, I expect to see a razor-blade, not an earring. It's a tiny fairy holding a moonstone orb. I have never seen anything like it. I put it into her outstretched hand.

"I'm going to check on Ethan now," I say inviting her to come along.

"You do that," she says barely concealing her anger.

"Are you pissed because I could help him or because you couldn't?" It comes out much harsher than intended.

"Both." She smiles. Then she adds more quietly, "I'm not mad at you, Sage."

"So you're in here punishing yourself?"

"Something like that. Man, you're such a buzz-kill," She cleans the blood from the floor with a bit of toilet paper.

"You sound like Finn," I say.

"Did you take away his lighter and matches?" She presses hard on the new cuts to stop the bleeding and then unrolls her pant leg.

"Me and what army?" We both laugh. "Is Ethan okay?" I rub the sides of my head again.

"Grandmother just about threw an aneurism, but Rachel talked her down, so Ethan got off with cleaning up the mess in the kitchen and a couple other restrictions."

"But is he okay?"

"He's worried about you." She turns back to the medicine cabinet and gets two Advil out of a bottle. She offers them to me with one hand, and she offers her gift with the other. I point to her empty hand, and she puts it gently on top of my head. Instantly my mind clears and the pain and stiffness are gone. I breathe a sigh of relief. Elena leads the way down the big staircase.

Chapter 8 (While the Cat's Away)

Wounds on the surface of the body scab over and eventually scar; the body knows how to repair itself. The cuts and bruises and burns beneath the skin open and bleed again and again, even long after the scars have formed; the psyche and heart could learn a lot from the flesh.

I'm not sure who is happier to see me up and about, alive and well, Ethan or Rachel. They're sitting outside at a table at the far end of the pool drinking lemonade. Ethan is writing or drawing in a notebook. He just about knocks his chair over when I come out the door. Rachel restrains herself, but the hours of worry are worn on her face. Her pained smile is exactly the same as the time when I got up after falling on my neck from the bars in a gymnastics meet when I was nine. Before Ethan makes it over to me, Rachel calls him back. She is not taking any more chances today with our weird touch and trade connection. I walk over to the table though to show them that I am fine. Ethan looks unbearably tired. He eyes are swollen and red-rimmed, and his voice comes out scratchy from all the crying and yelling no doubt.

Rachel says that after a fight the only appropriate conversation is small talk. It helps to normalize everything again. The concept seems to apply here too, so after a few minutes of small talk, I head home without touching either of them. They have stuff to "work" on. I just hope that Rachel's going to drop the whole doctor appointment thing.

I spend the next couple of hours doing dishes, dusting, vacuuming, and scrubbing every surface I can find. Maybe one of the side effects of being on the receiving end of Elena's gift is a desire to make things perfect. While I'm cleaning the house, the phone keeps ringing, but since I don't recognize the number, I let it go to voice mail. By the time Rachel comes in, the apartment is so clean even Iron Lady could live here. She takes in the transformation, and wraps her arms around me.

"Don't ever do that again, Sage," she says in measured, reasonable voice.

"Clean the apartment?" I half think she is referencing my abrupt exit to see Finn.

"Whatever it is that you did with Ethan in there, you scared me half to death."

"I was fine."

"You were NOT fine! You were yelling, 'Mama' and 'Lanie.' It was freaky. I was like you were Ethan."

"I was in the hospital when he was small. I think it was when his mom died."

"Interesting." She pauses and then takes my hand. "You need to dial back this thing with Ethan."

"I'm not sure I can," I say. Rachel looks ready to cry, so I change the subject. "The phone's been ringing off the hook. Some guy from Florida, Mr. Redman?"

"Raymond?"

"Whatever. He wants you call him back pronto."

Her face lights up like a Halloween pumpkin halfway between a grimace and a smile. "I'll return the call upstairs. You need to call your dad. You did something to set him off the other day, so maybe you should talk him off the ledge. It's not my job anymore."

"So you've said since I was five, and yet you do it so well."

"Not this time. Call him."

"Sure, Mom." My luck knows no bounds. She's apparently

forgotten about yesterday at least for the moment.

I wait till she's upstairs. Then I dial my dad from my cell. He doesn't answer, so I leave a message: "Hey, Dad. Sorry about last weekend. Something important came up. Kind of a boyfriend emergency. I hope I didn't worry you too much. Thanks for not narcing me out to Rachel. How about a rain-check? Dinner or something this week?"

I'm recording the morning's events in my journal when an insistent banging at the door interrupts my flow. It's Iron Lady, looking flustered and anxious. She pushes past me to meet Rachel at the bottom of the stairs. They go into the living-room to talk. I stay in the kitchen and keep my ears open.

"So they're in contact now. And it's really him. I can hardly believe it." Iron Lady tries to keep her voice low, but it carries because she's so worked up.

"I think you need to go, as soon as possible. I can stay with the twins," my mom says in a stage whisper.

"I don't know, Rachel. Maybe you can go and bring him back," Iron Lady sounds oddly unsure of herself, scared even.

"Lily, I can't be the one to go. He has no ties to me. You need to do this," Rachel says.

"I can't do it alone, Rachel." She sounds like Ethan. I hear her pacing around the room.

"I don't know, Lily. I could go with you, but what about the twins. Have you ever left them alone?"

"Never. Ethan requires a lot of supervision, but Elena already does most of it. She's just not very reliable in a crisis. Your girl can handle herself and them, though."

I bristle with something like pride.

Rachel is oddly silent. Finally she says, "I'll talk to Sage. Let her know what she's in for. We'll let her decide if she can handle it."

Iron Lady is appeased, "Good. I'll see you tomorrow then." On her way out of the kitchen she stops and makes eye contact, smiles grudgingly and nods before leaving.

Rachel comes in and stands by the counter. I look up from my journal. "How much did you hear?" she asks.

"Pretty much all of it."

"Hmm. So. . . what do you think?"

"I'm not sure," I admit. "That meltdown was majorly intense, and I'm not into dealing with the whole bed wetting thing. But maybe Elena can just take care of that kind of stuff. How long would you be gone?"

"A few days, a week tops, I think. But it may be trickier than I think."

"Who's in Florida, and what's going to be so tricky?"

"Sorry."

"Fine. So nuts and bolts what would I need to do? Lay it out for me."

"You would need to make sure that between you and Elena three meals make it onto the table every day, and that Ethan and Elena actually eat. You would need to keep up with the housework, dishes, floors, laundry, and yes, Elena can manage Ethan's issues. Other than that, it would just be a matter of keeping Ethan on the schedule we worked out and making sure Elena is not alone too much, if you know what I mean." I nod. "Oh, and make sure you don't burn the house down."

"Now, <u>that</u> I can manage!"

"Well, then the job is yours." She smiles, but it fades instantly as the worry-lines crease her forehead. "Really, Herbie, if it's too much, I won't go," I know she means what she says, but I also know that this is important. I'm pretty sure the guy they are going to see is the twins' father, so this could be huge.

"I've got it covered, Rachel. I can do this with my hands tied behind my back." I know I'm not fooling her. She'll check in four times a day, and I'll be happy she did.

The next morning after Ethan's swim, my run, and a couple of cups of Lily's really strong coffee, they sit us down at the kitchen table and get all the ducks lined up. Elena's in charge of keeping us on the schedule, and keeping the house clean. I'm on food. Ethan wants to know what he's in charge of, and Iron Lady rolls her eyes. Rachel tells him that he can be in charge of taking care of himself, getting dressed and showered and all that. She assures him that it would really help. I know where she's going with this, but I'm not hopeful about changing years of behavior patterns in a single week. We're strongly admonished about no visitors in the house. Rachel promises that Ben will check in on us, and we can call him if we need anything. Having that safety net makes me feel a whole lot better about the whole thing.

We spend the rest of the day cooking meals and putting them in the fridge and freezer and cleaning old lady's house down to the baseboards. I find this need to clean before travelling extremely odd. Rachel does it too. It's like they can't leave town unless strangers can eat off their floors. By 10 pm I'm beat. I snuggle down in my own bed for the last time until they come back, since I'll be staying at the house with the twins while Rachel and Lily are away. Despite my exhaustion, I have a tough time falling asleep. I decide to text Finn.

WAYD?

Hanging out with my dad, bonding.

Pants on fire.

How'd u no?

Bonding? Really?!

Over the top, I guess. WAYD?

In bed, trying to sleep.

WAYW?

Huh?

What r u wearing?

perv!

JJ.

u were not joking. not much :-)

Can u get out? meet me?

No way. I almost text him about taking Rachel to the airport in the morning, but something stops me and I text. *R is downstairs no way to get around her.*

Bummer. What about 2 morow?

Don't no. We'll c.

This sucks!

I agree. I miss u.

me 2.

That's it. Neither of us say good-bye or good night or anything like that. It's weird. I do miss him, and I want to see him. With Rachel away I may get my chance if I'm lucky.

On the way to the airport at the crack of dawn, Rachel has one more qualm to air.

"Sage, if something happens like the other day, and Ethan falls apart, please promise me that you won't do that thing again. Just let him go through his tantrum. He'll come out the other side without your help. Promise me."

I think hard about it. "I don't know if I can just watch him suffer like that when I know I can do something."

"Listen to me, Sage. He can deal with all that stuff; it's his stuff. Please say okay."

"Okay. I will be very very careful. I promise."

It's not what she wants to hear, but it is the best I can do. I let them out at the curb-side check in, and after I hug Rachel, Lily shocks me by hugging me too.

"Take care of them, Sage. I'm trusting you," she says, and I suddenly want to call it all off. I feel like I've taken on more than I or anyone can reasonably handle, but I bite my tongue as they wheel their bags into the airport.

On the way back home I imagine dire things, Ethan drowning in the pool, Elena slitting her wrists in the tub, and me being sucked into Ethan's nightmare with no way back to my own head. By the time I pull in the driveway I've pretty much freaked myself out, but Ethan is swimming laps, and Elena meets me by the pool with a cup of strong black coffee. We sit and chat with our feet in the water while Ethan swims, as though we've been living like this for years.

That hour of peace sets me up for an easy day, but a couple of hours later I am ready to break into the liquor cabinet. The trouble starts right after we come in from the pool to eat breakfast.

"Lanie, where's the vanilla cereal," Ethan whines.

"You said you wanted the chocolate, so I got the chocolate. Just eat it Ethan," Elena sounds exasperated so I'm guessing this is a fight they've had before.

I turn my attention to making another cup of coffee while they go round and round about vanilla and chocolate cereal with Ethan getting more high-pitched and Elena getting quieter and quieter until she's almost hissing.

Finally, I can't listen any longer. "Okay, guys, new rule. I'll put out what we're going to eat for breakfast, and there are no choices. Today we're going to eat the chocolate cereal." Ethan starts to complain, but I put up my hand, and he stops. "Later we can go to the store and get the vanilla kind and eat that tomorrow." They both nod and proceed to eat in silence. Note to self: get a magazine to read at breakfast. I remind myself that they've never been on their own before, so there are going to be some jitters to work out.

After breakfast, Ethan gets up and starts heading upstairs to change out of his swimsuit, but Elena stops him. "Can't you just wait till I finish clearing the dishes?"

"You don't need to help me. You heard what Rachel said." He looks to me for support, but all I can do is raise my eyebrows. I'm surprised by his initiative.

Elena's not. "Nice try, Ethan. I know what you're up to. You think because grandmother isn't here, you don't have to do what she told you."

Ethan does not back down like I expect. "I don't have to and I'm not gonna. She doesn't know anything and neither do you." He turns and runs through the archway and up the stairs. Elena is on his heels, and she's much quicker than I thought she'd be. In fact she's faster than he is. Ethan makes it to his room, but he isn't able to close the door before Elena's foot is wedged in beside the frame. If he pushed, she'd be no match for his strength, but he lets her shove the door into the wall with a bang. I wonder how much damage they've just done. I stay in the hall, back from the doorway, but I can see them facing off.

Ethan's room is huge like Elena's. In the far left corner he has a poster bed identical hers. The wet sheets are still on it and the blankets are hanging off the side. Across from the bed is a kind of art studio with paints, easels, and canvas. Closer to the door is desk and bookshelf as disordered as Elena's is neat. Across from the door is a deep window with a window seat and the dresser is beside it. Everything in the room is midnight blue except the walls which are one blue shade off of white. The effect is quite soothing, but the twins are far from calm.

"I don't need your help. Get out of here, now," Ethan punctuates his order by throwing a shoe at her.

Elena dodges it and then tries to make her voice calm. "E, you need to relax. It's not a big deal, and it's not a punishment. Grandmother is trying to help you--us get through this week without too much drama. Okay."

"Not OK!" He looks up and sees me in the hall. Then he looks at the bed and down at his feet as his cheeks flush. I expect him to give in to whatever this fight is about, but instead he looks up and says, "Go away." I'm not sure if he's talking to me or Elena.

Elena turns and sees me too. She leans back and a wicked smile spreads across her face. "Why don't we just let Sage decide?"

Ethan looks back at the floor for a long time and then at Elena, who continues smirking like a bad winner.

Ethan's cheeks burn a deeper scarlet, but he juts out his chin defiantly. "She knows anyway. It doesn't matter. You can tell her, and she can decide. I'll do what she says."

"Really, Ethan, you want to have this discussion with Sage? Are you sure?"

Ethan nods, but he turns away and covers his ears.

Elena says unnecessarily loudly, "Grandmother wants Ethan to wear a diaper during the day while she's gone, so you don't have deal with any accidents, but he clearly doesn't want to."

Ethan spins around. Narrowing his eyes at her, he says, "I'm not going to have any accidents."

"Sometimes you do," Elena shoots back.

"Sometimes I don't," he says biting his bottom lip.

I have to say that I am not liking the role of adult here. I want to just walk away and let them figure it out, but that is no longer an option since they are now waiting for my proclamation.

"Okay, Ethan," I finally say, "have it your way," The look of triumph on his face is almost worth dealing with the mess if he fails, but I have to appease Elena too since it will be her mess, not mine. I take a step forward into the room and wait for Ethan to make eye contact with me; then I add, "Ethan, if you have an accident, you clean it up, not Elena, and we go back to your grandmother's plan. Okay?"

"Fine," he mumbles.

Elena turns back to Ethan and says, "Get yourself dressed then and don't forget your sheets." She brushes past me in hall as she crosses over to her own room, slamming the door.

I'm about to head back downstairs to finish my coffee, when I think about Elena alone in her crimson room and the moonstone earring that I am suddenly sure she is using or about to use. I hesitate at the top of the stairs. I hate interfering. Her cutting is so oddly private like masturbating. But Rachel and Lily are both counting on me to take care of things here. So I reluctantly go back.

I knock on the door, but I don't wait for her to answer before going in. She's sitting on the floor by the window seat with a book open in her lap. I am relieved to see that I was wrong.

"What do you want, Sage?" The tone of her voice tells a different story, though, and she doesn't look at me, so I take a closer look.

"I just wanted to make sure you were okay with everything." I can see the trickle of blood on her forearm.

"I'm fine. You can go now." She knows I know, and she doesn't try to hide it.

"Elena, you can't do this while they're gone." I'm surprised at how hard my voice sounds.

"You are not here to babysit me, Sage. Go help Ethan change his bed."

I make a face. "As I recall, Ethan's your responsibility, I'm on food and refereeing apparently."

"Then you'd better get to the store and get that vanilla cereal or we're gonna be in trouble tomorrow." Elena laughs a little.

"No worries. If I get it, he'll want chocolate anyway," I say.

"But if you don't get it . . ."

". . . we'll really be in for it," I finish for her.

"I think you're catching on now," she says, pocketing the earring.

"Lanie?" Ethan is standing in the hall behind me, holding a hair brush and a bottle of detangler. She gets up and motions him over to the bench. I watch her gently work the tangles out of his hair for a minute, and then I head downstairs to clean up breakfast.

The rest of the day we spend working through Ethan's schedule that Rachel taped to the refrigerator. Because he's home-schooled, he doesn't take summers off. I expect that he's behind in in his studies because of the whole stuck in time thing, but he's actually way ahead of me and wickedly smart. I sit with him at the kitchen table while he totally rips through differential calculus like it's simple sums. I don't even know what half the symbols on the page mean, but when I look up the answers, he's got them all correct.

Elena does the French assignment with him. They work together on memorizing a poem. I wonder what the purpose of learning a language is for a boy who never leaves the house. Still, their voices ringing together in French are exotic and lovely. There is a lot of giggling and fooling around too, and it sure beats the bickering of the morning. Tomorrow we'll video tape him reciting it. He's not excited about the prospect of being on camera, but we make it into a game, and he's at least willing to consider it.

Lunch is another fiasco of finicky eating, but this time it's Elena who turns her nose up at the egg salad sandwiches I make. Ethan scolds her for not eating what's served, and I almost fall off my chair laughing. Ethan reaches out to catch me, but I catch myself first and pull away before he can touch me. He looks at Elena, confused. They move closer together, shutting me out of their silent conversation. I get up and stand by the sink, staring out at the pool, feeling like my heart must lie at the bottom of the deep end. When they're done eating, Elena takes Ethan upstairs. I watch them go, and Ethan looks back at me once, but I look away.

Elena comes back down a few minutes later. "What the hell was that, Sage?"

I hang my head. "I feel bad enough, Elena."

"Bullshit, Sage. What's your problem?"

I can't bring myself to say it out loud.

"Sage! Snap out of it. This is not the time for you to decide that you're suddenly squeamish. My brother is up there sure that he is being kicked to the curb because you think he's a baby. He thinks that now that he's trusted you with all his embarrassing secrets, you can only hate him for being so broken."

"You think I'm that shallow?! Jeez, Elena. It's nothing like that. It's me. . ." I hesitate, wrap my arms around my body protectively. "The other day, I . . . almost . . . I'm not sure how to explain it."

"Try," Elena's voice and eyes are ice.

"I got lost. We traded places, and I didn't know how to get back for a second. I don't want to go back there." My hands and voice shake.

Elena's eyes widen. "Oh."

"I'll go talk to him," I say. Elena nods.

It takes a serious act of will to knock on that closed door. There's no answer, and I consider letting it lie, but it's Ethan, and he's hurting, so I knock again. "Can I come in?"

After a long pause, I hear a small, "Okay."

At first I don't see him curled up in the window seat. He's got a sketchbook in his lap and an array of pencils scattered in front of him. I stand awkwardly in the doorway watching, feeling strangely hesitant about entering. I'm not sure why, but I can't go in.

"Hey, Mouse, you wanna to go sit by the pool?"

He smiles at the nickname, and after a couple of seconds looks up and nods. He gathers his pencils and the sketchbook and follows me down the stairs. I head over to the table where he and Rachel sat the other day.

"I saw your paintings in Elena's room. They're amazing," He doesn't acknowledge that I said anything. He opens the sketchbook and starts drawing.

"Can I tell you a secret, Mouse?" I ask.

He looks up.

"When we first moved in, the first time I saw you, I knew that we would be friends."

"How?"

"I'm not sure, but I really wanted to know you. Even from my window I could see that you were special."

He looks up at my window and then down at his feet. "I'm not special."

"How can you say that, Ethan? You’re so smart and you're an amazing artist and a great swimmer and absolutely beautiful to look at."

The tears are welling up and his chin trembling. "I'm all wrong, and you hate me. I knew that you would hate me if you knew--" his voice trails off.

"Look at me, Ethan," I wait until his eyes are looking right into mine. "I could never hate you."

"Then why won't you touch me? You think I'm a baby and I'm

awful like grandmother always says." He swallows back his sob, but the tears are falling.

"Ethan, there's nothing awful about you. I don't care about any of that stuff that's worrying you. Those things are not who you are. I wish I could make them go away because they make you so sad, but I don't care about them. The truth is I'm the one who's awful. I didn't touch you because I'm scared. I'm a big fat coward."

Ethan smiles through his tears. "You're not fat."

I laugh a little. "Remember the other day when you were really upset, and I took your place in that memory of the hospital. It was really scary for me, and I . . . I felt lost, like I didn't know how to get back to my own head. Do you know what I'm talking about?"

He nods. "But I wouldn't leave you there," he says looking right into my eyes. "Don't be scared. I'd never leave you. I promise."

Now it's my turn to well-up and look away. "I trust you, Mouse, but I'm still afraid."

"It's okay, Sage. I can wait for you to not be scared any more, but I miss you."

"I'm right here. You don't need to miss me."

He shrugs and blushes, "I miss . . . touching you."

"Oh," I say quietly. "Give me a little time."

"Okay," he says, and he goes back to drawing. We hang out there by the pool until we can't bear the heat for another instant, and then we race inside to change into our swim suits.

Elena's a little stressed about getting off the schedule, but she finally relents and joins us. On the way out to the pool she tells me that Rachel called to check in and tell us that they arrived safely. I wonder how much of our day Elena relayed back, but I don't ask.

We swim for the rest of the afternoon on and off. Ethan insists on playing our silly game of variations volleyball and trying to make a whirlpool. I get the importance of Rachel's schedule, but I let the afternoon stretch on without returning to it, despite Elena's pointed reminders.

When Elena and Ethan go inside to get snacks, I call Finn.

"Hey! I only have a minute."

"The voice is familiar, but I can't quite place it," he teases.

"Very funny. Be nice or you won't get your surprise."

"Ooo, a surprise. I can play nice for a surprise. What is it?

"If I told you, I'd have to kill you. And it wouldn't be a much of a surprise after that, would it? Just be at Exodus at ten tonight and don't be late."

"I'm liking this already."

"Gotta go, bye."

I hang up before he can say good-bye back, but Elena sees me put the phone down. When she gets to the table, she grabs it and looks at the call history. Even though she doesn't recognize Finn's cell number, she knows. "Finn?" she whispers in my ear, and I nod. She shakes her head in disgust.

Dinner is a somewhat whiney affair, but Ethan and Elena end up eating a meal between them. We get everything straightened up by seven, and we have a couple of hours to kill before Ethan's bedtime, so I suggest walking down to the strip mall for snow-cones. Elena loves the idea and looks hopefully at Ethan, but he shifts nervously from one foot to the other and wrings his hands.

"Ethan it's just a short walk, and you don't have to talk to anyone the whole time," I assure him.

"The snow-cone cart is outside, so you don't have to go inside anyplace," Elena adds.

"I'm not really that hungry," Ethan says, but I can tell he's thinking about it.

Elena keeps trying, "I know you love the blue raspberry."

Ethan smiles thinking about it. "What kind do you want?" he asks Elena.

"Maybe mango," she says winking at me. "Can we go?"

Ethan still isn't convinced.

"You can hold my hand all the way there and back," I offer.

Ethan smiles. "Really?"

I nod.

"Okay, I'll go."

Elena is ecstatic. She grabs Ethan's hand and races up the stairs with him. I'm thoroughly confused. They're back in a few minutes, and we head out. At the end of the driveway Ethan hesitates, but I hold out my hand, concentrating to keep it from shaking. Then I lock my mind on the details of the moment. Ethan slips his hand into mine and laces our fingers together. I wait for the jolt, but nothing happens. We're on the street, and the heat of his hand and body are flowing into mine, but my head is fine.

As we make our way down the block, I wonder how long it's been since he's been out in the world. Clearly, this is not an everyday or even every month event. Elena tries to distract him from his anxiety by pointing out strange, colorful and interesting things, but Ethan manages only a couple of fleeting smiles, as though the act of walking requires an intense effort. Across the street, a young couple passes with two huge dogs that bark at us excitedly. They wave hello, and Ethan grabs onto my arm with his other hand and looks down. Elena gives them a cheery, "Hello," and I wave distractedly. I wonder what they see. Do they think that Ethan is my boyfriend? I remember the conversation with Elena at the cafe when she talked about how people see Ethan, and I get it now. To that couple it probably looks like he's being possessive; they don't see the terrified little boy holding on for dear life.

Some cyclists buzz by us from behind, and the sudden noise stops Ethan in his tracks. I think about heading home, but we can see the snow-cone trailer just a couple of blocks up, and we've made it this far, so we might as well get the reward. There's a line of maybe seven people, but that's seven more than Ethan is willing to be near. I give Elena the cash and my order. Ethan wants a large blue raspberry, but Elena tells him he can only have a small. He doesn't even argue.

Ethan and I sit down on the curb a good distance from the line to wait for Elena. There's a group of three girls ahead of Elena in line, maybe fourteen or fifteen years old. They're trying too hard to look older, too much makeup, high cut shorts, skimpy tops. They glance coyly at Ethan and whisper behind their hands. Ethan squirms under their attention. "Why are those girls looking at me?" he asks.

I smile. "They think you're cute. They want you to notice them."

"I don't like it. I want them to stop," he's getting a little agitated.

"Just don't look at them. They'll get bored and stop," I tell him.

One of the girls, a tall blond, who will someday soon be the picture of trashiness, waves. Ethan looks down frowning. "Sage, I want to go home now."

"Elena's up next, let's just wait a couple more minutes. Look at me,

Mouse; don't look at them."

He turns around so his back is to them, and he's facing me. I rub his arm to comfort him and keep him distracted. The girls ahead of Elena get their snow-cones and head our way. I brace for impact.

"Hey there," the blond one says too loudly, looking directly at Ethan.

"Hi," I say coldly. "Can I help you with something?"

"Oh, hi." She says looking at me like she suddenly notices I'm there. "I wasn't actually talking to you."

"Oh, well, you are now, so what do you need?" I mimic her snotty tone.

Ethan's hand is squeezing mine so hard that his knuckles are turning white. My palm is on fire.

"Actually, I wanted to talk to your fine friend." Ethan glances up at her warily. "Hi. Can you settle a bet between me and my friends?" Ethan looks at his feet.

The girl is not sure how to deal with his lack of response. She takes a step back. Maybe she's figuring out that Ethan isn't "normal." Still she goes on, albeit less confidently. "We wanted to know if the girls you're with are your sisters or girlfriends." The other two girls, waiting a few steps back, giggle nervously.

Ethan whines in my ear, "Please, I want to go home." Elena starts heading our way, so I pull Ethan to his feet. He hides behind me like a little boy. At this point the girl is getting the picture, but I guess the awkwardness of the situation makes her feel backed against a wall or something.

"I think you should go now," I say, hoping she'll take the hint.

"Is he a retard or something?" the girl directs the question at me, but she doesn't wait for my answer.

"Lanie!" Ethan's cry for his sister is loud, but not exactly in my ears. Elena looks up like she hears it too. But no one else seems to react. "Hurry, Lanie. I want to go home NOW!" Elena gets to us in time to see the blond girl sauntering away and the other two giggling. Ethan's chin is trembling, and I know he's about to cry. I don't want those girls to have that satisfaction, so I walk away quickly, pulling him along beside me. Elena follows us, carrying the forgotten snow-cones.

When we're far enough away, we stop. Ethan immediately starts 'talking' to Elena. "Lanie, why did that girl say those things? Why did she do that?" The tears are streaming now and my stomach feels like I swallowed my own heart. His palm is still burning through mine and our fingers are fused. My brain is about to split open as all of Ethan's emotion pours through me: anxiety, fear, and humiliation. Elena is staring at me open-mouthed, and suddenly I realize that I'm crying too. "Ethan," I hear her voice in my head. "Ethan, stop crying now." Her panic is palpable. Ethan looks at me. He makes his breathing even, and mine evens out too. He tries to pull his hand from mine, but I'm back, and I don't let him. "I'm okay." I say in my head. They both open their eyes wide. Ethan pulls away quickly.

Elena doles out the snow-cones, and we eat them as we walk silently home, lost in the implications of what just happened.

When we get home, I let them go upstairs without me. I know that Ethan has had an accident and that thankfully Elena had prepared for that possibility before we left the house, but I have no idea how I know this.

I get my bag from the corner of the kitchen where I left it this morning and try to decide where I should sleep. Iron Lady offered her room, but I'd feel weird in her bed. I finally decide that the sofa in the upstairs game room works, so I deposit my pillow and sleeping bag there and go back downstairs to get ready for my "date" with Finn. I've got my hair braided and lip gloss on when Ethan calls me to come upstairs to say good-night. He meets me at the landing.

"You look pretty,' he says and wraps his arms around me. He buries his face in my neck. I focus on the softness of his curls brushing against my face.

"Sweet dreams, my little Mouse," I say in his ear.

"Sweet dreams, Sage," he says back. Then Elena leads him back down the hall to his room. I sit on the couch and wait. I'm soon rewarded with Elena's rendition of "Sweet Baby James," so much sweeter than James Taylor ever dreamed it could be. I nearly fall asleep.

When Elena comes out, it's 9:30, nearly time for me to jet. "That was kind of a disaster," she says. "I probably should have nixed that idea out of the box."

"It's my fault. I shouldn't have brought it up," I say.

"Sage, correct me if I'm wrong, but did you tap into Ethan's and my telepathy thing? I swear I heard you out there."

"I don't know about tapping in. I guess if I switch with Ethan, I can do that thing with you." I'm grasping at straws.

She's not buying it. "No, Sage. You were you, and Ethan heard it too. Did you hear us?

I nod.

"Could you hear us after we came upstairs?"

"No. It ended when Ethan let go of my hand." I admit. She's quiet for a moment, mulling it over.

I look at my cell phone. "I'm going out for a little while."

"With Finn?" her voice is icy.

"Is that a problem for you?" I know I shouldn't be such a bitch about it especially after the day we just had, but I can't deal with another obstacle.

"I'm just worried for you," she comes back, making me feel worse. "Finn is not nice. I know I told you that before. He did something . . . to me." Her voice catches like a frayed fingernail on silk cloth.

I think I know what she's implying, but I want to hear it from him. "I promise I'll be careful. I can handle Finn."

"Wake me when you get back." She turns away then suddenly turns back. "Sage? Why's your stuff out here? You better be sleeping with me."

I smile. "That sounds like heaven. See you in a couple of hours. If Rachel calls, I'm asleep already."

"You got it."

I hurry down the stairs and out the door. I decide against taking the car. Finn's waiting for me when I get there, and he looks like coffee is the last thing he needs. He kisses me hard, but it's nothing like the last time when his kiss was full of anger. He's already ordered me a vanilla latte, and I'm touched that he remembers my coffee drink, especially since he's never ordered it for me before. Two cupcakes are sitting in the center of the table.

"You trying to fatten me up for some reason," I ask.

"Fatten you up? Those are for me. If you're hungry, you'll have to get your own," he jokes.

"That's fine. I was thinking that my dessert would be a bit sweeter than cake anyway."

"That kind of dirty talk will get you everywhere, little girl!" His eyes twinkle flirtatiously.

I'm smiling now and relaxed. This is so easy. We eat cupcakes and drink latte's for a while, but Finn is not interested in talking all night, so we get on his bike and head to the lake.

The ride out is magical. The air is hot, and I could melt right through Finn's back into him. He smells so good, like pine needles and wind. At the stoplights, he kisses my palm, plays with my fingers, pulls me closer. I throw my head back and look at the stars, fixed points of light as the sides of the highway blur. I could ride all night on that back of Finn's bike like this, but too soon we turn and slow.

I've never been here at night, and it feels way more isolated than in the day. I slip off the bike, staying close to Finn. He takes the helmet off me and leans in for a deep kiss. Then he howls long and low at the moon.

I laugh and join him. He grabs a blanket and a couple of beers out of the bag on the back of the bike, and we walk hand in hand to the cliff over-hanging the water. We spread out the blanket, and Finn cracks the beers. He takes a slug then gets up and walks over to where a campfire has been set up a few feet to the left of the blanket. He gets the lighter out of his pocket and ignites the brush at the base of the pile of sticks and blows on it until the kindling catches. By the time he is settled beside me, the whole thing crackles brilliantly. He smiles at the effect.

"I thought I'd give you a little surprise, too. Do you like it?" Unfortunately, he's actually making me a little nervous, and he reads it on my face. "What? You don't like it?"

"It's beautiful - ," I hesitate.

"- But? I hear a 'but' coming."

"I don't know, Finn. Isn't there some saying about campfires and pyromaniacs?"

"Not that I know of," he tries to smile.

"Should there be?"

"Man, Sage, you are such a buzz-kill!" he says.

"If people keep calling me that, I'm going to start believing it."

He manages a half smile. He's not mad, which kind of surprises me.

"First of all I'm not a pyromaniac. What the hell did your mother say about me?"

"Nothing. I swear!"

"Whatev. Second, even if I was, this kind of fire wouldn't do it for me. It would need to be something destructive with damage, injuries, chaos. Third, it would be the fire getting me off, not you." He rolls me over easily and rests on top of me. Then he kisses me. He tastes like cinnamon and beer. I can't help myself. I kiss him back long and lingering. There's only one place this can go, and though I've been there before, I need to slow things down. He starts to unbutton my blouse, but I move his hand away.

"Saaage? What are you doing?" He says it kind of sing-songy, like I'm trying his patience.

"Can't we just be together for a little while."

"We are together; I'd like to be a little closer together." He moves in to kiss me again.

I turn my head. "Not yet. I want to get to know you a little better."

"You know everything you need to know about me, Sage. Even some things I'd rather you didn't know. Come on, the night ain't getting any younger."

I throw a bucket of cold water on him. "Tell me about Elena." I meant to ease into it, but I lose my head.

He rolls off me onto his back. I wait for him to yell or something, but he just lies there, watching the embers from the fire float up to the treetops and fade. I sit up crisscross and watch his face. I can't read his feelings in the fire light, but I doubt I'd be able to even in direct sunlight. Finally, he sits up facing me.

"What did she say?" he asks quietly, almost sadly.

"Nothing specific, just little comments about your level of niceness."

"Or lack thereof?" His voice has a growing edge to it. "I'm sure baby-brother had plenty to add to that discussion."

"Actually, he would prefer not to talk about you at all. You terrify him."

"Who doesn't? Oh yeah, that would be you. Poor little bastard probably doesn't even know what to do with what he feels for you, which would put us about in the same boat, now wouldn't it, Sage?"

I am not going to let this become about Ethan. "Off topic, Finn. I want to know about Elena. Keep in mind. You opened this can of worms."

He hangs his head for a second or two, and I think I might get off easy, but when he looks up, his eyes are blazing. I want to get up and run, but he'd be on me before I could get off the blanket. "I don't believe this shit! You play all kissy-face with me like it's about us, but it's always the same with you isn't Sage? You want everyone's dirty little secrets because you can't deal with your own. Have you had that talk with Daddy yet? Did you see him messing with your friend? Did it make you jealous?"

"You shit!" I murmur. My eyes are burning out of my head! "That's disgusting and evil. I hate you."

I get up and start kicking dirt on him. He grabs my ankles, and I come down hard on my back with my head so close to the fire I can taste it. It takes all of my strength to push him off me enough to move out of the heat, but I can't rise to run. A second later he has me pinned, and it's deja vu. His knees are on my forearms, and he's hovering over me, victorious. He kisses me, and I spit in his face.

"Real nice, Sage. You spilled the beer." His voice is totally calm. "Do you think Elena would call your niceness into question, Sage? Do you think she should? What are you doing to her brother, Sage? How nice are you being to little Ethan when you change his diaper?"

I'm totally powerless. The harder I fight, the further into the earth he drives me. Tears are streaming from the corners of my eyes, and I'm choking. He's winning. I take a deep breath and close my eyes. I picture myself home in bed with Elena. When I speak again, my voice is as calm and measured as Finn's. "Did you rape her?" I wait a beat. "Are you going to rape me?"

Finn's face changes. Slowly and deliberately he gets off of me and walks away. I get up and brush myself off. I have no idea where he's going, but I don't want to be left here alone. The bike is still standing where we left it, and Finn is nowhere near it. When I turn around again, I can see Finn through the fire. He's holding a huge branch like a shaman about to start a ritual. The moment the leaves catch fire, turning the branch into a giant torch, Finn smiles. He circles the branch over his head and then lets it fly into the dry grass behind him. The wind from the twirling and flying feed the fire to a bright flame, and the moment the branch hits the grass, the whole field seems to ignite. Instinctively, I grab the blanket and rush into the center of the blaze. I begin beating back the blooming flames, turning in an ever widening circle. I kick dirt and swing the blanket again and again until all the little monsters have been slain. When I stop swinging and spinning, Finn and the bike are gone. I'm drenched in sweat, and coughing hard from the smoke. I collapse onto the hard ground to catch my breath and figure out what I'm supposed to do next. When I reach into the back pocket of my shorts to call Elena, my cell phone is gone. It must have fallen out of my pocket in the scuffle. I crawl around in the dust searching for what feels like an hour. Just as I locate it, I hear a motorcycle approaching. I pray that it's a cop, that someone reported the fire. It's not.

Finn gets off the bike and throws dirt on the campfire until it's out. Then he hands me his helmet, and we get on the bike. In the peace and solitude on the back of the bike, I let the tears stream down, blurring the stars and the road ahead. He takes me to the end of the driveway, but he doesn't pull in. I pull off the helmet, and as I hand it to him, he grabs my wrist. "I didn't do what you said, and I'd never hurt you." His voice shakes.

I don't say anything.

"Did you hear me?" he asks.

"I don't know if I believe you," I whisper.

I close my eyes to his rage, but when he finally speaks, his voice breaks. I open my eyes. His are sparkling with tears. "You have to believe me."

He lets me go then, and I walk away. I'm almost to the door when I hear the sound of water splashing. I turn in time to see Ethan execute his perfect flip turn. I look at my phone; it's 1:35 am. I walk over to the edge of the pool and squat down. Ethan surfaces right in front of me.

"You're home," he says.

"Ethan, what are you doing up at this hour?" I go over and pick up his towel off the deck. I hold it out for him.

"I couldn't sleep," he says as he climbs the pool stairs and lets me wrap him up. "You smell like fire," he says frowning.

"Sorry about that." I take a step back.

Ethan looks me up and down. "You need a shower."

I laugh a little. "You got that right." He moves closer again, rests his head on my shoulder, leans his whole body into mine. "Where's Elena?" I ask wrapping my arms around him.

"She's sleeping."

"Ethan, what are you doing here?"

"Waiting for you to come home." He might as well finish the sentence with 'of course.'

I take him inside.

At the door I turn and see the taillights of Finn's bike pulling down the block.

Inside at the top of the staircase I hesitate. "Do you want me to get Elena?" Ethan shakes his head.

"I want to show you something," he says, taking my hand and leading me into his room. I know he's telling the truth about not sleeping because his sheets are dry. A light is on in the corner of his art studio. It illuminates an enormous partially completed canvas. Like Ethan's other paintings, it's mostly warm swashes of red, yellow, orange, and gold. As I get closer, I can see that in the cool center is a woman's face. She looks like Elena, but older. Her eyes are full of terror and a million other emotions. She is looking and reaching directly out of the painting and she's surrounded by flames. Somehow I know that the woman is his mother and perhaps this is the last time he saw her.

"Ethan, is that how your mother died? In a fire?"

He nods. His eyes are shimmering with intensity.

"You were there with her?"

He nods again slowly.

"Why are you showing me this?"

He looks away. "I knew," he whispers.

I remember the rain storm. It feels like it happened to me. "I'm so sorry. Have you shown this to Elena?"

"I can't," he says.

I'm silent for several seconds taking in the weight of what he's been carrying all these years. "Ethan, you know you couldn't have stopped it, right? There was nothing you could have done."

"But I knew." He releases my hand, turns away, and moves the canvas to the back of his closet.

When he comes back out, he looks down at his feet and asks, "Will you help me get ready for bed?"

I think about what Finn accused me of. "Ethan, I think you can get dressed for bed without my help." He looks disappointed, but not distressed. "I can stay and tuck you in when you're ready." He pouts as he takes down his swim trunks oblivious to my presence.

I turn around quickly and pick up the sketchbook on his desk. When I hear the crinkle of plastic under the sheet, I turn around. I pull the blankets over him, brush the curls from his face, and kiss him on the forehead. "Sweet dreams," I say.

"No," he protests. "You're supposed to say, 'my little Mouse.'"

I smile, caress his face again. "Okay. Sweet dreams, my little Mouse."

"Sweet dreams, Sage." He rolls over on his side to suck his thumb.

I take a second to hang his towel and swimsuit over the desk chair and turn out the light. Finally, I can take that much needed shower.

Ten minutes later I crawl in next to Elena. "Are you okay?" she mumbles.

"Never better," I whisper.

"What did you do?" she asks sleepily.

"Tell you in the morning," I say, but I have no intention of telling anyone about last night.

Chapter 9 (No Way Out)

Time is like an airport conveyer moving everyone in one direction at a certain rate. Whether we walk to rush that progress or stand still and allow the conveyor to take its sweet time, we each have to carry our own bags all the way to the end.

The next morning the sky is barely brightening when Ethan shakes me awake. I go downstairs with him but make him wait while I make coffee. I'm so tired that I'm dizzy, but I just can't send him away. Elena comes down about an hour later waving my phone.

"Your mom's friend texted you. He's gonna stop by this morning," she informs me.

Ethan and I are playing a game with the diving rings. I throw them, and he tries to get them all in one breath with his eyes closed. He doesn't hear Elena, so when the car pulls in the driveway, he's confused.

"Who's that, Sage?" he asks anxiously.

"It's my mom's friend, Ben. He's really nice." Ethan doesn't care about nice. He's out of the pool and in the house before Ben can get out of the car. Elena is kind of draped over one of the patio chairs in her Hello Kitty robe and pajamas. I run over to hug him.

"Well, the house is still standing. That's a good sign. Three teenagers still breathing. Check. Your mom said that the boy might be a little skittish. She wasn't exaggerating." Elena gets up and sweeps over to where we're standing.

"Hi, I'm Elena. That blur was my brother, Ethan. He's a bit shy."

"I'm Ben. How are you all getting along without adult representation? Wild parties? Drugs? Alcohol? Wanton teenage sex?"

"Definitely nothing wanton," Elena says.

Ben laughs.

I put my arm around Elena. "Come on in. We've got coffee - "

"- and two kinds of cereal," Elena adds with a smirk.

I make a move toward the door, but Ben puts a hand on my arm.

"Sorry, Herb. I'll have to take a rain check. Work is calling. I just wanted to check in. Rachel would not be happy if I didn't put in an appearance. Anyway, in the immortal words of the Terminator, 'I'll be back.'"

"You can tell Rachel, we're fine, great even," I say.

Ben gives me a hug, and shakes Elena's hand when she offers it. "Maybe next time I can meet your brother," he says.

Elena smiles sweetly. "I wouldn't bet on it."

"I like you," Ben says returning her grin.

"Back at you," Elena says.

We wave as he pulls down the driveway. Ethan peaks out the door. "Is he gone?"

"E, would it kill you to meet someone?" Elena sounds uncomfortably like her grandmother. Ethan looks like she just slapped him.

"Let's go eat breakfast," I say, heading inside. It's going to be a long day.

Ethan goes upstairs after sitting through breakfast sullen and silent. Elena doesn't chase him. I must have missed something last night, but I have the sense for once in my life not to ask.

Rachel calls a little while later, after Elena has gone up to get Ethan going on his schedule.

"Hey, Herbie. How's it hanging?" She's trying too hard to be upbeat.

"When are you coming back?"

"Ouch. That well, eh?

"We're fine," I say. "I just miss you."

"You're losing your touch, kiddo. That was a hair or two less than convincing," she says.

"You win. It's been a little harder than I thought," I admit. "But no worries. We're getting by."

"How's Ethan doing? Any meltdowns?"

"Nothing major. He's okay. I had no idea that he was such a math geek."

Rachel laughs. Her voice gets soft and tender. "Ethan's a mass of contradictions and surprises. And Elena?"

"I didn't expect so much bickering," I tell her.

"Siblings. That's totally and appropriately normal."

"Makes me glad I don't have any. What about you? Any luck with your mission?"

"I'll know more tonight. Hopefully, I'll be able to give you an ETD then."

"Sounds good. Make it speedy. Okay?"

"Do my best. Love you, Herbie."

"Me too, Madre."

After we hang up, I really want to indulge in a good cry, but Ethan comes down with his sheets, and Elena needs help setting up the camera to tape the French poem. No time to enjoy my own drama. In the middle of calculus my phone goes off. It's Jo, so I get up and take it outside.

"Jo Jo, what up, dog?" I walk around to the far side of the pool and sit at the table with my back to the house.

"Sage, you are about as ghetto as Taylor Swift, so please give it up."

"I can always count on you to keep me real," I say.

"So, how's life. Are you officially with the fire-boy now?"

"I'm not officially with anyone," I tell her.

"Not enough information. Details, please," she orders.

"You first." Maybe if I can get her talking about herself, I can somehow get around to my dad.

"I went on another date with Gene."

"Did you now?"

"Yes. And no comments about his name. He's very sweet and kind of funny in a geeky way."

"Was the kissing any better than last time?" I ask.

"Did I say anything about kissing?"

"Would you bring it up if there hadn't been any kissing?"

Jo laughs. "You know me too well. And since you asked, I will kiss and tell. It was good. Really really good."

"Jo, news flash, if the best word you can think of to describe a kiss is 'good,' then it probably wasn't."

"Sage, you are such a buzz-kill!"

"Have you ever noticed how over-used that phrase is?" I ask.

I don't hear Ethan come out, but suddenly he's beside me touching my arm. "Sage, when are you coming back in? You need to check my answers."

Jo is right on it. "Is that the boy twin? What's his name? Ethan."

"Good guess. Can you hang on a second?" I turn to Ethan. "Give me ten more minutes. Okay, Mouse?"

"Ten minutes!" he whines. "Too long! Come now, pleeeeez."

"Let me take your picture, and I'll make it five." I say.

He thinks about it for a second and nods. I move back a little in my chair and snap the shot. He's looking down and his lips are just a little parted, like he's about to say something. His curls look like a golden halo. "Thanks, Mouse. Go practice your poem while I finish my call."

He reluctantly crosses the patio and goes inside.

I get back to Jo. "Sorry about that, girlfriend."

"Sage, you sound like a mom," she says. "And since when do you negotiate with anyone about anything."

I send her the picture. "Just wait till you meet Ethan. Then you'll understand."

"OMG!" Jo practically yells into the phone. "Did you die and not tell me because that boy is surely some kind of creature from heaven. Can you say 'angel?'"

"He is beautiful, there's no denying that."

"So you're dumping the fire starter for the twin? Good choice." She doesn't know about Ethan.

"Don't think so. Ethan isn't really dating material."

"The best ones always play for the other team!" she laments, disappointed.

I laugh. "Not gay. He's kind of like a little kid. Rachel says he's stuck in time."

"Stuck in time? What exactly does that look like?"

I don't want to tell her about the bed-wetting or thumb-sucking, "It looks like someone who isn't growing up."

"Looks like he's got all the right parts to me."

"He does. He just doesn't know what to do with them."

"That's a shame, Sage. He seems kind of attached to you, though."

"I guess so." I don't want to talk about Ethan anymore. I want to talk about her. "Well, I need to get back inside and help him film his French assignment."

"Call me back when you're free."

"Sure. Do you remember how my dad always used to film us?" I know it's an awkward segue, but she takes the bait.

"We hated that stupid camera," she adds. "He was always there with it at the most inconvenient moments."

"Yeah, he never took the hint, though, did he?"

"That's the thing about your dad, Sage. He never takes 'no' for an answer." I can hear the anger building, so I fan the flame.

"Now he's got an even bigger and better video camera. What the hell does he need that for? He's certainly no Spielberg."

"It's just disgusting how he hides behind that thing, waiting for you to perform like a trained monkey." I'm not sure if she means me or the general you.

"I'd like to smash that damn camera into smithereens!" I half yell.

"Get in line. I want a piece of that action." She's almost there now.

"Sage, five minutes is up!" Ethan's voice carries across the pool.

"You better go, Momma Sage," Jo says.

"Bite me," I say.

"Tempting, but I'm too far away at the moment."

"Bye, Jo Jo."

"Later."

And that's it. I'm not going to get any more information out of her than that, because the next time I try to bring it up, she'll want to know what the fixation with my dad's camera is about, and then she'll put the pieces together and clam up again. What a waste!

Ethan and Elena are at it again. Ethan is holding the door opened, kind of standing behind it. "I don't want to do the video now. I want to go swimming. Sage, tell her that we're going swimming now," he begs.

Elena chimes in from the living room, "E, why are you being like that. You know the schedule and what you're supposed to do."

Ethan is agitated beyond what the situation warrants. "I don't want to do that stupid French video!" As soon as I come in, he sits in the corner of the kitchen on the floor with his knees drawn up to his chin. He wraps his arms around his legs.

I have no idea what's going on with him. Elena's no help. She comes in the kitchen, grabs his hands and tries to force him to his feet.

"Ethan, this is part of the schedule. French studies at 10, and today we do the video. It's all planned. Now get up!"

Ethan resists her easily. Even though he's small, he outweighs her by at least 50 pounds, and he's much stronger than she is.

"I don't want to do it. I want to go swimming." I wish I had the Rachel playbook for sibling disputes, but I'm hanging in the wind here.

Elena backs up and stands looking over him with her hands on her hips. "Ethan, did you wet yourself?"

He looks up, his eyes flashing. "No!" But he immediately puts his head back down.

"Then stand up and prove it!" she challenges.

He doesn't move.

Elena is livid. "I told you to go when Sage was outside. Did you just ignore me?"

He shakes his head, but he doesn't look up.

"What the hell, Ethan? What's wrong with you today?"

"Elena, enough!" My voice entering the fray surprises even me. "Let's just everyone take a time-out and relax for a second." I motion Elena to a seat at the table, and I pour her a glass of ice water. I do the same for Ethan and squat down to offer him the glass.

"Ethan, tell us what's wrong. Okay? Then we can fix it and get on with the day."

He's crying silently. I can see his shoulders shaking. "I didn't wet my pants," he murmurs.

"Okay, Mouse. Then what is it?" I ask.

"I just don't want to do that stupid video." He lifts his head to wipe his nose with the back of his hand. The circles under his eyes are almost bruise-colored.

"I think I know what the problem is," I say. Elena gets up and comes over. "It's my fault. Ethan waited up for me last night. I didn't get in till after 1:30 and we got up at what? 5:30?"

"Well that's just great!" Elena is even more annoyed. "We may as well just shred Rachel's schedule. Ethan, you aren't even trying to make this work!" She shakes her head. "Come on then. Let's go take a nap."

Elena's approach is all wrong, and Ethan bristles. "I'm not tired. You can't make me take a nap."

I'm so done with this scene. A nap sounds like a slice of heaven to me. I drag Elena into the living room. "You're not helping. Go upstairs and let me get this. Okay?"

"Fine," she says.

Back in the kitchen Ethan hasn't moved except to put his thumb in his mouth. I crouch beside him again. "You're so tired, Mouse. You can hardly keep your eyes open. I know because I feel the same way. Let's just go up and rest for a little while. You don't have to sleep, just rest. What do you say?"

He thinks about it, looking long and hard at my face. Then he reaches over and touches under my eyes. "Your eyes are so sleepy, Sage. I can tuck you in for a nap."

I laugh a little. "That's so incredibly sweet. You can tuck me in and then we can both get some sleep. What do you say?"

He looks down and then nods. I stand up and offer him my hand. As he takes it, I'm caught off guard by the jolt. The kitchen tips over; I'm in Ethan's bed looking at Elena. "Tell me where she went, Lanie!" I demand.

"Ethan, it's none of your business. I promise she'll be home soon. Just go to sleep."

"No! I'm waiting for Sage." Fear and frustration fuel my anger. "Did she go see <u>him</u>?"

"E! You can ask a hundred times. The answer is the same. GO TO SLEEP!"

"TELL ME!" I scream.

His fury jolts me back to the present. Ethan looks even more exhausted. I have no idea where the trade took him. We go upstairs hand in hand. Elena's waiting at the end of the hall where she ushers Ethan into the bathroom somewhat against his will.

"Thank you," I mouth to her before going into her room and collapsing on the unmade bed. I put the pillow over my head to block out their squabbling.

I'm nearly asleep when Elena comes in. "He wants you, Sage."

"No way. I can't move."

"Way."

"I can't," I whine. Elena pulls me into a sitting position.

"Yeah, you can. And you will."

Ethan calls from his room, "Saaage."

We both crack up. She gets behind me and shoves me off the bed.

"Argh!" I complain. "You, don't move. We need to have some words."

She's on her stomach smiling up at me. "OOOH! Are you gonna scold me?"

"I think you're enjoying this," I wink at her.

Ethan has given up on yelling. By the time I get there, he's sucking his thumb, and his eyes are closed. When I lean over to kiss him on the forehead, he puts his hand over mine. "Don't go," he whispers.

"I'll be right next door sleeping in Elena's bed. I promise I won't go."

"No," He mumbles. "Sleep here. You said I could tuck you in and we could sleep together." He moves over to make room for me. I hesitate. "Please," he begs.

"That's not exactly what I said, but I'll stay, just until you fall asleep." I climb up onto the bed. The plastic sheet crinkles under the coverlet. He rolls over away from me still holding my hand, and I curl in to spoon him with my arm around his waist. I'm not sure which of us falls asleep first, but I can't fight the comfort of the heat he radiates, the honey-sweet smell of his hair, and the rhythm of breathing together, deep, steady, and synchronized.

I wake up before Ethan and roll as quietly as I can off the bed. In her room Elena is laying on her back with her legs up in the air and her feet propped against the poster of the bed. She's drawing on her thigh with the moonstone earring, etching a picture in white scratches.

"Man, you're brave," she says rolling onto her stomach.

"What are you doing?" I ask pointedly.

"Look, no blood, no foul," she says, flipping over and sticking out her leg. "You're lucky you didn't get peed on." Her tone is nasty and accusing.

"Okay, Elena. Let's have it." I sit down across from her on the bed.

"What?"

"Obviously, you're angry with Ethan . . . and me. What's the what?"

She gives me her icicle stare. "You can't have them both!"

Didn't see that coming. I am decidedly uncomfortable with this turn. "Okay," I say, hoping that's all she has to say on the subject.

But she goes on. "And before you dismiss me as a jealous bitch, I fully and whole-heartedly admit to being jealous on so many levels that I'm turning a hundred shades from forest to chartreuse. I'm jealous that Ethan chooses you over me. I'm jealous that Finn wants you so bad he can't think straight, and most of all I'm jealous that you would choose either of them over me any day of the week."

"Oh." I'm thinking about how I can defend myself, but she keeps going.

"Now let's put all of that aside and get back to the point."

"Okay, but -" I start.

"You don't get to talk yet. You wanted to have words, well listen to these words carefully. You can NOT have both of them. It doesn't matter that they mean different things to you because that doesn't mean a thing to <u>them</u>. You'll end up breaking both of their hearts, and trust me neither of those boys will survive in any way that matters. Besides they won't let you."

"Are you done?" I ask.

"I think so."

"Are we talking about me, or is this about you?"

"Ouch! Didn't occur to me. Give me a second to contemplate." She's making fun of Rachel.

I can't help myself, I start giggling.

"Real mature, Sage," Elena narrows her eyes in mock anger.

"Okay, seriously. You're probably right, but I'm afraid it's a little too late to make any graceful exits, though things with Finn may be over anyway."

"Sweetheart, things ain't never gonna be over with Finn. If you think they are, then you don't know the first thing about Finnian Mulcahy." Elena's voice is playful, but I get her message loud and clear.

"Elena, I need to know what happened with you and Finn. What did he do to you?"

She starts scratching on her thigh again, concentric circles that end up looking like a bulls-eye. "I guess I should have told you all this before anyway. I'll start way back when it first began between me and Finn. Sixth grade actually."

"Damn. You do go way back."

"Six years. So in sixth grade Grandmother decided that she was going to toughen Ethan up by sending him to 'real' school."

"You've got to be kidding."

"The shrink that was seeing us at the time told her that a little peer pressure would help resolve his 'symptoms,' especially the ones that really bug her."

"The thumb-sucking and accidents, I'm guessing."

"Good guess. I'm sure that you can just imagine Ethan thrown into the lion's den of a public junior high armed with tape around his thumbs and a change of clothes in his backpack."

"Did he make it through the first day?"

"Not really. The school called on the second day insisting that grandmother send him to school wearing 'protective clothing,' and the kids had given him the delightful nickname of Peethan."

I try to hold in a snicker. "It's amazing the creative impulse that cruelty ignites."

Elena laughs, "You got that right!"

"I hated middle school, but at least I didn't have a nickname," I say.

Elena goes on. "All of that would have been bad enough, but then there was Finn. This happy hippy counselor at the school got all us nut-jobs together twice a week for group therapy. It was supposed to be all warm and fuzzy; it was anything but. That's where Finn enters the picture. He'd been setting fires for a couple of years by then, and he was really, really angry. Finn's dad had pounded on him from the moment of his mother's death a decade earlier, and Finn arrived at the ripe age of twelve full of testosterone and rage, desperately looking for someone that he could pound on in never-ending abuse circle-jerk."

"Ethan."

"Exactly. But he didn't count on me, or maybe he did. I don't know. Anyway he terrorized Ethan for a couple of weeks. Then we struck a bargain. He would leave Ethan alone if I was his girlfriend. At age twelve that wasn't too difficult. I had to sit with him at lunch and do his homework, crap like that. Before the year was half over, Ethan had a total break down and was hospitalized. Grandmother fired the shrink, and I thought I was finally Finn-free."

"Finn had other ideas?"

"Partially. What I discovered was that I secretly liked being Finn's girl. What I hated was the arrangement, the sense of servitude. Unfortunately for me, that was exactly what Finn got off on. For the next three years we played this ridiculous game. I would arrange for Finn to find out about something he could blackmail me for, and he would 'force' me to be with him until the information was unimportant or he got bored with me. Kind of sick. I know."

"Kind of, but you were young."

She rolls her eyes. "Flash forward three years. Ninth grade. Finn is setting serious fires, getting into all kinds of trouble, drugs, drinking, fights. I'm tied to home to Ethan, and I just can't keep up with the crowd he runs with. Plus, I don't really want to. I try to do the slow fade. All of a sudden, Finn is all about me. He's driving by the house with his posse and dogging my every move at school. One day after school, I'm hiding out under the bleachers, enjoying my favorite habit, and Finn follows me. Now he's got the goods on me for real, right. If he goes to the counselors, I'm gonna be ferried off to the funny farm or at a bare minimum hurried to some head shrinker, who's gonna try to make me stop."

I keep my mouth shut, but I really want to tell her that she should stop, that cutting is sick and not in a good way.

She goes on. "Now Finn wants more than homework answers. He wants me on my knees. I'm far from ready for that; it horrifies me, but there I am opening wide, every time he snaps his fingers. I hate him for making me do that shit, but every time I think, maybe he'll kiss me. It wouldn't be so awful if he'd just kiss me.'"

"Then one night he comes over, makes me sneak out to go to some party out in the woods. It's all fun and games. He finally kisses me. I'm on cloud nine, so I have a couple drinks to celebrate. Next thing I know it's the next day, my clothes are torn, I'm bleeding in all kinds of crazy places, and my memory's a giant black hole. Before you think roofies, remember I've got a history of losing blocks of time. Rachel says this selective amnesia is my way of coping with trauma. Anyway, the next Monday at school everyone's talking about how I gave it up to Finn in front of God and the world. Pictures of moderate incrimination circulate in cyberspace, but suddenly I've got this rep. Not that I had many friends to lose, but before that I wasn't a total pariah."

"The worst of it is that you and I both know I didn't give him a damn thing. Whatever he got from me, he took, and maybe there were drugs involved. Who knows? All of a sudden he stops snapping his fingers, won't even touch me, swears up and down that he didn't do anything, and it was all just trash talk, but I don't believe it. After all the dust settled, he just vanished. I didn't talk to him again until this summer."

"So you think he . . . ? You think he's capable of that?"

"Sage, people who suffer are capable of doing anything that will relieve their pain, even if only for a moment."

I watch Elena's ice cold eyes shift and wonder what she is capable of.

Chapter10 (Where There's Smoke)

One tragedy begets the next. A thunderstorm severs a branch from a tree. A child running down a hill trips on that branch, falling on stones that rip through the tender flesh of his hands and knees. The fall dislodges a pebble that tumbles into the pond sending ripples to capsize the leaf upon which a praying mantis sits. The tree goes on growing without the branch. The child weeps, bleeds, and survives the scars. The mantis drowns, and no one grieves.

Suddenly Elena's face goes ashen. She springs off the bed toward the window. "Ethan!" She darts from the room and down the stairs. I'm at the window in time to see her explode through the kitchen door into the yard.

Ethan is on the pool deck, trying to get to the house, but Finn is blocking him. No matter which way Ethan goes around the pool, he can't get past Finn. Ethan's yelling and crying; Finn's laughing. I can't hear what they're saying. Elena rushes at Finn, but he steps out of her way, and with a flick of his shoulder she's sent careening into the pool. It would be comical if it weren't for Ethan's reaction. Suddenly, his face goes hard and determined. Before he moves, I know what he's going to do. I break from the window and fall halfway down the stairs. I pick myself up and limp outside.

Elena is pulling herself out of the pool, but it's too late. While Finn is turned around laughing at her dousing, Ethan closes the distance between them. Without hesitation he grabs Finn's arm with both hands. Finn barely has time to turn to face Ethan before his face goes blank, and he sinks to his knees. A part of me hopes that Ethan sends him straight to the hell Finn authored for him in the sixth grade; the other part is terrified about where Ethan will end up in Finn's twisted mind. Elena and I reach them at the same time. I go for Ethan's hands, but Elena knocks me away. "I need you to be here! Not in there." She points to Ethan's head.

One by one she pries Ethan's fingers from Finn's bicep. Finn falls forward grabbing his head like it might come off, his mouth opens in agony. Ethan seems oddly calm, looking from Elena to me and back again. I squat down next to Finn.

"What the hell just happened?" he moans and seizes my wrist with one hand.

"You'll be alright in minute," I lie. I look up at Elena, but she has no intention of relieving Finn's pain. She puts her arm around Ethan protectively and starts ushering him toward the house. At the door Ethan stops and refuses to go in. He calls my name and reaches out for me. Finn continues holding me with a death grip. Elena scolds Ethan to go inside, but he's not going without me.

"Finn, what are you doing here?" My hand is going numb.

"Damn! What did that little freak do to me?" He's more confused than angry, but I expect that will change in the next two minutes.

"Ethan, go inside," I yell. Finn finally releases my arm and starts rubbing his temples and shaking his head like he's trying get a bee to stop buzzing inside it. I want to run inside with the twins, but I don't. Finn looks like he's about to totally lose it. "Finn," I say quietly and as calmly as I can, "Look at me. Take a deep breath with me." It takes him several tries to focus his attention. His brow is knit in pain, and his eyes are clouded and watering. His breathing is fast and shallow like he's hyperventilating. The last thing we need is for him to pass out. "Deep breaths, Finn. In . . . and out . . . Relax." I glance over where the twins are still waiting beside the door, watching. After a couple minutes, he seems better, or at least more himself. "Start talking now, Finn. Tell me what you're doing here!" I demand.

"I came to beat the shit out of your little boyfriend."

I hope he's lying. "That didn't work out so well for you, did it?"

"Who says I'm done." He starts to get up, but ends up sitting down weakly. The threatening gesture is enough to drive Ethan and Elena inside. "Shit, Sage. What did he do to me?" Finn whines.

"Nothing you didn't ask for."

"Come on. Tell me why my head is on fire. Did he give me an aneurism?"

"Really?" I laugh. "It's like consciousness swapping. You traded places."

"He was in my head?"

"And you were in his."

"That was his fire? Man, that's fucked up." Finn is still trying to figure it all out, but I know where Ethan sent him.

"Are you okay now?"

"Except for this splitting headache, I'm in one piece."

"Good. Then get the hell out of here!" For an instant he looks hurt, really hurt, but his expression changes so quickly I'm not sure I didn't imagine it.

Finn stands up and raises his voice. "We're not done, me and him. You hear me, Freak." Then he looks down at me and whispers, smiling, "I'm not done with you either, Stalker-girl."

"Maybe I'm done with you." I want to mean it.

He takes a deep breath and a step toward me. I hold my ground defiantly. He cups my chin and kisses me, not angrily like I expect, but like he means it. "You're not done, not even close, Sage." He walks away, trying to make a cool exit, but before he makes it to his bike, he stumbles and brings his hand to his head.

I turn away and hurry toward the house. Elena is standing at the door, watching. When I go back inside, Ethan is sitting at the table. He looks a little shell shocked, but he's not crying. Elena actually looks more messed up than Ethan. I sit down at the table. "E, you okay?" He kind of shrugs like he isn't really listening. "Elena?"

"I'm fine," she says too loudly. Ethan keys in on her distress.

"Lanie, are you hurt? Did he hurt you?"

"No, Ethan! I'm mad, really really pissed off." She turns her rage on him. "What were you doing down there alone?"

"I woke up, and I wanted to go swimming. You and Sage were talking about . . . bad stuff, so I just went by myself." He looks down at his hands.

"You're not supposed to do that!"

Ethan is taken aback. "I always swim by myself. Every morning. Why are you mad at me?" his voice cracks.

Elena shakes her head in frustration, "I don't know." Without further explanation she stomps upstairs, leaving us completely confused.

"Sage, I'm cold," Ethan complains shivering a little.

I go outside and get his towel from the pool deck. Back inside I wrap it around his shoulders. His teeth have begun to chatter. I check the AC, and it's set at 80. I kick it up two degrees.

"Come on, let's put on some warm clothes." He nods. We're climbing the stairs when Elena comes tearing down.

"I'm going out," she says, meeting us in the middle.

I don't need to ask. She's going after Finn. I'm not sure if she wants to help or hurt him.

"Sorry to leave it all on you, Sage, but I need to do this. If I'm not back by bedtime make sure Ethan's got a diaper on. Top drawer on the left. I've got my phone. Be good, E. I love you." She kisses him on the cheek.

"This is a really bad idea." I have to say it.

"He can't come here and threaten my family." She's resolute.

I just hope she doesn't find him. In Ethan's room we listen as Iron Lady's truck pulls down the driveway. Ethan has his forehead pressed against the window, and he's shivering even harder.

"It'll be okay, Mouse. Show me where you keep your warm clothes." He gets a pair of sweatpants and a hoody out of the bottom drawer. "You've got it from here; right, pal?" I ask on my way out the door. I wait in the hall. When Ethan comes out, his teeth are still chattering. His arms are wrapped around himself, and he looks miserable. I take him into the bathroom and blow-dry his hair. I get him to smile a couple times, but at this point I'm beginning to get worried. When I'm done, I get the quilt from Elena's bed and wrap him up on the sofa. I turn on the TV, and leave him there sucking his thumb and shaking to go down to make some hot soup. When I come back with the soup, he's staring at the TV more than watching it, and I have to say his name like three times before he turns and sees me.

"Ethan, where are you, sweetie?" I try to keep my voice from betraying my anxiety.

"In the TV room, silly," he says absently.

"I made some soup for you. Wanna try it?"

"I'm not hungry." He sounds far away.

"It might warm you up a little, " I coax.

He nods, and I spoon the soup into his mouth, but after four or five bites, he turns away, scrunching down into the quilt. I put the soup aside and let him lay his head against my chest while I wrap my arms around him and the blanket. He's still shaking at intervals in little spasms. The heat that he's radiating through the comforter makes the sweat drip down my neck. I'm sure if I touched his skin, it would scorch me. It occurs to me that he might be running a fever, but I'm not sure how I would know given that his baseline temperature is far from normal, and I don't know what exactly that baseline is.

"Do you want to talk about it?" I ask. I'm not really sure if this is a good idea.

"About what? Finn?" There's not a trace of emotion in his voice.

"Uh huh. Do you want to tell me what you saw?"

"Not really. Do I have to?"

"Of course not. We don't have to talk."

He snuggles closer. We lie on the couch not watching the TV until a knock at the door makes us both jump.

"I'll be right back. I'm sure it's just Ben," I say to reassure him, but his eyes don't reveal the usual panic.

I am stunned to open the kitchen door to my father of all people. My stomach lurches.

"Hey, Sage." He's all smiles. "Ready to have some dinner with your old man?"

I must look as confused and sick as I feel.

"Um, Sage, have you checked your phone lately?"

I scramble to remember the last place I saw it. "I must have misplaced it. Can you wait here a sec?" I race up the stairs to Elena's room. No phone. I must have lost it in Ethan's room. It's not on the table or the floor. I climb up on the bed and start looking through the blankets. Suddenly it occurs to me that the bed is dry. Good job, Mouse. I find it under the pillow.

Two messages from Rachel, an email and a text from my father. Shit! I dial Elena.

"What's wrong?" she answers.

"You have to come home. Like now," I say.

"I can't."

"I have no time for this. Elena, my father is here, and I have to leave with him. How soon can you be here?"

"Crap. Fifteen, twenty minutes I guess."

"Can I leave Ethan alone for that long? He's watching TV." I'm standing at door to his room looking at him down the hall.

"If he'll let you leave without a meltdown, it should be fine."

"I'll give it my best shot. Thanks."

"You owe me," she says.

"One more thing, I need a thumb drive. Please tell me you have one."

"Roll-top desk middle drawer. The purple one is empty."

"You're a goddess," I say.

"Good luck with Ethan."

"Thanks."

When I go back out into the TV room, Ethan hasn't moved. He's staring at the wall, not even pretending to look at the TV. His shivering has subsided. I crouch down beside him. "Mouse. Mouse?" He doesn't turn until I touch his face. "How are you doing?"

"I'm not so cold now."

"That's good."

"Is Ben gone? Come back." He sits up so I can lay down with him.

"It wasn't Ben at the door. It was my father."

Ethan frowns. "I don't like him."

"I know, but I have to go with him. It's important."

Ethan shakes his head slowly. "No you don't." But that's all the fight he's got. He sighs heavily and lies back down. Then he resumes staring at the wall beyond my shoulder, far away.

"I have to go now, Ethan. Lanie will be back in a few minutes. You just stay here and watch your show. Okay?"

He nods absently, like he has no idea what I've just said. I move his hair out of the way to kiss his forehead. "Back soon, little Mouse. Be good."

He puts his thumb in his mouth, and I just leave him there. I know as I go down the stairs, it's wrong. I already regret it when my father says, "Aren't you going to introduce me to your little boyfriend? I know he's up there." I suppress the pangs of guilt as I close the car door. I need to make this count. It may be my last chance.

"Hey, Dad, before we go out to dinner, can we stop by your place. I left my journal there last weekend, and I really need it."

"Are you sure? I didn't see it lying around."

"Of course not, Dad. I hid it so you wouldn't read it."

"That seems like a lot of trouble. Why didn't you just take it with you?" He's suspicious, but I have this covered six ways to Sunday.

"I couldn't do that because then the boy I was meeting might read about himself, or worse yet, about all the other boys. Too dangerous, plain and simple."

My father is smiling now. Probably proud of how smart I am. If he knew I was lying, he'd probably be even prouder. A chip off the old block alright.

"So tell me about this boy. If you live with him basically, then why are you sneaking out of my place to see him?"

I laugh. "The boy at home is not the boy I went to see. He's not my boyfriend."

"Okay then." He's laughing at me.

"So can we stop at your place or not?"

"Relax. We can just eat down near my apartment. I'm famished. How 'bout you?"

I don't tell him that I feel like I may hurl at the next turn. Instead I say, "Me too, but I'd really like to get my journal first if it's all the same to you." If this goes the right way, I'll get him to let me go up alone to get the imaginary journal. Then I can load all the files onto the thumb drive and get out of there with him none the wiser. I suddenly realize that I do not have a journal to "find." Strategic error. I'm thinking my way around it when we pull into his complex. "No need for you to run up three flights, I know right where it is," I tell him.

"Okay."

That was way too easy. I jump out of the car and bound up the first flight. The sound of his car door slamming stops me. I turn around to find him on the bottom stair. "Uh, Sage, you might need these." He's dangling the keys to the apartment."

"Silly me," I say, racing back down and grabbing them. "Back in a flash." Thankfully, he stays there at the bottom step.

In his apartment, I head directly to the bedroom and boot-up his PC. I plug in the memory stick and wait. Suddenly, the door opens, and my dad is there, looking at me across the expanse of the living room, putting two and two together as he says in slow motion, "I decided to use the bathroom - ."

As if on cue, we both lunge for the bedroom door. I make it first and get it closed and locked before he can push it open. I'm about to breathe a sigh of relief when I hear the living room slider. I leap across the bed and drop the stick in the track of the bedroom door. With only the glass between us, I can see the dread written on face. He watches me go to the computer and start pulling folders onto the stick. He's screaming loud enough for me to hear him through the glass.

"Sage! What the hell are you doing? God damn it, Sage. Let me in! NOW! What the hell?" He looks like a tiger trapped in a tiny cage. He picks up a plastic chair and smashes it against the glass. I cover my head in anticipation of flying shards, but the chair just bounces off. He bangs it again and again. I keep my focus on moving folders onto the thumb drive. As the copying progresses, I realize that now I have another problem. There's no way out of here except through the living room and even though it's my father out there, in the state he's in there's no predicting what he's capable of doing to me.

I wrack my brain for the answer to this puzzle until I have an idea. Maybe I can get out of here in one piece after all. When the download is nearly complete, I call Ben.

"Ben, I need you to come pick me up at my dad's apartment, NOW." I give him the address. He can hear the screaming and pounding coming through the glass.

"What's going on, Sage?"

"There's no time. Just come as quick as you can." I don't even try to mask my terror.

"On my way, but this better be good," He's not happy about whatever I am interrupting, but I don't really care.

After I hang up, I go to the window. "Dad," I don't yell because I want him to have to be quiet to hear me. "You're really scaring me. I don't want to call the cops, but I will."

"You just did, you bitch!" He yells back.

"I called Rachel. She's coming to get me," I lie. "You need to stay on the porch so I can come out."

"You aren't going anywhere with that memory stick. I don't know what you think you're doing, but you're in deep shit!"

"Just let me go home with Rachel."

"What do you think you're going to do with that stick? Everything on there is absolutely legal."

"That explains why you're so pissed, Dad." Perhaps sarcasm is not my best option at this point.

Spit is flying from his mouth as he yells, "I'm pissed off because my kid is playing some warped game of cops and robbers. You broke the one rule I gave you, and now you're turning it really ugly. What a nice kid I've raised!"

I want to scream "You didn't raise me!" But I need to calm him down, not spin him up any more than he is. "Why don't you tell me about the stuff on the computer? You might feel better."

He shakes his head, walks away from the window and then rushes it with his shoulder. Of course he bounces off the glass. I look at the time. Ben will be here soon. I go to the computer, eject the drive, and put it my bra. Then I look over at the porch. Instead of looking in, he's looking out over the balcony like he's going to jump. A few seconds later I hear the siren too. It's getting closer, and something tells me it's coming here. He's inside now at the bedroom door, and he's screaming hysterically, "LET ME IN! LET ME THE FUCK IN MY OWN ROOM." The casing buckles as he throws himself against interior the door. The wood cracks the second time he smashes into it. I hurry to the side of door, pressing myself against the wall beyond the casing. When he breaks through, he'll fall, and I'll have only as long as it takes him to stand to get out if I'm lucky.

With a huge crash the frame gives way, and the door goes down just as I predicted. I jump over the debris and sprint for the exit, looking back over my shoulder once. He doesn't waste time chasing me. He's at the computer, erasing his precious files. I hurry down one level and cross the breezeway to the back of the building. I duck into a doorway, so the cops who are racing up the stairs don't see me. Ben's car is pulling up a couple buildings away. I tear down the back stairs and come out in front of him. He reaches over and opens the door. I jump in sweating, out of breathe, and shaking like I have Parkinson's.

"Go, Ben, just go."

"Please tell me you aren't running from those cops."

"I'm not running from those cops. NOW GO!" He pulls around the squad car and waves at the officer in the vehicle nice as pie. I scrunch down in the seat. A minute later we're pulling out onto the highway. I sit up and take some deep breaths.

"Uh, Sage, why are you smiling? You're totally weirding me out."

"Can you say, 'adrenaline rush?'" I'm relieved and triumphant. I want to scream and war whoop, but I contain myself.

"Please tell me what the heck's going on."

"Not while you're diving, Ben. We can stop at Exodus. I'll tell you the whole story there." But by whole story I mean the part about my dad. There's no need to bring Finn into this.

The AC at the cafe is broken again, so we sit outside. He gets me a smoothie, and we make small talk for a while, until my heart-rate falls to relative normal. Ben is one of the most patient people I know, and true to his nature, he doesn't push. Almost an hour has passed by the time I'm ready. I tell him about the day I discovered the pornography and about the file with Jo's name. Then I retell the phone call that confirmed my suspicions. He totally agrees with me about her confirmation without ascension. When I make to the part about dad coming to the Paige's to pick me up, I start tripping on the high of what I did, and I manage to not bust out crying. Ben's stunned by the whole mess. All he can say in the end is "What a bastard!" over and over.

He looks at his watch and shakes his head. "It's been over two hours, Sage, and I was in the middle of making dinner with Joshua. He's going to think I've been abducted by aliens. You need to call Rachel and fill her in. I'll follow up later."

I hadn't counted on him bringing my mom into this. I'm begging him, "Please, please, don't tell Mom until I look at the files," but I'm drowned out by a fire truck barreling down the street. I watch it turn toward the Paige's house. A plume of smoke is rising over the trees, and I know - I just know. My smile drops, and I grab Ben's arm.

"Get me home!"

We race for the car and follow the siren up the block, another left and a right. I can see the flames shooting from the driveway. It's the garage, my apartment, that's burning. The cops are stopping cars at the end of the block. I leap out and race behind the houses, scaling the fences as I come to them. Finally, I make over the Paige's fence. Ethan and Elena are standing on the pool deck several yards apart from each other, watching the fire fighters hook up the hoses. One of them goes up to Ethan and yells at him, "Is there anyone in the building?" Ethan just stares into the fire without answering. The firefighter touches his arm and jumps back with his hand to his head like he's been stung. I have to get Ethan out of there. Elena is standing stiffly with her hands at her sides. Anyone else might think she was angry, but I can see the blood dripping from her knuckles because she's digging her nails into her palms.

I reach Elena first, "Elena! Elena! What happened?"

She releases her fists and looks down at her palms. "I just got back. Traffic accident. Ethan was here alone!" She's says haltingly.

"WHAT HAPPENED?" I yell. I never realized how loud a fire is. The trucks and water and people talking and yelling and the flames. I can hardly think. Ethan's skin is glowing red; Elena and I are drenched in sweat. The firefighter who touched Ethan is motioning us away from the blaze. I grab Elena's wrist and hurry to Ethan. I circle my arm around his waist, and move them into the house. Ethan stays by the window mesmerized by the scene outside. Elena is pacing like she's on the verge of an important discovery. I motion her over to the sink and wash the gouges on her hands.

"How did this happen?" I ask. Then Elena and I look up at each other at the same time with the same revelation, "Finn."

"He always goes to the same place after he sets a fire." She says.

"Where?" I stave off the blood with paper towels. Luckily the cuts are only as deep as her nails are long. The bleeding stops quickly.

"His mother's grave."

"This is my fault," I say. "I shouldn't have left." The flames are subsiding, but my guilt is rising.

The look she gives me does nothing to let me off the hook. "I need to go to Finn. He's in a bad way if he did this. You stay here and take care of Ethan. He'd rather have you anyway," Elena says feverishly.

I don't bother arguing with her. The shock of what I'm losing just beyond the pool is setting in. Elena gently turns Ethan's face from the window. Gradually, he focuses on her, and his eyes brim over with tears. He lets out one gulping sob and turns back away. She watches his eyes glaze over again and then kisses his cheek.

At the end of the driveway I see Ben hand Elena the keys to his car. I have no idea what she said to make that happen. He's managing the police and fire marshal. I'm grateful that I don't need to try to explain this mess to anyone right now. My mind starts travelling back down the road that led us here, and it ends up at Rachel. How many ways have I let her down? I feel the bitter taste of regret rising in my throat, but I swallow it down. I need to keep it together for Ethan. Tears are coursing his soot-stained face. I'm about to take him upstairs away from this when Ben opens the door, letting in the smoke and confusion. Ethan puts his hands over his ears, and doesn't look at Ben.

"What do you need, Sage?" He looks exhausted. He glances over at Ethan not sure about whether or not he should address him. I draw his attention back to me.

"Can you please call Rachel? Tell her what happened here, that we're all okay and not to rush back." I feel the tears starting behind my eyes. I turn away from him and take a deep breath. "You should take Rachel's car. Elena's going to be a while."

"She didn't really go to get her brother's medicine, did she?" Ben says.

I shake my head. "We can trade cars back tomorrow." I hand him the keys from the table.

"Your friend needs some attention," He motions to Ethan who's standing with his legs spread apart and a dark spot dripping from his crotch to his knees. "Is there anyone else I should call? This seems like a lot for you to manage." Ben says.

"No, I've got it covered." I feel oddly defensive. It's not exactly the first impression I wanted Ben to have of Ethan. "If you can call Rachel and handle those people out there, I can handle this in here. And please don't tell her about my dad."

"Sage, you've been through the ringer today, but I have to ask. Do you think your father might have had something to do with this?"

I suddenly regret my instant impulse to blame Finn. "I didn't think of that. I suppose it's possible. But, Ben, he doesn't know Rachel's out of town; he thinks she picked me up. If it was him, then he really wanted to-" I can't finish the thought.

I watch a lot of movies, <u>a lot</u> of movies. I always imagine what I'd do in the hero's place. I'd like to think if I was being hunted and someone was trying to kill me, I'd be Jason Bourne, taking the fight to them, not one of the stupid kids from *I Know What You Did Last Summer,* running around like a senseless rabbit. But finding myself in the position of potential target takes me to neither of those places. Right now all I feel is numb, not angry, not scared, just anesthetized.

Ben tries to comfort me. "Sage, you don't have to worry about that tonight. It was probably just a candle left burning or a broken pilot light anyway. Take care of your friend . . . and yourself. Call me if you need anything. I'll see you in the morning." He hugs me tight and kisses the top of my head. "You're gonna be fine." He says to Ethan on the way out the door.

I come and stand beside Ethan, careful not to step in the puddle. His brow is knit in distress and his lips are pressed tightly together in misery. "Mouse, can you look at me."

He looks down and his tears fall all the way to the floor. "I'm sorry, Sage," he mumbles.

"It's okay, E. Let's go upstairs and get cleaned up. Can you do that?"

He looks back out the window for several seconds. Then he turns back to me and slips his hand in mine. I'm grateful for the normalcy of this simple act, no trading places, perhaps because we're in exactly the same state of shock in the same inferno.

Upstairs in the bathroom I turn on the shower and wait in the hall for him to take off his wet clothes, but when I come back in, he's still standing there dressed by the tub where I left him, nearly catatonic, rocking back and forth on the balls of his feet. I take a deep breath and let go of the awkwardness of the situation.

"Ethan, do you need help?" He looks through me and nods. I start by loosening the string of his soaked sweatpants and slipping them down his thin hips. I pull the boxers down next. He holds on to me for balance when I free them from around his feet. When I stand up again we are face to face. For just a second he brings his forehead to mine and takes a deep shaky breath. Then I pull his arms from the hoody sleeves one at a time, and ease it over his tear-streaked face. I take off my shoes and guide him into the shower. With my clothes still on, I step in behind him.

He stands facing me, but not really seeing me. I reach up cupping the water toward his head to douse his curls. Then I pull him a step toward me, pour the shampoo into my hand, and rub my hands together. When I begin to massage the soap into his hair, I can feel him relax, muscle by muscle. I'm careful not to get the soap near his eyes. I guide him back under the shower and tip his head back to rinse. He closes his eyes. I have to reach around him, and when I'm done, he lays his head on my shoulder, wraps his arms around my back. I stand there for a long time holding him, frozen in time. When the water begins to get cool, I push him away gently to get on with the process.

He watches me soap the washcloth, and I offer it to him to wash himself, but he shakes his head, so I gently rub the soap over the soft blond hair on his chest and stomach nearly all the way down. I don't know how to do this. I hesitate and decide to move on to his shoulders. He watches as I soap the length of each of his arms. Then I turn him around to clean the golden skin of his back, and carefully, lightly go over the perfect curve of his hips and buttocks. I squat down to get his legs and feet, going only so high on his inner thigh. I stand up and turn him to face me. As I soap his face, his hot tears mix with the cool water of the shower.

I leave the shower running while I dry him off and wrap him in a big soft towel. I close the lid of the toilet and sit him down. Then I get back in the shower where I strip off my clothes and wash myself from head to toe in the same order I washed Ethan. I turn off the shower and pull my towel inside to dry off. I wrap myself before coming out. Ethan is sucking his thumb, but he stops when I get out, and he takes my hand when I offer it to lead him to his room.

In the top drawer I find boxers and pull-up diapers. I hand him one of each and take a pair of boxers for myself. Elena's clothes will never fit me, and Iron Lady is about twice my size. I slip the boxers on under my towel. They fit perfectly. He drops his towel to the floor and stands naked in front of me without self-consciousness and without dressing. In the next drawer down I find t-shirts. I pick out white for both of us. I turn away from him to put mine on, hoping he will get the hint, but when I turn back, he's staring at me, eyes wide and mouth open with his diaper and underwear still in his hand. I smile, shake my head, bring his shirt over, and slip it over his head. He helps me get the arms through so I can pull it down. I take the diaper from him and crouch down to slip it over his feet. He lets me pull it up, and then put the boxers over it, but he doesn't help. When I'm done, he leans against and reaches for my hand.

The detangler and brush are on the dresser where we left them earlier, so I guide him to the desk chair and start working on his hair. Bit by bit I smooth his curls. When I'm done, I pick up the towels and hang them in the bathroom. I put our wet clothes in the laundry basket from Ethan's room and wonder what to do with them now that we have no washer and dryer. This is a problem that can wait till tomorrow.

When I go back into Ethan's room, he gets up from the chair and silently motions for me to take his place, as if talking would take too much effort. I sit down, and he starts brushing out my hair. This small kindness coming from Ethan breaks me in half. Almost before he can take a second stroke with the brush, I'm sobbing.

"No, Sage, don't cry!" He kneels in front of me and rubs my arm. "It's okay. Everything's okay." I let him hold me for a few seconds, and then I pull away.

"I know. You're right. I'm just really tired." I take a breath and wipe my eyes with the back of my hand. He resumes his task. He pulls the brush gently through each section and then stops to feel for knots. He's a bit awkward, like he hasn't done this before, but his hands are warm and comforting on my head and neck. When he's done, I braid my hair over my shoulder and tie it off with a rubber band from his desk.

"Pretty," he says.

It's still early, and we're both pretty wired, so we pick a movie. Ethan gets settled on the sofa while I take the laundry basket downstairs to the kitchen. I take a few minutes to stand at the sink looking out the window. The fire is out. Only one truck is left cleaning up the gear. Crime scene tape encircles the garage. It doesn't look like there's much to salvage. I give in to another round of self-pity, but pull it together again while I wipe up Ethan's puddle by the window. After I wash my hands, I make some popcorn and a big bowl of grapes. I grab a Coke for myself and a bottle of water for Ethan. Then I find my phone and text Elena. No response.

I take the snacks upstairs and vow to forget everything at least until tomorrow. Tomorrow I will think about the huge mess I've made of things and hopefully figure out how I can fix it. Ethan isn't where I left him. I find him in his room staring out the window. From here you can see that the whole roof collapsed. My room is nothing but ashes. My computer, photos, stuffed animals, jewelry, clothes, every letter, project, CD, and memento gone forever. A sob catches in my throat. Ethan turns and wraps his arms around me. I know he wants to comfort me, but it feels all wrong.

"I'm sorry, Sage. I'm so sorry." My grief is upsetting him, so I shake myself free from his embrace and force a smile.

"I brought some snacks up. Let's go watch that movie, okay?" Rachel is a big fan of escaping into movies. She would never recommend it to her clients, but I've seen how it helps her cope. After the last boyfriend left us, she watched the entire *Star Wars* series, all six movies three times. When it was over, she was able to order take-out and do dishes and laundry again. We pick an animated movie, *Spirit*, about a horse. It's narrated by Rachel's celebrity crush, but I've never seen it before. I open the soda and water, offering Ethan the latter. He shakes his head.

"I'm not supposed to."

"It's okay tonight. You probably inhaled a lot of smoke. You need the water to get it out of your system."

"But, I'll wet through everything." His cheeks flush.

"Then we'll wash it. It doesn't matter, Ethan."

He thinks about it. Then takes the bottle from me and has a sip.

The movie is perfect, music and action, beautiful scenery, and most importantly a feel good ending where the horses all come together again, and the next generation is born.

I check my phone. Still no word from Elena.

It's been hours, and I have to make a conscious decision not to flip out. Ethan and I are both winding down, but neither of us wants to go to bed till Elena's back, so we play cards until Ethan can't keep his eyes opened. Then I insist.

"Will you sing to me?" he wants to know after we get through the bedtime routine.

"I'm not sure you really want that. I'm not much of a singer."

"I'm sure." he insists. He climbs into bed and moves over to make room for me. I sit down on the edge, and he frowns. "Snuggle. Please."

I fluff the pillow and sit all the way up on the bed beside him. He puts his head in my lap and I run my fingers through his soft hair. "Sweet, Mouse," I whisper.

He looks up, "I love you, Sage." It's so spontaneous like he's thought it a million times or we've said it to each other every day for a lifetime.

"I love you too, E." The comfort contained in those words is immeasurable. Everything is peace in this moment. I sing the only song I know all the words to, "Safe and Sound." I have a hard time making it to the end without crying, but the tears aren't tears of grief; they're something entirely different. Ethan is almost asleep. I gently move his head onto his pillow and slide down under the covers. He doesn't have to ask me to stay, this is the only place I could be right now. When I'm settled, he curls in to spoon me, and I melt into the warmth and safety that somehow miraculously surround us.

Chapter 11 (Lying in the Dust)

Before Smokey the Bear and Prometheus, fires scorched the land, wounding the delicate Earth. Years later lush meadows covered the scars, transforming devastation into paradise.

"Sage! Sage! Wake up!" Ethan is bouncing up and down on his knees next to me, grinning as the sun peaks over the window sill. "Dry, dry, dry. Everything's dry, even my diaper!"

I sit up. "I can't tell you how happy that makes me."

He laughs. "Let's go tell Lanie!"

I have no idea if she even made it home. "Why don't you go use the toilet? You wouldn't want to have an accident now; I'll wake Elena."

"Good idea." He bounces off the bed and races into the bathroom.

I cross to Elena's room. She rolls over and groans when I open the door. I breathe a sigh of relief and crawl into bed next to her.

"Did you swim over here," she mumbles her sarcasm.

"Actually, surprisingly, no. But I'll let Ethan tell you." She sits up a little.

Ethan comes tearing in, but as he passes the window, the smile leaves his face. He never makes it to the bed. He's drawn to the view like the rubble out there is calling him. He starts talking to himself in half-tones that don't make it to us as words.

"E. Come and tell me your good news," Elena coaxes. "Ethan," she says a bit louder. "What did you want to tell me?"

He turns part way toward us, but his eyes remain scanning the destruction of the night before. "I stayed dry all night," he says absently.

"That's great, E! Come on over here with us."

He wanders over like he's forgotten where he is. Elena throws a pillow at him.

"Hey! Why'd you do that," he demands, coming back to the moment. He climbs over me and settles in between us.

"Where is Sage going to live now?" He gives voice to the nagging worry that's been scritch-scratching at the back of my mind all night.

"I imagine that she'll stay here with us at least for a while," Elena says.

"Good." It was the answer Ethan had hoped for obviously. "She should sleep with me," he proclaims.

"Really," Elena says. "And why is that, brother?"

"So I don't wet the bed anymore." It's so logical to him.

Elena is not going to let him have this victory. "E, one night is not a pattern. Just because you had one dry night, and Sage was there for it, doesn't mean that she's like your magic cure."

"Twice!" Ethan insists. "I stayed dry twice when Sage slept with me."

"Naps don't count."

"Do too!" She's really pushing his buttons.

"Besides, Ethan, Rachel and Grandmother will be home today, and they will NOT allow Sage to sleep with you!" She is merciless.

"Why not? Why can she sleep with you and not with me? That's not fair!"

"Maybe not, but that's how it is because you're a boy and I'm a girl. Girls can sleep with girls, but boys can't sleep with girls."

"That makes no sense!" He sits up and faces her. "You're crazy."

"It doesn't have to make sense to you. It's just the rule. Go ahead and ask Sage."

Ethan turns to me.

"I'm afraid she's right, Mouse." I hate to back her up, but she is right.

"But you slept with me two times. Did we break the rule?" He's so confused.

"Yes, I guess we did break the rule." I admit

"So I can't tell Grandmother and Rachel that you made me stay dry?"

"Yeah, probably not," I say. He looks crestfallen. "You can tell them that you stayed dry, just not that I slept with you. Okay?"

He thinks about it. "Okay. I can keep a secret."

"I bet you can!" I pull him down into a bear hug, and Elena rolls over on top of us, hugging us both.

When Ben shows up around 8 o'clock, Ethan makes a mad dash upstairs. To his credit Ben doesn't ask Elena where she took his car; he just plays along with the medication fiction. He stays for coffee and not so subtly hints that he needs to talk to me alone. Elena joins Ethan upstairs.

"Rachel is totally freaked out. You need to call her the second I leave if you haven't yet. Please tell me you called her."

I roll my eyes and feel uncomfortably guilty. "Check. Call Rachel ASAP or sooner."

"One more thing, the cops will be around this morning. They want to talk to all three of you."

"That is not going to be possible." I'm not telling him anything he doesn't know.

"I'm afraid that's your problem, Sage."

"What did you tell them?" I want to prepare myself for what kind of questions they might ask.

"I can't really divulge that. They asked me not to discuss it with you. I'll tell you this much, they don't think the fire was an accident. I'm pretty sure they're calling it arson."

All I can see is Finn's file. I need to talk to Elena before the cops show up. Elena comes down to say goodbye to Ben, but Ethan hides on the stairs, peaking around the corner.

"Call your mother. NOW!" Ben hugs and kisses me goodbye, and hugs Elena too while she thanks him profusely for loaning her his car. He thanks her for returning it one piece, and they are the best of friends. The minute Ben's gone Ethan is back in the kitchen. I suggest that he go upstairs and paint for a while. He declines. Elena takes the situation in hand, though, and forces him to go up and get his school work together.

He's barely out of the room when I begin the interrogation. "Did you find Finn?"

"Did you think I wouldn't?"

"Did he do it?" I cut to the chase.

She doesn't get to answer. A sudden wrap on the door puts an end to my fact finding mission. The police officers are polite, but their timing couldn't be worse. They ask if it's alright to come in ask us a few questions. I know that they wouldn't be here unless they'd already obtained consent from Iron Lady and Rachel to question us as minors without their presence. The very first question they ask sends us scrambling.

“I'm Henderson, my partner is DeSocio. We were informed that there were three minors residing here. Is that right?" The female officer speaks, scanning the living-room as she makes the introductions.

Elena looks at me. "Yes. My twin brother lives here too."

"Is he here now?" she asks. I look at Elena. I want her to lie. Ethan will not be able to deal with this.

"Um. Yes, but he's not really available," she fumbles.

The male cop looks like he's in no mood for nonsense. "Look, we need to talk to each of you separately. We can do it here or we can down to the station. Your choice," he says, staring me down.

"Here would definitely be better, " I say. "The issue is not the time or the location, the problem is that he kind of suffers from PTSD."

The cop rolls his eyes, "Don't we all, kid."

"No, not like that." I'm fumbling too. "He's got severe, really severe social anxiety, plus he's got the emotional maturity of a four year old."

"Hey, Henderson," he addresses his partner, "Sounds like your last boyfriend."

"Nice, DeSocio! Real sensitive." she fires back with a sardonic smirk.

Then he turns back to me. "Look, kid, I don't care if the boy wears diapers and sees giant purple kangaroos. We need to talk to him."

Elena chimes in, "Well, he got half of it right anyway." I throw her eye darts.

This is going to be a monumental train wreck and there's nothing I can do to stop it.

"Now Henderson here is gonna go with one of you to bring the other one in here, so you don't get a chance to square your stories."

He's really pissing me off. My mouth is moving before my brain knows what's happening. "Don't you think we would have gotten all our stories straight already. We had all night, ya know." I don't mean to, but I mimic his accent and cadence.

"Let's assume you aren't that smart," he jibes.

"All right then, but your partner there is going to question 'the other one,' not you." I point to the female cop.

"Who's calling the shots here? You or me?" He stands up straighter.

"You, but you should listen to me because if you try to question Ethan with that attitude of yours, you're gonna get nothing but a meltdown that I'm gonna have to spend the day cleaning up after."

“My attitude!” he mumbles, but he's kind of done with me, so he turns to Elena. "So this is how it's gonna work. Two of you in here with one of us, and the other one of you questioned by the other one of us out there." He points outside. Then he turns to me. "You got any problem with that, Missy?"

I think about it for a minute. "Actually, the best way to do this would be for you to interview Elena while Henderson interviews me. Then one of us can be with Ethan while Henderson interviews him. Yeah, and the name is Sage, not Missy."

"My god! Where are the damn parents here? Are you always this bossy?"

"Is this part of the interrogation?" I ask.

"Henderson, get her outa here before I take her in for being a smartass."

Henderson smiles as she leads me out to the pool deck. "You're winning him over."

She's nice, but I know that friendly means loose-lipped. "Let's just do this, okay?" I say.

Her smile fades. "Fine. Let's start with where you were last night before the fire. The fire chief has you showing up after the trucks."

"I was with my Uncle Ben at the Exodus Cafe."

"And before that?"

Shit! I can't really lie to the cops. Besides I'm pretty sure Ben told them. "I was at my dad's apartment, south of the river. We were supposed to have dinner."

"Your father is Jacob Wester. That right?"

"That's right."

"How did you end up with your Uncle Ben?"

"My dad and I had a fight. I called Ben to pick me up."

"Were you aware the police responded to a domestic violence call at Mr. Wester's address yesterday around 6:30 pm?"

"It was a loud fight. I left before the officers arrived."

Henderson pauses and takes off her hat. Her hair is a pretty auburn color. Her eyes soften along with her voice. "Are you afraid of your father, Sage?"

"No." I say it too quickly and I look away. She knows I'm lying.

"Did he know that your mom was out of town?"

Damn it Ben! He planted this line of questioning in their minds. "My dad would never hurt me or my mom. He's not a great dad, but he's not violent." I see the door go down and the wild look in his eyes. I push it from my mind and hope that Henderson can't read my thoughts.

"What did you fight about, Sage?"

"Stupid teenage stuff. I snuck out to be with my boyfriend last weekend." I know it's the wrong answer before I finish the sentence.

"Who's your boyfriend?"

I am sooo stupid! Now I've involved Finn, even if Elena manages to avoid it, but why would she? His record will come up, and this time he won't be mandated to therapy. "Do I have to answer that? I'm sure he's not involved."

"Then it won't hurt anything to tell me who he is." She's not letting me off.

"Yeah, well, the thing is, my mom would freak if she knew I was dating this guy."

"Not really my problem, Sage." Her hat's back on at least figuratively.

I shift nervously from foot to foot, but I'm not talking.

Henderson looks me up and down. "Look at this, Sage." She points to what's left of the garage. "This was NOT an accident. Someone who may have thought you and your mom were home trashed this place. They tried to kill you, and I'm not being melodramatic. If you don't help us do our job right now, the next time this happens, you won't be talking to me the next day. Do you understand?"

I nod solemnly. "Finn Mulcahy."

"How did you and Finn meet?"

"Through my mom." It's not a lie.

"Son of a friend or something?"

"Or something."

"One of your mother's patients?" She's quick; I have to give her that.

"Afraid so." Right now all I can see is Rachel's face when she realizes what I have been doing behind her back. I just want to slip out of my own skin and find a better person underneath.

"Sage, you need to focus. We're almost done. I asked how you and Finn are getting along. Any fights?"

Damn this sucks worse than anything. I could just blatantly lie, but then Elena or Ethan could totally contradict me. "He's been kind of jealous lately."

"Why?"

"I spend a lot of time with the twins here."

She gives me a look. "He does realize you live here."

I nearly slip and say they have history, but I recover. "I've been kind of neglectful . . . as a girlfriend."

"Second thoughts?" I can hear the acerbic barista yelling "buyer's remorse" in the back of my head.

"A little, maybe." No reason to lie about that.

"This Finn guy, has he ever been violent with you?"

"No." Too fast, too loud again. I just want this to be over.

"You sure about that?" She takes a step closer.

"Yes." I look down at my feet.

"Sage, you're a smart girl and a terrible liar. You seem pretty together, responsible and all, so I'm gonna ask you something that I normally wouldn't ask a witness. If you were a betting girl, who would you put your money on for the arsonist here?"

I'd put my money on Finn . . . or my father, but saying either one out loud is not in me. "I really have no idea. The idea of anyone wanting to hurt me or my mom is absurd. I'm afraid I've got nothing."

She puts her hat back on. "Okay let's go talk to the boy," she sighs disappointedly and looks up at the house. Ethan has been watching us from the upstairs window. He's sucking his thumb. Perfect!

Henderson looks at me like she's convinced now.

I fill her in on what to expect. "Look a couple of ground rules for dealing with Ethan. First, do NOT touch him. All hell will break loose. Second, remember that he's a four year old. I know he looks like a teenager, but trust me he's not. Keep it simple. Third, don't expect too much. He doesn't really talk to strangers."

"I'll be gentle with him," she promises sincerely.

She follows me up the stairs. The door to Ethan's room is closed. I knock on it quietly. "Hey, E, it's me. Can I come in?"

"Only you, Sage. No one else."

I motion to Henderson to stay in the hall while I go in. I leave the door open. Ethan's sitting in the window seat.

I sit down next to him, take his thumb out of his mouth, and hold onto his hand. "Hey, E. The lady who was talking to me outside wants to talk to you too. Do you think you can do that?"

He shakes his head. "I don't want to talk about the fire."

I think hard about how to make this happen. "Do you know who that lady is?"

Ethan nods nervously, eyeing Henderson who's lingering outside the door. "I talked to the police at the hospital. I don't want to again."

Henderson interrupts, "I didn't see anything in the report about anyone being transported to the hospital."

"Different fire, long time ago. Unfortunately, this isn't his first rodeo." I explain.

"Different fire?" Ethan seems confused.

I get up and put my hands on his shoulders to point him toward the window, but everything goes wonky, and my last thought is, "Not now, Ethan."

The woman from the painting is pulling me up the stairs. Her face is inches from mine, and her moonstone fairy earring glitters in my eyes.

"Ethan, just come with me, and you'll be safe. Hurry!"

"No, no. I don't want to. I want to leave."

She's pulling me into the bathroom. Elena is there too, a skinny little girl with long messy hair. She reaches out to me, but I'm trying to pull away to get out of there. The tub is running. Mommy closes the door and locks it.

"Please, Mommy! Let's go get ice cream or drive to grandmother's house." I'm desperate.

"Not now, Ethan!" She yells.

The charred and collapsed garage comes into focus. I try to remember where I was in the conversation. "Remember last night, Mouse." I pant, pointing out the window, but he won't look.

"I don't want to talk anymore," He turns in to me, wraps his arms around me and buries his face in my shoulder.

Henderson must have come in while I was out of it. She's standing next to us. "Just four questions, Ethan. I promise to keep them simple." Her voice is soft and soothing.

Ethan pulls away from me a little and looks at her. "I'm tired."

"I understand. It will only take two minutes. Can you try?" She's really good at this.

Ethan shrugs, but he turns to look at her. He holds onto my hand with both of his and leans against me.

"Thank you. Question one: Were you here alone when the fire started last night?"

Ethan glances down for a minute like he's trying to remember. "Yes, I think so."

"Good job!" She makes a move like she's going to touch him. I inhale sharply, and she remembers not to and pulls back. "Okay, second question: What happened before the fire yesterday?"

"I took a nap with Sage, and then Finn came when I was swimming alone, and then I couldn't get back all the way. I was so cold, but Sage wrapped me up in the blanket and then she had to go with her dad, but Elena was supposed to be at home soon and she wasn't. That's all I remember." He's out of breath and squeezing my hand a little too hard.

"That was a lot. You did great. Take a deep breath." Ethan takes a deep breath with her. "Okay. Third question: When did you realize the garage was on fire?"

This question seems to stress Ethan out more than the others. He looks away and shuffles his feet uncomfortably. After what feels like an unbearable wait, he mumbles, "I smelled smoke and gas in the kitchen. Can three be enough?" he asks me.

"You're doing amazing, Ethan. Only one more," Henderson is not going to let three be enough. "Last one: What did you do when you smelled the smoke and gas?"

He looks at her almost angrily, "I went outside."

"Why did you do that? Why didn't you stay inside away from the fire?"

He's really agitated now, and he lets go of me. "We have to get out of the house if there's a fire. If you stay inside with the fire, you'll get burned!" He throws his left arm out to show her his scar.

She's a little shocked by his reaction, but she recovers quickly. "Ethan, the fire wasn't in this house; it was in the garage."

Now the tears spill over. "That isn't a question, and you lied! That was six not four. No more questions and no more not-questions!" His voice is loud and angry in a way I have never seen before.

Even Henderson knows that the interview is over. I follow her to the door.

Ethan calls silently to Elena. I don't hear it, but I know.

She's already on her way up the stairs. She looks at me accusingly and closes the door behind her.

"I think he was confused." I say.

"Really?" Henderson counters. "He seemed perfectly clear to me."

"In the other fire, when he was four, he was trapped in the house. That's how he got burned." I don't know why I'm being so defensive.

"Good to know," Henderson says dismissing me. "Thank you for your time this morning, Miss Evans. We'll be in touch." She hands me her card and sweeps through the kitchen. DeSocio follows on her heels like their exit has been choreographed.

I watch the cruiser back down the driveway and pull away. Then I sit at the table with another cup of coffee and call Rachel.

She picks up on the second ring, "We're okay, Mom."

"Sage, why didn't you call me right away?"

"What happened to 'I'm glad you're alive?'"

"Sorry, Herbie. I'm just a little worried about what's happening there, and the damage, and then there's all the stuff here."

"I know, Madre. I'm so sorry. I really screwed up."

"Did you set the fire?"

"Mom! Of course not."

"Then how is this your fault? Look, I don't have a lot of time. We're on a layover. They're about to call for us to board. We'll be home by dinner."

"Okay, but we're all just fine."

"That's awesome because we're bringing someone home to meet the twins."

"Just give them a couple of days to catch their breath. The cops just left here, and it was not pretty."

"Sounds like good advice." She pauses. "I want you to know I'm really proud of how you've handled all of this."

"Thanks, Mom." I hang up feeling like this may be the last time I ever hear my mom tell me she's proud. When she finds out what I did with Finn, and how I played spy with my dangerous, crazy father, and that one of them burned down our house and tried to kill us, I'll be lucky if she doesn't send me away to military school. The thing that has me completely flummoxed though is why I didn't hand over the thumb drive to the cops and fry my dad's ass. What am I waiting for? Finn deserves to be heard out, though, and I still don't know what went down with him and Elena last night. My head is reeling by the time Ethan and Elena come back down. They're dressed and ready for the day to begin.

We sit at the table in silence for a while. All I can think about is how I did this to them.

"I'm so sorry, you guys. This is all my fault." My voice is choked, and I put my head in my hands. Elena reaches across the table palms up.

"No, I deserve to feel this guilt," I tell her.

"That's beside the point," she says.

I put my hands in hers, and immediately the sun is brighter, the walls are whiter, and all of this seems so temporary and easy to fix.

"Now what should we do today? Rachel said that they will be back by dinner time." I say.

"We should clean up the house," Ethan suggests.

Elena smiles at me, "Well played, Sage."

We divide the tasks and send Ethan upstairs to tidy the TV room and the bathroom. When we're finally alone, Elena doesn't waste any time.

"I found Finn last night, but it took a while. He was not where I thought he'd be. After the graveyard, I went by his house. His dad was barely-standing drunk, but he remembered me or should I say he remembered my mother. He called me Lana . . . and a bitch . . . and a dyke. Whatever! He told me that I hadn't aged at all. Duh! I'm like seventeen. It was freaking weird. He kept saying I ruined his life. After a while, I got him to tell me that Finn usually hangs out with his boys at the Tavern.

I found them there upstairs shooting pool. The guys confirmed that they had just gotten there, and that Finn wasn't with them earlier. He wasn't with his dad either judging by how drunk he was. In fact I don't think anyone had seen him since he left here after the incident with Ethan."

"Did you talk to Finn?"

"He showed up at the Tavern about twenty minutes after I got there. He was not happy to see me there and ignored me until he was good and drunk. He was really messed up by Ethan. He talked a lot about the fire he saw in Ethan's mind, but not a word about the one here last night. I just let him ramble, waited for him to trip up. Nothing. I drove him home after closing. He wants to see you, Sage. He was adamant on that point. I really want to say he did it, but I'm not completely convinced. You should to go talk to him." She pauses. "I mean today."

I check the time, 11 o'clock. "He'll be waking up about now," I say.

"You better change first. You're cute as hell in Ethan's clothes, but I don't think Finn will appreciate it."

"Roger that." I run upstairs and change into one of the four outfits I now own, the only clean one in fact. Ethan meets me in the hall.

"Where you going?"

I hate lying to him, but it's better than upsetting him. "I'm going out for some groceries. Is there anything you want?"

"Cherries," he says quietly.

"I don't think they're in season, but I'll look for them." I kiss him on the forehead and turn to go.

"Sage, I'm sorry I got mad before."

"It's okay, Mouse. You did fine. Don't worry about it. Okay?"

"Okay," he says, but he doesn't seem okay.

I go back and give him a hug. "I won't be long. Help Elena get the house cleaned up."

I feel like I'm taking only half my heart. It's harder to breath and it hurts to move. I wonder if Ethan feels like this too.

Outside of Finn's house I stand next to the car and assess the damage this visit could do. If his dad answers the door, I could cover by giving a made up name, or I could just hope Finn's dad doesn't know that his shrink has a kid with my name. It probably doesn't matter anyway since Rachel is going to know about me and Finn from the cops anyway. My inner debate is silenced by the commotion coming from the house. Finn's dad throws a duffle bag out the front door onto the lawn. He stumbles on his way back in and leaves the door hanging open.

"Get the fuck out of my house," his dad slurs loud enough for me to hear from across the street.

Finn moves into the hallway where I can see him casting about for solid footing. "Who was on the phone? Damn it!"

"Figure it out, genius! Every chance you get to fuck up, you're just gonna take it! Aren't you?"

"You can't throw me out! It violates my parole. They'll throw me in jail." His voice is shaking, desperate.

"You're going to jail anyway, asshole!"

"What the hell are you talking about?" Finn's voice is plaintive.

"You dumbshit, you can't play me like that. I know what you did yesterday. You stupid fuck!" Finn's dad kind of laughs coldly. "I am done with you, boy! Get out of my house!" He grabs Finn's arm and tries to haul him out the door.

"Just tell me what I did." Finn spins out of his grasp. Despite his father's inebriated state, he manages to pull back and land a powerful punch squarely into Finn's jaw. The force is so fierce that Finn falls backward, smashing his head against the wall. He ends up on his knees at his father's feet. Even from here I can see the blood trickling from the side of Finn's mouth.

His head is down, but I can hear the tears in his voice, "Please, dad . . . please."

"No more," his dad says. I think he's going to walk away and just leave Finn there in the hall, but he turns back around, and as Finn struggles to his feet, his father plants his foot in Finn's back and sends him careening out the door and down the concrete steps. Finn lands in a face-plant on the walkway. He doesn't bother getting up; he rolls over onto his back and stays there. I'm just about to run across the street to him when his father comes back out. He hurls a set of keys at Finn's head, but misses by a mile. Then he says in strangely calm voice, "Take the damn bike. Maybe you'll kill yourself and put us both out of our misery." He doesn't go back inside. He stands there staring at Finn with loathing. Then he sees me. Finn must see his focus shift because he sits up and turns to see what his father is looking at.

I can't read the look on Finn's face because he gets up quickly, wiping his arm across his eyes and then his mouth. Keeping his back to me, Finn picks up the duffle and keys and attaches the bag to the back of the motorcycle in the driveway. He gets on and guns the motor as he pulls out. Almost without stopping, he tosses me his helmet and grabs my wrist, pulling me onto the back of the bike. I have no idea where we're going, but I pull the helmet on, wrap my arms around his chest, and press myself against his back like the night he had the nightmare. This time there's no question; I can feel the spasms of his sobs and his tears splashing down onto my hands.

By the time he stops the bike at the cliff, he's calm. The ground is scorched from the other night; it reminds me to tread lightly with Finn, especially in the raw state he's in right now. He gets off the bike and walks to the edge of the cliff like he's going to jump. I follow at a distance. Suddenly he spins around.

"What were you doing at my house?" It's an accusation.

"I needed to talk to you." I hesitate before going on. "About what happened yesterday?"

"First Elena; now you. I must have really scrambled the freak's egg." He's smiling, but it's all bravado, misdirection.

"Actually, this isn't about Ethan; it's about you . . . and me."

"Are you gonna kick me to the curb too." He tries to play it off by clearing his throat, but his voice breaks.

I have business to take care of here, but my heart is calling out to him too. I want to put my arms around him and tell him that I remember the night he rescued me, and now it's my turn to rescue him, but what if he started the fire? What if he's that jealous, that dangerous? How stupid would I be then? "No, Finn. I don't want to kick you anywhere."

He smiles a little and moves closer to me. "Good." He takes my hand, and we start walking. There's a trail head about a quarter of a mile up the road. We've passed it before. For a long time we hike through the woods in silence. Then the trail emerges into a clearing, and the whole gorge opens in front of us with the river snaking far below. Above the path is an out-cropping big enough for three or four people to sit on. We scramble up to it. From the path below no one would know anyone was here.

"What are you going to do?" I ask after we get settled and take in the view.

"About what?" He's far away, but my question brings him back. "Nothing. Lie low, wait for my dad to sober up and remember that he loved my mom, and I'm all he's got left of her even if he does hate my guts."

"I'm sure he doesn't hate you." I think about the fact that there's a fifty-fifty chance that my father tried to kill me last night.

Finn laughs. "I'm sure he hates me." Maybe he's right. After a couple minutes, he starts talking low and sad. "You know how moms and dads kiss their kids good-night or good-bye when they leave for school. They always say, 'love you,' like it's no big deal. Sometimes kids say it back, sometimes not. It doesn't matter, because the kid gets the message. After a while the parents don't even have to say it anymore. It just takes a look. I bet you know what I'm talking about."

I nod, "Sure. Rachel used to say it so often I had to tell her to stop sometimes."

"Yeah, I can see that. Rachel is like the first person who ever made me feel like I mattered to someone. Then you came along." He looks out at the horizon. "Anyway my mother was like that. I wasn't even three when she died, but I remember her telling me every second of every day that she loved me. Maybe she tried to get it all in 'cause she knew she wouldn't be here now." He doesn't even try to cover it. The tears are streaming down his face. He doesn't want my comfort though. It's not like when Ethan cries, and he just wants to held and rocked. This is different, and it hurts me too, like there's an icepick slowly piercing me all the way through just above my left breast.

When he's composed again, he goes on. It's like this story has been building inside him just waiting for an audience. "Back then, before she died, I guess maybe my father loved me too, but he never said it. I don't know. Maybe he only ever really loved her. I remember them fighting though. He was sad a lot." He should be telling this to Rachel. She would know what to do, what to say.

He looks at me, and suddenly leans in and kisses me deep and slow. It takes away some of the ache in my chest. He turns away then and looks down at the river far below us. "When she was there on the floor, shot, bleeding out quart by quart, all the love he had in him spilled out onto that floor too. The empty space in his veins and arteries filled with black miserable hatred that he pours out onto me. I think he blames me for that gunshot like I was the one who pulled the trigger. I would give anything to go back and relive that night. Do it different."

"Do what different, Finn? You were like two years old. How could anyone blame you?"

He raises his eyebrows like this never occurred to him. "I guess if someone tells you that something is your fault enough times, you just believe it. You start to wish that you were different, blameless. You just want to undo everything."

I want to ask why he shot her and how Finn could possibly be to blame, but that would be the worst thing I could do right now. Instead I turn his chin toward me and kiss him.

He takes off his shirt and folds it into a pillow. I lie down on the cool stone and let him unbutton my blouse. He lies beside me, touches the skin of my neck, around the top of my breasts like he is trying to absorb me through his fingertips. When that's not enough, he kisses me, tastes me with his tongue. The dirt from his hand falls onto my belly, and he sweeps it carefully away, before kissing me there, slowly, gently, again and again as he unbuttons my shorts and slides his hand inside. I can barely breathe. Then he slips my shorts down following their path with the tip of his tongue down my inner thigh.

My turn. I guide him onto his back and free him from his shorts, lick around the tip until he moans. I giggle; it makes him smile. He flips me onto my back. Kisses me again. He takes a break to get a condom out of his wallet, but he doesn't slip it on right away. While he's busy with that, I get rid of my bra and shirt. He takes the hint and teases my nipples with his tongue until I squeal. He lies back and looks at the clouds. I climb on top of him let my hips play out what I want to do when my panties are off and he's finally inside me. With my fingers I trace the shape of his face, fine lines of his chest, and the curves below his belly, memorizing his lines. His eyes are deep and contented. I could swim there forever.

He sits up and pushes me to standing, strips me naked, unsheathes the condom and rolls it on. Then ever so gently he lowers me onto him, so we are sitting chest-to-chest, face-to-face. I have never felt any pleasure so deep, this feeling of him inside me, around me, utterly connected in every way. We grind in a rhythm that sets my brain on fire. The sweat is trickling down my back as the heat builds. Now I'm the one moaning, pressing into him harder and harder as I feel the approaching explosion. Then time stops. The meager clouds understand as they freeze in place. I close my eyes and let the release spread through every pore from my center up through the top of my head. For a moment I don't even need oxygen. I am only spirit and senses until I take a deep shaking breath.

The power of speech eludes me, and Finn thinks that this is the most amusing thing he has ever seen. He's laughing even as he changes our position, so I am on my back. Then he is all business, lacing his fingers through mine and holding my hands down above my head. I wrap my legs around his back to help him. After a couple of false starts, we find our rhythm again. I watch his face get more and more intent as he gets closer and closer to climax, and I hold my breath with him as he crests the wave.

This time he doesn't roll off and dance away. This time he stays inside me until he can't anymore. Then, we wrap ourselves around each other and hold on as though a tornado may come and blow us apart. I breathe him into every cell as he tangles his fingers through my hair.

"You turn me inside out, Stalker girl." he mumbles sleepily.

"Back at you, Fire-boy." The minute I say it, the reason for being here comes back to me like a headache. Without getting up or looking at him, I just say it. "Finn, our apartment, the Paige's garage, burnt down last night."

He doesn't say anything. I turn my head and look up into his eyes. I can't read the myriad of emotions playing across that sea, so I wait.

"You think I did it," he finally says.

"I didn't say that."

He pushes me off him and gets dressed. I follow his lead. "At least I know why Elena showed up last night and why my dad wigged out on me."

"Tell me you didn't set the fire. I'll believe you."

"No, you won't. I wouldn't even believe myself." He pulls me into a hug, and kisses my forehead. "Thanks, Sage."

"For what?" My head is reeling.

"For today. For telling me. For giving me a chance."

"What are you gonna do?" I want to take him home, protect him somehow.

"Get a hotel room, pay in cash, give a fake name. Same old, same old. I've done it a hundred times since I was fourteen."

"Where will you get the money?"

He laughs. "Don't worry, I'm not going to boost a liquor store or anything. Since I turned twelve, every Friday my dad leaves five hundreds on the kitchen table. He thinks that means he's taking care of me. Most of the time I just save it. I have thousands of dollars in the bank. At one point I thought I might use it for college. Now I use it for shit like this." He jumps down from the ledge and reaches up to catch me.

"That's great, and it sucks at the same time," I say.

He laughs again. "What a way with words you have."

On the way back to the bike we argue about him telling me where I can find him. He says that he's not going to tell me because he doesn't want me to lie to the cops. I lose that one, but before we go back into town, I have one last bit of business to attend to, and I need a win. "Finn, you have to stop this thing with Ethan."

He frowns. "No, Sage, you have to stop this thing with Ethan."

How can I make him understand? "It's not like that with him."

"What is it like then, Sage? And before you answer, remember I took a little trip through his mind too."

I have no idea what to say to this. It worries and fascinates me that Ethan could think of me the same way Finn does.

"I'll make this easy for you, Sage," he says. "Just tell me you don't love him." He waits while I struggle with my thoughts. "Yeah, that's what I thought."

"This is stupid, Finn! Being jealous of Ethan is more ridiculous than being jealous of Elena."

"If the idea of you and Elena together wasn't so hot, I might be jealous of her too. Don't give me any ideas." We're at the bike and he's handing me the helmet, effectively ending the discussion. There's just no winning today.

Chapter 12 (Earth, Wind, and Water)

A philosopher thousands of years ago suggested that time flows like a ribbon in space, all of time existing always. We are tiny ants on that ribbon walking in a line, everyone moving in the same direction on some urgent business that consumes our perception, so all we can desire is what lies ahead and all we fear is chasing us from behind.

By the time I get home with cherries, the house is spotless, and the guy from the pool company is cleaning out the debris and trying to adjust the pH.

"Where's Ethan? I brought him some cherries."

Elena's at the sink putting the last dish in the dishwasher. "He's beside himself about not being able to swim until tomorrow." She turns around to face me. "OMG! What did you do Sage?"

She's looking at me like the words "I just had sex with Finn" are written across my forehead. "What?" I ask as innocently as possible.

"You didn't! Please tell me you didn't." She's in full-on mom mode.

"What are you going on about?" Admit nothing, I tell myself.

"At least go take a shower before you see Ethan. He's upset enough about you going to see Finn. He will freak if he smells Finn on you like that. Jesus, Sage. Hasn't any of this made an impression on you?"

"You told Ethan where I was?" I'm incredulous.

"I didn't have to tell Ethan where you were. He probably knew where you were going before you did. I thought you were catching on here."

I'm a total idiot. The cherries were a diversion. He knew, and I should have seen that.

Elena stands with her hands on her hips. "So what did he say?"

"It wasn't Finn. The fire. It wasn't Finn," I say without conviction.

"Says the girl who's so easily seduced. Wow! I'm convinced." Her sarcasm is deserved.

"Now who's the buzz-kill," I throw back, heading upstairs.

Ethan comes out of his room before I can duck into the bathroom all the way. "I got you some cherries, Mouse," I say from behind the door.

"I missed you," he says as I close it.

I peek back out. "Five minutes, E. I really need a shower. I missed you too."

He sits down in the hall across from the bathroom to wait. I wish I could go out and give him a hug right now. After my shower, I put Ethan's clothes back on. Even though I wore them all night, they still smell like him.

Rachel and Iron Lady show up at dinner time as promised. Elena and I have managed to put a pretty respectable welcome home dinner together for them. We're all in the kitchen when Ben's car pulls up the driveway. Seconds later Rachel sweeps in ahead of Iron Lady, gathers me into her arms, and holds me so tight I can't breathe. Iron Lady barely wraps her arms around Elena, but I can see tears in the corners of her eyes. Rachel moves on to Elena, who she hugs much more tenderly, while Iron Lady thanks me for keeping the house so nice. Ethan hovers in the doorway of the kitchen like a humming bird, part of the excitement until Ben comes in with the suitcases. Then he's gone, hiding on the staircase as usual. I excuse myself and follow him. He's sitting on the stairs about halfway up, where Iron Lady goes to listen to Elena sing him to sleep. He moves over to make room for me.

"Hey, Mouse. What are you doing out here?"

"Too loud, too many people," he explains, laying his head on my shoulder.

"You know, Rachel and Lily are happy to see you too. They've been worried about you."

"I know."

"You should come down to dinner and show them that you're okay. Can you do that?" I ask.

"Can that man leave first?"

I laugh a little. "That man is Ben. He's a really good friend to me and Rachel. You should give him a chance."

"I don't want him here." He takes hold of my hand for comfort.

"Ethan, sometimes, lots of times, actually, we have to do things that scare us, and after we do them, we aren't scared anymore. Do you remember the first time you met me?"

Ethan nods. "I was really scared."

"Aren't you glad we met now?"

He laughs, "Of course!" his smile dissolves quickly. "He won't like me."

"Of course he will. I liked you right away when we met."

Ethan looks at his feet. "He saw . . . when I had an accident."

"Oh. E, it was a bad night for everyone. Ben isn't going to hold that against you. I'm sure he understands how scared you were. Come on, you can do this." Everyone in the kitchen is taking their seats around the table. Elena leaves the two nearest the door for us.

He peaks around the corner, and sits back down, thinking about it. I stand up, and he reluctantly follows me into the kitchen in much the same way he followed Elena the night we met, one hand holding mine and the other holding my arm. Most of the meal consists of Rachel giving us the third degree, and Ben and Elena exchanging sarcasm and well-matched wit. Even Ethan laughs at their banter and manages to leave Ben with a much better impression than the last time they met. He makes it all the way through the meal holding my hand, then jets before dessert is served. Iron Lady takes a bowl of ice cream up to him while Elena and I clear the table.

As soon as dessert is done, Ben heads out, and Rachel takes charge of me. "Get your stuff together, we should go too. It's been a long day, and I'm sure Lily would like to spend some time with the twins. I found us a nice hotel just north of here."

Lily won't hear of us leaving, "Nonsense, Rachel. After all you and Sage have done for us, the least I can do is put you up. Sage can bunk with Elena, and you can have the attic room."

I didn't even know there was an attic room. Based on Rachel's reaction, she didn't know about it either. Iron Lady leads us through the archway in the living room to a room behind the kitchen, her room. I'm wishing now that I had stayed here. The room has two levels. On the bottom level is the bed, dresser, like a normal, simple yet elegant bedroom. In one corner a spiral staircase leads up to a cat walk about three feet wide that encircles the perimeter of the room eight feet up. The wall of the walkway is floor to ceiling bookcases filled with novels, plays, and poetry books. At the far end of the cat-walk is a cozy alcove with two chairs and a balcony overlooking the lower level. She leads us up to the alcove where there are two doors, one that goes to a bathroom and the other that leads up a steep stairwell to the attic. The attic room is long with a slanted roof, a big iron bed at one end, overstuffed chairs beside fancy little tables, and a long mahogany desk built into the wall. The floors are polished hardwood covered with bright rugs that look Guatemalan. It’s hotter than hell up here, but Iron Lady throws a switch that initiates the low hum of the attic fan, and in about five minutes the temperature is almost comfortable.

"We'll have to share the bathroom in the loft, but you can stay here as long as you need to," she says to Rachel.

Rachel looks like she's going to cry. Iron Lady leaves us there alone to catch up. I collapse on the bed while Rachel unpacks her suitcase into the antique dresser.

"How are you doing, Herbie? The truth,"

I've been holding it together all this time so I can take care of everyone else, and now faced with the prospect of someone taking care of me, I hesitate. If I let myself feel anything, then the pain is going to be bad, really bad.

"I feel pretty numb to tell you the truth, Madre. I can't let it be real yet."

"I get that."

"Did you look at the damage? I ask.

"I couldn't," she says. "Have you?"

"Only from a distance."

Rachel hesitates, then says, "Sage, you know that the fire was not accidental, right?"

"The police told me that," I confirm.

"There's a possibility that one of my clients is involved in this."

I know she means Finn. This is it, my chance to come clean with her and tell her about our relationship. My heart pounds in my ears so loudly, I can hardly hear her go on.

"The boy I'm talking about has a history of starting fires, and this fire looks a lot like the other fires he's started. Though I'm sure if he is involved, he wasn't trying to hurt anyone. He knew that I would be away for a week at least."

I want to say, "Are you talking about Finnian Mulcahy? Actually, I know him, so do Ethan and Elena. In fact I made love to him just a few hours ago." Argh! There's no way to do this! I really want to do the right thing. Instead I say, "Are you sure it was him?"

She looks at me a little strangely. "You think it could be someone else?"

I'm going to jump off a different cliff here and assume that Ben blabbed about the fight with my father. "I had a huge fight with Dad. It was really bad. It happened a couple hours before the fire started."

Rachel is the picture of concern, but I can tell she isn't taking me seriously. "What happened?"

How much do I spill? I want to at least look at the thumb-drive before I throw my father under the bus. "Here's the twitter version: I broke his rules, lied, and stole from him. It was all for a really good reason, but he freaked. We're talking wounded-animal freaked. I've never seen anyone so angry in my life. I can't get into the details. Please don't ask."

"Sage, if you're in danger, I need to know exactly what's going on."

"I promise I'll tell you tomorrow. I just need to sleep on it tonight, sort through the whole thing in my head. Please. Nothing's going to happen tonight."

Rachel thinks about it, then concedes, and shifts gears. "Ben said that the night of the fire things got kind of crazy here. Do you want to talk about that?"

"Mom, the garage was on fire, and the twins were probably both having major PTSD flashbacks. Elena just needed to get out of dodge, so I told her to borrow Ben's car. I think she went to a movie or something because she came home really late, but totally fine." I hate lying about this, but I keep going. "Ethan had a bit of a meltdown, wet his pants, kind of went semi-catatonic on me, not a big deal considering everything."

"Okay then. What about you, kiddo?"

"I wasn't here when it started. I was at Dad's and then with Ben. If I had been here . . ." My voice is rising like I'm angry, but I'm not angry, at least I don't think I am.

"It's okay, Sage. I am sharing that guilt in a big way. I shouldn't have left you with all of this; it wasn't fair." She sits down next to me on the bed and rubs my back. Maybe I am a little angry at her for leaving me here. "I'm sorry about the police this morning too. Lily and I gave them permission to question you guys. I didn't think it should wait. Plus, I wanted them looking in on you in case there was any further danger. How did that go?"

"About like you'd expect. Elena got defensive, I got mouthy, and Ethan cried."

Rachel laughs at my depiction of the inquisition. "Those poor cops."

"Hey, what about us? Poor us!"

"Of course, poor, poor Sage!" She rubs my hair into knots.

In the pause that follows, I have a thought that could save us all. "Mom, what if Lily just forgets about the whole thing? Can't she just send the cops away or something? I mean it's her property that burned and no one was hurt."

Rachel laughs ironically. "That isn't likely. Lily is . . . how can I say this nicely? . . . a determined woman with an ax to grind. She isn't interested in why the fire was started. Someone needs to be made to take responsibility and it's not important who that someone is."

"What if it was one of the twins?"

Rachel raises an eyebrow. "As their therapist, I can tell you that neither of the twins is capable of arson. They have anger, but it's all turned inward. Frankly, though, I doubt Lily'd even let them off the hook. Lily has some anger issues too." She shakes her head wryly.

"She would have to press charges to get the insurance money anyway."

"Oh," I say quietly.

"Why would you ask such a thing?" she asks gently.

"I don't know. I'm just confused, I guess. I don't understand how anyone could do this." I lay my head in my arms.

"You look exhausted, Herbie. Why don't you go to bed?"

"You too, Madre." She gives me a half smile. I pause then ask, "Hey, can I borrow your computer tonight? Mine is kind of dust." I say it as a joke, but it makes me feel like I was punched in the stomach. "Just plastic and circuits," I mumble to myself.

"Of course. You'll need to use the guest login that's set up." She goes to the desk and writes the password for me and hands me the computer bag."

"I'm gonna go now, 'kay? Sweet dreams, Madre."

"You too, Baby."

I make my way back through Iron Lady's room and marvel again at the library-like elegance of it. I pause to browse the bookshelves. Everything from Cervantes to Umberto Eco; Iron Lady and I have this in common for sure. I wonder if she loves movies too. Probably not.

"You can borrow whatever you like," her voice makes me jump. She's sitting in the alcove with a cup of tea and a book. I'm not sure how I missed seeing her when I came down from the attic. "You like reading?"

I nod. "I've read some of these." I point to the section with D.H. Lawrence and Charles Dickens.

"Hmmm. Old Brits. You're something else, Sage. More than meets the eye."

"Thanks, I guess." I start to head toward the spiral staircase.

"Please, take a book with you," she insists.

Even though I've read it before, I take D. H. Lawrence's *The Rainbow* off the shelf. "Thanks," I say showing her the book.

"Interesting choice. Good-night, Sage."

When I get upstairs, Ethan and Elena are playing cards in the TV room. They don't see me at first. Ethan's back is to the stairs, and Elena's head is bent in concentration. From the changing expressions on their faces, I can see that they're "talking." I wish I could hear what they were saying. Ethan is ready for bed in his boxers and t-shirt. I'm sure he's been waiting for me. Elena looks up.

"Lurking on the stairs. Really?" She asks, raising an eyebrow.

"Did you really just use the word 'lurking?'" I respond.

"Were you spying on us?" she shoots back. “Answer truthfully or suffer the consequences.” She throws out a pointed finger like a witch casting a spell.

"No! No! Not the consequences,” I recoil in mock terror.

Ethan laughs at us. Maybe it's the best sound in the universe. He jumps up and pulls me over to join them. "Now we can play spoons. You have to have three," he says.

He grabs two spoons from the table by the couch. "Grandmother and I had ice cream for dessert," he explains. "But don't worry; I washed them."

"Good thinking," I say, placing the spoons in the middle while Elena deals the cards.

The first round is quiet, subdued, but each round gets more and more raucous. It feels good to scream and tousle for the spoons, but no matter how much I want to be, I'm not fully there. The thumb-drive is waiting ominously just down the hall. Suddenly, Iron Lady appears on the stairs to shush us.

"What in God's name is going on up here? The neighbors will be calling cops," she scolds.

"No!" Ethan cries. "No more police, please!"

Elena leans over and whispers in his ear. He relaxes a little.

Then Iron Lady looks at Ethan and her watch. "And, you, young man, what are you still doing up? It's after ten." Elena gets to her feet reluctantly and reaches down for Ethan’s hand. As they make their way down the hall, he tugs against her like he doesn't want to go. They turn toward Ethan's room.

"Bathroom first!" Lily yells, shaking her head.

I watch her go back down the stairs. Lemon love, kind of sour. The thought makes me smile. I grab the computer and head into Elena's room to set up. Just as I locate the memory stick, I hear Ethan calling my name. It's easy to leave this behind to go to him.

Elena is sitting up on the far side of the bed. Ethan is snuggled down in the center. I slip in next to him under the covers. He lays his head on my chest, wraps his arm around me, and puts one leg over mine. I kiss the top of his head and inhale his sweet smell.

"This is the best night of my life. I wish we could stay like this - Lanie, Sage, and Ethan, together forever," he says, looking from one of us to the other before putting his thumb in his mouth.

When we're settled, Elena starts singing. Tonight she chooses the Beatles, "Golden Slumber," and then because Ethan says that one is too short, "Strawberry Fields."

Ethan's asleep before the second song is over, and I'm barely conscious myself when Elena shakes my shoulder.

"Come on, Sage. You can't stay here."

I could stay here forever. What is she talking about? "Mmmm." One consonant is all I can manage.

"Saaage," she sings. "Waaaake uuup."

"Why?" I get a whole word out this time.

"First of all, I guarantee you won't be as lucky tonight as you were last night. Trust me waking up peed on is no picnic. I speak from long hard experience."

Ethan shifts a little closer to me in his sleep like he's protesting her accusation, asking me to stay. I think hard about the repercussions. Ultimately, it's not the thought of being peed on that makes me slide out from under Ethan's arm and leg; it's the thought of Iron Lady walking in and finding me here like this. Then I remember the memory stick. Ethan protests my exit by mumbling in his sleep, but he doesn't wake up. I kiss him one more time and whisper in his ear, "I love you, my little Mouse." When I turn around, Elena is already gone. I close Ethan's door on my way out.

Elena's sitting at the desk in front of Rachel's computer about to insert the thumb-drive that I left on top of the case.

"Man, talk about spying! What exactly do you think you're doing there?" I say.

"Just helping you out." She stands and motions for me to sit down.

"Any chance I can get some privacy to look at this?" I ask.

"It's my drive, so you need to share. What is it? Dirty pictures of Finn? Hmm?"

"Actually, it's kind of personal. I'm not really in the mood to share."

Elena shrugs. She picks up *The Rainbow* from the desk and retreats to the bed. "Have it your way. Nice choice by the way," she says waving the book. "My grandmother lend it to you?"

"Yup."

"You are definitely in her good graces, girlfriend."

I get the headphones out of the computer bag and plug in. The menu from the memory stick comes up with all the girls' names, and my temples start to pound. I scan for Josephine, hoping that I imagined it, but it's there about two-thirds of the way down the list. I wonder if I'm going to throw-up for a second, but I get control of myself before I click on it. It opens in the same room as the other girl's video, but this time the frame is empty. I can hear voices off camera though.

"Okay, so like, we can like include all her favorite stuff in the video. I want to like sing her favorite song. Maybe you can come and film at my house and I can play piano. It will be so much better. But today we can film like that dance she and I did for the talent show last year, and I can just make my message. What do you think, Mr. Wester?"

"Please, call me Jake."

I pause it to breathe. The voice, the cadence confirms it. It's Jo, my Jo, and she's talking to some stranger who sounds a lot like my father. I'm suddenly thankful that I had my last name changed to my mom's for my twelfth birthday. I don't even want that small connection with him.

I give myself a minute to assess what's there. They're making a birthday video for me, obviously, but the fact that I never received it is a giant red-flag. I steel myself and click the arrow to play. Now Jo comes into the frame. "Hey, Mr. Wester, I mean Jake." She giggles nervously and turns to face the camera. Two years ago about, that's when this was filmed. Jo's hair is long in a ponytail, and she's wearing her red 'I've got your Bach' t-shirt and a pair of short white shorts.

"What is this room? I've never been in here before," she says.

Two years ago my dad lived in an old Victorian downtown with four of his bachelor buddies. It was a great place with dozens of little rooms tucked here and there under dormers and eaves.

My father's voice comes from behind the camera. "It's my camera room. That's why we're doing Sage's video in here."

Jo goes over to the bed and picks up the animals one at a time. "Hey, aren't these Sage's?"

There's a brief hesitation before he answers. "Yeah. Sometimes she comes up here to relax. She must have left them."

I stop the payback again. Despite recognizing the house, I never saw that room in my life. My hands are shaking so badly I can barely scroll to the button that restarts the video.

My father's voice comes on again, "Why don't you start with the dance, Josephine. I have the music all queued up."

Jo snorts, "Yuck. Please don't call me Josephine. It's ugly."

"Oh no, sweetheart. It's not ugly at all. It's a name for a queen. It's power and elegance. It's a very sexy name."

On screen, Jo's head shoots up. She isn't sure how to take that comment. It's my first clue that something is going to go horribly wrong here. Maybe she sensed it too.

"Just Jo is good," she says setting up a boundary. "The dance is fine. I'll start there."

The music starts, and she dances clumsily to the ridiculously amateurish choreography we plagiarized from the drum line routine that year. The pressure behind my eyes begins building.

"That's really good, Jo, but let's film it again a little slower with more hips. Relax a little."

The music comes on again and Jo dances slower. He asks her to do it three more times before she protests. "Hey, Mr. Wester, it's really hot in here. Can you turn on the air or something?"

"I'm sorry. The AC is broken up here. Why don't you change into something cooler? A piece of clothing sails into the frame. Jo examines it dubiously. "Okay. I'll just go downstairs and change."

"That's not necessary. I'll go down and get you some water. You can change here. The camera is off." I can hear the door close. Then Jo strips to her underwear and puts on the sexy little sundress my father gave her. She examines herself in the mirror, and then as an afterthought slips off her bra.

"Better?" My dad's voice makes her jump on camera, and I jump too. "Lovely. Really. Feel free to keep it when we're done."

"Uh. Okay. Thanks. What are we going to film next?"

Now my dad comes into the picture. He takes the water over to the bed, sits down and then motions for her to sit next to him, which she does. As he's handing her the water, he spills a little onto her legs. Not enough to make her flinch, just enough for her to brush it away.

"Let me help you," my dad says, and he puts his hand on her thigh really high up. Jo pushes him away and jumps up.

"What are you doing, Mr. Wester?" her voice is shaking, but she's holding her own. Good girl, Jo Jo! I think.

"Don't you like me, Josephine?"

"Sure, but like my best friend's dad, not like that."

"Fair enough," he says. And both Jo and I relax a little. "What if we try something different here? I'll go back to the camera, and you can relax for a minute on the bed."

Jo takes the bait. The camera zooms to her breast, legs, shoulders, crotch. I want to scream, "Get the hell out of there!"

"You know making this video is taking a lot of time and money. Maybe you can pay me back, by doing a couple little things for me while you're there on the bed. Nothing bad, just little things. Nothing really."

The camera pans to Jo's frightened expression and follows her as she rushes to the door, only to find it locked.

"Don't worry, Josephine, you're perfectly safe here with me."

"What are you doing, Mr. Wester? Are you crazy? You need to open this door now." Her voice is shaking.

"In just a few minutes. Let's finish the video first."

"You mean Sage's video. Your daughter's video. For her birthday. You mean that one, right?"

"Right, that one. Now go back and lie down on the bed like a good girl. I promise I'll stay back here, and I won't touch you if you do as I say."

At that point the picture blurs as Jo rushes the camera. The frame flips and then goes dark. There's no more. When I pull out the head phones, I realize I'm gasping for air. Elena is behind me, and before I can take another breath, her hands come to rest on my shoulders. My mind clears, my heartbeat returns to normal, and the rock in my stomach dissolves to dust. I turn around in the chair and pull her over where I can wrap my arms around her tiny waist and bury my head in her belly to cry.

And therein lies the limitation to Elena's gift. It can take away the pain, but not the knowledge. She reaches around me and closes the laptop. Then she strokes my hair until I'm cried out.

When we're lying next to each other in bed, she says, "Tell me that wasn't your father."

I realize she's never seen him, only Ethan has. "It looked like my father and sounded like him, but it acted like a monster. I don't understand."

"Yes, you do, Sage. You know better than anyone how well people can hide their shadows," she says almost sadly.

"Are you talking about Finn? He's not the same now as when you knew him. He would never do those things now."

"Really? I know you've seen flashes of his cruelty. You just choose to overlook them. Focus on those dimples and deep blue eyes, and it's easy to think he has a heart."

I know she's right, but my heart doesn't believe what my head might know. It's a puzzle to be sure, but what Elena is really getting at is that if I can see past Finn’s dark spots, why can't I extend the same mercy to my father.

Elena interrupts my train of thought, "Do you know the girl in the video?"

"You could say that. She's been my BFF since kindergarten."

"Did she tell you about this?"

"No. I had no clue that my dad did this to her. None."

"How long ago was that filmed?" she asks.

"I think it was about two years ago, near as I can tell. I didn't exactly check the timestamp."

"Man, that's some friend. She stuck with you after that. You sure nothing changed?"

I think back. “Jo had mono that year. She and I mainly talked on the phone. When she got done with school, if she made it, she went home and slept the rest of the day. Maybe I was too self-absorbed to realize . . ."

"Sage, you, self-absorbed? Never."

I have to smile at her sarcasm. "Yet, here you are. Sharing your bed with me," I say wryly.

"I like self-absorbed. I understand it." Elena smiles sincerely, sweetly and then leans down to kiss me.

"Mmmm, mango." I smile. Her sweet kiss doesn't last long enough to block out my rushing thoughts. "Elena, what am I going to do?"

"What does your heart tell you to do?"

"Tell Rachel. But that's just passing the buck. It's just making my problem hers. Isn't it?"

"Sage, you're a kid. This is too big for you to handle alone. I think your heart has the right idea."

"I need to call Jo too. I have to know what happened after the camera went dead."

"Why?" Elena is seriously surprised.

"Really? So I can know what he did to her."

"Why, Sage. Asking her a lot of questions is not going to help her. It's just going to open old wounds. If she never told you, then she must have had a good reason. If I were you, I'd consider it a gift that she stayed friends with you, and let it be."

Elena's probably right as usual. "Okay. I'll sleep on it, but I don't think I can just pretend I don't know. I think we need to talk about it."

"You are such a shrink's kid. Did you ever think that sometimes it's best not to talk about things?"

I take her arm and push up the sleeve. "I can see how well not talking about your pain has worked for you."

"Ha! For all you know I talk about it all the time, and this is the result of all that talking."

"Riiiight." I borrow her tone.

Elena feigns indignation. "Okay, let me tell you about my pain. I have to share my room for god knows how long with a nosy drama queen who is in love with a total loser and my brother, who by the way hate each other."

"Pa leez! I am not in love with anyone!"

"Then what are whispering in Ethan's ear? And why are you doing it with Finn if you don't love him? Hmmm?"

I prop myself up on my elbow. "Where is this coming from?"

She looks away. "I'm just kidding around."

"Are not!"

"Whatever, I'm going to sleep now. G'night." She rolls over to face the wall.

"No way! You little green-eyed monster."

She rolls back over. "Could you be any more arrogant? I am so over you wanting Ethan and Finn more than you want me."

"Um. That wasn't what I meant. You kind of flipped it."

"Oops. You meant that I want Ethan and Finn to want me not you. Not that I want you to want me more than you want them." She starts to giggle.

"Do you want me to want you, or do you want them to want you?" I start laughing too.

"What I really want is for you to want to stop this ridiculous conversation." She can barely get the sentence out between giggles.

I can't even respond. I'm just trying to catch my breath. Finally, we get our silliness under control. "Okay, Elena, I'll just say it. I love you the most. You are the only one who could make me laugh like that on possibly the worst night of my life."

She rolls over to face me. "Goodnight, Sage," she says as she gently strokes my cheek. Then she faces the wall again, so I snuggle in close to spoon her. Sleep comes almost instantly.

Chapter 13 (Sins of the Fathers)

Sometimes the broken pieces can't be put back together. Shards too small to see are blown away, and the parts that are left fit imperfectly. Sometimes no amount of glue, dexterity, or patience can make something broken whole again.

Bright sunlight peaks around the edges of the curtain that someone closed. Elena is breathing lightly beside me. The hair curls at her temples. It's uncanny how like Ethan she looks right now. Twin angels, I think.

"Stop staring," Elena mumbles without opening her eyes. "It's annoying."

"Sorry, I thought you were asleep."

"How can I sleep with you staring so loudly?" She's trying to sound serious, but I hear the giggle under her words.

"How did we get to sleep in so late?" I ask, reaching for my phone to check the time. "It's 9:38."

"Damn. What happened to Ethan?" She sits up lazily. "He's always up at dawn."

At the same time we both bolt for the door to check on him. He's not in his room, though. Elena can't resist pointing out the fate I escaped. “Bet you’re glad you slept with me now.”

I go to the window; he's not in the pool either. She starts to strip the sheets off the bed, but I stop her. "Ethan needs to do that," I say.

"You're right." We race down the stairs and into the kitchen. Ethan and Rachel are at the table working on some kind of behavior modification chart. I don't catch the theme, because Rachel's computer is set up in front of her, and the thumb drive is still dangling from the USB port. The screen is up, which mean she woke the system up. If she wasn't looking closely, she might have just clicked out of the last blank frame of the video and been done with it, but if she was even half awake, she would have seen the open browser with the file names.

"Finally!" Ethan sighs, bouncing up from the chair. "You guys are so lazy! Rachel made me let you sleep in."

"You so rock, Rachel!" Elena says giving her a little hug from behind. Then she kisses Ethan on the cheek. "Good morning, little brother."

"I'm not littler than you," Ethan protests. "We're the same age, and I'm taller." Elena ignores him as she rummages through the refrigerator looking for something to eat. I distract him from the argument by pulling him into a hug.

"Hi, Sage. Wanna go swimming?" he asks.

"Maybe," I say, looking at Rachel to assess the damage.

"Sit down, Ethan. Let's finish this. Then we'll figure out the rest of the day." Rachel says in her talking to a little kid voice. I get a cup of coffee and sit next to Rachel on the other side. While her attention is on the chart she and Ethan are working on, I slide my hand over to remove the drive. Before I can extract it, Rachel's hand comes down on mine gently. Without turning to look at me, she says calmly, "I think I should hold on to that, Sage. We can talk later."

I swallow and extract my hand. "Hey, Ethan, can I borrow some more clothes?" I ask, standing to leave.

He nods, glancing curiously at Rachel and then me. I wonder if he already knows in his way about the agony that lies inside the circuits of that little purple drive. Upstairs I rifle through Ethan's drawers looking for something more presentable than boxers. Hopefully a shopping trip will be on today's agenda. We'll also need to do something about the laundry situation.

When I'm dressed, I go back to Elena's room and sit in the window seat, staring at the charred building below. I take a mental inventory starting with furniture: the old green couch that sagged at one end with the coffee stain on the arm -- happy to see that eyesore gone; the special dishes that Rachel and I painted together at the ceramics shop every weekend my dad didn't show up the year I was 11. (We did the same pattern on all of them so they would be a set. I did the bluebonnets and Rachel added butterflies and bees.) -- I loved those dishes; the deluxe coffee maker with the timer that we splurged on for Christmas last year -- major bummer. We probably won't replace that. I'm turning the phone over and over in my hand, wishing Finn would text me, but knowing he won't. I nearly jump out of my skin when the thing rings.

I can hardly believe the display. "Hello?"

"Hey, Sage. What's going on? You're being a bit formal today."

"Sorry, Jo Jo. I'm just surprised you called."

"I haven't talked to you in like two or three days. Now that you have the mysterious twins and your dangerous boyfriend, I guess I'm just no longer noteworthy. Not even missable. It's sad, really."

"Not true at all. In fact I was thinking about you right before you called."

"Cool, it's like BFF ESP. LOL." She's giggling, but it's forced, and I can't join in. "Sage is something wrong? You like always laugh at my jokes, and what could be funnier than three acronyms in a row?"

"Sorry. It's been a crazy couple of days. Rachel left town with the twin's Grandmother."

"So you've had to be responsible. Tough gig. How's that working out for you?"

"Not so well, actually. The last thing Rachel says to me is "and don't burn down the house." Now I'm sitting here looking at a pile of ashes. On the bright side, it was only my house in the garage, not the old lady's house."

"Oh my god! You aren't kidding, are you? Was it the pyromaniac boyfriend?"

"Jo! No! No, it wasn't; at least I don't think so. I hope not. Everyone thinks it's him though."

"Is Rachel in the know then?" she asks.

"Not yet, but it's only a matter of time. Believe it or not having my house burn down was not the worst thing that happened to me in the past three days." I'm ready now. We have to talk about this.

"What could be worse than losing everything you own in a fire and being on the cusp of an earth-shattering fight with your mom about the first boy you ever did the deed with."

I resist the urge to tell her that I know she's been through worse. I want to give her a chance to tell me. "Finn is not the prime arson suspect in my mind."

"Who else could have done it? One of the twins?"

"No way!" I take a deep breath and dive in. "Actually, I think it might have been my father." The last word leaves a bad taste on my tongue. "Just before the fire, we had a huge fight about those videos I found on his computer."

"Oh." She says it so quietly I almost don't hear.

"Did you know he had a video of you?" I ask gently.

"I suspected he might when you mentioned it the other day," she says. Her tone is slightly biting.

"Is that why you're calling me now?" I ask.

"I needed to know if he taped . . . it," she admits.

“Why didn't you tell me what he did to you?" I try not to echo her anger.

"What would I have said, Sage? You never would have believed me. Hell, my own parents thought I made the whole thing up."

"Jo Jo, I would have believed you."

"I tried to tell you a hundred times that year I was in and out of school with mono, but you brushed me off every time. You had other stuff that was way more important to discuss. You're kind of self-involved, no offense."

"Well, I'm listening now."

"Sage, I've worked really hard to get passed that day. I don't want to talk about it."

I'm not hearing her; I just go on, "The video goes blank after you rush the camera. What did he do? You have to tell me."

There's total silence on the line, and I think maybe I lost the connection.

"Are you there, Jo?"

"Uh huh. I'm just trying to figure out how I can spit in your face through the phone."

"What?" I am not prepared for her rage.

"You total bitch! You want me to relive that nightmare to satisfy your twisted curiosity? Un-fucking-believable!"

"No, Jo. It's not like that." I feel the gravitational pull between us shift.

"Don't bother. I know you, Sage." She brandishes the blade that she's going to use to severe our friendship.

"Please, Jo Jo," I beg. "Forget I asked. How can I fix it?" I'm crying now.

"Fix it?" There's no mercy in her voice. "For two years I carried this shit inside to protect you, and you never cared enough about me to ask me even once in all that time."

"I didn't know. How was I supposed to ask?"

"That's the point. You should have known!" She's right. I know I don't deserve her forgiveness. I wait for the heat of the blade; she doesn't prolong my anticipation. "I'm done with you, Sage."

"Please, Jo. . ." I have no words only tears. Then the line goes dead.

I slide from the window seat onto the floor and curl into a ball to hold all my shattering pieces together. My heart is flying apart like a Cuisinart blade is ripping through it. Memories of cartwheels and crushes, shopping trips and school projects, bikes and badminton fall through my fingers like ashes. I can't breathe. I hate my father; I hate myself.

I don't hear Ethan come in, but I feel him kneel down next to me. I can't look at him. I just want him to go away. I don't want to be here right now. I wish I could just disappear and materialize on the moon. For a fraction of a second I flash on the view from the outcropping where I made love to Finn.

Suddenly, with a simple touch, I'm gone. It's Christmas time. The house is aglow with colored lights even though the sun is shining. The decorated tree looks huge. Presents just opened are strewn everywhere along with wrapping, boxes, and bows. A tall thin man with delicate features and a deep voice is singing to the little girl on his lap. It's Elena. She's three or four years old. In another room a melodic soprano voice sings along. I am holding onto a big soft stuffed dog, rubbing it's fur against my face. I go to the sofa to sit with the man and the girl. I want to be part of them.

"No, Ethan, you need to get changed before you can be on the couch." The man's voice is not kind. He pushes me away. "Lana, come take care of the boy before he ruins the new sofa."

The pretty woman comes into the room; she looks at me and shakes her head; then she reaches down for my hand and smiles. She turns to the man and says, "Jeez, Jesse, would it kill you to change a diaper?" Then she turns to me, "Come on, little angel, let's get dressed so we can go outside and play with all your new toys." I am happy to be with her.

Suddenly, time shifts; the room is dark. I'm sitting on the stairs alone. I can hear a woman crying nearby. In another part of the house a little girl is laughing and a deep voice responds playfully.

"Don't cry, Mommy," I say. "I love you, Mommy."

Her voice comes back in a gravelly whisper, "Ethan, leave Mommy alone now. Mommy needs to figure something out. Don't worry, baby. Soon everything will be better. Daddy will be gone, and we'll be happy. I promise."

The space contracts and waivers; then I'm in my kitchen at the Paige's garage. For a second I think I'm in my own head; it's a couple of days ago. My hand is shaking as I reach for the door handle. I'm having trouble seeing and breathing.

Then the lights seem to come on. I'm sitting on the floor in Elena's room with my phone in my hand, and Ethan's beside me. I realize that he just gave me the best comfort memory he could find, like I did for him the day of the doctor's appointment meltdown. The act of pushing the memory left me totally exhausted and disoriented. It seems the effect on him is similar. He sits back on his heels and brings his hands toward his temples. "Sage?" His voice is lost and far away.

"I'm right here, Ethan. Are you okay?"

He looks at me like he doesn't recognize me or like he's really seeing me for the first time. He places his hand on my face to caresses it. Then he cups my chin. Despite the strangeness of this action, I am completely unprepared when he leans in and kisses me, gently and then deeper. This is not the kiss of a child; it's a lover's kiss, eyes closed, lips parted, full of desire. Half of me knows that this is wrong on a hundred and one different levels. Half of me knows this is maybe the one right thing for a seventeen-year-old boy to do. I put up my hand to push him away, but when I finally find his shoulder, I can't.

Our lips part momentarily, and Ethan opens his eyes. I expect to see surprise, confusion, some childlike view into the little boy I know, but instead I see the same hooded pleasure, albeit less self-assured, that I see when I kiss Finn. Before I can follow that thought to a logical conclusion, Ethan is kissing me again, pulling me up onto my knees like him so our bodies are pressed together. The shock of his excitement hard against me makes me push him away, ever so gently.

"Ethan," I pant. "What are you doing?"

"Yeah, Ethan, what are you doing?!" Elena's voice is like a bucket of ice water on us.

Ethan looks down embarrassed. He pulls his shirt down over his pants, shifts position so he's sitting with his knees up to his chest, like the day he sat in the corner of the kitchen to hide his accident. He looks from me to Elena and back again. I'm frozen on my knees. Finn's words about taking a trip through Ethan's mind and the implied accusation scream at me from my memory. I can't look at Elena's face.

"What are you three up to?" Rachel asks from the doorway. Ethan looks at Elena.

"Please, Lanie, don't tell. Please." His plea is silent.

Elena speaks out loud, "Just figuring out what to do with our day."

"Thank-you," I think. Elena and Ethan's heads shoot up, and they both look at me.

"How are you doing that, Sage?" They think it almost in unison.

"It's not on purpose," I think.

"Looks to me like the three of you are thick as thieves, up to no good," Rachel says coming into the room. "Plotting mutiny, perhaps?"

Ethan pulls his knees in tighter.

"Nothing so malicious, Madre." I get up and draw her attention away from Ethan.

"You guys need to get out of here," I think.

"Well, whatever you're planning, it's going to have to wait." Before they can move, Rachel turns back around to face the twins. "I need to talk to Sage for a minute, and then we have to do something about the laundry and buying some clothes for Sage and me. Elena, you're going to be on laundry detail. Ethan, you can get the sheets off your bed and help your sister load up the truck. Then you're off to the laundr-a-mat, Elena"

"Okay," they say in unison.

"You don't need new clothes, Sage. You can wear mine," Ethan thinks. "I like when you wear my clothes."

I don't mean to, but I think, "Me too. I love the smell of you near me all day."

"That's disgusting! Stop it now!" Elena think-shouts, looking back and forth between us angrily. I can feel the heat of embarrassment traveling up my neck and onto my cheeks. Ethan's grinning.

"Am I missing something here?" Rachel asks out loud.

"No," we say in unison.

"Okay, then." Rachel turn her attention back on me. "Sage, do you have a fever? You're awfully red."

"I'm fine. Probably sunburn."

Ethan giggles a little, then stops abruptly when Elena thinks, "Cut it out, E!"

Rachel looks dubiously at the three of us. "Ethan, Elena, you have your marching orders. You can go now."

Elena grabs Ethan by the upper arm and hauls him to his feet. Keeping a tight grip on him, she shoves him roughly ahead of her out the door. "Ow! you're hurting me, Lanie," he says out loud.

"Good," she responds. Once they're across the hall, she slams Ethan's door closed.

"Any idea what that was about?" Rachel asks me.

"Not a clue. Sibling stuff, I'm sure." I try to 'listen' to what's happening across the hall, but they seem to be out of range or something because I can't hear their thoughts anymore.

"We need someplace more private for our discussion, Sage. Let's go to the attic."

I follow behind her. Both dreading and relieved to bring her into this insanity with my father.

Unfortunately, we never make it to the attic. As we're coming down the staircase, a carillon-like bell rings through the house.

"Someone's at the door," Rachel explains.

I'm standing behind her when she opens it, only half interested in who it might be. The man is tall and well-dressed, expensive suit, clean-shaven, with the bluest eyes I've ever seen next to Finn's.

"Sean, please come in," Rachel says pleasantly, though I can tell she's surprised by his presence.

As he enters, I turn my back to him quickly, suddenly realizing who he is, but I'm not fast enough.

"Please, don't leave on my account," the man says to my back.

I turn around slowly and catch the knowing sparkle in his eye. I can see what Finn will look like in twenty years. His father has the same dimples when he smiles, but Sean's smile is dripping with something between malice and satisfaction.

"Sean, this is my daughter. She has some chores to do. We can talk in the kitchen."

"Thanks, Rachel, but I'm actually here to see Sage."

Rachel looks confused. She turns to me. "Sage?"

"It took me a little while to find you," the man continues addressing me like Rachel isn't there, "but since I still pay for my son's cell phone, I have access to the records. A call to a contact at the police station and imagine my surprise to see my boy's shrink listed as the owner of the number with all the suggestive little text messages." He turns back to Rachel. "For about half a second I thought maybe you were having an inappropriate relationship with my boy." He laughs. This man is terrifying. More terrifying than the out of control drunk I saw the other day. He's a snake, cold blooded, waiting to strike where he can do maximum damage. I can see the sums adding up for Rachel, he doesn't need to paint her a picture. "Then I remembered that you had a teenage daughter. Do people ever tell you that you two look remarkably alike? Finn and I get that a lot." Except Finn has a heart, I think.

Rachel finds her voice, finally, and she addresses me as she stares the man down. "Sage, I think you should go up and help the twins." Her tone is all mama-bear-don't-mess-with-my-cub, and it wipes the smug smile from Sean Mulcahy's handsome face. I telegraph my intent to beat a hasty retreat, and suddenly a very strong hand is gripping my upper arm. I involuntarily yelp.

"I'm sorry, Rachel, I don't think you heard me. I'm here to see Sage. I promise I won't keep her from her chores for long." He places my body between his and Rachel's, so she can't lash out at him physically.

The sound of feet and voices on the stairs pulls all of our attention. Ethan is carrying the laundry basket which blocks his view of us, but Elena, coming down ahead of him, sees what's happening. She momentarily freezes on the stair, but she can't retreat. Ethan's progress forces her forward into the living room. At the bottom of the stairs she moves in front of Ethan to shield him from view as much as she can.

"Well, hello there. Ellen . . . no . . . give me a second . . . Elena. That's it. How strange! All my son's sluts under one roof. No wonder he liked therapy so much." He pauses and addresses Ethan. "I recognize you too from the bully incidents." Ethan looks like he wants to run but can't. Sean turns to Rachel to explain. "He's the special needs kid that Finn terrorized in middle school, gave him a nervous breakdown or something like that." Then he says to Ethan. "I can't tell you how sorry I am that my kid put you through all that." He almost sounds sincere, but Ethan isn't listening. I can't read his thoughts, but I'm afraid he might rush the man to switch places.

"Ethan," I say out loud and wait for him to look in my eyes. "I'm okay. Finn's dad and I are just going to talk for a minute outside. Okay?" A little stream is running over the floor boards at Ethan's feet. Sean's grip on my arm relaxes as he realizes that Ethan's wetting himself. I use the distraction to pull away, but I don't run. I turn and walk purposely out the front door. Finn's father follows me, slamming the door behind him and holding onto the handle so my mother can't open it.

"What do you want?" I ask and in my head I add, 'you bastard!' to the end of the sentence.

"Where the hell's Finn." The viper's fangs are out now, he's done with his hypnotic little dance.

"He wouldn't tell me where he was going. I don't think he wants to be found."

"You lying little bitch! I know you know where he is. That boy can't go three days without tail, so spare me your bullshit."

I take a couple steps back so he can't reach me without releasing the door handle. "I don't think you're going to hit me out here in front of god and everyone because you aren't drunk enough today. So I'm going to lay it out for you. You beat up your own son in front of me, which is low enough. He begged you to stop and you didn't, which makes you an even lower life-form. So make no mistake, there is no force in the universe you could exert on me that would make me hand him over to you. You don't love him. You only want to hurt him."

Sean Mulcahy deflates by half a degree. "Yeah, and let me guess, you love him. The boy comes over here and burns your place to the ground, and you're going to stand here and tell me about how you love him. Let's see how much you love him after he destroys some more of your life, little girl. My son, the one you saw beg for my mercy, he has none. The more you love him, the more he will burn, until everything you care about is in ashes. Then we'll see how much you love him." Tears are playing under the man's eyes, and I think that despite everything, maybe he does love Finn. Maybe?

"Why do you want to find him?" I ask with less venom.

Rachel and Iron Lady are rounding the side of the house as Sean releases the door handle and sits down on the front steps. I motion them away.

"The cops like Finn for this fire." He continues wearily, "I just want to say goodbye. They're gonna put him away this time, and I won't be around when they let him out."

"I'll give him the message," I say. I walk away toward Rachel and Lily, leaving him there on the steps. Then it comes to me that if Sean Mulcahy figured out that I was the last one to see Finn, and the cops already know about our relationship thanks to my big mouth, they must already be watching me pretty closely. If they really want to arrest Finn, I'm their best bet for finding him. Finn probably knows this too. He'd be crazy to contact me. I might never get a chance to give him that message. When I get to Rachel, I let her close her arms around me, and I give in to the wave of sadness that that realization carries in its wake.

In the kitchen Rachel stops to get me a glass of water. Then we head up to the attic for a different discussion than the one we were about to have twenty minutes ago. I sit on the edge of the unmade bed and wait for the hail of guilt to rain down on me. Rachel paces the length of the room, shaking her head in disgust or disbelief. I'm not sure if I should say something or just wait.

"Mom?" I can't stand her silence any more. "What are you thinking?"

She turns and stares at me like she just realized I was in the room. "Let's see, where do I start? I 'm trying to figure out who the hell you are. My kid doesn't lie to me. She doesn't keep secrets from me. We're a team, my kid and I. I have no idea who you are."

"Maybe that's because you stopped paying attention. You knew me and then you forgot about me." I say it quietly. I can't look at her.

"Don't you dare put this back on me! You do not get to play the neglected child card! Finnian Mulcahy! Really, Sage? How exactly did you miss the crucial fact that he's mandated to therapy? Shouldn't that have been a clue to you that there might be something wrong with him? Really?"

"Not everyone who sees a therapist is broken beyond repair, Mom."

"True, but the kids I see are more broken than the average kid in therapy! Aren't you the one who always calls me a 'therapist of last resort?' It makes my head spin to think how many times you lied to me in the last . . . how long? How long have you been seeing Finn?"

"I don't know. Maybe six months, maybe more, maybe less. A while I guess."

"Are you having sex? drinking? drugs? Don't lie, please."

Shit. I am so done in. "Yes, twice, and we used protection. Yes, once in a while, but only beer. And yes, once, but only pot."

"Perfect! You have it all figured out, don't you? Breaking the rules and lying are okay if you don't take it too far. Any excuse for every stupid choice!"

"Can we talk about Dad now?

"That makes sense since your behavior is giving me flashbacks to living with him. Tell me about what's on this thing." She takes the drive from her pocket and holds it up to my face.

I tell her everything from the day I used his computer all the way up to Jo cutting me off. I manage to make it through the whole story without breaking down, though I have to stop a couple times when I get to the phone call with Jo. "What are you going to do, Mom?"

She sits at the edge of her chair, looking over my right shoulder, like the subtitles are printed on the wall. She doesn't ask a single question or seem surprised by any of it. I wonder how much she knew or suspected about my father. "I'm not sure what to do, but the police need to know everything for Finn's sake," she says quietly.

I smile a little. She cares about Finn too. On some level she gets why I chose him.

There's a sudden knock on the door. "Rachel, you need to come down. Now!" Lily's voice is urgent and annoyed. Rachel hurries down the steep stairs and opens the door. Before she can ask, Lily says, "Jesse is here." Rachel puts the thumb-drive in her pocket and follows Lily downstairs. I follow too at a distance.

"I thought we agreed that he'd wait till tomorrow to come over," Rachel says.

"He said he couldn't wait," Lily says. "Elena and Ethan are up in Ethan's room. He was pretty upset by what happened earlier."

Rachel turns to me, "Sage, the man who's here is the twins' father. Go up and prepare them as best you can. I'm trusting you to do this right. I know it's going to be a shock, but hopefully a good one."

Rachel and Lily head into the kitchen while I race upstairs. I knock on Ethan's door.

"Hey, it's me. Can I come in?"

Elena opens the door, but not all the way. She blocks my entrance. "Sage, you need to just stay away from my brother. Ethan is behind her, looking at me with big frightened eyes.

"Don't you think that should be Ethan's decision?" I ask, trying to look past her.

"Trust me, that is his decision," she says. Ethan shakes his head slowly and then looks down at his feet.

"Whatever, Elena. I don't want to stand here and argue with you about whether or not I can come in. I really need to talk to you both right now. It's about Lily and Rachel's trip to Florida."

Elena opens the door a little wider. When I don't go all the way in, Ethan steps forward. Elena puts her arm out to keep him back from me and says, "Fine. Talk."

"Rachel and Lily hired a private detective, this Raymond guy, to find someone, and Raymond found the man they were looking for in

Florida. They went down there to convince the guy to come back here with them, and he did. He's here now, and in a few minutes we're all going to go downstairs to see him."

Elena's respiration rate has increased, and her face is flushed. "Back here. He was here before? Sage, what does this man have to do with us?"

"Everything," I say, and she knows. Her expression goes from disbelief to shock to anger to fear and ends in joy.

"Sage, it's him isn't it?" She's as happy as that little girl at Christmas. I realize how much Elena has missed her father. I nod. "He's downstairs right now?" I nod again. She is out the door like a shot. We can hear her squeal of delight all the way up here as she yells, "Daddy!" I can imagine her jumping up into his arms that adoring child reborn in an instant.

Ethan sinks to the floor. His face goes blank as he pulls his knees to his chest, wraps his arms around them, and starts rocking back and forth. I sit down on the floor beside him. I reach over and caress his cheek. "You okay, Mouse?"

He shakes his head. "He hates me. He hurt my mom and made her go away forever. I don't want to see him." He starts to shiver. I jump up and get a blanket from his bed to wrap around him.

"Is that better?" I ask. I reach out to hold his hand, but he pulls away.

"What's going on, E?" I ask.

"Lanie says you can't touch me, and I can't touch you anymore. Ever." He lowers his head to his knees, puts his thumb in his mouth, and rocks himself. I want to hold him, but I just sit beside him waiting for whatever's going to happen next.

We don't have to wait long. Elena comes up first and stands in the doorway. "Ethan, Daddy wants to come up and see you. Would that be okay? You don't have to come down."

Ethan starts to cry. He knows that whatever he says doesn't matter. The meeting is inevitable. More footsteps sound on the stairs. I move a bit closer to Ethan in case he decides he wants to hold on to me after all. Almost immediately he leans against me. Elena gasps, frustrated by our noncompliance with her recent edict, but Rachel, Lily and their father are here before she can make a move.

Rachel introduces me to a tall thin man with blond hair, sad gray eyes, and delicate features as Jesse Paige, Lily's son and the twin's father. He looks different than in Ethan's memories, smaller and less scary. Ethan doesn't look up or take his thumb from his mouth. He leans against me hiding his face.

"Hey, boy," Jesse says awkwardly. "You got a hello for your old man?" Ethan turns even further away from him. "What's wrong with you, boy?" The question is nether kind nor cruel. He's confused by Ethan's behavior. Surely Rachel prepared him for meeting Ethan. "Okay then. I'm gonna go. I'll be back again later. Maybe we can talk then. 'kay?" Ethan does not respond. Elena hugs her father goodbye, and the adults go back downstairs.

"I've got from here, Sage," Elena says coldly. I start to get up, but Ethan holds onto my shirt.

"It's okay, Mouse. Lanie's here. I need to go now. You'll be okay." He lets go reluctantly, and Elena takes my place on the floor. I walk out the door, and close it behind me with a strange echo of finality.

Chapter 14 (Fighting Fire with Tears)

There is a generally held misconception that ghosts are manifestations of the dead. The fallacy of that premise is that there is only one way to be dead. In truth there are more ways to be dead than alive, and the ghosts of these varied dead are everywhere we turn.

Rachel likes to talk about burning bridges. I think it's a stupid metaphor. In my experience there's never two people standing on opposite sides of ravine with a symbolic bridge between and a box of matches in one party's pocket. It's more like two people fail to pass through the same door and the one who exits (or enters depending upon the situation) simply closes the door and locks it, shutting the other out. Each person is left with no idea what could possibly be happening on the other side.

So for two days I trip along on eggshells, trying to make amends as best I can. Still, Elena sleeps on the floor in Ethan's room, sticking to him like paint on a canvas, and Rachel ices me out completely. With Jo as history and Finn on the run, I get no calls, no text messages, not a single source of meaningful contact with anyone. On the third day I give up. I stay in bed all day with the curtains drawn and read all of *The Rainbow.* Iron Lady brings me a tray with dinner and though I'm asleep when she brings it, I know it's her because of the book left with it, *A Secret History* by Donna Tartt. Appropriate title I think. I eat the food cold and cry through the whole meal in gratitude for her kindness.

When the house is dark and silent, I go downstairs to get a soda. I find a half-empty bottle of wine in the fridge and take it out to the pool with my journal. I spend the whole night drinking, writing, sobbing, and trying to make sense of how I could have systematically destroyed every relationship in my life. My heart cries out for the one person who could possibly understand how I feel, but there's no way to reach him. All I've got is this damn icepick taking up residence in my chest above my left breast. Every color blue is only there for me to compare to Finn's eyes, and every sensation on my skin leads me to the places he touched me. That's what it's like to be awake. I'm stupid and hopeless and above all lonely to the point of madness.

At some point in the night in self-defense I fall asleep with my head on the glass table. Strangely, it isn't Finn who haunts my dreams. I see Ethan at the window looking down, and in a flash he is there with his arms around me, telling me that I'm not dead yet, pulling me into the same kiss again and again, pressing into me with a desire that makes me wake up panting and painfully guilty.

The sun is cresting the horizon as the sky glows orange. I ditch the wine bottle in the neighbor's trash can and wait for Ethan to come down. He appears at the window briefly, but he doesn't wave, though I know he sees me. A few minutes later he creeps out the door, and I rise to meet him. He's glancing back nervously even as he hurries toward me. Without hesitation we hug each other like we've been apart for months. I inhale the honey sweetness of his hair, rub my cheek against his, and find his lips.

The banging of the screen door wakes me. It's Elena and Ethan. She sees me, shakes her head in disgust, and turns him around before he knows what's happening. They're there and gone without a word.

Now that the living inhabit the house again, I scuffle back to my comfortable prison upstairs to wait out the sunlit hours. In the afternoon I can't stand the confinement and isolation anymore, so I venture down to the kitchen where they're all gathered for lunch. The conversation falters when I come in. I look from face to face for some sign of forgiveness or residual love, but come up empty. Even Ethan won't make eye contact with me.

"Rachel, can I borrow the car to go to the library, please," I ask quietly.

Rachel looks at me like I've just asked her to buy me a small island in the South Pacific. Then she shakes her head and says, "You've got to be kidding."

I don't respond. I just walk out the door and map out the four mile trek in my mind. The last thing I need is more time to think. I take out my phone and headphones and try hard to concentrate on some music as I walk.

At the library, I enlist the aid of the reference librarian who is delighted to have a mission. We search the digital archives of the local paper and within an hour Finn's story in four installments is printed and in my hand.

"New Year's Tragedy at Attorney's Estate Shocks Community" 1/1/1996

Local socialite Sabine Mulcahy was DOA at St. David's hospital late last night in a holiday celebration turned tragedy. According to her husband, local attorney Sean Mulcahy, he was showing off his wife's Christmas present a 40 caliber Glock 23, when the gun went off. The bullet pierced his wife's brain in a through-and-through. Also present was the couple's 2 year-old son and several close family and friends who had gathered to celebrate the holiday. The investigation is ongoing.

"Attorney Held without Bond in Wife's New Year's Eve Shooting" 1/8/1996

Attorney Sean Mulcahy was ordered held without bail following the shooting death of his wife Sabine at a New Year's Eve Party. Charges were filed after it was revealed that Sabine was involved in an extramarital affair that her husband had recently discovered. Mulcahy maintains his innocence, claiming that he was showing off his wife's Christmas gift a 40 caliber Glock 23 when he was startled by his young son who had awakened and entered from another room. The gun discharged accidentally, according to Mulcahy. He claims that he and his wife were working out their problems. Alcohol is considered a factor in the shooting. A trial date will be set for early in the spring. The Mulcahy's two-year-old son has been placed in foster care pending the results of the trial.

"Attorney Cleared of Charges in Wife's Death" 5/10/1997
Local Attorney Sean Mulcahy has been found not-guilty in the shooting death of his wife at a New Year's Eve Party in their home last year. The jury deliberated for only two hours before returning the not-guilty verdict. One juror commented following the trial that it was Mulcahy's dramatic performance on the witness stand that tipped the scales of justice in his favor. At this writing Mulcahy is expected to regain custody of his three year-old son, and will return to his local law practice following an extended vacation.

Finn's mother's obituary is short. Beside it is a photo of a tall handsome woman, who you can imagine wielding a gun. She was definitely a force to be reckoned with. Her list of causes extended far beyond the hospital and Junior League nonsense usually associated with women in her social position. It's obvious that she managed everything about Sean's life and that without her, he was utterly lost. Whether or not he killed her on purpose, despite the trial result, remains a question in my mind. I wonder how many others continue to suspect him. The stories confirm that Finn witnessed the shooting and his mother's death, though how much a two-year-old could actually remember about such a traumatic incident is surely questionable. If Rachel ever speaks to me again, I'll have to ask her about that.

By the time I'm done my heart is ripping through my chest. If I thought researching Finn's past would help me miss him less, I was crazy wrong. Sitting in this forced silence under artificial lights is making me want to scream and cry. I check out a book on PTSD in children, hoping it may shed some light on the twins too, and hit the road, hoping to walk off this impossible angst. Before I've gone half a mile, I am done in. Over a hundred degrees in the shade, reflecting off the pavement leaves me soaked in sweat and dying of thirst.

I have no money, but I stop at Exodus to keep from collapsing from dehydration like some caricature of the survivor of a plane crash in a desert, crawling across the burning sand. I'm also secretly hoping Finn will show up.

I settle myself in the corner of a couch with a glass ice of water and start reading. At around four the acerbic barista who accused me of buyer's remorse comes in for her shift. She recognizes me right away.

"Hey, it's you. I have something for you," she says like she's going to hand me a summons. She doesn't wait for me to respond. She goes to the back of the shop and returns with an envelope.

"Man, your not-so-sure boyfriend sure is sure about you, Bitch. And may I say he is all kinds of hot in a brooding James Dean kind of way." She hands me the envelope.

I'm so excited I almost forget to thank her. "Hey, thanks."

"Yeah, well don't make it a habit; I'm not the damn post office!" She's smirking, maybe the closest she gets to smiling, so I'm guessing she really doesn't mind all that much. Leave it to Finn to think of this. The cops probably won't notice a gesture this subtle. Still, I know this is a one-time deal. He won't take the risk of repeating it.

I savor the moment. Hold the envelope in my hands as long as can before I open it. My name is written in tiny script across the seal, like he wanted to keep the contents confidential. I imagine him taking off his helmet and sunglasses when he comes in. I see him charming her with his dimples and sparkling eyes as he orders. I conjure him here sitting beside me now; then I rip open the end of the envelope and pour out the contents.

The note is written on hotel paper, but the insignia has been torn off. I check the envelope for a clue and find nothing. This is the first time I've ever seen Finn's handwriting. It's very careful and neat, as though he doesn't want the message misconstrued.

Hey Stalker-girl,
I can't stop thinking about the last time I saw you. I wish I could make all of this right somehow so we could be together for real. You told me the other day that if I told you I didn't do it you

would believe me. So I'm telling you now; I didn't do it. I've been thinking hard about who did. I know your dad must be on the short list of suspects, but what about my dad. If he figured out about us, this would be a great way to get rid of me. I think you also need to consider one or both of the twins (unless they were with you when it happened). They would be the only others with access to the apartment. Anyway, I am so sorry it happened, and I know you are going through hell with your mom since she probably knows about us by now. I hope she will forgive us. I totally care about you, Sage. You should know that in case I don't see you again. Don't miss me too much. F.

I read the note about ten times. I guess he's had a lot of time to think about how this all went down. He must be plenty frustrated about hiding when he didn't do it. My brain hurts from thinking about our fathers. my dad, the pervert, and his, the murder. We fit, Finn and I; maybe it will all work out. I try to picture a possible resolution, something like the cops finding evidence against my dad or his, and Finn being cleared. Even if that happened, where would Finn go and how would we get around Rachel. I'm in knots that are slipping tighter and tighter around my chest. I'm going to suffocate. I want to close my eyes and let it happen, but somewhere in some corner my brain the fight hasn't entirely drained out of me. I get up and head home.

Home. Technically, I don't really have one anymore on any real level. I remember travelling with my mom when I was like four or five. We went to the west coast for a vacation or something. The whole time we were away I kept saying, "I want to go home!" Then for months after we had returned, I continued to say it. Rachel knew that it really meant that I wanted to feel safe. If I had anyone to cry to right now, I would cry like a baby and beg to go home, but there's no point in tears; they only make me tired and snotty.

I arrive at chez Paige footsore and sunburned. I sit in the shade and soak my feet in the pool. I have Finn's letter tucked into my bra next to my heart. I try to focus on that as I watch Rachel, Elena, and Lily get ready for dinner. Ethan is nowhere to be seen. Elena must be taking a break from baby-sitting him since I've been gone. Lily glances out the window and nods, acknowledging my presence, but to Rachel and Elena I'm little more than a puff of smoke, a ghost who has no power in their realm.

What about Ethan? Being separated from him is almost worse than being kept from Finn. Of course I don't believe that Ethan's choosing to avoid me. I know that Elena is controlling him. If Elena told Rachel about THE KISS, then she's probably in the keep-Sage-away-from-Ethan camp too. I scan the upstairs windows for him, but he isn't there. I look back down at the water, splash my face and arms. The water immediately evaporates off my skin. I might melt into the pool deck and vanish into vapor like I never existed at all. I get up and go around to the front door, slip inside and up the stairs. As I'm opening the door to Elena's room, I hear a click across the hall. Ethan peeks out from behind his door.

"Hi, Sage," he whispers.

"Hi, Mouse," I whisper back. There's a strange pause as he hides behind his door, and I start to move behind mine.

"I miss you, " he says so quietly I'm not sure if I really heard it.

"Me too," I say, opening the door wide again.

He takes a step into the hall. "I'm sorry, I did that." He blushes. "When I kissed you the other day."

"Don't be sorry," I say. "It'll be okay. Elena will get over it eventually. You doing alright?"

"Not so much." He looks down at his feet. "I had a really really bad dream last night, and too many day accidents. Elena's very angry with me."

I take a step toward him. My arms ache to hold him, but the footsteps on the stairs send us scurrying into our separate rooms.

Elena's voice echoes in the hall, "Ethan, are you ready for dinner?" She knocks on his door and goes in without his invitation. I can't hear the rest, but a few minutes later I hear their footsteps on the stairs.

I entertain myself by writing in my journal, making up little metaphors that make me feel numb.

> *I'm not real anymore. People lining the streets can't see me except for the few I choose to touch, but seeing me is nothing*

short of a curse because the ones who catch a glimpse are regarded as crazy beyond hope.

I would give anything for a bottle of whiskey or handful of the painkillers the dentist gave me when I had my wisdom teeth out. Both might be even better; coma sounds like a blissful option to my ghostly existence. I lie on the bed and press my palms against my eyes until colorful patterns form. I focus on the whole picture because if I try to look at a detail, it all goes white. I played this game when I was little whenever I had to wait for a long time somewhere I didn't want to be. It's comforting for some reason, and eventually it lulls me to sleep. When I wake up, the house is quiet. Elena has come and gone, I'm sure, and someone has left me a coke and a glass of ice. Some of the ice is still unmelted, so it wasn't too long ago.

I go into the bathroom and pour out the water. I stop to look in the mirror. My usually silky hair is frizzy, greasy, and frayed at the ends from sweating and sleeping on it. My face is red from the sunburn I got on my travels today, and even my eyelids sting. The swelling around my eyes makes my cheeks look sunken. A ghost or a zombie, I think. One night I will eat them all in their sleep, except Ethan. I am lost in this rather dark tangent when I am startled out of my skin by Ethan screaming. He's hysterical. I can hear Elena yelling to try to wake him, but he keeps crying and yelling, inconsolably.

I'm just about to open the door and go in when Elena comes out. "Get Rachel," she says, wide-eyed and anxious.

I meet Rachel at the bottom of the stairs. All the way in the attic she could hear Ethan's screams. "Night terrors?" I ask. Rachel looks at me like she doesn't know me. "I've been reading about children's responses to trauma," I explain.

"Okay kiddo, so what are you supposed to do?" she asks.

"Very little," I say hurrying up the stairs nonetheless.

Elena lets me through without a fight. I can see why she's so disconcerted. Ethan is sitting up, screaming with his hands over his ears. He's kicked all the covers off the bed. His eyes are wide open and terrified. It seems like he's awake, but I know he's not. It would be too easy to be switched into his nightmare, so I concentrate on the details of the moment before putting my hand on his shoulder. I don't try to wake him. Instead I rub his back, hold his hand, and whisper to him until he's calm enough to lie back down. I sit beside him till his breathing is nearly normal. Elena and Rachel are watching, so I leave without kissing his forehead. Rachel follows me out.

"Good job, kiddo, she says approvingly.

"Good enough to be forgiven?" I ask.

"One thing has nothing to do with another." Rachel says flatly and goes back to bed.

Now I'm wired. I pace back and forth until I hear Elena moving around in the bathroom next door. She's in there for a long time. I know what she's doing, but I don't care about stopping her. Whatever gets her through the day is fine with me. I listen for her to leave, so I can shower.

After about 45 minutes, it's quiet, so I go in. "Holy shit!" I yell-whisper. Elena's passed out on the floor in the corner between the tub and the sink. Her left arm is hanging limply on the floor with blood running down it and pooling by her hand. I swear it looks like a botched suicide attempt.

"What the hell?" She jumps when I curse.

"That's my line! What the hell back at you!" I say horrified.

"Jeezes, Sage, it's only a little blood." She licks it off her arm and smiles. She sees that it bothers me, so she does it again.

"That's disgusting!" I say.

"Don't knock it . . . " She gets up and calmly cleans the floor with some toilet paper.

"That's a lot of blood, Elena! Let me see your arm." She's already pulled down her sleeve.

"Don't worry. It doesn't hurt, not nearly enough anyway. I'm gonna get some sleep. You go ahead and do whatever it is you do all night."

Before she disappears behind Ethan's door, I pose the question of the day. "Are you ever going to forgive me?"

She turns slowly back to me. "I'm not sure you understand, Sage. It's not really about forgiveness. Forgiving you would be easy since Ethan's the one who kissed you. This thing between us is about trust. Ethan's my brother. It's my job to take care of him because he isn't really able to care for himself. He's fragile and innocent, and you're an emotional bull in china shop, just inches from shattering him and not even aware of what you're doing. I don't trust you with him."

Talk about shattered. This is not something I can fix. I turn and head down the stairs. In the kitchen I stand over the sink, running the water to mask the sound of my retching sobs. I hold on to the counter with both hands because my knees can't bear the weight of the realization that Elena hates me not for what I've done, but for what I am. Finn has navigated this sea of self-loathing. I need him to help me find my way.

I turn my back to the cabinets, slide down onto the floor. Through my tears, I look up, and like a sign from the almighty goddess, I see the glitter of Rachel's keys next to the coffee pot. I catch my breath and stand up. I turn off the faucet and without another thought I grab them and head out to the car. The stars are perfectly aligned. Rachel left the Volvo parked on the street, so when I start it, no one in the house will hear. I have hours till I need to be back, hours away before anyone knows I've been gone.

I roll down the windows to try to simulate the feeling of being on Finn's bike and head for the only place in the world that feels safe to me, the only place I could possibly find Finn.

I don't park by the cliff where we swim; I drive further down to the trail head and park behind some bushes so the car can't be seen from the road. I haven't exactly prepared for this excursion, but I find a little penlight flashlight that works intermittently and an old picnic blanket in the trunk. It's all I need.

Hiking at night is not the safest of activities. I trip several times and then concentrate on taking it slower. The moon is fairly bright where the trail opens, but in the woods it's pitch dark, and staying on the path proves oddly challenging.

You'd think that the woods would be quiet at night, but I swear every creature in Texas has come here to party. A group of owls acts as sentry asking for my identification. A family of armadillos steps out of prehistory to guide me. The small ones approach me curiously when I stop moving, and the mother almost rushes me. My ridiculous screeching and jumping around scare them away. A posse of raccoons hangs out in some cedar trees, staring at me the same way the kids in the lunchroom at school do, with distaste and amusement.

I finally find the out-cropping. It takes me three tries to scale the small cliff that seemed so easy a few days ago during the day, but I manage it and settle myself on the blanket. The view over the ravine in the moonlight is eerie and surreal. All the colors are silver, gray, and ghostly white. A part of me is excited like a kid on Christmas Eve. Finn will be here; I just know he will. I send him a psychic message that I'm sure he can hear. Another part of me feels like the desperate fool that I am, sitting on a rock in the middle of nowhere waiting for nothing, and risking everything to do it. Just shoot me now, someone. Do me this one small kindness.

I wait all night, flicking away the spiders and millipedes, jumping at every little noise, but when the sky begins to lighten, I give up. I really give up. I jump down and land on my knees, scraping them. The sting of cool air on the open wound gives me an excuse to let loose the tears that I've beaten back all night. I wrap the blanket over my shoulders and cry all the way back to the car. I sob as I drive home and don't stop until the car is parked.

The one thing that would make my misery complete would be Rachel waiting for me in the kitchen. I steady my nerves for the encounter, but miraculously, luck is with me, and no one is up, not even Ethan. I put the keys back where I found them and make a pot of coffee. When it's done, I pour a cup and go back outside.

I'm standing there looking out over the pool at the ashes and soot of my former life, wondering for the bazillionth time how I got here. Then for no rational reason whatsoever I abandon my safe comfortable little cup of coffee and the clean world of the pool to walk myself right through the crime tape and into the mess that was once my home. At first I'm very careful of where I step, and I try not to touch anything to avoid getting too dirty. Then gradually I begin to accept that I am part of the debris, not above it. I am splinter and ash; only a miracle of timing left me in this corporeal form. I work my way over to what was once the kitchen and my room above. They are smashed together now like the layers of a lasagna. Then I begin to dig.

I grab a broken beam and use it as a shovel to move a pile of the roofing. Under that layer, I see the mirror that hung over my old dresser. The metal frame is bent and twisted, and the glass is partially melted. I take the beam and swing it as hard as I can into the glass that's left. The explosion of shards and the sound of shattering are exceptionally satisfying, so I hit it again and again. I dive back into the ashes and move the rubble with my hands. I find a piece of the duck cookie jar that Ben gave us when I was little. It's only the beak and one eye, but I shove it into my pocket. I clear another place to stand, scraping my arm on a metal spring that was once part of my mattress. A clean incision stretches from my shoulder to my elbow and crimson droplets appear immediately. No matter.

The next treasure I unearth is a pearl. It must have come from my grandmother's necklace. The string burned away of course. I wonder how many of the pearls I can find. Maybe I can have it restrung. I come up for a breath of air that isn't full of soot, and I hear voices yelling. Rachel and Lily.

"Sage, get out of there! The structure is not stable!" My mom's frantic, but I wave her off in my mind.

I'm totally safe here; ghosts can't be injured. To get to the living room, I have to really dig deep. Under the top two layers there's a pocket of space; in this area several items survived. I'm pretty sure the fire must have started upstairs because this stuff would be okay if it weren't for the water damage and collapse. I clear out a space where I can crawl under the wreckage. It's dark and damp below the surface, but right away I find another pearl, so I know this is the direction I'm supposed to take. There's too much ambient noise outside with all those people shouting at me, and the quiet in this little cave is welcome even if it is hard to breathe here.

I salvage everything that isn't smashed, burned, or drowned - precious little. I make a pile just outside my little hole. The strangest things survived under here. A coffee mug managed to sustain only a small chip out of the handle, a bic pen still writes, a totally Goth candle holder with a snake wrapped around the base, a gift from Jo, is completely intact. I keep my eyes peeled for pearls, and find two more. I have no idea how much time has passed, but I'm hungry, and I need to pee. I know that if I come out, they won't let me back in. I'm not done, so I push those needs to the back of my mind and continue sifting through the ash.

A while later I hear someone else moving through the rubble. Whoever it is, isn't screaming or freaking out, which is good because

I'd have to use my mirror smashing technique on anyone who got in my way. I peek out from my current position near the stairs. It takes me a minute to figure out who it is, but I like his gentle features and tired eyes.

"Hi there, Sage." he says. "Remember me?"

"Hi, yourself. You're the twins' dad, right?"

"Yep. Whacha doing?

"Looking for stuff," I say, ducking back down into my current excavation.

"What kind of stuff are you lookin' for?"

I stop for a moment. I'm not sure how to explain this. "Pieces that can be put back together, I guess."

"You're scaring a lot of people out there."

"What are you talking about? No one who lives in that house gives a shit anymore. I'm dead to them. I'm a ghost. Know what I mean?"

"Kid, I wrote the book on bein' a ghost. I been dead to so many people that sometimes I feel like I should just live in the damn graveyard."

"What did you do?" I ask.

"You first." He's not willing to part with his secret just yet, but I can't get rid of mine fast enough.

"Where do I start? . . . My mom, Rachel, is pretty awesome, ya know."

"I noticed that," he says grinning sadly.

"Well, anyway, she gave me one little rule, and could I honor it?"

"I'm guessing not."

"Then you're right. Do you know why I broke her simple little rule?"

"Not a clue."

"Well, that's too bad because I don't have a clue either. Maybe that's what I'm looking for in here. Wanna help?"

"In a minute. So what was the rule?"

"That isn't the point. The point is that breaking the rule, which by the way turned out to be a reasonable rule, managed to end in this." I gesture around us. "It hurt too many people to count, people I love, who don't or can't love me anymore."

"Sage, can I tell you something I learned about love from being a ghost?" Jesse asks.

"Bring it."

"People who you think can't love you anymore, they do. They manage to go on loving you no matter what you do. Sometimes they act like they won't ever forgive you, but they find a way . . . in time. Besides, Sage, I have a feeling that at least some of this damage happened around you, not because of you."

I look at him in the dim light. I think about the flashes of Jesse and his wife: Lana pulling Ethan up the stairs, and Lana saying that Jesse would be gone soon. I remember the closeness Jesse shared with Elena, and I come to a nearly blinding realization.

"You didn't start the other fire, did you?" I blurt out.

Jesse takes a step back, and nearly falls. "What the hell?" he mumbles to no one in particular.

I don't feel like explaining my connection with Ethan. "It was their mother, wasn't it?

Jesse looks like he might cry. "No one would believe me. Lana was in love with someone else. She told me and I laughed. I wouldn't let her go, but I wouldn't forgive her either. So, no, I didn't strike the match, but it was my fault sure as if I had."

"She could have left you. You can't keep someone who doesn't want to stay. Why'd she stay?"

"Not because she loved me. She was afraid I would keep the twins or at least Elena. Besides, her lover was killed by her husband."

"Her affair was with a woman!"

"Yeah, that was my reaction too."

My mind churns into overdrive as I remember the articles from the library. "Let me guess - the woman was married to an attorney, who the shot her on New Year's Eve and was arrested for her murder and cleared eventually."

"Are you like Ethan?" Jesse is really thrown.

"What do you mean?"

"Like, do you know stuff . . . that's going to happen or that happened to other people?"

"Not at all," I laugh. "It's just a fucking small world; that's all." It strikes me that Ethan's gift scares him more than a little.

He relaxes. "Well, it's a small town anyway. The truth is I punished

Lana, made her crazy, used our kids against her. I deserve the accusations and the prison term, but I couldn't face that then, so I ran. I'm not sure what'll happen to me now, but I can't stay a ghost. It's no way to live, halfway between here and there."

"Sometimes you don't get to choose. If others want to ghost you, you're just gone." I say. Then I turn back to digging. Jesse moves in closer to help. He finds a drawer that can hold some of my larger finds like an old cast iron skillet, a brass Eiffel tower lamp (no lamp shade of course), and a metal ruler. Jesse finds three more pearls.

After a while, he stops and watches me work. Finally, he says, "Sage, I think we should take a break. We've been at this for a couple of hours, and they said you were out here for at least a couple hours before I got here. Let's go get some food and water, maybe take a shower.

I shake my head. "I haven't found it yet." I start digging more aggressively; something large shifts above us.

Jesse looks up anxiously as the beam groans. "There's nothing to find here, Sage. This is just stuff. What you're looking for is out there." He points to the table by the pool where Rachel is pacing, Ethan is curled into a chair sucking his thumb, and Elena is biting her nails. Lily is there too, standing at the edge of the police tape, trying to keep me in her sights. "No one's ghosted you, Sage. That's all in your head."

I need to pee pretty badly at this point, so I concede with a slight nod. Jesse reaches for my hand to pull me up. When I stand, my shoulder hits the beam. Wood, ash, roof tiles, and tons of other crap begins to rain down on us. Jesse has a clear shot out of the avalanche, but my leg is more than knee deep in a pile of stuff that I need to climb over. I try to shake my hand free from his, but he holds on with an iron grip and yanks me out of the hole and up into the air. I end up crashing full-on into him, knocking us a couple of feet away from the collapse. He rolls over to shield me from the stuff that's coming down. When it stops, Jesse stands up and throws me over his shoulder. I'm upside down, watching a stream of blood follow us across the pool deck. With all the strength I can muster I reach up to rub my temple because it itches, but when I get there my fingers slide over the slick surface of my skin, and I realize it's my blood pouring out behind us. Then I give up the fight and let it all go black.

I wake up in the living room with Lily pressing down on my temple. "Not so hard." I try to wave her off, but she keeps the pressure steady as I try to make my eyes focus on the ceiling. Jesse is cleaning off the cuts on my arm and shin, and Rachel is on her cell phone giving the address. I turn my head slightly to assess the source of crying on my right. Two blurry figures huddle together on the stairs. Elena's holding Ethan; he's crying inconsolably, saying, "No hospital, no hospital," over and over.

I try to sit up, but Lilly and Jesse are pushing me down. It's maddening! Finally, I just scream, "Argh! Just let me go use the damn toilet!" Iron Lady and Jesse back off. Rachel cancels the ambulance and runs over to help me stand up. "I'm fine. I can walk," I insist, but I have no idea which direction the bathroom is in. Rachel steers and hovers until I shut the door. Nothing in the world feels better than a long pee after holding it for hours and hours. When I get up though, I realize that maybe I should have let Rachel come in, because the floor tilts dangerously, and I turn around just in time to hurl into the toilet.

I unlock the door. Rachel rushes in. "Hospital!" she insists.

"Okay." I say. I let Jesse carry me to my mom's car, and he slides into the back seat beside me. Lily drives and Rachel rides shotgun. I realize she must be too upset to drive. It's kind of touching.

At the hospital they stitch up cuts on my arm, shin, and head. They take a bunch of x-rays and scans and pronounce me hard-headed. Rachel thinks that is hilarious and responds with, "You don't know the half of it." The ER docs want to keep me overnight for observation because I have a slight concussion, but I absolutely refuse. I want a shower and soft bed; besides Ethan is probably in a bad way thinking about me here. Jesse and Rachel promise to keep me awake all night, and they finally release me around 9 pm.

At home they set up shifts to watch me, but once I'm ensconced in bed, Elena busts out a deck of cards and sends them all away. At about 3 am she fades out, and I'm on my own.

There's no way to fight sleep in that bed with her calming presence, so I get up and sneak into Ethan's room. I sit in the window seat and watch the moonlight play on his angelic face. He's lying on his back with the covers at his waist. His golden curls are spread out like a mane on his pillow, but the soft down of peach fuzz over his chin and under his nose remind me that he's not really a little boy. I remember in vivid, painful detail the way he kissed me and his surprise at his body's reaction to it. And suddenly, silently I am crying. I'm aching for him to find a way out of his wreckage. I want to pull him out the way Jesse pulled me out, but that's not possible. I turn away to look out the window.

Ethan's sheets crinkle and his bed squeaks. When I look over, he's sitting up watching me.

"I'm sorry, E. I didn't mean to wake you," I say, trying to keep my voice from betraying my tears.

"Why are you crying, Sage?" He slips out of bed and comes over to the window seat.

"I don't know," I lie, standing to meet him. He steps in closer and wraps me in a hug. It takes me a minute to realize that he's shaking and crying too.

"I'm sorry, so sorry, Sage," he mumbles.

"Sweet, Mouse, what could you possibly be sorry about."

He ducks out of my hug and goes into the closet where he keeps his secret painting. He comes out with a large box and hands it to me. I couldn't be more perplexed.

I sit down on the floor and open it. Inside I find my computer, photos, yearbooks, stuffed animals, and jewelry, plus a hundred paper butterflies.

"Ethan, how. . . ?" I reach up and take his hand.

He's crying really hard now. "Lanie!" he calls for her in his head, and I hear it clearly.

A moment later she's there at the doorway. Several strange scenarios play out in my mind: Ethan knowing about the fire before it happened and rescuing my things; Ethan starting the fire, not a chance. Elena? She looks at me and the box. "Ethan you shouldn't have done that," she says silently. I'm still holding Ethan's hand, and I hear her.

Finn was right.

Chapter 15 (Forged in Rain)

During the Apocalypse most will panic, run willy-nilly like insects; others will sit and wait patiently for the end, inured to pain and loss simply because of their irrelevance; still fewer will rise up, the survivors, getting done what needs doing to keep going; finally, the fewest of all will sift and analyze the evidence, gathering the facts and data, desperate to find the logic, the pattern, the reason that will make it all make sense.

My brain is exploding like the grand finale at a fireworks show. I don't remember getting up and leaving Ethan's room or putting the box in Elena's room or going downstairs or leaving the house. When I return to a semblance of conscious thought, I find myself sitting fully dressed on the bottom of the swimming pool crisscross like I'm playing mermaid tea party. I have to hand it to Elena, burning the garage was the one event that would force Finn out of the picture with the cleanest stroke. I would reject him out of hand for his insane jealousy and possibly he would even go to jail, accomplishing the ultimate blood-letting, Elena's revenge.

Crazy like a fox, but oddly out of character as Rachel pointed out. Elena seems more protective than destructive. Her anger is generally turned inward at herself, hence the cutting. Why would she suddenly be striking out? Is she that desperate to preserve my relationship with Ethan? Probably not, since if that were the case she would have been happy about the kiss, not angry about it. I just don't get it. When I come up for air, Elena is sitting on the deck with her feet in the water. I might as well ask.

I come up and swim over to her. When she is looking fully into my eyes, I ask, "Why?"

"Why what, Sage?" she looks up as if she's annoyed. I turn away from her, disappointed. I wish she'd be straight, but she's going to play dumb. Perhaps the reason she's been keeping me away from Ethan is because she suspected this would happen if we were together. She was afraid he would give her up.

"Did Ethan get back to sleep?" I ask, looking up at his empty window.

"Yes, I sang to him. Puts him out like magic every time." She reaches toward me to touch my arm, but I dodge her. I don't need her magic clouding my mind just now.

"I didn't mean to wake him up," I say.

"He's fine," she says. "Are you okay?"

"Sure. I just got back all the things I thought I'd lost. I'm totally jazzed." My voice is flat, subdued.

"He didn't do it," she says. "He didn't start the fire." I'm not looking at her so I can focus on her voice. The cadence or pitch is different, all wrong somehow.

"I know that," I say. "As if he's even capable of it."

I get out of the pool and sit next to her on the deck. She finally gives words to my jumbled thoughts. "You think it was me."

"Was it?" Maybe she'll give me the truth now.

"No." She says it quickly, quietly, like she doesn't want me to hear. "As long as we're getting down to it, and we have all night, why don't you tell me about what I walked in on the other day?"

"Ooooh, the KISS." I try really hard not to smile and fail completely.

"This is NOT funny or trivial! Damn it, Sage!"

"Why are you so worked up, Elena? Ethan is seventeen. Whether or not his mind or his emotions are or aren't, his hormones are. He's seen me kiss Finn and . . ." I am interrupted by a strange realization.

"And what?" Elena is shaking her head.

"Holy shit!" I turn and face her. "Right before we kissed, Ethan pushed a memory to me. I was upset, and he wanted to help me the way I helped him the day of the doctor appointment meltdown. Just before it happened, I was thinking about Finn. Maybe when we switched, he got caught up in my memory somehow. Remember how pushing the memory to him messed me up. I think it had the same effect on him."

Elena thinks about this, and the tension drains from her like an unclogged a sink. "Sage, you're a genius!" she exclaims. She goes in for the hug and then realizes I'm all wet, so she kisses me instead.

I wish I could feel so resolved about her part in all of this, but my suspicions are still running high.

Elena goes inside and makes a pot of coffee, and we stay the rest of the night by the pool. At dawn Ethan appears in his swimsuit looking uncertainly at Elena and me before starting his laps. When he's done, I meet him at the steps to wrap him in the towel while Elena watches. His bright smile tells the story of how relieved he is to have our little group back together.

We're talking and laughing, eating graham crackers and marshmallows for breakfast when the police cruiser pulls up the driveway. Ethan makes a move to bolt inside, but he can't get to the door without passing the cops, so he shrinks down in his chair and brings his knees up to bury his head.

"They can still see you," Elena whispers to him. I giggle nervously. It's our old friends, Henderson and DeSocio.

As usual Henderson does the talking, "Hi, Sage. Ethan. Elena. Sage, is your mom home?"

I nod. "I'll go get her." Henderson and DeSocio follow me into the kitchen and stop there while I hurry up to the attic.

Rachel throws on a robe and comes down with me.

"Sorry to bother you at this early hour, Ms. Evans," Henderson says, "but we have some news."

I'm torn between leaving and staying. I'm terrified they're going to say they found Finn. I move toward the door slowly.

"Please stay," DeSocio says, blocking my exit. "This involves you too."

I move back over to Rachel, and she puts her arm around my shoulder protectively.

Henderson continues. "Early this morning we got a call at 15 Clearview Drive."

"Finn's house," I whisper, moving closer to Rachel.

"A neighbor reported shots fired."

I can feel my knees give out. Rachel guides me to a chair as Henderson goes on.

"When we arrived, Sean Mulcahy was DOA from a self-inflicted gunshot wound to the temple. He left two notes. One for his son and one for you." She hands an envelope to my mom.

Rachel fingers the paper like it's covered in blood, and she doesn't open it. "Please, Ms. Evans, we need to take it back with us as evidence."

Rachel sits next to me and opens the letter. She reads it aloud in a shaky halting voice.

Dear Rachel,

I want to thank you for all you have tried to do for my boy and me. I am so sorry that we paid you back by destroying your home and terrorizing your daughter. (Please apologize to Sage for me.) If you are receiving this letter then I have been successful in exiting this life. Maybe I'm in a place where I can be with the one person I ever loved. But it's not important where I am anymore. The fact is my boy doesn't need me. I've never been any good to him anyway. But I think he needs someone to take care of him, though he is technically almost a man. I am begging you to be that person for him. Take him in and give him some of what I couldn't. It might not be too late for him. I have provided for him financially in my will so he won't be a burden to you that way. I'm sorry to put this on you, especially with all the legal trouble he's facing, but you are the one person he trusts, and I trust you too.

Sincerely,
Sean Mulcahy

Rachel's crying by the time she finishes, but I'm just relieved that

Finn's okay.

"Sage," Henderson's voice makes me jump. "Now would be a good time for you to tell us where Finn is. In an hour, maybe less, this will be all over the news and Internet; it would be a shame for him to find out about his father that way."

I stare at her blankly. Poor Finn! Maybe he won't have the TV on. Maybe he won't see a newspaper. Maybe he won't boot up a computer. You can bet the cops will take this opportunity to put Finn's picture out there too, which means he won't be able to hide much longer. Soon everyone is going to recognize him. This is a perfect storm. "I really don't know where he is or how to reach him, " I tell the officer.

"Sage, we just want to talk to him," DeSocio says, exasperated. Henderson leads me to the other room. "I don't think Finn is our guy. If I can talk to him, then I think we can get this all straightened out." She stares harder at me as if that might convince me to cooperate.

"I swear I don't know!" I yell, and I run upstairs. I'm dialing Finn's cell phone, as the cruiser pulls away, but I know he doesn't have it. He left it at his dad's house, so they couldn't track him through it. I wish he was less paranoid, worse at disappearing. Rachel is suddenly at the door.

"Mom, I need the car, please."

She shakes her head. "No can do, kiddo. You shouldn't be driving with a concussion. Besides the cops will follow you right to him. You need to sit back and wait. Finn will either turn himself in, skip town, or show up here. My money is on the last option. And who would know him better than his shrink?" She smiles and opens her arms.

"Thanks, Mama." I hold onto her for a good long time, comforted by her smell, her warmth, and her impeccable instincts. I hope she's right.

At noon the doc from the ER calls to check on me. She gives me the green light to sleep since I haven't had any symptoms. I want to stay up and wait for Finn. At 3 o'clock when I knock over the ice tea trying to get an apple out of the fridge, Rachel finally forces me to get in bed. I'm out before she can kiss me good night.

I wake up I don't even know how many hours later. The sky is already dark and everyplace I have stitches and everyplace I don't aches like I have been beaten senseless by five big guys. White noise like static echoes around my aching head, and I try hard not to move, but beside me Elena is snoring incredibly loudly. I roll over to poke her. For a second I think I'm still asleep or I got hit in the head harder than I thought because it's not Elena snoring; it's Finn.

OMG! It's Finn sound asleep next to me like it's no big deal! I'm torn between waking him and letting him sleep, but I have no will power at all. I turn on the light, but that doesn't do it. He always sleeps with the lights on. I try blowing in his ear and tickling his nose. Nothing. Finally, I semi-yell, "Finn, wake up."

He groans and rolls over. "Sage? How long have you been awake?" Then he jumps up. "Jeez, sorry. I didn't mean to fall asleep."

"What are you doing here?" I guess I didn't think he would really come.

"My dad . . .," his voice trails off.

"I know. The cops were here this morning. How did you get here?"

"Elena hid a ladder in the back behind the roses."

"How'd she know?"

"Man, that girl can really keep her mouth shut," Finn says in awe. "I've seen her like almost every day. She knew where I would be. Her old man is staying there too, so no one's the wiser that she keeps going to that hotel."

"How did she know?"

"It's a place I used to go back in the old days. She figured it out right away. We've been meeting at the HEB, Starbucks, a Walgreens. There's this guy, Brad. He's my connection. He works as manager over at the HEB. We used to hang back a ways, but he's not like one of my regular boys, so no one's watching him. Elena knew him too because his parents died in a car wreck when we were in the fourth grade, and he was one of the 'Loser's Club' at middle school. Anyway we've been passing notes through Brad. I knew he'd have my back because he's got something to lose if I get picked up."

I am trying to take it all in. Elena is kind of blowing my mind all of a sudden. Why would she be helping Finn if she set the fire to get him out of our lives?

"You okay? You look a little freaked," he says.

"Freaked pretty much covers it, " I say. "But also relieved and happy to see you. When the cops came today and they said something about gun shots, I thought you were . . . or worse, that you did your dad. Damn. I'm so glad you're here!"

I let myself fall into his chest, and he holds me tight like he wants to keep me from floating away. Then he relaxes, and we lay down with my head on his shoulder. He strokes my hair in silence for a while. I almost fall asleep again, but the elephant in the room keeps me awake. Finally, I have to ask. "What are you going to do?"

"Right now I'm going to enjoy as much time as I have with you before someone else figures out I'm here. Then . . . well . . . I'll figure that out when it comes."

It's not the answer I had hoped for, but I'm not sure what he could say to make all this okay.

"Do you want to talk, you know, about your dad?" I look up to gauge his emotional state.

He half frowns, half smiles. "Okay, Rachel, we can talk about that if it'll make you feel better."

Sure, I think. I can play this game if it helps him open up. "This isn't about my feelings, Finn. It's about yours. I think talking about it will make you feel better." I imitate Rachel's voice and hand gestures.

Finn sits up. "Very scary," he says. "You've got her down cold."

"Well, she is my mom," I say proudly.

He takes a deep breath and settles back into the pillow. "Don't do that again, okay."

"Sure," I say. "It's all me now. What's going on in there?" I touch his temple and his heart with my index finger. He takes it from his chest and kisses the tip.

"I'm not sure. It's like a fucking twister inside my head. Everything about him dying and the night my mom died is all jumbled up and swirling around. I can't make sense of any of it because it's all whipping by so fast and furious." He's a little breathless. He inhales deeply then he goes on shakily. "It's all my fucking fault, you know. All of it. Do you want to know why I sleep with the lights on? It's not about fear of the dark, monsters and that shit. See, every time the lights go out, in the dark, out of the corner of my eye I see a spark and smell sulphur, like after you light a match or shoot a gun. Then all these feelings rush in, and that hole in my middle gets ripped open wide, and I can't breathe because my throat feels raw and torn." He takes a minute then goes on. "The shrinks all say that I was too young when my mom died to remember the shooting, but I know this much, it was dark when I came down the hall. I yelled for my mom to come. Then the gun went off. My father, on the nights when he was so drunk he couldn't get undressed without my help, would hold onto my arm so tight that it would leave bruises. He'd tell me that story again and again until he passed out. He wanted to remind me that it was my fault that my mom died. If I had just stayed in bed like a good kid, she would be alive. Maybe it's like a false memory, made up in my head, but maybe he told it right. A part of me thinks I should just turn myself in and let the chips fall, even though they'd be putting me away for the wrong crime."

I sit up so I can see him. "It's not your fault. Your dad made his choices. He screwed around with a gun at a party when he was probably drunk. He blamed someone else for his stupidity and loss, and he shot himself because he couldn't live with the guilt. It all could have happened with or without you."

Finn shakes his head, grinning. "I've said it before and I gotta say it again, you've got a way with words, Stalker-girl." He pulls me over and kisses me deep and slow. It takes me back to the way he loved me on the overlook, and I want a repeat performance in this big soft bed, but the timing is all wrong; we have stuff to deal with or our options will dwindle to none. Finn knows it too. He's not interested in making love to me. He pushes me away and holds me at arm's length. "I can't take the thought of not seeing you again, Sage."

I touch his face. "We're going to figure this out. I know we will." He leans against my hand, kisses it. Just then the door opens. There's no time, but instinctively I move in front of Finn to block him from view.

"Sage?" Ethan's voice is small and needy. He keeps moving toward the bed in tiny footsteps. "Your light was on. I can't sleep, I want . . . " he suddenly realizes that I'm not alone in the bed and stops in his tracks. "No. Oh no." In the second that he's frozen by his fear of Finn, I jump off the end of the bed, and throw myself in front of the door, closing it with a bang. At almost the same moment Ethan tries to bolt, but he careens into me and falls to the floor.

"Ethan, please, wait," I plead. "It's okay. Just hang on a second." Finn gets out of bed, but he doesn't come over. Ethan gets back to his feet slowly, staring me down with a look that is angry and heart-wrenching. Then he turns to Finn, like he's ready for a fight, terrified, but ready. Finn looks at Ethan and backs away, "Hey, pal, there's nothing going on here. Just relax okay?" His palms are out, urging Ethan to keep his distance.

It's odd from my vantage point; I don't know which of them is more frightened of the other as they start to circle each other like cats with their backs up. Finn knows what's coming this time and if Ethan comes at him, Finn will lay him out with a hard punch to the face. I don't want Ethan to be hurt. I do the only thing I can do. As Ethan makes his move toward Finn, I step between them, facing Ethan. I know he's going to send me to his private hell, but I focus on the day we played volleyball in the pool.

For half a second I see Ethan's gray eyes as he tries to pull away, but I wrap my arms around him in an awkward embrace. I feel us go down on our knees together like the day we kissed. Then the room goes dark and silent. I smell gasoline and hear the swish swish of it in the can I am carrying up the stairs. I feel strangely disconnected, like I'm doing an errand for someone else, and I'm not really sure why. I go into Rachel's room and pour some of the gas over the bed and carpet. Then I go into Sage's room (my room). It looks bare like I've moved out. A big box sits by the door. After I pour the gas on the bed and carpet, I put the box under one arm and spill what remains in the can down the stairs. I leave the can in the upstairs hallway and go down to the kitchen. I put the box on the table and pull the matches from my pocket. I take one out and try to strike it, but I've never done this before, and I don't really know how. My hands are shaking. I know this is wrong, but I can't stop it now. I've gone too far already. I stand over the sink to practice on a few more matches. Finally, I figure out how it works, and I can do it. I feel strangely victorious about my new skill. I take the box outside and go back in. I stand by the stairs and strike the match like an expert. I drop it in the puddle of gas on the bottom step. The whoosh of flames is horrific and I jump back, but I stay there in the kitchen to watch it climb the stairs.

Suddenly, I'm terrified; I'm in a bathtub full of ice cold water. I pee in my pants to try to warm the water up. It works for a second. Elena is there with me and so is Mama. The room is filling with smoke, and someone is outside pounding on the door and screaming. "Lana, you stupid bitch, come out! Please! You're all going to die in there! Lana, what the fuck are you doing?" It's Daddy's voice, slurred and sobbing. Elena tries to get out of the tub to let him in, but Mama struggles with her to keep her in the water. Elena rips the little fairy moonstone earring from Mama's ear, and Mama yells, but she gets Elena back down in the tub. The pounding stops and we're alone: me, Elena, and Mama. Mama's crying and blood is tricking down her neck from where the earring got torn out. She hands us wet washcloths and tells us to breathe through them as the flames start leaping around the door. Then she sits crisscross by the tub, holding our hands, Elena on the left and me on the right. Soon the fire is all around her. Elena screams and pulls away from Mama in terror. I watch her sink under the water, and I hold on to Mama tighter. As the flames lick at her clothes and hair, Mama howls in agony. She turns red then black. The smell makes me throw up. Her face is gone and she's not moving, but I can't let go; I can't stop staring. I watch the flames moving up my arm too, but I don't feel anything. Then the glass window above us rains down on our heads and strong arms lift me out of the now hot water and through the opening.

My arm is burning even after I come to; I can't catch my breath. Ethan is calmly holding me like we just exchanged a kiss. I shove him away and scramble backwards. No fucking way! This is not happening, did not happen. It couldn't be Ethan. Finn is behind me, crouching down with his hands on my shoulders. I hear a long, low moan, like grieving dog, and I realize that it's coming from me.

"What the hell did you do to her?" Finn is angry, but not willing to engage. He stays behind me.

Ethan falls backward when I push him, and he ends up sitting with his legs splayed apart. From a million miles away I watch him crawl into the corner and curl into himself with his thumb in his mouth.

Elena chooses this moment to make her appearance. "What the hell is going on in here? Are you trying to get caught?" Her focus is on me and Finn in our weird little tableau, but then she turns to see Ethan. "Oh shit!" she says in quiet resignation, like she knows the whole story, and my guess is that she does. This thought is enough to propel me to my feet.

"It was Ethan!" I can barely get the words out. I want to hit her. "You knew, you bitch, you knew! That's why you helped Finn! That's why you pretended to be mad at me about kissing your brother!" Oops, I turn in time to see Finn's told you so reaction. Then he retreats to the bed to leave Elena and me to have at it.

"Damn it, Sage! Everything's not about you!" She goes over to Ethan and cradles him against her chest. She gently takes his thumb out of his mouth and holds his hand so he can't put it back. "I didn't know what to do. When I got back, I could smell the gas on him, the fire had just started, and he was standing there holding your box of stuff. I took him inside and cleaned him up, threw the clothes into the fire. By then the sirens were approaching, so I pretended to just be arriving on the scene."

I shake my head in disbelief. I go over to where the twins are huddled and squat down till I am eye-level with Ethan. He sits up to face me. "Why, Ethan? Why?" Half of me wants to shake him.

He looks down, "I wanted him to go away and never come back."

"Finn? You wanted Finn to go away?"

Ethan nods.

"What made you think that burning down our apartment would make that happen?" I'm yelling.

He looks up at me in surprise, like I should already know this. "He did!"

I turn and look at Finn who has moved to the bench at the end of the bed. "What?" Finn says. "I have no idea what he's talking about."

"Yes you do, " Ethan says with a strange conviction. "You were thinking about it. You thought about how you would do it and everything."

Finn squirms under the accusation. Elena and I are staring at him. "Finn?" I ask.

"Jeez! Okay, I thought about it. I think about burning down a lot of stuff. It's my thing. Right?"

"Ethan, why did you think the fire would make him go away?"

"He thought about that too." He pauses and quietly adds, "When the fire happened before, everyone went away, Mama, Daddy, everyone except Lanie."

Finn stands up defensively. "Look, Sage, I never would have done it. I'm sorry I ever thought it." He turns away.

"I'm sorry too," Ethan says. His eyes search mine for forgiveness. As shocked as I am, I can't find a way to blame Ethan. I caress his face and kiss his forehead.

Finn steps forward. "So he gets a pass, Sage? Really? I can't fucking believe this shit."

I stand up to face him. "Suck it up, Finn! There's enough blame to pass around here, but all that isn't going to get us anywhere, is it?"

"You giving me a pass too?" His voice is angry, but his eyes are as childlike as Ethan's.

I caress his face and kiss him softly too.

"Very sweet," Elena says sarcastically, joining Finn and me in the middle if the room. "Now that the cat's out of the bag, what's the plan, Chief? Turning Ethan in to the cops is out of the question, right?"

"Agreed," I say looking at Finn.

"Yeah, yeah! The cops would never buy any of this mind-reading shit and he'd end up in nut house till the end of time. I don't need that on my karma. But I shouldn't have to take the blame, either." Finn says.

"I think we need Rachel," I say. I'm expecting a chorus of objections, but there's only one.

Ethan's small tearful voice comes from the corner where Elena left him. "Please, don't tell." It's a hopeless plea, and he knows it.

I go and take him in my arms. "We have to." I whisper in his ear. "But I promise, it will be alright. No one is going to be mad."

He shakes his head. "No, it won't be alright. Everyone will be mad at me. Please, Sage, make another plan."

I wipe his tears away with my thumbs. "Ethan, this is very serious. You set all of this in motion, and I can't stop it, so you're going to have to be really brave and help us do whatever Rachel tells us to."

He buries his face in my shoulder and cries for a few more seconds. Then he sits up and nods. "Okay, get Rachel," he mumbles.

I leave the three of them in Elena's room and sneak quietly through Iron Lady's room to the attic stairs. I don't knock because I don't want to wake Lily. When I get to the top of the stairs, I'm shocked to see Jesse pouring two glasses of wine, and Rachel draped over his shoulder. I must be pretty stealthy because it feels like an hour passes while they're all over each other, and I'm just standing there like a stupid fly on the wall.

"Mom!?" It's interesting how much subtext can be packed into a single syllable.

"Oh my god, Sage. We didn't hear you." She and Jesse part like the Red Sea to let me through.

"Hi, Sage," Jesse says a little sheepishly. I suppress the desire to give him 'the look.'

"Jeez, Mom!" I'm beyond grossed out, but I immediately regret my reaction. I really have no talking room since Finn is up in Elena's room.

"What do you want, Sage?" Her voice is ice cold.

I need her help, so I take it down a notch. I'm just thankful I didn't walk in on them in bed. "I . . . we have a situation, and well . . . I need you . . . NOW."

Rachel puts down the wine glass, "Is it Ethan? Elena?" Jesse asks.

"Sort of. But not you, Jesse. Sorry. Just Mom."

Rachel looks me up and down like somehow my emergency can be ascertained through my body language. "Does it involve the twins?" I nod. "Then he's in." I can tell it's nonnegotiable, and we're wasting time, so I don't argue.

"Just be quiet on your way through Lily's room. This party is already way too big."

We sound like a herd of buffalo on the stairs, and I'm about to lose it, thinking of Lily waking up and calling the police. I can almost see them cuffing Finn and dragging him away when I notice that Lily's bed is empty.

“Relax. She's out decompressing at a movie,” Rachel explains.

Sweet luck may just be on our side tonight, but I cross my fingers, just in case.

When we get upstairs, Elena and Finn are in one corner arguing. They stop when we come in. Finn steps back and looks hang-dog at Rachel. "Rachel! I am so sorry about all of this," he mumbles gesturing toward me.

She walks slowly to where he stands and puts a hand on his arm. It's all the encouragement he needs. He puts his arms around her and she hugs him back much more warmly than I would expect. "We're going to figure all this out, Finn, don't worry."

"Hey, Jesse." Finn and Jesse shake hands like old friends.

Rachel is completely thrown. "Jesse?"

"We've been sharing a hotel room for a few days now," Finn explains.

Jesse looks at Rachel and shrugs. "Cut me some slack. The kid's in exactly the same boat I was in 13 years ago."

Elena is nodding, looking like she might explode. "See, Finn, it's the perfect solution!"

"Shut up, Elena!" Finn's tone backs her right down.

Rachel suddenly reminds us that everyone is not up to speed yet. "Finn, are you turning yourself in?"

"Mom, Finn didn't do it," I say.

"Sage, I know you want to believe that, but . . . " I cut her off before she breaks Finn's heart.

"We know who did it. And I mean KNOW, not a guess," I say.

Rachel looks hard at Elena, then me, then Finn. Finally, her eyes travel down to floor where Ethan is sucking his thumb with his eyes closed. She gets it on the first try. "Oh no, please tell me I'm wrong."

I move her to the far end of the room. "You're not wrong, but it wasn't his fault . . . in a way." I have no idea how to explain Ethan's gift. Rachel sinks down on the side of the bed. "Okay this is going to be a lot to take in. Ethan has a kind of 'gift.' You know how when people touch him, they get headaches and strange thoughts, well, that's part of it. Ethan can like trade consciousness with people. Okay, long story short, he traded with Finn and saw something that he then carried out because the exchange confused him."

"Huh?"

"I'm sorry. Let me break it down for you. Ethan was channeling Finn's thoughts when he burned down the garage." I say it louder than I mean to.

Rachel takes a step back. “The police assured me that the MO was Finn’s, plus he had motive and opportunity.”

Elena jumps in, “That’s what Sage is telling you. Ethan followed

Finn's MO to the letter because he used Finn's memory or more accurately Finn's fantasy."

Finn looks away when Rachel tries to make eye contact. Then she gets up, crosses the room, and crouches down beside Ethan. "Did you really do this, Ethan?"

Ethan nods miserably.

"And it happened the way Sage and Elena say."

Ethan sits up and looks around the room. "You used to let Sage climb the big willow tree in your front yard even though it scared you. I saw the tree and the little yellow house in your memory."

Rachel shakes her head in amazement and stands to face me. "Call me a believer."

"Fuck this! Enough about him. What about me?!" Finn has reached his limit.

Jesse has been pacing the length of the room. He stops suddenly and turns to Finn. "I been where you're standing, only no one, and I mean no one, was behind me. Granted I had about ten years on you. Anyway, I know how this will play out for you if you turn yourself in, and I don't think it would feel right for anyone in this room. I ain't about to let you go it alone, son. I ain't no father to my own boy. Hell, I can't even touch him without being in pain for 24 hours. But, you, son, you I get. What do you think?"

Rachel touches Jesse's arm. "Are you sure? You came here to clear your name."

"Looks like the universe has a different plan in mind," he smiles a little sadly.

I think I'm being slow on the uptake because everyone else seems to get it, but I'm a little lost. Rachel's hand is over her mouth like when she watches a tear-jerker movie or a Hallmark commercial, and Elena is smiling. Ethan is curled up as small as he can make himself with his head in his sister's lap. I can't think about what they are suggesting. I get the blanket from the bed and put it over Ethan. Everyone is watching me. Finn comes behind me and turns me to face him.

"Sage, I'm gonna go with Jesse."

"Where? Back to the hotel?"

"No, Sage. That place is probably crawling with cops by now. I need to go further away. Jesse's been off the grid for 13 years; I think he can keep me safe."

Jesse jumps in. "We ain't got much time, boy. If Lily comes home, the cops'll be here 'fore ya know it."

I don't like this plan even a little. “Lily won’t prosecute Ethan.” I say with as much conviction as I can muster. “Finn doesn’t have to leave.”

“Sage, you know she’ll send him away. This is just the excuse she’s been waiting for. Please . . .” Elena’s voice is plaintive, desperate.

I go to the window to try to think of something else. The night seems darker than usual, and everything is glistening wet. The rain courses the window like tears, and I realize that the tapping in the back of my mind all night has been the rain hitting the glass. One more thing to lose. One more moment of grief. I wish I could put Finn in a box like Ethan did with my photos, so I could wake up tomorrow and discover miraculously that he wasn't lost after all; he was here the whole time.

Finn puts his arms around me. "You know, Sage, you could come with us."

I look at Rachel; she nods slightly.

"NO!" Ethan is on his feet suddenly, his eyes wide. He grabs at my hand, holding it desperately. "No, Sage you can't go. Please, don't leave. Please." He wraps himself around my arm, and Finn takes a step back.

Elena called it. Ultimately, I have to make a choice. Oddly it's not as hard as I imagined. Perhaps the choice was made long before any of this ever happened.

Chapter 16 (Geodesy)

> *After the Apocalypse, the ones who are left will settle into some pattern, some semblance of the life before. They will endure each day and even plan for the days to come, but in the silent loneliness of the night when sleep eludes them, they will replay each detail of the final moments, trying to find the one mistake that if undone through some miracle of time travel would evade the entire disaster.*

Jesse is a professional runner. He knows just what to pack and the routes the cops won't bother to cover. He scrolls through Google maps, making notes for about thirty minutes then makes a call to a friend in Florida who can set up fake identities, real authentic ones, good enough to pass for school enrollment, jobs, even plane tickets, though that is a risk not really worth taking. Jesse lives in a house down there on a gazillion acres where he tends the horses and cattle in exchange for rent, food, and cash. It will be months before anyone even knows someone is living there with him.

Getting out of this house is going to be the trickiest part of the venture. We have to move before daybreak. The rain though uncomfortable and inconvenient has brought in good deal of fog with it, which helps us immeasurably. Elena sneaks around to the back of the house and sets up the ladder she left for Finn. She stays in the garden and waits for us to climb down. Rachel is wearing my coat and taking her car out to hopefully draw the cops off if they're watching the house. If they don't follow her, she will meet us in the alley behind Exodus where Finn hid his bike. At the window she hugs Jesse for about ten minutes, but she doesn't cry. He gives her a final sad look before disappearing out the window. She wishes Finn a safe journey before he climbs down. I'm the last one to go. She grabs me before I can put a leg over the sill and presses her cheek to mine saying, "Good luck, Sage." Then I'm out the window too.

Ethan will ride in the car with Rachel. He's dressed in Finn's jacket and his hair is shoved up under a cap. I was shocked when he insisted on coming. There was no dissuading him, so Rachel agreed that he should ride with her, dressed like that he could pass for Finn. If the cops follow them, then they'll just keep going and circle back home, but we are counting on them meeting us.

Exodus is closed and the alleyway is as quiet as a church, except for the scurrying of bugs and rats in the dumpster. We attach the packs to back of the bike and wait for Rachel and Ethan to show up. Jesse paces. He doesn't like waiting, but he reminds us or himself perhaps that Rachel deserves at least 10 minutes. I'm not worried; no one's going to find us here.

Finn stands with his arms around me, his hips pressed into mine. The quickness of his pulse has nothing to do with my proximity. The pitch darkness in the alley is making even me anxious. I can only imagine how it's affecting Finn.

Finally, we hear the hum of Rachel's car. The headlights briefly blind us, which is oddly comforting and nerve wracking at the same time. Rachel parks at one end of the alley and runs to meet Jesse halfway. If there had been any question in my mind about them before, it is surely answered by the passion of the kiss they exchange now, right out of a ridiculous romance novel. I can't hear what they are saying to each other, but Rachel keeps wiping Jesse's cheeks and sniffing loudly. They part by increments, finally releasing hands and turning away. Jesse gets on the bike facing away from the car and Rachel. He doesn't look back. Years of practice. He knows how this is done.

I don't. At summer camp while all the other kids clung to each other, crying out those final moments, I'd be the first to slip out without shedding a single tear. Now faced with this apocalyptic good-bye, I'm paralyzed. I have no frame of reference. It's like being crushed under an avalanche of snow, suffocating and numbing. I don't know how to let go.

Finn kisses me long and tender. "Later, stalker- ," he can't finish, so he brings his head to my shoulder and lets me stroke his hair. I am shaking with silent sobs that I can't let out.

From the corner of my eye I see Ethan pull free from Elena and run toward us. When he gets close, he takes off Finn's jacket and hands it to him. "Thanks," Finn mumbles, and after a couple beats, Ethan walks back to Elena, watching us over his shoulder. I wish he wasn't here.

Finn pulls back to put the jacket on. I reach for him again, and he turns away. "Time to go, Sage." I shake my head, but no words come out. He gets on the bike, puts on his helmet, and revs the engine. He follows Jesse's lead by keeping his eyes on the road ahead. The bike disappears down the alley, consumed by the rain and fog. When engine drones out of range, it feels like it was all a bad dream, except for the icepick piercing me through. I double over from the pain and let a silent scream tear through me.

Rachel eventually leads me back to the car. I sit in the back with Ethan on the drive home. I can't hold onto Finn with Ethan's leg pressing against mine and our hands woven together. His honey-sweet smell and his head resting against my chest heal like a balm. I know it's just deferring pain that is destined to return, but I let it work its magic. None of us talks. Lily pulls into the driveway behind us, and I trust Rachel to take care of the excuses. Ethan holds my hand on the way into the house and upstairs. While I'm drying his hair, he asks, "Why didn't you go?

I take off his shirt and dry his chest, arms, and back before I answer. "I couldn't leave you."

Ethan turns to face me. "You love me more than Finn?"

"It's not really a contest, E. I love you different than I love Finn. You need me and I need you too. I can be without him, but . . ."

"Not without me?" He says it sadly with his eyes on the floor.

"What's wrong, Mouse?"

"I want you to love me the way you love him."

I could ask why, but I'm not ready to hear his answer, so I go to his room and wait while he changes back into the pajamas he left on the bathroom floor.

I get a t-shirt and shorts for myself. I really need to go shopping. I put them on and turn around. Ethan's at the door watching me. I search his eyes for some hint of the sexual attraction I felt when we kissed, but the closest I can see is curiosity.

I pull back the covers to make sure the sheets are dry then Ethan slides into bed and moves way over to make room for me. I slide in next to him and let him snuggle into me with his head on my chest and his leg draped over mine. He takes a deep contented breath and puts his thumb in his mouth. I sing "Here Comes the Sun," softly and horribly off key, but I can feel him grow heavy with sleep. He wakes a little when I move his head to the pillow to slip out.

"Don't go, Sage. I promise I'll stay dry. Please." he mumbles.

"Rules, baby, there are rules." I kiss him lightly on the lips, and he opens his eyes, surprised.

"I love you, Sage."

"I love you too, Mouse." This is why I stayed.

I watch him from the doorway until he's asleep. Then I go across the hall. Elena is half-gone too. "Finally," she mumbles. "Did he try to convince you to stay with him again?"

"You know it," I say as I climb onto the bed without getting under the covers.

Elena sits up and holds my hands. "I'm glad you stayed."

"Me too," I say, and I mean it even though I feel like I'm going to cry again.

"I can help with that," she offers pointing to my heart.

"Tomorrow," I say. "Tonight I need to mourn."

"Okay," she says and kisses me gently, sweetly. I stare into her cerulean eyes, and they feel like home.

"I'm gonna go sleep with Rachel," I say getting off the bed reluctantly. "See you in the morning."

I'm opening the door when her voice drifts over. "The kiss with

Ethan . . ." I stop. ". . . it wasn't all from Finn. You know that, right?"

"I know," I say, but I can't turn to face her.

In the attic Rachel is sitting up in bed with her computer in her lap. She's nursing a glass of white wine, maybe what was left over from the date I interrupted just a few hours ago. I imagine being in her shoes, thinking I'm about to get lucky and then without any warning, watching it slip away. If I was her, I would hate me.

Her eyes are puffy and red, and there's a pile of tissues on the floor next to the bed. She looks up suddenly like I made a sharp noise. "Herbie?" She's surprised to see me.

"Can I come in?" I ask.

"Okay." She pauses the movie she's watching.

"I'm really sorry, Madre," I say snuggling in next to her with my head on her shoulder.

"Me too," she says. "You gonna be okay?"

"Eventually. I was my decision after all. What about you? I guess you never saw that coming. Did you?"

"Not in billion years." She turns the movie, *The Bourne Identity*, back on and wipes at her eyes.

'Nothing like the healing power of a Matt Damon movie," I say.

She forces a smile. "You wanna stay?"

"Sure. As long as I don't have to sit through *Good Will Hunting* again, I'm good."

We watch in silence as Jason Bourne and the hot foreign girl travel through Europe and finally make out in the bathroom. Then Rachel pauses it again. "What are you doing here, kiddo?"

"I wanted to make sure you were okay?" I say.

"Is that so? And. . . ?

"Also . . . I wanted to know . . ."

"About me and Jesse," she finishes the sentence. "Sage, you are the kid that has to know everything, aren't you?"

"Guess so. Are you gonna tell me or am I going to have to hack your email and steal your phone to read the text messages?"

Rachel reaches behind her, grabs the pillow, and whacks me over the head. The computer nearly falls off the bed, but she catches it in time and moves it safely to the night stand. "Jesse is different, kind of sweet and vulnerable, but strong too in a survival kind of way." I make a sign like I'm going to puke. Rachel shakes her head. "Do you want to hear this or not?"

"I didn't know you were going to go all gushy on me." She rolls over and reaches for the computer.

I grab her arm. "Go ahead, you obviously need to spill this."

She smiles and goes on. "Jesse needed me, and it felt good to be needed like that. I'm sure you of all people can understand that. Besides he's so dreamy." She puts her hand to her forehead melodramatically. "His eyes are the same shade of gray as Ethan's and that Southern drawl . . . yum."

She is totally making me laugh even though we're both in agony. Then she gets all serious again, "The whole thing really started in Florida. He came back here for me."

"I'm so sorry, Madre. I never meant to screw up your life. Well at least not this much."

"You didn't screw up my life, only my date. Whatever is going to come of me and Jesse will happen the way it's supposed to and when it's supposed to." Rachel sound so clear like she really believes the crap she's spouting.

I change the focus, "Jesse's coming here for you is nice . . . for you. Not so nice for his kids," I say.

"That bit was more complicated. I think he thought that seeing them would hurt them worse rather than helping them," she reasons.

"True enough in Ethan's case," I say.

"Sage, can I ask a personal question?"

"More personal than did I have sex?"

"Okay, maybe not that personal. Why didn't you go with Finn? Don't you love him?"

"Talk about complicated," I say rolling my eyes. "I do love Finn. I mean I must love him; I let him get pretty deep past my defenses, but . . ."

Rachel cuts me off. "You know I would have come too. We could have made that work. You and Finn, me and Jesse."

"I don't know if that would work or not, for real, but this," I gesture to include the whole house, "this works for some reason."

"What do you mean by 'this?'" she asks.

I commit halfway. "This house. Lily. Me. You. The twins. I couldn't leave."

"You mean Ethan," she says in her know-it-all voice.

I nod.

"Oh, Sweetie, there's not a lot of hope for him, you know. The prognosis even with medication is pretty sad. Agoraphobia, social anxiety, PTSD, enuresis, emotional regression. The list is kind of endless. He's a little boy who is going to age like a man, but will always be a child."

"Mom, I have hope for him." I say it quietly and decisively. She doesn't argue.

She turns on the movie again, and I scrunch down and let the voices lull me to sleep.

What feels like five minutes later there's an insistent knocking at the kitchen door, and the sky peeking through the window is light gray. Below the loft Iron Lady curses loudly. I put a pillow over my head. A few minutes later she's standing at the foot of the bed. "It's the police," she says flatly.

Rachel tells me to stay upstairs, that she will take care of it, but my curiosity is stronger than my exhaustion, and I sneak down into Lily's room to press my ear to the wall her room shares with the kitchen.

The officers are not Henderson and DeSocio. I hear two male voices saying something about my dad. I'm only catching a few phrases here and there, but it seems like they're looking for him. An air raid siren goes off in my head. I run up the stairs and tear the attic room apart. I wrack my brain for the last time I saw it. Rachel had it in her hand. What did she do with it? I can't find it anywhere. I'm still searching when Rachel comes back up. "What are you looking for?" she asks.

"The thumb-drive? Where is it?" I ask a bit more hysterically than I intend.

"Okay, here we go."

"Mom, please tell me you didn't turn him in."

"I can't do that, kiddo." She sits on the edge of the bed and pats a spot next to her for me to sit, but I don't move from where I stand across the room.

"How could you do that without telling me? What part of my friend, my dad, my problem did you not understand?"

"What part of my child, my responsibility, my mistakes, do you not understand?"

I shake my head. "Go ahead, enlighten me."

"Why do you think your dad and I split up?" she asks.

"He's a narcissistic cheater."

She laughs, "That too. He had problems when we were married. I knew something was terribly wrong with him . . . sexually." I wince and she puts her hand up to calm me. "I'm not going to give you any details, obviously. But I knew, and I closed my eyes. I didn't want to face what I suspected. After we split up, it was easy to push away my suspicions. My cowardice put you and your friends in danger. I am sick about what he did to Jo. I am sicker that if I had been braver, confronted him about his bizarre behavior, it might never have happened." She's trying hard to hold back the tears.

"You knew? You sent me off with him and you knew?" I am having a hard time processing all of this.

"Sort of knew, Sage. I loved him. I couldn't accept that he could be capable of anything like that. I was stupid! I am so sorry. I had to turn him in once you told me what he did. I had to get him off the damn streets!"

"I get it, Mom," I say quietly. "But you should have told me what you were doing."

"You were a little off your nut. You know what I mean?"

"Is that the clinical term for it?"

Rachel smiles, "I didn't want to push you any closer to the edge. I'm sorry you're hurt now, but I'm not sorry I did it."

"Is he going to jail?" I ask.

"I think so, as soon as they find him. They have a lead." Rachel looks so tired. "I'm going back to sleep for a bit. Care to join?" She's already under the covers and curled up on her side.

"Ethan's going to be awake in about five minutes, and he'll be in here bugging us as soon as he figures out where I am. I'm gonna go."

As expected, Ethan's awake when I get upstairs. His bedroom door is open, and he's taking off his diaper, his back to the door. He doesn't see me watching. He stands up and gets his swimsuit from the desk chair and in that moment I am able to admire his beauty: the golden glow of his skin and hair, the sinewy muscles of his arms, back, and thighs, the perfect taper of his waist, and the other gifts he's endowed with. Breath-taking and heart breaking. He pulls on his trunks, turns, and sees me. I am so busted.

"Sage!" His cheeks flush suddenly. Then he smiles and hurries to hug me. “I missed you.”

“Me too, Mouse.” I bury my face in his curls and don't let go.

Chapter 17 - Epilog (More than Memory)

I used to think that knowing someone's secrets gave you power over them, the kind of power that could make you a hero or a hell-raiser. Either way every time you expose a hidden wound you become responsible for what happens to the secret and to the person it belongs to.

The sun is coming up over the houses on the next street. Any moment the screen door will creak, and Ethan will walk out into the half-light of dawn. We have been living in this house high on a hill near the university for six months. This morning I managed to sneak out to the patio without waking him to work on an essay for my writing class.

The door bangs, and I smile.

"You left me," Ethan says, pouting.

"You looked so peaceful, how could I spoil that? Besides I needed to study."

"Okay, but next time, wake me up." He drapes his towel over the chair and slips into the water without a splash. It's October now and a bit too cold out for swimming at 68 degrees, but the pool is heated, and even if it wasn't, he'd get in. I watch him cut through the water like a shark, all power and speed. I'm smiling at the image of Shark-

Ethan when he comes up.

“What are you smiling about,” he asks.

“Nothing . . . you,” I say, trying not to laugh.

“You better watch it, or I’ll come drip on you,” he threatens before disappearing again.

A few minutes later, I hear a car pull up in front of the house. All balance is instantly restored to the universe. Seconds later, Elena comes through the screen door.

"Knew I'd find you two out here." She puts her arms around my neck from behind and kisses my cheek.

"How was the super-power training?" I ask. Elena has been in Florida at a parapsychology laboratory where they’ve been testing her gift and paying her for that privilege. It's been a tough three weeks here with just Ethan and me, but we managed.

“Super!”

Ethan sees her and scrambles up the pool steps. "Lanie! I missed you soooooo much." He tries to hug her, but she dodges him nicely, putting the chair between them.

"Missed you too, Mouse," she says, reaching over to caress his face. "Hugs later, okay?"

"Okay. Guess what?" he says to her, grinning at me.

"I'm sure you're going to tell me."

He nods. "One month, 30 days, no daytime accidents!" He’s smiling like he just won the lottery.

"If you make through today, "I remind him.

He ignores me and asks Elena, "Do you want to see the chart?"

"E, that's amazing! You can show me when we go in." But he runs in to get it." She turns to me, "Miracle worker."

"Motivation," I say. "I'll only sleep in his bed with him if stays dry all day."

"So thirty dry nights too, then?"

"I'm not that lucky."

"You do like to live dangerously," she laughs and throws her arms around my neck again. "Damn, I missed you, girl!"

"Likewise," I can’t stop smiling.

Ethan comes back and shoves his chart into her hands. "Are you coming to the museum with us? Jo Jo is meeting us there for lunch."

he says. "It opens at ten. We're going to try taking the bus again."

"You nervous?" she asks.

Ethan nods, his eyes wide. "Last time wasn't so good."

"We don't have to relive it, E. It was a while ago. This time will be better," I say.

“I know,” Ethan says confidently.

"I think I'm going to pass on the outing," Elena says, "I need to check in at the Bean Scene so Marco can get me back on the schedule. Oh yeah, the gallery sold two more of Ethan's paintings last week! $3,000 bucks. Nice job, little brother!"

"I'm not little -"

I cut him off. You should go get ready, E. If you hurry, we'll have time to get bagels before the museum opens." Ethan forgets the argument, racing into the house and up the stairs.

Elena follows me into the kitchen and puts Ethan’s chart back on the fridge. She touches my shoulder and whispers in my ear, "Letters and gifts from Finn and Rachel in the front suitcase pocket in our room." My heart skips a beat. "He still misses you like crazy. They . . . Finn wants to know when you're going to get down there."

Rachel joined Jesse and Finn in Florida when we moved here. I can call her, but only when she’s away from the ranch. With GPS and all it’s just safer for Finn. Rachel says he rarely leaves the grounds, but he’s almost never at the house with her and Jesse. He sleeps in the loft in the barn or out under the stars.

Elena is staring when I come back to myself. I shrug noncommittally and take the stairs two at a time

While Ethan showers, I sit on the floor and read Finn's letter a dozen times, trying to picture his eyes and dimples. It's been over a year since that rainy night when he and Jesse rode away. More than a year since we made love, more than a year since I held him or heard his voice. In some ways he isn't real any more. His flaws have faded, and purified version of Finn remains. It's that Finn I am faithful to, that Finn I wrap my mind around at night before I fall asleep. Real Finn misses me, but I'm not fool enough to think he's waiting.

Sage,

I’ve been trying to write this letter for a month without success

and now it's down to the wire. Elena is putting her suitcase in the car. I tried to write something cool and sarcastic, but I'm not really that guy anymore. I've had to come clean with myself out here. Everything about the way I lived was about keeping people at a distance so I wouldn't hurt them or be hurt by them. Distance felt safe. Now it feels like distance. Spending days alone with only a horse to talk to will teach you a few things. Anyway, I'd be lying if I said I'm miserable; I'd be lying if I said I'm not. Jesse and Rachel are awesome, the parents I always wished I had, but I'm too old for storybooks and goodnight kisses (unless they come from you, lol). As it turns out, I love the ranch! I'm pretty good at the work. Even so there's this strange emptiness I can't escape. When I ride out deep into the night as far as my horse can go, I always end up at the same place. You. Girl, you may be a million miles away, but you are here in the palm of my hand too, the hilt of a knife that cuts out my heart. Guess it goes without saying I miss you. Guess you know that my invitation to join me here is not time limited. Guess that's all there is to say, cause Elena needs to get to the airport. Then, now, always, you turn me inside out, Stalker girl!

F.

I try to imagine this new Finn, part cowboy, part philosopher. If I went down there, would it be the same between us, or is he in love with a distilled and perfected version of me too?

Ethan comes in dressed, and I shove the letter into my pocket before I help him wrap his thumbs in duct-tape so he isn't tempted to suck them in public. I comb out his hair and step back to admire him. He is striking in the off-white Henley and khakis. With his hands shoved in his pockets, he looks like any hipster college boy all scruffy-faced and brooding. No one would ever know.

Ethan runs down to show Elena his new sketches, and inspired by Finn's prose, I take a minute before showering to finish my essay.

Before it happened to me, I thought love would be simple, like falling into a soft bed. One person moving ever closer to me until we became one; from a distance love seemed safe. But when love came, there was no violin music in the background; it was accompanied by the deep growl of an approaching avalanche, the crackle and hiss of a fire storm, the howl of a tornado blowing through without warning. There was nothing safe about it. Love was a terrifying expanse that had to be bravely crossed every day. It became the ache in my gut when I leave Ethan at home alone, the sleeplessness when Elena's away, and the empty place just above my left breast where an icepick used to pierce clear through. Even thousands of miles of road and years apart can't dim the sparkling-blue eyes that burn inside my lids just before I fall asleep. When it comes to love there is no feather bed, no safe distance.

ACKNOWLEDGMENTS

Many thanks to all the people who encouraged me in the process of writing this book, especially Susan Jarvis, Connie Kilgore, and my book club girls: Helen Mayhew, Bridget Kane, and Jessica Vance who were there for me from the start to love my story and remind me that the I owed it to the characters to tell it all.

Thanks to Ernest Gaines and Joseph Andriano at the University of Louisiana who mentored my writing as a graduate student and gave me the tools and confidence to follow this path.

I also want to recognize the writers in my life who inspired me to get on with it already: John Fleming, Andrew Michael Roberts, Chris Michalski, and Alicia Hartzell.

Thanks, more than I can say, to Wahab and Batina for letting me stay in their cabin whenever I needed the space to write.

A special shout out to the writing group who provided so much valuable criticism at the beginning of this project and helped shape it into what it became: Stephanie Wenger, Mike Walker, Clay Woomer and the others (you know who you are).

For all the tantrums and little boy behaviors that made Ethan more real I owe my nephews Chase and ZJ Hays.

For the information about police procedures and laws, I am grateful to my friend, neighbor, and APD officer Adam Collins.

Last, but not least, I totally owe my daughter Skye a debt of gratitude for her patience through all the "café days," her design of the geodesy logo, and her insightful ideas for making the characters and story more engaging.

Coming in February 2014

STELLAR NAVIGATION

Elena's Story

Susan Michalski

GEODESY
BOOK 2

Keep reading for a sneak peak.

Chapter 1 (Back Home)

"Or liken me to a shoe
Blackened and spit-shined through
Kicking back home to you
Smiling back home
Singing back home to you
Laughing back home to you
Dragging back home to you."
(Shawn Colvin, "Polaroids," 1992)

The heavy ocean air breathes me. I am a grain of salt dissolved in wind, both less and more than when I first stepped onto this strand. Before then, I had never been to a beach or much of anywhere really. I had never been drunk on my own power or aware of my ultimate insignificance. I moved through a life that was only half mine. It's like landing on a planet light-years away. The air has substance; I can wrap my arms around it or spread them wide and let it lift me off the ground as it sings my name, Elena. The birds call out in a language that strips away all pretense. They are in charge here, creatures of air and water, ordering the pitiful flightless humans to do their bidding. Even the ground has a will and desire of its own, shifting and sucking my feet until I tire of fighting it and collapse into its warm embrace. The horizon stretches into a silk thread and falls away just beyond my imagination. I am inconsequential under the burnished sky, and at the same time the secret me inside rises up with the tide, authentic, suddenly whole and real and more than what I was before.

Every afternoon for three weeks poor tortured Finn was there beside me, but not really with me as he stared expressionlessly out at the water, waiting for it to quell the flames licking at his head and heart. I should hate him for the things he's done. I should thank him for things he's done. But our past feels like nothing more than a weathered shell that has no purpose anymore. If he'd just let me, I would help him. I would reach inside, find the source of his agony, and extract every shard and ember. All it would take is a touch. I reach for his hand again and again, but he pulls away every time. Maybe his torment is too much a part of him to be without it; maybe I get that more than I'd like to admit.

Downstairs the door opens and bangs shut, pulling me back to the present. I get out of the tub and wrap the towel around myself as Ethan climbs heavily up the stairs. I got back from Florida this morning and begged off the museum excursion that my house-mates, my twin brother, Ethan, and bestie, Sage, had planned. Of course, I missed them over the three weeks I was away, but I wasn't ready to struggle with where I fit in this world that dances to Sage and Ethan's beat. I wanted to have a few more hours to be Elena alone and simple, just me.

I am about to open the bathroom door, but Ethan beats me to it. I know by the inward curve of his shoulders, the tremor in his chin, and the lines creasing his brow what happened, so I don't ask. I touch his hand, but he won't lift his gaze. I close the door behind him. Not so long ago he would have reached out to me for comfort, asked me to help him get sorted out. Now he will suffer the humiliation, angry and alone as he changes out of his wet clothes. It is a bitter pill that I can heal anyone I touch, except the one person I am most connected to, the one person who needs my healing gift the most.

Voices drift up from the living-room. Sage is not alone. I dress quickly and sprint down the stairs. Jo is standing at the bottom of the stairway like she's thinking about coming up. I leap into her open arms from a few steps up and wrap myself around her, almost toppling her onto the sofa. Luckily I'm tiny and she's strong. She laughs low before kissing me and putting me carefully down. I run my fingers through her short dark hair, while she twirls one of my shoulder length curls, and I close my eyes to imagine holding her kiss much longer, savoring it like the last bite of a dark chocolate mousse.

"You're blonder," Jo says smiling her approval. Sage drifts in uncomfortably through the archway from the kitchen. Jo drops her hand, and I follow her lead.

Jo and Sage have known each other beyond forever, but I came into the picture as Jo took a brief hiatus from Sage. When she came back, I had taken her place in Sage's life. It would make sense for her to resent me, but our mutual attraction to Sage and then each other dissolved that potential energy and a much more complicated dynamic has emerged.

"What a fab surprise." I can't stop smiling.

"Wild horses couldn't keep her away," Sage says. Jo shifts away from me a little.

"Guess we aren't celebrating tonight," I say to distract from the awkwardness. I look up at the stairs where Ethan went.

"It was my fault. I forgot how long it would take to get home during rush hour even in a car. At least we weren't on the bus or in the museum." Sage says.

"He had a great day, though. And even when he . . . you know . . . lost it, he didn't lose it completely like he used to. You know what I mean?" Jo says.

I have to smile despite the sadness of the subject, but I don't prolong the conversation because Ethan is descending the stairs, head down with a handful of ink pens in different colors clutched in his hand. He doesn't look at any of us as he makes his way through the room. We follow him into the kitchen where he takes the chart off the refrigerator. He was so excited to show it to me this morning when I got home. "30 days," he had said. "If I make today, I will have a whole month with no daytime accidents." At nineteen this is a huge accomplishment for my precious and problematic twin, who spent fifteen years of his life as a four year old, living and reliving the trauma of the fire that took our mother and sent our father on the run. Now he looks at the chart like it has betrayed him. For half a second I think he is going to rip it up or crumple it. Instead he sits at the table and begins to draw on it.

"Hey, Mouse, tell Elena what we saw today," Sage urges, trying to bring him back to us.

"Later." He doesn't look up.

I take a step forward to see what he's drawing, but he shields it with his arm like a kid taking a test in school. Jo comes up behind me and slips her hand into mine. Her touch is magical in the corniest of ways. I just want to take her upstairs and close the bedroom door.

"Who's cooking tonight?" I ask absently.

Ethan looks up at Sage, and I wonder if he's communicating with her telepathically, the way he and I used to but rarely do anymore.

"No one," Sage says. "We're going out to dinner tonight to celebrate your home coming."

I raise my eyebrows. "You sure you're up for that, little brother?" I ask, putting my hand on his shoulder.

He shrugs it away. "Why not?" His voice has an edge that I've never heard before. It stings like a sharp flick to the temple.

I let it go. "Is Jo coming?" I ask.

"Sorry, sweety," she says. "I'm just the taxi service today. I have music stuff, rehearsal, you know, big performance coming up. Next time for sure." She motions with her head toward the door.

I walk Jo out to the car, stopping to look in the back window to see how much damage Ethan did to her upholstery.

"You gotta love leather seats," she says reading my concern. "Sage cleaned it up, no worries."

"Thanks for being such a good sport." I shuffle a bit closer to her.

"What am I gonna do? Be mad? It's Ethan. How could I be mad at an angel?" Her eyes go soft as she talks about him.

"Sage should've made him wear a diaper." I shake my head.

"Controlling Ethan's not Sage's gig."

"I see," I say half insulted, "That's my gig."

"Hey, if the fiddle fits . . ." She flashes her adorable tough girl smile.

I stand on my toes and kiss her. "When do I get to see you?" I try not to sound as desperate as I feel.

"As soon as I can get my shit together. Promise." She looks into my eyes until I have to look away.

"Tomorrow?" I ask.

"I'll do my best," she says, and then she's in the car, backing down the driveway. I could have done with one more kiss, but Jo's not there yet.

Back in the kitchen, Sage is putting dishes from the sink into the dishwasher. Ethan and his pens are gone.

"Check it out," Sage motions toward the chart on the fridge.

I take it down to examine it. There in the box labeled with today's date is a tiny picture of a boy with curly hair, a sad face, a dark spot on the crotch, and a puddle on the ground. I bust out laughing. "At least he's developing a sense of humor about it," I say. "That's good, right?"

"Maybe. It's a way to deal with his embarrassment and disappointment at least," Sage says.

Ethan comes into the kitchen. He takes the paper out of my hand, holds my eyes for a beat, and puts the chart back on the fridge. "Let's go eat. I'm starving," he announces. Then he whispers in Sage's ear. Sage grins like a chimp.

"Whisper whisper," I mock.

"Don't get your panties in a twist, sister. We have some surprises for you." Sage laughs.

Ethan hands Sage the keys and her purse, then bolts out the door ahead of us. Sage locks the house then makes a great show of sauntering to the driver's side of the old Volvo we share. She's swinging the keys in spiral on her finger. Just before she opens the car door, she lets the keys fly in a high arch over the roof of the car. Ethan plucks them from the air with one hand. I hold my breath as the two of them circle around the car like a Chinese fire-drill and take each other's places. Ethan slides into the driver's seat. Sage looks at me over the top of the car, and I mouth, "Have you lost your fucking mind?" She shrugs and drops into the seat next to Ethan. I get in the back hesitantly and fasten the safety belt with exaggerated care.

Ethan turns the engine over, checks the rearview mirror, and backs out of the driveway. My mouth is catching flies, no doubt, but

I have temporarily lost control of the muscles that might close it.

On the way to the restaurant Sage patiently coaches Ethan through the intersections and on and off the highway ramps. It's clear that this not his first time on the road. He is calm and adept in a way I would have never imagined. Even his parking is smooth and accurate. "Wow," I say when he turns off the engine. He smiles brightly, confidently, maybe the happiest I've ever seen him. He puts up his hand for a high five that Sage returns along with a little hipster fist bump. I can only shake my head. On the way into the restaurant I grab Sage by the upper arm to let Ethan go in ahead of us. "What in the name of hell and all its manifestations made you think it would be a good idea to teach Ethan to drive?" I demand when he's out of earshot.

Sage stares me down. "He's a teenage boy. What do normal teenage boys love almost as much as girls in tiny bikinis?"

"Cars," I say quietly.

"Ethan needs to feel normal to be normal."

"Sage, he's not 'normal,'" I remind her.

Sage looks away and then back at me. "You need to let go of that, Elena. Let him grow up already."

A part of me knows she's right, but she's wrong too. She can't make him into something she wants him to be. Her expectations are too high.

Ethan comes back out of the restaurant. "What's taking you guys so long? I'm hungry."

"You're always hungry, Mouse!" Sage says as she slips her arm around his waist, and they put their foreheads together.

Inside the restaurant I pull back and watch them. Sage gives the hostess her name and asks for a booth. Ethan hides behind her, like a little boy. What's new is that when the hostess says hi, he responds in kind, making eye contact albeit briefly, and he shows no sign of the terror that would have consumed him in a situation like this a year ago. I'm sure he appears shy to her, but maybe not abnormally so.

After we're seated, there is no avoiding Ethan's elation. "What do you think, Lanie? I can drive a real car!" He throws his head back and laughs like a little kid. "By next month I'll be ready to take the test if I want."

"Really?" I say shaking my head at Sage.

"Sage says I'm good enough." A small flash of anger colors his cheeks and tone.

"You drove amazingly well, E. I'm really impressed. . ."

Sage signals me with her eyes to not continue the 'but' phrase that was set to follow. I bite my tongue and leave it at that. We will have to talk about it later, but I can let him have this moment.

I let my eyes scan the restaurant. We come here to this little roadside Italian dive a lot. It's usually pretty empty, and the tables are oceans apart, so Ethan doesn't feel crowded. Repetition and routine are the keys to success when it comes to my brother. I'm not sure if Sage has internalized the rules.

A group of girls a couple years younger than we are comes in. They look sweaty and happy like they've just won a soccer game. Every one of them slows as they pass our booth to gaze at my brother. They stare in hungry admiration as he holds hands with Sage and she whispers in his ear. They don't see him though. They see the pretty wrapper: the golden surfer-boy curls carelessly framing his gentle face, the bright red lips shaped into an angelic pout, the intense gray eyes with impossibly long blond lashes, and the turned up nose that makes him look much younger than he is. What they don't see is that he's gripping Sage's hand for dear life because their attention is making him panic, and she's whispering words not of love, but of comfort to assuage his anxiety so he doesn't freak out, start crying or worse. If those girls knew the truth about this boy, their stares would be quite different. Not normal, not close.

Ethan and Sage have one more surprise for me. When the waitress finally graces us with her presence, Sage nudges him gently. Ethan swallows and looks down at the menu. He points to the chicken Marsala and mumbles his order without looking up. The waitress writes it down on her pad completely unaware that she is witnessing a milestone, a miracle. I let it sink in. Ethan ordered a meal in a restaurant. It's a small thing for most people, but for a boy who never left the house for six years and hid in his room anytime anyone new came through the door. This small act is earth-shattering. I am so thrown that I almost forget about the news that I have carried from Florida. Almost.

I have had a week to mull it all over, and I am still a bit flummoxed by the development I have yet to impart. I have no idea how Ethan and Sage will take it. I plan to break it to them slowly, give them enough information to figure it out for themselves, so there's no killing of the messenger if that's the upshot. It could really go either way, though. I know I'm taking a big chance throwing this at Ethan in a public place, but what the hell. If he can drive a car and order a meal, this should be easy. I hope. When the food arrives and silence settles over us, I edge off the cliff.

"How long have your mom and our dad been living together?" I ask Sage.

"Rachel and Jesse?" Sage answers, "Six months I guess, about as long as we've been in the apartment."

I pause for a few seconds. "How old is Rachel?"

"Ask weird questions much, Elena?" Sage is looking at me kind of funny, and I think she might guess my news.

"Just answer the question," I say.

"Forty-five," Ethan says, happily joining the game.

I wink at him.

"Sage, do you think of us as family, like siblings?"

"Really, Elena, enough with the disconnected questions." Sage puts her fork down in annoyance.

"Yes or no, please," I insist calmly.

"Of course, I do," she says looking nervously from Ethan to me. "Where are you going with this?"

"Well . . . in about six months we're going to be related for real."

"What the hell are you taking about? Rachel would never ever ever get married again, even to Jesse. Besides he can't marry legally; that would put him back on the grid." Sage is shaking her head like I've lost my marbles, but Ethan's eyes are growing huge with the realization that he stole from my mind. 'Cheater,' I think, but he doesn't care.

"A baby?" he thinks. "I'm going to have a brother?"

"Or another sister, if you're very very lucky," I respond in my head.

The smile spreads across his face slowly as his imagination goes to work on the idea of a baby in the family.

I watch him and think, 'one more reason for you to grow up fast, little boy. Let's see if you can get out of diapers before the baby does.' It's a cruel thought, but it's there before I can stop it, and Ethan reads it. In an instant his smile vanishes, replaced by the creases in his brow and tilt of his chin that signal the peculiar pain of shame. I might as well have punched him. Ethan starts to bring his thumb up to his mouth, but I reach out and catch his hand in time. He pulls away and sits on his hand scowling at me. 'I didn't mean it, Mouse. I'm sorry,' I think as loudly as I can. I don't know if he hears me.

All this drama goes on without Sage. She is still trying to add up the sums.

I finally spell it out for her. "Rachel's pregnant, you big idiot!"

Sage's mouth falls open, and her eyes go blank for a second. Then in typical Sage fashion, she explodes. "No fucking way! Rachel's too old! I can NOT believe this! Great timing, Madre mio! All those years I begged for a sister and now that you decide to give me one, I have to share her! Really, Mother!"

"Ah yes, I forgot. It's all about Sage." I lean over and give her a playful punch in the arm. She looks at Ethan for support, but he's lost in his own thoughts. His eyes are sparkling with the tears he's fighting thanks to my unfortunate mean streak. That's new too, Ethan fighting back tears and not just melting into them. He succeeds in regaining control of himself, and picks up his fork. I watch him push the food around his plate. He glances at me because I'm staring, and manages a fairly vicious return glare. I look away, completely chastised by the thought he directs at me. 'At least I'm trying; I don't see any charts on the refrigerator dedicated to your little problem.'

"Who are you?" I say out loud. He turns away from me, frowning.

The rest of dinner is a combination of Sage's restless self-centered energy, Ethan's barely concealed disappoint with me or himself or both, and me desperately jumping through hoops to make everything seem fine. On the way out of the restaurant Ethan turns the keys over to Sage and gets in the back seat, where he curls into himself and immediately begins sucking his thumb. I give up trying, and Sage drives us home in silence, each of us lost in the reality of what it could mean to be a sibling, or for some of us what it already means. On the way through the kitchen Sage grabs Ethan's chart off the fridge while he heads upstairs to get ready for bed.

"What do you need that for?" I ask.

"Ammunition," she explains. "He's going to expect me to sleep in his bed with him."

"Right. Because of your magical motivation intervention in my absence," I say.

"Hey, it worked. Didn't it? 29 days without an accident is a record I think," she says.

"But he didn't make it today, so no reward tonight, right?" I ask. I want Sage with me.

She nods. "That doesn't mean he won't try to negotiate anyway."

"I think I'll just stay down here while you guys work that out." I collapse onto the sofa.

"Suit yourself, but you'll need to go up and spend some time with him before bed. He missed you like crazy." Sage stands over me.

"Sure," I say, but I'm not sure. "You go first and I'll be like the clean-up crew that follows the elephants. I'll get all the shit that follows."

"Very funny. You can go up first if you want to," Sage offers.

"I'll take it." I jump up with an enthusiasm I don't really feel.

"Sold to the highest bidder," Sage drops into my place, and takes Finn's letter out of her pocket.

"You haven't read it yet?" I delivered Finn's letter to her this morning as soon as I got home.

"I haven't memorized it yet." She smiles sadly. A year and half is a long time to not talk to someone that you're in love with. I'm sure that letter is small comfort.

"Better get to it then," I say and begin the long climb to Ethan's room, completely unprepared for who or what might be lurking around the next psychic bend in the labyrinth of my twin's mind and heart.

He meets me in the hall, ready for bed.

"Where you going?" I ask half-smiling, hoping he's forgotten my nasty comment.

"Downstairs to hang with Sage," he says without returning any of my good will.

"E," I put my hand on his arm to force the connection. "I am so sorry for being so mean at the restaurant. I don't want you to be mad at me. I missed you. Didn't you miss me too?"

He looks down at his feet and nods. I take his hand and lead him back into the bedroom. His room in our little rental house near the university is tiny with barely enough space for the bed, dresser, and small desk. Sage and I share a slightly bigger room, so that the third bedroom, the largest, can be used for Ethan's art studio. A gallery in town sells his haunting paintings. While it's hard for lots of people to imagine, Ethan brings more money into this house than Sage and I combined. Ethan sits on the edge of the bed while I fiddle with the stuff on his desk -- sketches, notes, and elaborate math problems with symbols I don't understand worked out in perfect miniature print that fills three or four pages front and back. "What's this?" I ask, holding up a page.

"Don't mess those up!" He jumps off the bed and grabs the paper from me. He organizes it back into the pile while I look over his shoulder.

"Sorry," I mumble.

He turns around to face me, and I feel oddly intimidated. Ethan is nearly a full head taller than I am, though no one would describe him as tall. At 5' 8" he and Sage are actually about the same, but in the last year or so he's put on a little weight, filled out some through the shoulders and chest, so he doesn't seem as small to me. I step back to let him through and notice the sprinkling of blond whiskers over his top lip and on his cheeks and chin, one more thing to add to growing list of changes in him. "So what's the stuff on those papers?"

"Dr Roschan from the university started working with me on Skype a couple weeks ago, remember?"

"Oh, yeah. I forgot Sage set that up. How's that going?"

For a second Ethan forgets his annoyance, and his eyes light up. "He's giving me extra problems and stuff he does with the graduate students. It's way cool." His voice drops at the end.

"Sounds awesome. What's the prob?" Ethan sits in the middle of the bed cross-legged with his head down. After a couple seconds, he looks up halfway.

"He wants me to come to class at the university. He thinks I should be a normal student, but . . . I can't."

"Too scary," I say, and he nods. "Nobody's going to make you go, E."

"I know, but . . ." He doesn't finish. He pulls at the fuzz on the blanket and his eyes cloud over.

"What is it, E?"

He takes a deep breath and looks at me with something akin to desperation. "I don't want to be afraid of everything anymore. I want to be like you and Sage, not like me." Now the tears spill over and I feel him reaching out for me emotionally. I sit next to him on the bed, and he puts his head in my lap, curls in knees to chest and puts his thumb in his mouth. I run my fingers through his tangled hair, trace the lines in his forehead.

"Give it some more time, E. Look at how far you've come in the last six months: riding the bus, going to museums and restaurants, driving a car." I give him a playful poke, and he manages a fleeting smile. "Who knows? Maybe next year you'll be ready. Maybe by next year it won't seem so scary."

"Maybe," he says wistfully, wiping his eyes with the back of his hand. Gradually, Ethan relaxes and a comfortable silence settles between us. I wonder if he's falling asleep.

"Hey, Lanie. What did they do to you in that place in Florida?" Ethan asks quietly.

I shift a little, and he sits up to face me. His brow is knit in concern. Since when does Ethan worry about me? When he was stuck in time as a four-year old, his selfish concerns and anxieties took all his energy. How old are people when they begin to worry about others? Eight? Ten?

Now that Ethan's unstuck, this age thing is becoming a kind of obsession for me. I ask Rachel, as Ethan's and my therapist, over and over, "So how old do think Ethan is now?"

"Nineteen, same as you," she laughs. "The mental age measurement is not that literal," she explains. "He'll make amazing progress in some areas, like the agoraphobia, and no progress at all in others, like the enuresis."

It's a reasonable explanation, but I still wish I could have an age thermometer so I knew what to expect from him.

"Lanie? You're staring at me that weird way again. Why do you do that all the time?"

I look away. "I don't know, E. I guess I just don't recognize you sometimes."

"You're kind of freaking me out. Can you stop?" He gives me a little grin.

“Freaking you out? You sound like Sage." I reach out and caress his face.

"What did they do?" he asks again, leaning into my hand.

"Actually it was kind of amazing, like something from the future or a movie." Ethan isn't looking at me anymore, so I pause and follow his gaze. Sage is standing in the doorway.

"Mind if I join?" she asks.

I motion her in. "Saves me from having to repeat myself," I say

She walks around the bed to sit behind Ethan. He immediately relaxes against her, and she wraps her arms around his waist. I envy the easy comfortable way they fit. Before Ethan can put his thumb in his mouth, she gently catches his hand in hers. The way she caresses his thumb has to feel much better than sucking it. She rests her cheek against his head, and they breathe in sync. Sometimes I think that maybe this is how it is meant to be, that Finn was some sort of temporal disturbance in the force that is Ethan and Sage, and all of that is over now. Then I remember the fire in Finn's eyes on the beach and the catch in Sage's voice when she says his name. And I know without a doubt it's not over yet, not by a long shot, and my heart aches for my brother.

"You're doing it again, Lanie," Ethan whines.

"Sorry, little brother," I tease. Sage rolls her eyes, knowingly, waiting for Ethan's indignant response to the moniker, but Ethan's not stuck at four anymore.

"Just tell your story, littler sister," he responds, giving me a mock glare.

I have to smile. "Well played, E," I say. "I'll tell you the story." But the not the whole story, I think. Not the part about Jamie. Not the part about you, Brother.

Ethan's gray eyes lock on mine, and in the back of my head I just make out his thoughts like a voice whispering from across a noisy, crowded room. "I already know the whole story. I knew it before you did. I knew it before it happened."

ABOUT THE AUTHOR

Susan Michalski has been creating stories for as long as she could understand words. Because she rarely sleeps, reading and writing have filled the dark hours since childhood. With degrees in literature, drama, creative writing, and secondary education, Susan has been able to find work as an actress, high school teacher, college instructor, web/UI designer, private tutor, online course writer, curriculum designer, technical writer, waitress, and swim coach. She dreams of quitting her day jobs to live in an alternate reality full-time. Because surviving trauma and how it affects our interactions with each other is one of the most interesting conundrums of the human condition, Susan made it the focus of her first book. She is a believer in paranormal phenomenon of many kinds. Susan Michalski lives, works, and occasionally sleeps in Austin, Texas with one genius child, two devoted dogs, two immortal hamsters, and a guinea pig named Butterscotch. *Safe Distance* is Book One in the *Geodesy* series. Go to www.geodesyseries.com to enter the Geodesphere..

Made in the USA
Charleston, SC
30 September 2013